THE
PHILOSOPHER
PRINCE

PAUL WATERS

THE PHILOSOPHER PRINCE

THE OVERLOOK PRESS

NEW YORK

This edition first published in the United States in 2012 by
The Overlook Press, Peter Mayer Publishers, Inc.

141 Wooster Street
New York, NY 10012
www.overlookpress.com

For bulk and special sales, please contact sales@overlookny.com

First published in Great Britain in 2010 by Macmillan,
a division of Pan Macmillan Ltd.

Copyright © 2010 Paul Waters

Map designed by Raymond Turvey

Library of Congress Cataloging-in-Publication Data

Typeset by Ellipsis Books Limited, Glasgow
Printed in the United States of America

1 3 5 7 9 10 8 6 4 2

ISBN 978-1-59020-718-5

www.overlookpress.com

For K. W.

Ah, but a man's reach should exceed his grasp,
Or what's a heaven for?

Robert Browning, from *Andrea del Sarto*

There will always be men who will revolt
against a state which is destructive of humanity
or in which there is no longer a possibility
of noble action and of great deeds.

Leo Strauss, from *Restatement on Xenophon's Hiero*

THE ROMAN EMPIRE, circa AD 360

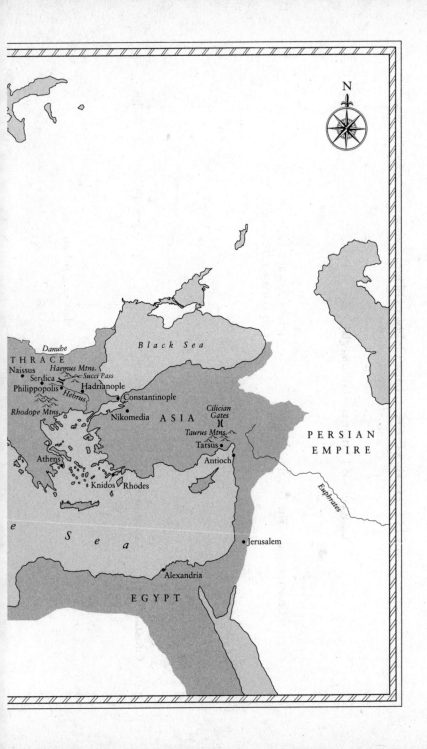

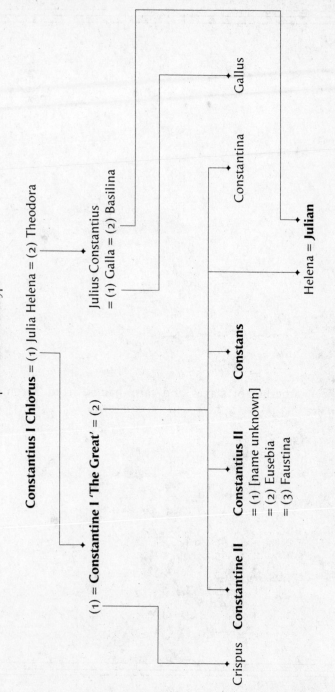

THE HOUSE OF CONSTANTINE (Simplified)

Emperors are in **bold** type

Constantius I Chlorus = (1) Julia Helena = (2) Theodora

(1) = **Constantine I 'The Great'** = (2)

Julius Constantius
= (1) Galla = (2) Basilina

Crispus **Constantine II**

Constantius II
= (1) [name unknown]
= (2) Eusebia
= (3) Faustina

Constans

Constantina

Gallus

Helena = **Julian**

ONE

THE PYRE HAD BURNED down at last. Marcellus, who had watched unflinching, turned now and wiped his brow with his hand. He took a breath, and drawing himself up he stepped from his mother's side, away from the solemn gathering of slaves and farm-hands, from Tyronius the steward, and from faithful old-man Clemens who had, in the end, outlived his master. At the altar of solid stone he paused, and taking a last fist of incense he cast it into the bronze fire-basket. The incense hissed and spluttered, and a strand of blue smoke wound up into the chill British air, curling over the old shrine with its pillared door and sloping roof, then drifting and dispersing between the surrounding poplars.

The youngest of the slave-girls wiped her eyes with her hand. Marcellus glanced up and gave her a brief smile, and for a moment, as he turned, his grey eyes met mine. I had scarcely dared look at him while the fire raged and his grandfather was consumed. The heat had reddened his square features; the undertow of pain, which showed in the fine lines about his mouth, had made him beautiful.

My heart filled. I knew he was holding his grief in check, for the sake of the others, and for his own pride.

He had told me, when we were alone, that this was no time for weeping. Aquinus had lived a noble life crowned with glory. He had shown there is a dwelling place for goodness in the world; he would not have wanted tears and wailing. He had stood against tyranny, and had pre-served the province of Britain, and had died in peace, in his old age, in his own home. Count no man happy, he had once said, till he is dead, and the mocking hand of fate can touch him no more.

I took a step forward and gave Marcellus a nod. He met it with a private frown, as if to say, 'Well, Marcus, it is done, and we are on our own, you and I, to find our way as best we can.' Then, returning his mind to the busi-ness of the ceremony, he crossed back to the place of the fire, knelt down on one knee, and gathered the wine-cooled ashes into the alabaster jar, ready to join those of his ances-tors in the ochre-painted tomb behind.

As he finished, his mother, who till now had remained silent, said in a tone as sharp as the frozen air, 'And thus the line is ended.'

Marcellus hesitated. I felt a tightening of the muscles in my back. This was the old fight between them; and I was the cause.

For the smallest instant he stared down at the ashes in his cupped hands. I saw the contours of his face harden, like a man in battle. 'No, Mother,' he said in a level voice, 'there is me.'

He waited, not looking up. But she said no more; and after a moment he completed his task and set the cover on the jar. Then he stood, took the cloth from Tyronius, and cleaned the dust from his fingers. And she, whose features during the whole of the ceremony had remained still and cool as the embossed wreaths on the alabaster jar, continued to look out beyond the shrine to the middle distance, as if her words had not drawn blood.

I frowned, and considered her across the burnt-out clearing, feeling the beginnings of anger for his sake. He had wanted this day to be right, a final offering to his grandfather; but she would not let go her quarrel, even here. I was the enemy; but it was Marcellus, her son, and the man I loved, who had denied her what her heart longed for, when he failed to bring home a wife of her choosing, and produce a child to preserve the bloodline. Even Aquinus had chided her in the end, in his gentle, amused way, telling her she lacked proportion, that she should trust to the gods and the passage of time. But she had no trust in gods, and time had robbed her of her husband, Marcellus's father, long ago. So in place of trust she had tried to order the world in accordance with her wishes; and the world had not obeyed.

I looked away, down to where a half-burned fragment of juniper-wood still smouldered near my foot. Who was I, I asked myself, to blame her? I had what I wanted, after all, while pain had made her brittle and remote. Some kindly god had brought Marcellus to me. He filled my life, he kindled my heart. Whom, I reflected, did she have, to set against the circuit of the seasons and the years? I knew she resented me, and I wished it were not so; yet I could not hate her. I had known too much of loss and solitude for that.

I let out my breath and watched it diffuse in the cold air. Already the frost was descending. Beyond the circle of poplars, the pale disc of the sun was drawing down over the canopy of forest, and above the tree line the evening star shone out, white and glimmering.

I returned my eyes to Marcellus. He was dousing the altar flame with wine from a silver pitcher. Across the remains of the pyre, silhouetted against the light, his mother was watching him from under her veil. Suddenly her head went up. I thought, at first, her gaze was directed at me, that she had divined my thoughts. But she was looking past me, out over the land. Then, in her precise, crystal voice, she said, 'Who are those people?' and everyone turned to stare.

Out below the ridge, caught in its long shadow, a line of horsemen were picking their way single-file down the track. 'Is this some business of yours, Marcellus, today of all days, when you have your family to attend to?'

'No, Mother,' he said, 'of course not.' He handed the pitcher to the steward and stepped out beyond the light of the torches. I moved up beside him. Unconsciously, with the habit of my training, I felt at my side, where my dagger should have been. But I had dressed for Aquinus's funeral, not for war. My dagger was at the house, lying on the table beside my bed where I had left it, in its latticed sheath of leather.

In a low voice intended only for me, Marcellus said, 'See, they sit like soldiers, all but that squalid-looking one – you see him there? – the one second from the front, in the brown cloak.'

'They are no soldiers I know. Where are their uniforms? And why do they come from the west, over the fields, and not from the road?'

He narrowed his eyes at them. 'They did not want to be seen. They did not expect to find us out here in the open.'

'We have no weapons,' I said.

He nodded, then said, 'I know.'

He threw a quick glance over his shoulder, towards the high-walled enclosure of the great house, judging the distance. It was built to resist a small army, in this time of barbarians, and there we should be safe. But already the horsemen were spreading into the low valley, closing the gap between.

He met my eye, and made a small angry gesture with his arm. 'I am not going to run like some peasant before bandits, least of all today.' Then he turned back to the others, the servants from the house and the landsmen. They were stirring now, and gaping in alarm. Raising his voice, Marcellus said, 'Be still. These men have the look of soldiers. We will wait here, and see what they want.'

So we waited. We had little choice. I could see about thirty riders; I wondered how many more there were behind the ridge.

In the valley they spread out and paused, looking at us warily and conferring. One of them pointed towards the oak gates in the enclosure wall, and the man beside him nodded. The gates stood open still, from when we had made our progress from the house, bearing Aquinus's body on its last journey. For a moment they glanced about confused; and I knew, if I had been armed, and with a troop of my men, that this would have been the time to strike. But it did not take long for them to realize we were defenceless, exposed in the open and at their mercy.

They divided. Some wheeled round and made for the house and high fortified walls of the enclosure; the rest, about twenty of them, led by the squalid-looking rider who sat so poorly on his horse, climbed the path to where we stood by the shrine and altar and burning torches. I frowned out at them, trying to make out the intention in their faces, preparing myself for violence. Recognition stirred. In the deepening gloom I shielded my eyes against the torchlight and looked again.

'What is it?' asked Marcellus.

'That one, the squalid one who rides like a slave. I know him.'

He had his hood up; but as he turned on the path the torchlight had caught him. He was older than I remembered; but childhood pain stays in the mind. His mean, self-satisfied face was one I could not forget.

'It's the bishop's creature,' I said. 'Faustus, the deacon. I am sure of it.'

Marcellus glared, but there was no more time to speak. The other riders circled us and dismounted, showing their swords. Then, when he was sure he was safe, the deacon clambered down from his horse.

'What do you want, Faustus?' I cried.

He peered at me, narrowing his eyes, and his sly face took on an expression of mock surprise. 'Why Drusus, son of Appius, you are here too! But how not? Two doves with one trap, as the hunters say.' To the armed men he nodded and said, 'The traitor's son; the father was executed.' Then he turned and made a show of taking in his surroundings – looking with raised brows at the altar and implements, and the open doors of the mausoleum with the torches burning in their sconces on either side.

'What is all this,' he said, jabbing his finger. 'Necromancy? Are you conjuring the dead? The penalty for necromancy is death.'

'It is a funeral, you fool,' said Marcellus. And his mother said sharply, 'Who is this vulgar man?'

'He is the bishop's underling,' I told her. 'His name is Faustus.'

'Whoever he is, he is intruding on family business. Tell him to leave, and take these men with him.'

'That will not be possible, madam,' answered Faustus smoothly. He reached into his cloak, and with an attempt at a flourish withdrew a crumpled document. 'I have a warrant, you see, for the arrest of your son and his friend here. Now please, step away. These are not women's matters.'

'What warrant?' cried Marcellus, stepping up. One of the soldiers warned him back with his sword. 'The bishop has no authority. Is that why you come here, like thieves in the night?'

Faustus gave him a brief, false smile; then he sniffed, rubbed his damp nose with his fingers, and wiped them on his cloak.

'But who is speaking of the bishop?' he asked with a pleased air. 'This is an imperial warrant; it comes from the notary Paulus himself.'

'I do not believe you. The emperor stripped him of his office.'

'Yet the need calls forth the man. But have you not heard? Then I shall be the first to tell you. His eternity the emperor Constantius has reappointed Paulus to attend to the rebels and traitors in Gaul. The emperor knows his friends in adverse times, and there is none more loyal than Paulus. And the bishop, of course. And,' he added, with a gesture at himself, 'and me . . . So I am afraid your hopes have run away with you. The notary is waiting at Trier – see for yourself, see here, this is his seal.'

Marcellus took the warrant from his outstretched hand and studied it in the torchlight, then handed it to me. The deacon continued, 'So I advise you to obey. We do not want the lady here to suffer any inconvenience, above all in these troubled times, with no one to protect her. And if you are innocent, well, then you have nothing to fear.'

'No one is ever innocent to the notary. Everyone knows that. The man is a murderer.'

Faustus merely shrugged.

'I suppose your master is behind this,' I said to him.

'Bishop Pulcher is a man who helps his friends. It would have been better for you if you had remembered it . . .

Oh, but I almost forgot. Where is Aquinus? He too is summoned; indeed it is he the notary wants most of all.'

'Then,' said Marcellus, 'you are too late.'

'Too late? Must I remind you . . .?' But then a vacant look settled on the deacon's face as realization dawned. He craned his head and squinted with new interest at the bed of white ash. 'Oh,' he said. He shifted uneasily, then glanced round, like a man who finds he has been the victim of a trick. Pulling himself up, he went on, 'The notary will not be pleased. Still, I suppose nothing can be done.' He paused, and scratched his ear. Then, his confidence returning, he swept his arm in front of him and declared in a mocking voice, 'I do not know why you trouble over the corpse of a pagan. You should have tossed him on the midden, like a dog.'

The guards were ashamed. I questioned one of them as he was tying me, but he only mumbled that he was doing his job, and would not meet my eye.

They were all uneasy; I sensed it like a smell. They would not wait for the dawn; and as soon as the others returned from the house we set out, travelling by starlight and the quarter-moon, following seldom-used tracks.

Only Faustus spoke. He chattered on, mocking and crowing in his toneless voice. But at length, finding himself ignored, even he fell silent, and concentrated instead on his horse, which had grown sullen and resentful from his constant shifting and snatching at the reins.

We travelled south. Whenever the guards saw the glimmering lights of a settlement, we left the track to avoid it. We saw no one. Eventually, in the first grey of dawn, we came to an abandoned hamlet beside a muddy tidal creek. There was an old jetty, half-collapsed from age and neglect, and moored on one side of it a seagoing cutter.

Here we dismounted. Faustus's humour, such as it was, had ebbed away during the long cold night. Now, with no more attempt at pretence, he merely said, 'At last we are rid of you.' He paused after this, then added in a loud, intoning voice, 'If the eye offends, then pluck it out.' It sounded like something he had picked up from the bishop, or from one of his sacred books. For a moment he looked pleased with himself; then he snapped his fingers at the guards and we were dragged off to the ship.

The deacon knew well enough the particular hatred that the notary held for us; the shipmaster, a slovenly man with a dirty vessel, did not care, so long as he was paid. He inspected the purse of coin the deacon gave him, then he ordered us down into the hold. Here we were carefully chained, because those had been the deacon's instructions. But thereafter we were ignored – not fed, nor given water. But at least not cast overboard in our heavy manacles, as I had partly feared – for these, I knew, were the notary's methods. It was little comfort. I knew too that if we were spared drowning, it would only be because the notary had something worse in store. He was known across the empire as a master of torture and slow death. It was his pride.

It is seldom one can say of the barbarians that they have brought one something good. But chaos, which is the enemy of civilized life, is sometimes the enemy of tyrants too. When we made landfall in Gaul the first sound that met our ears was an angry disagreement on the quayside. 'What now?' muttered Marcellus with a grim look at the rusted grille above our heads. 'Is even murder too difficult?'

We listened to the muffled disputing voices. At one point I heard the shipmaster's voice shout, 'But these are the orders, see for yourself, look at the seal!' and another voice responding in a flat, uninterested tone, 'Orders or no orders, I can't conjure men from nowhere. It should have been arranged.'

They argued on. Eventually heavy feet sounded on the deck, the grille flew open and the shipmaster's heavy face appeared in the opening, flushed and angry.

'Out!' he ordered.

The boat was moored at a long stone quay lined with warehouses. The warehouses looked abandoned, with open doors and empty space within. At one end of the quay, a line of drab fishing skiffs lay tied one to the other, like craft laid up for winter and then forgotten. There was a town on the rising ground farther off. Its walls shone russet-red in the glow of the late sun.

'Where is this place?' I asked, rubbing my chafed wrists.

'Boulogne,' said the shipmaster, 'not that it matters to you.' And then, with an angry sweep of his arm at the official who was staring up at us from the wharf, 'Go on! What are you gaping at? Go and fetch them!'

The man sniffed and strutted off.

'So what now?' asked Marcellus.

'It's not my concern. Your deacon friend said a detail from the notary would be here; but that fool' – stubbing his thumb in the direction of the official – 'doesn't know what I'm talking about. "It was not arranged."' He mimicked the official's voice.

Soon the port official returned with a detachment of men. They were not imperial troops, but some sort of local militia, little more than youths got up in rough, makeshift uniform. But they moved with sturdy pride, and their weapons – hunting knives or odd swords – were oiled and polished. There followed more discussion in the lee of the warehouse. I could not hear what was said. Once or twice their leader, a young captain with a broad, farm-boy face, glanced up with a furrowed brow. But the shipmaster, at least, was smiling. He was rid of us; and after some brief negotiation we were led away, out through the walled gateway of the docks.

We passed through a run-down quarter of ships' chandlers, coopers, sail-makers, and the kind of low taverns one finds at any harbour. Most were shuttered and closed. From a doorway a gaunt-looking street-trull called out and flashed her breast at Marcellus; but then she noticed our fettered wrists, and seeing there was no business to be had she abandoned her pretences and hawked and spat.

'Why is it so quiet?' I asked the captain. 'Where are the people?'

The captain frowned. 'There is no work. They have gone away.'

He had an honest, open face, and it seemed to me he was not happy with the task he had been given. So with a smile I asked how the town managed for itself, with all the trade gone.

He gave me a wary look, to see if I was somehow trying

to trick him. No doubt he had been told I was a dangerous criminal. But then, with a shrug, he answered, 'We manage well enough. We have to. Now stop talking.' And after that he moved away from me.

That night we were shut up in an ancient cell built into the bricked inner arches of the town wall, the kind of place municipal authorities use for common thieves and such people. It was dripping-damp and smelled like a latrine. But before he locked us in for the night the young captain unchained us, and tossed in an armful of clean straw from the horse-manger outside. Next morning he brought goat's cheese wrapped in a cloth, and milk and rough barley-bread, and allowed us to stand in the open and wash at the trough.

As I splashed my face I glanced about, taking care to be discreet, for the captain had told his men to kill us if we tried to run, and they were as tense as hounds on a hunt. We were in a paved open area just within the town gate. Around us, a convoy of men and transports was assembling. I asked someone who was standing at a mule-cart what was happening.

He eyed my clothing – I was still dressed in the formal tunic I had worn for Aquinus's funeral, dark-red heavy wool, with a black cloak over – and asked where I was from. When I told him he said, 'The roads are not safe to travel. Is it not so in Britain? No? Then you are fortunate. No man will go alone if he can avoid it. The barbarians lie in wait and pick off the unwary, like wolves taking lambs, and the emperor does nothing.' He kicked at the wheel of his cart as if he hated it. It was laden with crude earthen pots and dishes, packed with straw. 'I was a rich man once,' he said. 'I had a thousand iugera of land beside the Rhine. Now I am reduced to this.'

'What happened, sir?' I asked.

'What happened?' He regarded me sidelong, to see if I was mocking him. But judging I was in earnest he continued, 'It is a story told a hundred times, why tell it again? The Franks came from the forest across the river. They burned my home and took my land.' He made a blowing sound at his raised palm, as if he were blowing away a speck of dust. 'All gone, everything I worked for; and now I am here. We live like prisoners behind the walls. My wife takes in sewing, and I am reduced to peddling this cheap ware, which once I should not have deigned to eat from.'

Someone called him. But before he walked off he added, 'My wife calls it fate. She takes it calmly.'

'But not you, sir?'

'A man should be master of his fate,' he answered. 'We had what we had, and we have lost it. Well I have said enough. It is treason to speak thus.'

It was well after sun-up before we set off.

I had supposed we were the only prisoners; but before we left, six old men were led down in chains from the town. They had well-bred, intelligent faces, and were dressed in what once had been fine clothes. They were the kind of solid citizens who form the backbone of any provincial city, and just those whom the notary liked to implicate in his webs of treason, so he could confiscate their wealth. They gazed hopelessly at the ground, and did as they were ordered. I could not speak to Marcellus, for we were being kept apart, but I caught his eye and he frowned back at me. We had seen the same oppression in Britain, before we drove the notary out.

The old men were loaded onto an open cart, and we were told to climb up after them. Then the captain shouted the order for the gates to be opened.

From Boulogne we moved east, passing through good, flat farming land. But good though it was, the fields had been left untended, and were growing over with tall grass and saplings; and if we saw a farmhouse or settlement, it had a wall thrown up around it, crude work of wooden pikes or scavenged masonry, put up in a hurry. Then, arriving at Rheims, we found the city gates shut against us, and no traffic on the road, though it was daylight still.

We halted, and the captain shouted up at the grey, corbelled walls. From the gatehouse heads appeared, townsmen with spears. Were we mad, they called, when they had found out who we were, thinking to travel at such at time? Had the captain not heard then? German tribes had swept in from beyond the Rhine; word was that the fortress city of Cologne had fallen. No one knew how far the barbarians had penetrated, or how great were their numbers. But great or few, there was no Roman army to oppose them, and each city of Gaul was forced to look to its own defence.

So at Rheims we waited. It seemed that no one knew what to do. Days passed; but every delay that kept us from the notary was welcome.

We were kept on the upper floor of a disused townhouse,

with bare boards and crumbling plaster, and a window that gave out onto a muddy court.

One early morning, the young captain appeared with the guard who brought our breakfast. He stood leaning at the door while we ate; and after a while he spoke. His orders, he said, had been to take us to Trier, the Western imperial capital. But now, since the road was no longer safe, he had decided to take us to Paris, where he could hand us over to the authorities and be done with us.

He had spoken awkwardly, and when he was finished he waited, shifting uneasily from foot to foot. He was a simple farm-lad with an unruly mop of curling, corn-coloured hair; he would have been happier building hayricks, and there was too much decency in him not to feel shame at holding prisoner men who were old enough to be his grandfather.

Sensing he was eager to talk, I asked if he would eat with us. As I had guessed, this was the lead he had been waiting for, even if he did not know it himself. He came forward and squatted down, and one of the old men pushed the common platter of bread and cheese to him, and asked him about his family.

His father, he said, farmed a plot not far from Boulogne – you could see the fields from the high part of the town, where the old temple was. He had two brothers; he was the third son – the youngest.

'I too have a son,' said the old man. 'He is in the army, serving the emperor on the Persian border. I expect I shall not see him again.'

The captain paused and looked at him. 'I am sorry, sir,'

he said through the food in his mouth. 'I do not understand why the world is as it is.' He fell silent, and chewed
with a furrowed brow. After a few moments he said, 'There
are baths close by. If I take you there, will you promise
not to try and run?'

'Run?' said another, giving a bitter laugh. 'Where to?
We are too old to run. We have no money; we are already
half dead. I will not lose the last of my dignity.'

So we got our first proper bath for many days, a naked
row of grim, unhappy old men, the captain, Marcellus and
I.

We fell to talking, as one does at such times, and soon
the talk turned to the barbarians.

'Sometimes weeks pass and you do not see them,' said
the captain, shaking his head, 'and then, when you think
it's safe again – there! They have you.' He made a motion
across his throat with his finger. He knew of whole
families – father, mother, children, grandparents – who
had been found cut to pieces on their farms, when they
could just as easily have been spared. On one farm he had
found two young children, a son and a daughter, strung
up from the trees behind the grain-store. 'The girl,' he said
frowning, 'was naked. She was six years old. My brother
knew the family.'

'Is that why you joined the militia?' asked one of the
old men.

The captain paused before he answered. 'I wanted things
to be better,' he said.

The old men looked at one another. It seemed cruel to
ask the obvious question: why he was escorting helpless

townfolk far from home when he should be protecting his farm and family. I suppose he sensed it, for presently he said unprompted, 'I try to do my duty. I don't know what else there is.'

I asked what had happened in Gaul. He told me how last year the emperor had sent a general to set things to rights, but instead of fighting the enemy the general had declared himself Augustus. So the emperor sent another general to remove the first. Then the prefect had been caught plotting, and he too was ordered back to court. Little wonder, he said, kicking the water with his naked foot, that the German tribes were tearing Gaul apart.

After this, one of the old men said, 'And what then of the notary Paulus?'

The captain pulled a face. He threw a quick, wary glance across the steam-filled room before he answered. Narrow spears of winter sunlight were shafting in from the little windows under the tiled, domed roof. No one else was there. Even so, he lowered his voice before he spoke. The notary, he said, was supposed to be at Trier, where he had taken up residence in the imperial palace while he conducted his inquisitions. He paused, then added, 'But one of my men has got it from a tavern-keeper here in Rheims that the notary fled when the German barbarians took Cologne.'

'Where to?'

The captain shrugged. 'Who can say? All of Gaul is like a stirred-up wasps' nest. No one knows anything for sure.'

Private looks were exchanged. Marcellus said, 'Who then is at Paris?'

'I heard the emperor's cousin is on his way. The emperor has promoted him to Caesar, and sent him to Gaul to save us.'

'What, Julian?' cried the old man beside Marcellus. 'Can the emperor do no better? Julian is little more than a boy, and certainly no soldier.'

'So people say. But word is he is surprising everyone of late. He has been fighting the barbarians in the south, and now he is marching north. They say he is an honest man.'

'Then he must be rare as a butterfly in winter,' said the old man bitterly. But he had little else to cling to, and so he said no more.

And thus it was, that winter, in my twenty-first year, and all because Cologne had fallen and the barbarians had come swarming across the Rhine, that I came to Paris, a small city I had never heard of. It changed my life forever.

It had rained all day, grey gusting swathes of it, driving in from the west. But, as we approached, the clouds finally frayed and parted, and the sky flared into a towering sunset, reflecting on the river in the valley ahead, and glancing off the wet terracotta tiles of the city spread before us. The town itself was unwalled – the first in Gaul I had seen without walls – but in the middle of the river, on its own boat-shaped island, a squat, ancient-looking citadel rose up, its sheer walls mottled in the slanting sunlight.

As we descended into the low valley the road divided. The eastern fork led to a square-walled army fort on the hill; the other, which we took, continued south, down to the bridge and the island citadel.

The cressets had been kindled by the time we reached the inner courtyard. We were received into a high, vaulted chamber that was divided into iron-barred pens, like a place for sheep or cattle. Here we waited, while a bored-looking clerk copied the details of the warrant onto a wax tablet, and called each of us before him.

When my turn came he peered at me, peered again at the warrant, then with a flick of his hand beckoned Marcellus up from behind.

'Wait over there,' he told us, gesturing to one side.

We waited, watching while a steady traffic of officials passed to and fro, dressed in their long dark tunics, clutching papers and tablets and scrolls, some deep in conversation, others staring fixedly ahead, all seeming busy, none of them noticing for an instant the prisoners and clients waiting to be seen.

'All this activity,' muttered Marcellus, who had no time for bureaucrats, 'and yet the province burns.'

But presently a dapper young man in green and scarlet livery came up and asked us to follow him. He wore a wide belt of brown leather, studded with silver. It was fine and showy. I noticed it bore no weapons.

He seemed rather pleased with himself, but he was civil enough. He conducted us from the chamber, along one of the many corridors, and then up a flight of ancient stone steps, worn down by generations of footfalls. We climbed for some time, past tiny window embrasures that showed the river and land beyond, until we emerged at last into a wide high-walled courtyard somewhere in the upper part of the citadel.

In the middle a huge old cedar grew black against the darkening sky, rising from the flagstones. On one side, high up, a wooden walkway followed the line of the outer rampart, below the parapet. Here and there, narrow window-slots looked down from stone walls; but no lamps burned in them, and there was no sign of life, no sounds of voices – only the distant sweep of the river far below, and, in the boughs of the cedar, the indignant chirruping of some night-bird.

'This way,' said the liveried youth.

Soon he paused at a studded door with an iron handle. He unlatched it, and gestured us inside, saying others would come soon.

Then he left us.

Something was not right. I frowned to myself, trying to think. The room was long and whitewashed and unadorned, with a narrow mullioned window at one end. Someone had lit a lamp for us; it flickered from a recessed ledge. By its light I saw there were two beds, neatly made up with clean sheets and bolsters; and against the wall a table and a washstand.

I was about to comment on this to Marcellus; for one did not, in my experience, encounter prison cells furnished in such a way. But before I could speak, he called from where he was standing by the window. 'Come, Drusus, look here!'

He had opened the shutter and was fingering the stone mullion. 'See, there are no bars. It is narrow, but we could get through.'

I moved up beside him. 'Yes,' I said, tapping the rough stonework, 'I think so.' I paused and frowned. Then, with a jolt, I realized what had been troubling me. 'But wait, Marcellus!' I cried. 'Did you see keys or locks? Did you hear the guard close the bolt?'

He looked at me. And then I leaped past him to the door, and heaved on the iron-wrought handle. The latch clicked, and the door swung open.

I peered out across the dark courtyard, with Marcellus pressing up beside me.

'I don't understand,' he said, 'unless—' But before he could finish I caught his arm and hushed him. On the far side of the great courtyard a door had opened, showing distant figures silhouetted by the light within. We drew back inside, and eased the door closed. Soon footsteps sounded outside on the flags. There was a tap, a silent pause; then the latch stirred, and two servant-boys entered, bearing in their arms a pile of towels, and, on top, two neatly folded tunics.

'I am sorry, sirs,' said one, 'for keeping you waiting. I expect you are tired after your journey, and will be wanting to wash and change. I have sent for warm water. It will be here directly.'

I stared at him, and after a courteous pause he eased past me and set down the towels on the washstand, while his companion began unfolding the tunics, one on each bed. They were of fine white linen, with a waterleaf border embroidered in green.

Seeing me staring he turned with a look of concern. 'I know, sir; forgive me. But I could find nothing better at this short notice. If you will tolerate it for today, I shall have something more suitable made up by morning.'

I gaped, first at the clothes, then at him. He smiled, then gave a small, polite cough. He must have supposed I was simple.

'My lord Eutherius sends apologies,' he continued, 'that he has not been able to greet you personally. But he hopes you will feel disposed to join him later for dinner.'

I looked at him, but it was Marcellus who spoke. 'Delighted,' he said, in his best charming voice.

It was as well he was there. I do not think I could have uttered a word.

I thought my twenty years of life had been eventful and varied; but nothing had prepared me for Eutherius.

We had stripped and washed, and dressed in the fine new clothes that had been brought for us. Later the servant-boy returned. He escorted us through the citadel, along dim corridors lit by bare lamps, through cavern-roofed halls, and down stone stairways, until we came to a part of that great rambling fortress that looked less like a barbarian stronghold and more like a rich man's palace.

We came at length to a room that put me in mind of some costly woman's tiring-chamber, decorated with silk hangings of vermilion and pink. Silver lamps in the shape of swans burned on a wrought standard, suspended on little chains. At one side, three upholstered couches had been placed around a low polished table. Arranged upon it, in green glass bowls, were figs and sweetmeats, and tiny cooked eggs garnished with herbs.

'Please,' said the servant, making a civil gesture for us to sit. The lord Eutherius would be with us directly.

So we sat. The servant went off, and we waited, alone and unguarded, and stared about at the festoons of silk, and at the little glass bowls, and at each other.

Presently voices sounded outside. The double-doors with their painted panels opened, and a large middle-aged man swept in.

'Forgive me!' he cried, spreading his big fleshy hands in a gesture of supplication. 'How rude you must think me, to have kept you.'

He was dressed in a bright ankle-length tunic of crimson and dust-blue, with embroidered edges and a belt of woven gold. The sweet smell of apple-scent hung about him. 'No, no, please don't stand,' he cried, seeing us move. He eased himself down onto the couch opposite. 'I have been obliged,' he went on with a sigh, 'to attend unexpectedly to matters of state: the new prefect has just arrived, you see, far earlier than anyone expected.'

He spoke in careful precise Latin, with a hint of the sing-song cadence of Greek. He smoothed down his clothes, and arranged his large body on the couch, saying, 'But you have had the most arduous journey, I am sure; nothing must disturb your comfort further.' He turned with a smile to a dark-skinned, exquisitely dressed boy who had entered with him, who had gone off to stand beside the hangings. 'We will have our wine, I think, Agatho. And – if these gentlemen do not object – you may give word to the cook that we are ready for him at last.'

Earlier, waiting for the servant to fetch us, we had determined that we should try to escape that night. The unbolted door must surely have been a foolish oversight; either that or, amidst the muddle of our arrival, we had been taken for someone else. Best to be gone, then, before some clerk discovered his error.

Yet this man Eutherius seemed to be expecting us. And now, after wine had been poured and passed around by the pretty servant-boy, Eutherius turned intelligent dark eyes on me and said, 'I gather, young man, that you have fallen foul of our friend the notary?'

I swallowed. The wine – fine and cool and fragrant, the kind my uncle used to import from the Rhine for his richest clients – suddenly tasted bitter on my tongue. I had allowed myself to hope, fool that I was. I should have guessed the notary would not be content with a quick death. He would want to twist the knife: he had made slow murder his life's business. Torture was his art.

I set down my gilded cup. 'Then you know,' I said, in a slow, even voice. I was about to go on, and tell him he could set aside this absurd pretence; but before I could speak the doors flew open and a team of liveried men marched in, bearing platters of food high in their hands, which they presented to Eutherius, and then set down before us: mushrooms in honey; diced fragrant chicken; mullet cooked with almonds and red berries; glazed pork on sticks; and other delicacies in small covered pots.

'Excellent! How wonderful!' cried Eutherius, beaming at the silver plates. But Marcellus coughed and frowned. His face was beginning to show the strain. 'Forgive me, sir. I do not understand. Are we prisoners here? You treat us as honoured guests.'

'And so you are,' said Eutherius, turning to him.

Marcellus looked into his face, waiting. After the hardships of the journey I could tell his patience was at an end. I suppose our host saw it too. With a sigh he set down the little embossed dish he was holding and said, 'I see I shall have to explain, if I am not to spoil this banquet of ours. But please eat . . . and while you eat I shall tell you.'

The notary Paulus, he said, was not the only man to make use of spies. It was a sad reflection that even spies and their masters were watched – the notary included. 'But there it is. Spies are spied upon; guards are guarded.' And after the disaster he had caused in Britain – which, said Eutherius with a nod, Marcellus and I knew of at first hand – Constantius the emperor had decided Paulus had criminally exceeded his orders, and demanded his presence at court. 'The emperor,' he added, with a dry look, 'wisely ensures that he bears no responsibility for the faults of his subordinates.'

He paused, ate a honeyed mushroom, then went on, 'Well, as it happens, I myself was at court in Milan when Paulus arrived. He came by sea, all pomp and retinue and swaggering attendants – not at all what the divine Constantius wanted to observe when he had just received word of yet another rebellion. Really, it was a most injudicious move on the notary's part.' He puckered his lips, and surveyed us with wide innocent eyes. 'As for you, we knew you had been taken, but in all the confusion we did not know where. Then my' – he paused – 'my contacts, let us say, in Rheims, brought word. You may have noticed your appalling journey improved a little thereafter. Now do stop staring, and try to eat. You both look lean as stray dogs.'

We did as he bade us, and as my emotion subsided, I realized how hungry I was.

While we ate he went on, 'Between you and me, I can tell you that I too have had occasion to disagree with our esteemed notary. He is—' He raised a finger, and pulled a face as if he had swallowed vinegar. 'Well, perhaps best not to speak too freely of a man with such a reputation. So let us merely say that he can be contentious.'

Marcellus, eating mechanically, was watching him with eyes as attentive as a greyhound's. The servant-boy Agatho stepped up and refilled my wine-cup. I drank it quickly down.

'However you look at it,' Eutherius continued, 'the emperor has been badly advised. Now Britain is in turmoil and barbarians range over Gaul at will. So he has appointed his young cousin Julian as Caesar, and that is why I am here.' He slipped a berry into his mouth, and inclining his head to Marcellus said, 'So, to return to your question, you are most certainly not prisoners. You are free to leave, even now, in the midst of this feast. The unfortunate men who accompanied you have already been offered passage home. And you, if you wish, are at liberty to go with them . . . But perhaps, when you see for yourselves that all I tell you is true, you will consider staying for a while. Julian will be here this winter. I should like you to meet him.'

Two

NEXT DAY WE LEFT our room and walked about. No one stopped us.

We had been housed in the oldest part of the citadel, all thick ashlar walls and stone passages; but elsewhere there were newer additions in the Roman style: handsome panelled rooms with mosaic floors, frescoes and pilasters, built around a cloistered garden planted with neat plum trees and bordered with rows of box hedge.

We retraced our steps, and going by a different way we came to a long cavernous chamber flanked by squat columns and hung with heavy faded tapestries. It was some sort of room of state, with a dais and high-backed chair at one end. Grey winter light filtered in from narrow window-slits; an iron-wrought cresset hissed and flickered against the wall.

At the far end was a high ceremonial doorway with a postern in it. We walked through, emerging onto a balcony with a flight of steps which descended into the paved court-yard below. Around us on three sides the sheer walls of the citadel rose up; on the fourth there was a stone gateway, and beside it a guard dressed in imperial uniform.

Marcellus frowned down from the balcony. 'Now,' he said, 'let us see if we are truly free to go.'

We went down the steps, crossed the great square court-yard, and strode up to the gate. The guard's eyes moved. He nodded at Marcellus, and let us pass without a word.

We strode on, scarcely daring to turn. But when I glanced behind, no one was following.

I let out my breath. I had not realized, till then, that I was holding it in. After weeks of captivity, and sleepless nights on stinking straw, and days filled with the corrosive dread of sudden, violent death, it seemed we were free, just as our strange new host Eutherius had promised. I felt almost ashamed to have doubted him. But Marcellus said, 'We had to know, Drusus. Words are one thing; deeds are another.'

We wandered without hindrance. The island where the citadel stands is the oldest part of Paris, with the rest of the city spreading out to the south, across the river. Out-side the citadel walls is an old town of narrow streets and shadowy iron-gated courtyards; and, beside the river, on the eastern side of the island, an old temple set upon a raised base. We came across it on that first day. As we drew near I looked up at the gable-end. Written in sculpted bronze was the dedication: IOVI OPTIMO MAXIMO.

'Jupiter's temple,' said Marcellus, gazing at the verdigris lettering.

We climbed the marble steps to the podium, and walked along the colonnade of acanthus-topped columns, pausing at the ledge and looking down at the fast-flowing water below.

'What do you think?' said Marcellus, returning to the question we had been discussing all morning: whether we should stay or go.

I was watching a pair of moorhens as they darted on the water, dipping down, then bobbing up like glistening black corks and shaking themselves.

'There is still Paulus the notary,' I said.

Each time, as we had talked, we had returned to this.

He nodded. 'Yes. I thought we were rid of him.' His voice was bleak and angry.

'I too. But now we know differently.'

I recalled the day I had dispatched the terrifying, hard-faced notary as a prisoner from London to answer to the emperor for his crimes. He had torn the province of Britain apart with his treason inquisitions. He considered himself above the law, like all of the emperor Constantius's black-clad secret agents. It was I, and Marcellus, and Marcellus's grandfather Aquinus who had stood against him in the end, and helped the people of Britain to drive him out. But too many had died. The province would never be the same. That day, on the quayside in London, he had said in a voice that chilled my soul that I had better hope we never met again. And now he was free, and restored to power. So much, I thought bitterly, for imperial justice.

I glanced up from the swirling water to Marcellus's face, then gestured out southwards at the undulating green land

in the distance, with its leafless fruit trees, and old enclosures, and black vine stocks on the slopes. 'He may have
fled from Trier, but he is out there somewhere, and the
emperor has forgiven him his crimes, or does not care.'

I saw Marcellus's broad, strong hand clench and
unclench, showing the tendons in his wrist. He raised his
arm and pushed his fingers through his mane of hair, in
the unconscious way he had when he was troubled. His
hair was the tawny colour of old bronze. It always turned
that way in winter.

'I will not live like a caged animal.'

I nodded; then said, 'I know.' It was one of the things
that made me love him.

'If we go back, Drusus, we will never rest easy; we will
never know when he is coming for us – he and his agents
and that creature Faustus, lurking like thieves in the
shadows, waiting for our guard to drop. He hates us too
much to forget. Every stranger's visit, every creak in the
night . . .' He paused and frowned. Then he said, 'I ask
myself what Grandfather would have done.'

I too had asked myself this question. Aquinus had stayed
true to his honour, and to what befitted a gentleman. He
was gone; but his lesson stood before us. He had never
consented to slavery, either of his body or his mind.

'Then,' I said, 'we must see this onwards to its end, wherever it takes us.'

He nodded slowly, and gazed downriver.

It had been a day of cloud. But now at last the sun had
broken through, horizontal spreading bands of purple and
brilliant orange, set against the rain-soaked land.

'There is something I like about Eutherius,' he said, after a pause. 'He may dress like a springtime flower, and drench himself in scents, but he is no man's fool. I trust him, don't you? If he thinks so highly of this new Caesar called Julian, then perhaps we should wait, and see him for ourselves.'

Grief wears many faces, as in the time that followed I began to understand.

Some men weep, and tear their hair, and like a summer tempest it is gone. This is the grief we see in the theatres: all show and noise, that makes the people stare. But even the young, if they stop to reflect, will know there is another kind. It sits in the heart, and dwells there like a banked-up fire, smouldering unseen.

Marcellus had loved his grandfather deeply. In the absence of his father, who had died when he was young, his grandfather Aquinus had made him what he was, fashioning by his example every fine and pious and noble part of him. And since the last short illness that brought his death, Marcellus's mind had been forced to his duty – to Aquinus himself, to his brittle mother, to the farm, the hands, the household. They had all turned to him, placing on his shoulders the burden of their need. And he, because it was in his nature, had borne it, as Atlas bears the world.

He was twenty-one, my age. We had fought together and loved together; and when I saw he did not stumble I looked no further. I did not see what it cost him. But now, at last, I began to sense a change, the first flickerings of the hidden fire.

As always, when we were with others, he was faultlessly

courteous. He had been bred to civility, and good manners came to him as naturally as drawing breath. But when we were alone I would catch him gazing silently at the lamp flame, or out to the empty horizon, absorbed in some private melancholy.

He was too generous to burden me with it; yet I could feel his sadness. If, at such times, I broke in on his reverie, he would look up and smile, and say something light; and for a time seem to shake off the mood. But always later it would return.

Near the Paris forum, on the south side of the river, we had found the town baths, and the palaestra behind, with its grassy spaces and colonnaded athletics courts. Here, in the time we waited for Julian to arrive, we took to exercising. I had never known Marcellus fail in anything; so when he began seeking out the wrestlers and pitting himself against far stronger men, brutes for whom the gymnasium was their life, I supposed he knew what he was at.

They thrashed him, time after time. Yet always he would go back for more, sitting afterwards in grim silence while I tended to his grazes, never crying out, keeping his pain within by some act of angry will. Perhaps the violence purged him of something. Whatever it was, he did not speak of it, even to me.

Yet at times the mask would slip and he would grow angry at some minor thing – a broken bootstrap, a lamp wick that would not light, or some mislaid piece of clothing. Sometimes, at night, I would hear him stirring and groaning in his sleep, until eventually he would start awake. I would speak his name in the darkness, and he would pad naked across the floor and crawl beneath my covers, and fall into a deep slumber without a word.

And next morning he would wonder how he got there.

Thus the days passed; and it seemed I could not reach him.

In those first weeks, we saw Eutherius often. Dressed like some large exotic bird, in oranges and yellows and mauves, he told in his sing-song voice of his life in Constantinople among the corrupt, self-seeking officials of the Consistory; or he lamented the crudeness of northern Gaul, which he regarded as brutish and uncivilized. But always there was irony shining in his dark eyes, as if he had known much worse.

As indeed, I soon discovered, he had.

It was one evening during dinner that we found out. He had happened to mention that he had passed that day along the street behind the forum, where the brothels are, adding with a shake of his large expressive face, 'An appalling sight. Even the courtesans lack art. They move with the gait of farm-girls, paint their faces as if they were whitewashing a barnyard wall, stare and spit and pick at their noses. I wonder that they persist in their trade at all; I can hardly imagine they make a living . . . Not, of course, that I should be one of their patrons.'

Marcellus and I answered quickly that we were sure of it. We had already drawn our own conclusions about his tastes, and they did not include the backstreet whores behind the forum.

'But do not be deceived, my dear Drusus,' he continued, divining at least in part my thoughts. 'You will find it is often the finest peacocks that chase the dullest hens, and the most fastidious men who secretly relish the mire. One notices – being deprived of such pleasures oneself.'

I agreed, even though I did not quite follow what he meant. He was clearly a man of means, who could afford whatever pleasure he cared to purchase. I concealed my sidelong look, but he must have noticed, for he said then, 'You did not know?' And, seeing my confusion, 'Well, after all, why should you? I had assumed . . . but one should not assume.'

Then he sat back on the wide upholstered couch, gently smoothed his clothes, and told us his awful story.

He had grown up in Armenia, in a wild hill-village on the fringe of the empire. It was a land that had been often fought over. One day, when he was eight years old, tribesmen had come raiding across the mountains. They burned his village, and killed everyone they found, forcing the women first. He would have died along with his father and mother; but he had been a pretty child, and the raider had stayed his sword.

He quickly learned, however, that he had not been spared out of pity. At the next market-town his captor sold him to a Roman merchant. 'At first I could not understand it, for I was not ill-treated nor set to slave-work, and indeed my surroundings were immeasurably more lavish than what I was used to. But then, half a month later, when I was stronger and had ceased to cry all day, my new master, who had been kind to me, came one morning and told me I must go with two friends of his who were waiting in the hallway.

PAUL WATERS

'And so I went. They took me out of town, to a farmstead set in an olive grove. I heard the screams as we drew
near, but even then I did not struggle, for in my innocence
I did not know they gelded boys.'

Marcellus had been eating, picking at a dish of dried
apricots and figs. Slowly he set the dish down, and stared
at Eutherius with an appalled look. 'By the gods,' he whispered.

'It was long ago. One forgets.'

'What happened?' asked Marcellus. 'How is it that you
serve the emperor?'

He told us. After that day he had never seen his master
again. As soon as he recovered, he was sold to men who
traded in such goods, and they took him on the long
journey to Constantinople. There he was purchased by an
agent of the imperial palace. He was given an education,
and, proving able, was put to work as a clerk. He excelled,
and was promoted.

'I have often reflected that, but for those cattle-thieves,
I should be hoeing scree and tending goats on some sun-
parched hillside, as my parents did, and theirs before them.
But now I read pleasurably in four languages; I have a
delightful house of my own looking out on the Bosporus,
I have wealth and friendship, and I dwell at the centre of
power. It was a trade no man would choose to make. And
yet, after all, perhaps it was a good one.'

There was, of course, no answer.

Marcellus and I drank a good deal of wine that night.
Later, as we lay in the darkness of our bedroom, Marcellus, who had been a long time silent, whispered, 'You

know, Drusus, I am glad Eutherius told his story tonight. I think I was meant to hear it. I was letting myself forget that there is misfortune everywhere. No man can escape it; it is how he faces it that matters.'

After that day I sensed a change in him. Often I would find them together, he and Eutherius, walking slowly about the paved gardens among the box hedges, or along the colonnaded walkways, deep in talk, Marcellus, straight-backed and handsome, his muscular, well-shaped hands moving as he made some point; and Eutherius, tall and large and gentle, ambling beside him like a silk-clad bear. Had he, I wondered to myself, seen further than I, and given Marcellus what he needed? I could almost have been jealous.

But if Marcellus warmed to Eutherius, he soon came to detest the newly arrived prefect, whose name was Florentius.

Florentius was the kind of man who has never for an instant doubted his own merit. He was of middle age, with a lean, haughty face, and a tight-knit nest of chestnut hair, an effect he achieved by having his slaves curl it for him each day with hot irons. He also had a fine-tuned sense of his own dignity, and was entirely devoid of humour.

Both Marcellus and I disliked him from the start, and I daresay we should scarcely have crossed his path – which would have suited us well – but that he got into his head that all eunuchs were a centre of intrigue. And so, deter-mined not to miss anything that might concern him, he forced himself into Eutherius's company.

Though Florentius was sensitive to the smallest per-ceived slight to himself, he was capable of the grossest rudeness. He would keep those he had summoned waiting outside his office half a day; he would cut people short; he interrupted; he made remarks that caused those with him to blush with impotent fury. For though, as prefect, he lacked military powers, he was not a man it was wise to clash with. The emperor Constantius himself had appointed him, and any decision he made would be given unquestioned approval at court. He could punish and demote at will within his extensive bureaucratic domain, and his subordinates lived in terror.

Eutherius never let on what he thought of him – he was too much the diplomat for that. But Marcellus loathed him, and when he was with him Marcellus retreated behind a wall of distant civility.

A better-bred man than Florentius, sensing this, would have let it pass. But Florentius responded by needlessly disputing with Marcellus, seeking his opinion only to dismiss it, forcing him into barbed conversation only to put him down. Mostly I do not think he was even aware of it himself; but he had grown used to flatterers, and his sensitive nose had sniffed out that Marcellus was not one.

Just then, what irked the prefect more than anything was the career of the new Caesar Julian.

Julian had been studying at the university in Athens when his cousin, the emperor, had summoned him to the court in Milan, there appointing him Caesar, and sending him to Gaul. At the time no one had expected much to come of it, for, as Eutherius explained, everyone knew that Julian was more concerned with books than war, and had never fought in battle, let alone commanded an army.

But he had surprised them all. He had marched into Alsace, fought back the barbarians and restored the fortresses that guarded the undefended plains beside the Rhine. The German chieftains, outraged at being thwarted after years of raiding at will, had massed their armies to extinguish this presumptuous Roman. Having assembled a horde of thirty thousand men, they advanced on Strasburg, led by their high-king Chnodomar. They had assumed their victory was sure. But in the battle that followed, the German armies were routed and Chnodomar was taken. Six thousand barbarians died in the fighting, or were trampled in the rout, or drowned in the Rhine as they tried to swim to safety. Out of thirteen thousand men, Julian lost only two hundred.

When news of this victory arrived in Paris there had been joy. Everyone praised the young Caesar, who had so unexpectedly shown himself to be a great general – everyone, that is, but Florentius. He had risen by careful stages, never taking risks, never crossing his superiors. He had plodded through his career like an ass at a waterwheel, and to him Julian's sudden rise was a personal affront. So amid the general happiness he observed sourly that Julian's success was no more than beginner's luck.

We soon learned that there were other men, too, for whom Julian's victory was unwelcome. That winter, Eutherius received a letter from Julian, saying he had been delayed. He had clashed with his Master of Infantry, a man by the name of Barbatio, who instead of supporting him, had thwarted his efforts all through the year's campaigning. Now Julian had dismissed him; and Barbatio, wishing to forestall criticism at court, had hurried to Constantius complaining of Julian's conduct, saying he was exceeding his authority.

'So Julian has asked me to travel to court and put his case to the emperor,' explained Eutherius. 'No one else will speak up for him; the intriguers and backbiters are already doing their work.'

'But does Constantius not trust even his own cousin, whom he appointed?' I asked.

Eutherius smiled, as a mother smiles at a charming, naive child. 'Constantius grew up with courtiers. He trusts no one. Remember that, my dear Drusus, and you will understand him.'

The court, which moves from city to city, following Constantius, was at that time at Sirmium in Illyricum, a journey of some weeks. 'Pity me,' Eutherius went on, 'for it will be a wretched trip – snow; mountain roads; miserable inn-food – and I do not travel well. But I hope you will stay while I am gone. Julian still plans to be here – though he cannot tell quite when.'

So we promised to wait; and next day walked with Eutherius's litter and small entourage to where his carriage and baggage-train were waiting at the limit of the city, and there we saw him off.

And when he was gone, Florentius made his move.

It was early one morning, a few days later. A clerk came rapping at the door and curtly announced that the prefect's secretary required us at once in his offices. When we appeared before him he looked up with an expression of assumed boredom and said, 'Ah yes; the Caesar Julian will be wintering at Paris, as no doubt you have heard. Therefore there is no longer space to accommodate you. You will have to make other arrangements.' He gave a strained smile, and then with a languid gesture of dismissal returned to his papers. It was the revenge of a bureaucrat.

Eutherius, in his kindness, had left us a little money. His dark-eyed servant-boy Agatho had brought it in a calf-skin purse tied with leather cord, on the day after he had departed. The money was enough for our needs if we had remained in the citadel; but it was no great sum otherwise. We discussed it. We did not intend to be driven off by Florentius. So now, finding ourselves suddenly homeless, we searched around and asked at the usual places in the forum, and in the end found lodging at a rundown farm close to town.

The farmer owned an orchard and a few fields, and needed help, offering in return two draughty bare-wood rooms in an outhouse, with hens clucking in the yard and a view out to the apple trees of the orchard beyond. His wife, he told us as he showed us this, had died some years before, leaving him with a daughter to raise alone. Now she was eighteen, and was more trouble to him than the farm. She stood at the porch on the day we moved in, hand on hip, regarding us with wide insolent eyes. Her name was Clodia, and she was to prove a trouble to me too, in a way I had not guessed at.

We moved to our simple quarters and set to work, clearing ditches, repairing dry-stone walls, and cutting back the neglected vines on the low slopes. Like all of northern Gaul, the place was pitifully neglected. Many of the farmer's labourers had fled, or had been conscripted during one of the barbarian invasions and had not returned. But worse even than the lack of men's labour was the flight of knowledge itself. We saw it everywhere, in every botched and half-done thing. The ancient skills were slipping away. They had not been passed from father to son, because the father had died too soon, or the son had seen no use in them, thinking a shoddy job would do just as well. While I worked – sweating in the cold fields, hammering planks, clearing bramble from the water-courses, or pruning the overgrown orchard – Marcellus brought something of far greater value: he brought ideas and schemes he had learned on his grandfather's estate in Britain, where the long thread of land-knowledge had not been broken. It is knowledge hard learned, till it dwells in the bones. But knowledge does not outlive the knower.

There was a peace in such simple work. The days passed one into the next, and each night I slept deeply. As for the farmer, he was glad to find he had taken on more than a pair of strong young men. Then, one grey, windless after-noon, while I was stacking bales in the barn, I heard shouting from across the fields, and when I asked the hands what it was they called up that it was the Caesar's army, come at last.

That day, Marcellus had gone to market with Clodia and her father. I jumped down from the stack of hay and hurried out, clambering up with the others onto the water cistern to see. Already, on the sloping grassland beyond the river, the horsemen of the cavalry, dressed in their scarlet cloaks, were rounding the camp wall. Behind them came the infantry cohorts, with their dragon-headed shields, painted gold on red. They wheeled and divided as they prepared to march through the gateway of the fort. Now and then, carried on the still, winter air, came the sound of their marching song, full of strength and pride. 'And why not?' I thought, feeling my heart stir with it. They had defeated the German barbarians, who supposed they could raid across the Rhine at will; they had given them a bloody nose, and sent them back to their endless forest to think again. So why not be proud? They had earned it. And if this young scholar Julian had restored their pride to them, winning victory against such odds, then it seemed to me he was not such a fool as the prefect Florentius made out.

All of us strained to see, hoping to glimpse this new young Caesar. But from so far off, each rider looked the same as the other, with none singled out in gold or white or purple. Perhaps, after all, he was not with them, for the army moved in stages as it divided itself for winter quarters.

But afterwards, returning to my work on the bale-stack, I felt a new impatience with my lot. I wanted to be with those men at the camp on the hill, working at what counted; not clipping vines and shifting stones on another man's land. Then, for the first time in a long while, I thought of my father, and was glad he could not see what my life had become.

I confess too that there was another thing preying on my mind just then, though it shames me to tell of it. For now I come to speak of love, and of my own failings.

43

It had not taken me long to realize Clodia did not like me. She was slim and brown-eyed and, I suppose, pretty, except for a certain hardness about the mouth, which settled on her when she thought no one was looking. I have always hated slyness. I began to notice how she affected a laughing, careless manner when Marcellus was around her, which ceased as abruptly as a slammed door as soon as he was gone. She did not trouble to put it on for me.

Even so, I was always careful to be civil; but perhaps, with a hunter's intuition, she had read something of my secret heart. As for Marcellus, what he saw in her I never quite understood. Certainly her physicality and rude manners were unlike the cooped-up, high-born brides-to-be he had known in London, whom his mother had tried to force on him. Besides, she put on a good act, or so it seemed to me, and I thought it mean and small of mind to tell him what I saw.

Whenever he ran errands to town for her father, or took the mule-cart to the fields, she found a reason to accompany him. And I, seeing it all and feeling ashamed that I even noticed, found reasons to occupy myself elsewhere. Her advances were gauche and heavy-handed: a lingering touch, a thrusting accidental glimpse of her breast, a too-long smile that died on her lips if I happened to catch her eye. I found myself wondering if they did anything. If so, Marcellus did not mention it, and I did not ask.

So, from before the time of the army's arrival in the citadel, and after it, I began to find excuses to go out alone, walking the field tracks, or wandering without purpose about the city, as I once had done when I was still a boy at my uncle's house in London. I fell to brooding. I did not understand myself – or chose not to.

And so it was that I came, one late winter afternoon during my wanderings, to the spot overlooking the river where the temple of Jupiter stands, on its high ashlar base overlooking the river.

Already the light was fading into leaden dusk. For a while I sat on the ledge, my elbows on my knees, idly watching the swirls and eddies on the surface of the water. I do not know how long I remained, lost in my own turbulent thoughts. Eventually, across the river, I saw glimmerings of light as the first lamps were kindled.

I stood, and made my way back to the steps. Under the porch at the temple's front I saw that the tall bronze double-doors stood ajar, which earlier had been closed. I hesitated, and peered inside. The dusk was deeper within. There seemed nothing to keep me. But, being in no hurry to return to the farmstead, I decided to go inside and look around, just to see. I edged between the gap in the doors and entered.

The air inside was cold and still. It smelled of damp stone and old incense. I stepped forward, watching where I set my feet, for the floor about me was scattered with a covering of dead leaves and pieces of broken stonework. I paused, waiting for my eyes to adjust to the gloom. And then, against the far wall, seated upon a throne of carved red granite, I discerned the god. He sat as tall as four men, bearded and mighty. The powerful face had been hacked, and one great marble hand had been axed off. It lay among the wind-gathered leaves at the foot of the plinth. The frieze too, which ran around the statue's base, had been chiselled and scarred, and daubed with Christian signs.

I had not set foot inside a city temple since London, when I was attacked and almost killed. I recalled Marcellus's words to me: it was madness to go to such places alone, now that the Christians took it upon themselves to kill a man rather than leave him to his gods. But now, once again, I felt the pull of something old and timeless. I knew I needed to be here, on this day, at this hour; though I could not tell why.

Advancing, I turned my palms upwards and spoke the words of a prayer, using the ancient formulas I had once heard Marcellus's grandfather speak, fine old Latin, like sculpted stone. And afterwards I knelt down and brushed the leaves from the broken marble hand, and raised it up. It took all my strength to lift it. With difficulty I set it on the plinth, at the god's feet. It was an offering of sorts.

My efforts had disturbed the silence. Now, as it returned, I had a sudden feeling that someone was watching me, though I had seen no one. I stilled my breathing and listened, and felt my hair prickle on the back of my neck.

There was a tiny sound, no more than a stirring, like a shift of leaves. I swung round. Twenty paces away, silhouetted in the twilight in front of the high door, a man stood regarding me.

'Who are you?' I shouted angrily.

The man took a step towards me, and as he moved I saw he was sturdy and broad shouldered, with the gait of a legionary or a peasant. Instinctively, like any man with a soldier's training, I felt at my belt. I had no sword; but I had found an old hunting knife at the farm, and had cleaned it up. My fingers settled on its old birch-wood handle.

'Forgive me,' the man replied, pausing in the place where he was, 'I did not mean to startle you.' His voice was friendly; his Latin had the lilting accent of the East. He turned, and said something quickly in Greek. There was a movement, and from the shadows another man, thinner and fine-boned, stepped out into the shaft of grey light.

I watched them warily, preparing to move. The one who had spoken lifted his hands to show he had no weapon. 'We mean no harm,' he said.

'Then what do you want?' I said back at him.

They stepped forward and looked up at the tall statue of Jupiter enthroned. I could see, now he was closer, the shadow of day-old stubble on the man's jaw. His hair was carelessly, unevenly cut. A common soldier, then; yet somehow he did not have a common soldier's coarseness, and his delicate-looking friend did not look like a soldier at all. He peered at the base of the statue, frowning at the scribbled alphas and crude daubed crosses. 'You see, Oribasius?' he said, gesturing. Then, turning back to me, 'We were here when you came; you startled us or we should have spoken out.' He paused, and when I did not speak he went on, 'Did you come with the army, friend?'

'No,' I said.

'Then you are from Paris?'

'No again.' My answers were cold and wary. I was in no mood for small-talk. I was angry that they had secretly watched me, when all the time I had supposed I was alone. Besides, there was a covert air about them, as if they were keeping something from me, or playing with me.

Sharply, with a stab of my thumb at the broken frieze, I asked, 'Are you Christians?' And I thought to myself, 'If they came looking for a fight, then I will give them one.'

'I did not do this,' he said carefully, keeping his eyes on me. 'I would never do such a thing. It is sacrilege.' He paused. 'But tell me, if you are not with the army, then with whom?'

To shut him up I answered, 'If you must know, I am a guest of a certain Eutherius, who is friend to Julian the Caesar. I daresay you have heard of him.'

His brows went up at this, and I saw the two of them exchange a private look. 'Indeed we have,' he replied. And the other, the one called Oribasius, said, 'Truly we mean no offence. But what is your name? It may be that we have heard of you.'

I answered that I doubted it; but seeing no harm in telling them, I said, 'I am Drusus.' And at this, to my surprise, Oribasius asked, 'Then do you have a friend called Marcellus?'

I stared at him, taken aback. But his burly friend laughed and said, 'You see, we too are friends of Eutherius . . . But the prefect said you had gone away.'

'So we did. The prefect turned us out. He said there was no room at the citadel.'

'Did he now?' He frowned, and once again they exchanged a glance. 'What will you do now?' he asked.

I shrugged. I had heard, I said, that the Caesar was

looking for good men. Perhaps, when Eutherius returned, I should try my luck there.

'Well, whoever told you that was right. But Eutherius will be away some time.'

'Then I suppose I must wait.'

He considered, rubbing at the stubble on his chin. 'Yet perhaps,' he said, 'there is no need for that. I think I can help you . . . Will you come and see me at the citadel tomorrow – you and your friend?'

I allowed myself a private smile. No doubt this man was some junior infantry officer who thought he had his commander's ear, and wanted to make himself seem like someone. Still, he had an honest look; it seemed churlish to decline. So I said I would see him next day, as he asked. I did not have the heart to tell him that with Florentius the prefect as my enemy, I doubted I should even be admitted at the gates.

He nodded and gave a small, grave smile. He was not, I could see, a smiler by nature.

'Then good,' he said. 'Until tomorrow then?' He made to go.

'But wait,' I cried. 'Whom shall I ask for?'

He looked surprised at my question, as if it had not occurred to him. He glanced quickly at his slim, dark friend, and seemed almost at a loss.

'Say you have come to see Oribasius,' he said. 'I shall be with him.'

It was night by the time I returned. No lamp was burning in our outhouse, and at first I thought that Marcellus was

49

not there. But when I went striding in I found him sitting in the dark, on the rough-wood three-legged stool in front of the stove. He was resting his chin upon the heel of his hand, frowning into the red charcoal.

'Marcellus!' I cried, and began to tell him what had happened.

He looked up startled. His cheeks were flushed from the heat of the fire. His brow looked creased and troubled. But it was something else that gave me pause. I turned, knowing already what I should find. Beyond the circle of light, beneath the shuttered window, the farmer's daughter was reclining on the couch, propped up on one elbow, regarding me with eyes that shone in the reflected glow. She pulled herself upright with an angry flick of her hair. Her dress was loose on the shoulder, showing her pale neck, and the breast she was so proud of. But at least she was clothed; for already it was dawning on me what I had stumbled upon.

In a cold voice she said, 'You are interrupting. Have you forgotten how to knock?'

I felt my colour rise, and my anger with it. 'Then I am sorry, Clodia,' I said, 'but I did not know, and it is dark. But now I am leaving.'

I had picked up the stool beside Marcellus's. I was still holding it in my hand. As I set it down, Marcellus caught me by the wrist. 'No, Drusus, stay. It is freezing outside.'

For a moment I hesitated, caught by something in his voice – not frustrated lust, which is what I had expected; but a note of melancholy. I looked at him again; but in the dim light he did not see the enquiry in my eyes. Then,

behind me, I heard Clodia draw her breath in an impatient sigh. My gut tightened, and I thought: What am I to
her? Am I a rival? What, by all the gods, Marcellus, have
you told her that she should think so? I was about to speak
out, but I stayed my tongue. I had rather die than let her
see my naked heart.

I pulled myself free from Marcellus, more roughly than
I meant, knowing I needed to be alone, away from them.
I heard him call; but already I was at the door, and ignoring
him I fled into the night.

Only when I was among the dark trunks of the apple
orchard did I pause, and as I stood kicking at the long
grass, collecting my wits, one of the farmer's she-dogs came
loping up. I crouched and ruffled her ears. Then I moved
on, bounded over the low wall, and followed the cart-track
off between the fields.

Marcellus was right: the night was freezing, and in my
haste I had not picked up my cloak. Well, I thought wryly,
it was too late now to return for it. I rubbed my arms and
walked on. Above me, long strands of silver cloud were
stretched across the sky, illuminated by a hidden moon;
the breeze of earlier had dropped, and a hard frost was
descending. Presently, with no clear sense of where I was
heading, I came to the low-lying ground near the marshes.
A carpet of mist had settled on the land, and as I walked
it swirled and parted at my ankles.

Soon I came to a grassy hillock, a place I knew. In the
luminous night it rose up like a low island in a sea of mist.
I trudged to the top and sat, ignoring the bitter cold, staring
out to the far-off lights of Paris, and the citadel beyond.

I told myself the girl was not important; and yet my heart spoke differently. In this one thing, which should not matter, I saw I was not master of myself, and it made me wretched. I shook my head, and cried out at the night, and tried to think. I wanted to fill my mind with easier things. Yet I saw, like a climber lost in the wooded foothills who glimpses through the trees the sunlit peak, that here, somehow, lay a truth which must be faced.

I sat for a long time troubled, torn between my reason and desire. I spoke out loud, and called reproach to the waxing moon; and it seemed she answered me, saying, 'But why complain? I have shown you the way, Drusus; but it is for you to follow. Be master of your desires, or they will master you. Only then will you know yourself. That is the freedom God has given you. If you will not, no other can.'

And I remembered what I knew in my bones and in my deepest heart: that no man may possess another, or what he yearns for dies in his very grasp. Love must be free, or it is not love, but something baser. And desire, if not ruled by reason, is no more than a fire that consumes the very thing that gives it life.

And so I sat, alone beneath the glittering dome of heaven, and scorched my soul. The time passed, and I did not notice it. When next I stirred, the moon was gone, and the frost lay settled on the grass and on my clothes. I stood, and shook myself, and made my way back across the fields. A stillness had come upon me.

The house was dark; the fire in the stove had died. Silently I closed the door and tiptoed to my bed. I pulled off my clothes and shivering buried myself beneath the pile of blankets. I had thought Marcellus was asleep, but now, from the other bed, I heard him whisper, 'I looked for you.'

'I am here now,' I said.

There was a shifting, and I felt a tug at the blanket. 'You are cold,' he said softly. 'Move over; there is room in here for two.'

In the morning I told him about my strange encounter at Jupiter's temple, and the invitation to the citadel.

'Then we should go,' he said. 'Maybe this soldier can do as he says, if he is a friend of Eutherius.'

I thought of the scruffy, self-conscious, slightly odd young man I had met in the temple. 'It may be so,' I said, 'but don't count on it. I doubt he goes so high – except in his dreams.'

We were sitting on the edge of my bed, the blankets pulled around us. His body was warm beside me, but the room was bitter cold and our breath showed in the air.

I saw him give me a quick, sidelong glance. 'And then,' he said slowly, 'there is Clodia.'

I took a deep breath, and frowned out at a red-breasted robin I had been watching on the window ledge outside. Until now, we had not spoken of the night before. Marcellus turned to face me, pulling his legs up under our shared blanket. His knees touched mine and rested there.

'Drusus,' he said, 'I need your advice. You were with the army in London; I expect you know more of these matters than I.' He paused, and rubbed his face with his hand, and then pushed his fingers through his sleep-tousled hair. Lines of worry and concern showed about his mouth. I saw he had gone a little red. 'The truth is,' he went on, 'I do not know what to do about her.'

His eyes studied my face, full of trust. It brought a lump to my throat, and made me feel cruel and base.

I said, 'She does not matter. It is not important.'

His brow creased in a frown. 'She is very persistent.'

I swallowed, and wondered how the god was mocking me. 'Well,' I said, 'I suppose that is her way.'

There was a pause after that. I started to speak, to tell him he could take a girl whenever he chose, that it would not come between our friendship. But he silenced me, saying, 'I know that, Drusus; but it is something else.' He stared at the opaque glass of the window and gave a sigh. 'She was fighting with me last night when you came. She said many things. She accused me of wanting you more than her.'

I laughed. 'And do you?'

'It's not the same. You know how it is. In the end, when she went on and on, I told her to believe what she liked. That was when you walked in.'

I recalled her face upon me, accusing and resentful. 'She does not matter,' I said again. 'It was my own demons I had to wrestle with.'

And then he said, 'She claims she wants me to marry her.'

'What?' I cried, looking at him with amazement. 'But why? Is she with child?'

He shook his head. 'No; nothing like that. She has thought it all through; she talks of business, of uniting my land with hers; she thinks Britain would suit her very well.'

I stared at him, and thought of what his mother would make of Clodia. I could almost have laughed, except he looked so grave.

'Does she, indeed?' I said eventually.

'Well, yes; but I do not want it. Not now. I do not know where all this came from, Drusus, if you want to know the truth of it. It's not as though . . . well, never mind. I fear I do not understand women at all.'

I thought to myself, '*I* understand this woman well enough.' But I said, 'Women are a mystery. And we are young still.'

'Yes,' he said, nodding. 'And she should not have spoken to you like that; I told her so . . . I love you, Drusus; we belong together, and she can make of it what she likes.'

'I will always be here. You know that.' And then, with a grin, for there had been too much seriousness, 'Still, you must not forget the bloodline, or I shall be blamed for it.'

This was an old joke between us. He smiled, then laughed, and gave my shoulder a shove, sending me back into the pile of blankets.

And then, as if I had brought to him some unexpected gift, he kissed me.

Later that day we crossed the bridge to the citadel.

At the gate I gave Oribasius's name, and waited to be turned away. But instead the sentry pulled himself straight and called me 'Sir' and summoned his superior. A liveried steward conducted us inside, through the inner court with its pleasant columned cloister, box hedges and plum trees, along a wide bright gallery painted with landscaped gardens and hunting scenes. Beside me, Marcellus touched my arm and muttered, 'I thought you said this friend of yours was nobody.'

I pulled a face and shrugged. I had expected to be taken to some barrack-room.

We came eventually to a bright room with high windows and a painted, coffered ceiling. No one was there. But the steward, before he went off, turned and said, 'The honourable lord Caesar will be with you shortly.'

'Wait!' I cried, almost running at him. 'What "lord Caesar"? There has been some mistake; I am not here to see the Caesar. He does not know me. I came for Oribasius.'

The steward looked at me oddly, as if my words made no sense to him; but, before I could go on, there came the sound of approaching voices. I looked round, wondering how I was going to explain my presence to the cousin of the emperor. But, instead of some imperial prince, I saw advancing in the midst of the entourage the same man I had seen at the temple.

'Drusus!' he cried, striding towards me across the polished floor. 'You see, Oribasius, I told you he would come. And you must be Marcellus. Well, greetings to both of you, I am glad you are here at last.'

He turned and said something to the steward. It was only when the steward replied with, 'Yes, Caesar' that the truth finally came to me. He had smartened himself up, though not by much; he was dressed in a well-worn light-brown tunic bordered with a pattern of meandering scarlet, and someone had made an attempt with his hair. He was speaking to Marcellus, asking if we had been admitted without hindrance, and saying we must return at once to lodge in the citadel. Marcellus, poised as always, was answering with his usual well-bred civility – he was never awed by authority or title.

Around us, meanwhile, the room was filling with courtiers and servants and officers in uniform. There was a stirring in the outer chamber, and then Florentius the prefect strode in.

His auburn hair had been coiffured and sculpted into tight, artificial curls; he wore a fine cloak of dark-blue, clasped at the shoulder with a jewelled brooch of gilded filigree. People turned and looked, pausing in their conversation. One might have supposed, indeed, that it was he who was the Caesar. He was talking to his secretary, the man who had expelled us. But as he spoke he was glancing about, seeing who was present. For the smallest instant, as his eyes scanned my way, they paused; and though he tried to cover it, I knew he had seen me. He moved towards Julian, who was surrounded by a press of officials; but before he could reach him, Julian turned and called to me and Marcellus, 'Come, let us go somewhere quiet where we can talk.'

I saw Florentius halt as if he had been struck. With an effort at smoothness he turned back to his secretary. Julian did not notice.

We went to an adjoining chamber. Oribasius followed, and shut the door. The room was small and plain. There was a table under the window, a few simple oak chairs, and a lattice-doored cupboard filled with books. It might almost have been a room at an inn, except for the books.

'I hope you will forgive me for last night,' said Julian. 'I think you scared us more than we did you. Even so, I did not like to hide in the shadows like that, when you thought you were alone. It was shameful really, but I had to be careful.' He glanced at Oribasius, then added with a hint of a smile, 'It would not do, you see, to have it known that the cousin of the great Constantius was poking about in a temple of Jupiter.'

He crossed to the table and picked up a letter of rolled papyrus from under an onyx weight. 'This came from Eutherius. He says he has been delayed at the court.'

I said I was sorry to hear it. I had not yet recovered from finding out who he was, and had been going over in my mind my sharp words when we were in the temple. But he seemed not to care, and when I remembered to add, 'Lord Caesar' – which was what everyone else was calling him – he waved it away with a motion of his hand, saying, 'Just call me Julian. It is enough, between friends.'

He paused and looked at me, and gave an awkward, slightly embarrassed smile, like a shy but courteous child. Then, looking serious once more, he lifted the letter and indicated a small tear in the corner. 'You see?' he said. 'It is where the court spies broke the seal; they did not even trouble to conceal it.'

He followed my eyes, and nodded quickly when he saw I had understood.

'I imagine you are shocked; but one grows used to such things. Eutherius will have expected it, and he will have written accordingly. Listen . . .' He opened the page, scanned it for a moment, then read, '"And besides, I am pleased to report that the divine Constantius continues to be advised by the best minds in the empire."' He looked up with a short laugh. 'That,' he said, 'is his way of telling me the grand chamberlain Eusebius is still dictating policy – so much the worse for me!'

He took a breath to continue, but Oribasius, who up to now had stood silently near the door, gave a slight, discreet cough. Julian glanced at him, and seemed to think again. 'Still,' he said, after a short pause, 'there is no need to trouble you with the chamberlain.' He looked back at the letter in his hands. 'But what I wanted to find was the part where he said you would be here in Paris, that you were friends and I could trust you . . . Ah, here it is.' And he read out the words happily, as one might pass on a compliment heard from another, and when he had finished he set the scroll aside, and placed the onyx weight on top of it.

'You know,' he said, turning back from the table, 'I think some god had a hand in our meeting, don't you? It was not just anywhere we met, and I doubt another soul has set foot in that temple for a year.' He looked at his friend. 'Now don't tell me, Oribasius, that *that* does not mean something!'

The sound of voices could be heard, carrying from the great reception room beyond. Julian frowned at the door.

'And now,' he said, 'I suppose I had better go to them. But Drusus, Marcellus, will you come and dine with us tonight? . . . and do please forgive me for the little deception at the temple. It was necessary.'

59

THREE

WE RETURNED TO THE citadel, not to our old small room under the spreading cedar, but to a fine new suite which looked out over the inner court. It had a floor of chequered marble, and on the wall a fresco of a river scene, with boats plying the water, and men on the terraced bank, gathering the vintage.

Marcellus was standing at the window, gazing out at the rising ground beyond the river Seine, where the horsemen of the cavalry were wheeling and breaking as they practised their manoeuvres. We had been talking of Julian.

'Have you noticed,' he said, 'he's shy, and hides it by talking? And – I don't know – I get the feeling there's something else.'

'What else?'

'I can't tell. Something private, as if he and Oribasius share a secret.'

'Well, they came from the East together. They have known each other for years, after all.'

'Yes, perhaps that's it.' He fell silent and watched the horses for a while. Then he said, 'Yet there's something more, I sense it. As though there is something he wants to tell, but dare not.'

I was lying on my bed, my arms crossed behind my head, idly surveying the pleasing scenes on the frescoed wall as I listened. I nodded to myself. I too had sensed something private, some secret unwillingly hidden from view. 'Well, he is the emperor's cousin. He didn't want it talked of that he had gone to the old temple.' And remembering the letter he had shown me with the broken seal, I added, 'Even he is watched, it seems.'

Marcellus shrugged. 'Yes. So much for trust.'

'Did you notice Florentius?'

He gave a laugh. 'He wasn't pleased to see me.'

'He wasn't pleased to see me either. He caught me looking at that ridiculous bird's-nest on his head.'

'What does he expect? His hairdresser must have been an hour at it. Why do it at all, if he doesn't want people to look?'

I smiled; but then I said, 'Even so, for all he is a fool, he is a powerful one.'

'I know – and he is the first to make sure no one forgets it. Still, we are guests of the Caesar now. He cannot tell his lackey to throw us out again. Florentius didn't even have the courage to do it himself.'

'That's the kind of man he is. Have you noticed how he looks down his nose at Julian? You'd think he was another one of his clerks.' And then, after I had thought about it for a while, I added, 'I wonder if Julian realizes what he thinks of him.'

Earlier we had gone to the old farmer to tell him we were leaving. He shook his head and wondered what he would do without us; but he was not greatly surprised. He knew we could not stay, and took it with good grace. He thanked Marcellus for the many improvements he had made; and Marcellus, in his turn, reminded him of what still needed attending to – the vine stocks on the far slopes; the ditch in the south barley field; and the old granary behind the house, which was damp and needed airing when the fine weather came.

I watched the old farmer's resigned, careworn face as he listened and nodded and frowned. I felt sorry for him; he was honest and decent, and much put upon by fate. But I was not sorry to be leaving, not least, I admit, because of Clodia. While we were busy with our farewells, she sat apart on the step, absently stroking one of the farm cats and glaring with a face like a storm cloud.

Presently Marcellus went off alone to say goodbye to her. I waited in the dirt road outside the gate, making small-talk with the farmer. Whatever they had to say did not take long. I heard a door slam, and when he returned he was looking rather awkward. I made no comment, then or later. After all, she had only seen in him what I myself had seen.

And – I knew this too – it is easy to be generous in victory.

*

Oribasius was a native of Pergamon; he had studied as a physician, and was now engaged in the great task of writing, as he told us, an encyclopedia of medicine. He had known Julian from the time that Julian was a student at the university in Athens. If Julian was a talker by nature, Oribasius was a listener. They understood one another. He was the audience to Julian's protagonist, and there was, it seemed to me, a genuine trust and friendship between them.

But right from the start Florentius, judging others by his own measure, suspected Oribasius's motives were venal. If Oribasius attached himself to Julian, it must be that he wished to gain from it. He snubbed him in the colonnades and passageways of the citadel; he passed barbed, sarcastic comments, not caring who heard. He supposed sneeringly that it must be useful to have a friend so highly placed, and imagined the imperial residences throughout the empire were a welcome comfort. He wondered, with an ironic arching of his brows, how much of a fortune a doctor devoted to study and pursuits of the mind could possibly need.

Oribasius let pass these comments with nothing more than an amused look in his dark, intelligent eye. But Julian noticed, and knew the attacks were really directed at him.

Nor, as I soon came to learn, was Oribasius the only cause of friction with the prefect. Where Julian tended to good-natured familiarity, Florentius was stiff and formal and obsessed with place; and such opposites seldom mix. In another life I daresay they would have kept apart; but Florentius, being responsible for the civil administration of the province and the supplies to the army, could not be ignored. Julian needed him, and Florentius knew it.

Moreover, Julian was by nature impulsive. If he wanted to do something he did it, ignoring the cat's cradle of petitions and approvals that turned a day's activity into a month's work. He had driven back the barbarians by moving fast. The bureaucrats could catch up at their own slow pace. All this Florentius took as an attack on himself. He thought Julian was trying to undermine him, to make him look a fool. As for Julian, he saw Florentius's obsession with process as absurd, when all about him circumstances called for swift decisive action. Neither man understood the other.

That winter, Julian offered us places in the officer corps. I chose the infantry, which I knew from my time in London; Marcellus the cavalry.

The Master of Cavalry, whose name was Severus, had just returned from the Rhine, where he had been inspecting the defences and surveying the ruins of Cologne. On the way he had encountered Frankish skirmishers laying waste the farmlands south of the Meuse. At the sight of Roman troops they had fled north, but as soon as Julian heard of it, he called us together for a war-council. The barbarians must not be allowed to raid at will or consolidate their positions; how soon, he asked, could the army be ready to march?

In the pause that followed, Florentius, who was standing behind, gave a loud, artificial cough.

'Yes, Prefect?' asked Julian, turning to him.

Everyone knew, said Florentius, with the air of a schoolmaster correcting a slow child, that it was the habit of these barbarians to strike when the army was scattered in winter quarters. 'By May,' he said, 'they will have gone back across the river to their own lands.'

'And next year,' retorted Julian, 'they will return. That too is their habit.'

'It is the middle of winter, Caesar; you cannot fight now. Everyone knows that.'

'It seems,' said Julian, 'that no one has thought to inform the barbarians of it. If they can fight in winter, then so can we.' He turned to the map spread out over the table. 'Victor, Arintheus, this route is the best, if it is passable. Send scouts to find out. Valentinian, you see to the mustering of the troops from winter quarters. You, too, Drusus.'

Everyone crowded round – all except Florentius. The colour had risen in his face, but he said no more. While the others talked and planned, he stood with his chin up, half-looking out of the window, as if something in the still courtyard outside had drawn his eye.

A few days later, shortly before we were ready to depart, Marcellus returned late to our rooms. He had been out training the new cavalry recruits, Severus having discerned straightaway his skill with horses. The recruits were young Romans from Gaul for the most part, eager youths fired with the taste of success; but they were rough and raw still. They had learned to ride well enough on their fathers' farms, but knew little of mounted combat, or moving in formation.

Marcellus pulled off his heavy winter cloak and tossed

it on the chair, then sat on his bed and began unstrapping his boots. His cheeks were flushed from the cold, and from a hard day of physical work.

'You smell of horse,' I said.

'So would you, if you had been with me. But have you heard? Florentius has announced he is marching with us.'

'Whatever for? What use can he be?'

'None at all. You should have heard Severus cursing when he heard about it . . . He would have made a centurion blush.'

I smiled at the thought. Severus was a burly African from Carthage with a weathered face and short-cropped grizzled hair. He had a blunt habit of speaking his mind, which endeared him to Julian – and made Florentius bristle. He made no allowances for the prefect's precious airs, and it was no secret that the two men could not stand one another.

'Well,' I said, 'he doesn't have to come. He will hardly be among friends, after all.' And while Marcellus pulled off his clothes we joked at the thought of Florentius out on campaign with his hairdresser and manicurist and the rest of his entourage.

'I suppose,' said Marcellus, standing naked at the washstand, 'he thinks he will miss out.'

'More likely he wants to keep an eye on Julian . . . or someone else does.'

'Yes, perhaps.' He turned, serious now, and regarded me through the folds of the towel as he dried his face. 'I had not thought of that. Eutherius said everyone is watched. What does that do to a man? It's sickening.'

He ruffled up his damp hair and threw the towel aside. We were learning to understand the ways of the court.

Two days later, on a damp grey morning, we assembled for the march north.

I was sitting on my horse among the other officers, watching while the troops assembled in formation before the fort. In the distance, across the Seine, I could just make out the old farmhouse, and the hay-barn and water-cistern beside it, where I had gazed out on the day the army had first arrived. I shrugged and smiled, and reflected on my change of fortune.

Severus came riding up on his tall, chestnut horse. He spoke a few words to one of the tribunes, talking of some military matter; as he spoke he glanced towards the citadel. Then he paused and looked again; and the tribune beside him laughed.

I turned my head, following their gaze. In the distance, riding up the hill on a white dappled stallion, was Florentius, resplendent in shining dress-armour, with a thick, fur-lined riding cloak flowing from his shoulders and cascading over the horse's flanks.

A buzz of amused comment passed along the line, and there were many bright smiles, until Severus barked out for silence. Julian, seated on a plain army-issue mount, glanced briefly round, then looked away again, affecting not to notice.

We advanced northwards, taking the roads as far as they led, then skirting water-meadows and frozen marshes. There was a bitter north wind, which blew against us all the way. As we drew closer to the Meuse we passed abandoned settlements, their roofs and windows gone, and fields untended and returning to the wild. Julian, pointing this out to Florentius, said it was a disgrace that so much land lay idle, when half of Gaul went hungry. The prefect, cold and bad-tempered under his furs, told him that the inhabitants had gone to the cities. 'They have gone for safety, sir, as I am sure the Caesar realizes.'

Julian frowned at the wasted fields. Already sapling trees had taken seed – bramble and whitethorn and fast-growing rowans. Within a generation it would be forest once more, and no one would know it had ever been farmed. He told the prefect this, saying, 'Yet men must still eat, and all this is good fertile land. We must encourage them to return, before it is grown over. We must make it safe for them.'

'As you say, Caesar,' answered Florentius, with a cold, pinched smile.

I saw Julian preparing to speak again, his mind working with his plans. Florentius saw it too; but rather than wait he twitched the polished reins of his horse and wheeled off.

Julian watched him go, and for a moment his eye caught mine. I had expected to see anger in his face. But instead what I saw was hurt and sadness. It was like the face of an intelligent child, who is treated cruelly when he does not expect it, and is unwilling to let it show.

We advanced into the borderlands. There was no sign of the Frankish raiders, except the destruction they had left behind them. Soon we found out why. Alerted to our approach, they had withdrawn to one of the many abandoned frontier posts along the Meuse, left empty when Magnentius and then Constantius had stripped the province of troops to fight their civil wars. While the men were setting camp, digging ditches in the hard ground, pitching their hide tents and erecting a palisade, we surveyed the perimeter to see how the fort could best be taken.

It had a high, stone gateway, facing south-west. The gate itself was gone; the Franks had barricaded the entry with piled-up masonry and old roof-beams from the ruined barrack-houses inside. They eyed us from the ramparts as we approached; and when they thought we were near enough they began hurling down missiles and shrieking abuse in their uncouth guttural tongue. They were outraged that we had dared to come and challenge them.

We kept back, out of their range. Soon, as this dawned on them, they saved their weapons and contented themselves with insults.

'It will take time to shift them,' commented Valentinian, observing the wild barbarians with distaste, 'they are well dug-in.'

'Yes,' said Julian frowning, 'and in our own fort too. But we are outside, and they are in, and I doubt they have laid by much food. They have grown used to our weakness. They think we shall just march away and leave them to their looting. But I will have them out, if it takes all winter to do it.'

Florentius was not with us. He had remained at the camp, to supervise the erection of his tent – a tall, striped pavilion with an entrance porch of red-painted ash-wood poles. I was passing with Marcellus and our comrade Arintheus just as the furniture was being carried in. It lay spread about on a patch of square canvas, waiting to be borne inside by the slaves – stools with cushions, an inlaid writing table, lampstands, an upholstered couch, and in the midst of them a bronze bath embossed with garlands. As we paused, taking all this in, one of his liveried upper-servants came striding up. The prefect, he said, wished for a word.

'Ah, gentlemen!' cried Florentius, from between the half-unpacked boxes. 'Now we are here in this wasteland at last, perhaps you can talk some sense into our great general.'

'Sir?' I said.

'Come now, he will not listen to the voice of experience, so perhaps he will listen to you. The Franks have come and gone through these lands for years; it is no surprise they see it as their own. Does Julian not understand he is giving offence? They will complain to their brothers across the Meuse and the Rhine. Mark my words: by stirring them up we shall have trouble all along the frontier, and then he will have something to answer for to the emperor.'

'Do you wish us to tell the Caesar this?' asked Arintheus.

The prefect shrugged. 'Tell him what you wish; I doubt he will listen. Either way, he will learn soon enough. He cannot go marching about like this in the depths of winter. Who does he think he is? . . . You there!' – suddenly crying

70

out at a group of his slaves who were pulling on a guy-rope – 'stop tugging and heaving like that, you fools, or you will bring the whole thing down into this wretched mud!' He turned back to us. 'You are soldiers, are you not? So make him see sense, before his schemes bring chaos along the whole frontier.'

Later, when we saw Julian, Arintheus mentioned Florentius's words – though he omitted the haughty tone.

'He is right in this at least,' said Julian, 'that the Franks do not like it, and they will have sent to their heartlands for reinforcements. But otherwise our conclusions differ. He believes that therefore we should do nothing, lest we make them angry, and what sort of policy is that? No, we will show them we are ready to defend what is ours, and if they have sent for reinforcements, we had better make sure we take the fort before their friends arrive.'

While he spoke, his eyes had been gazing across the river at the dense forest beyond. But now he turned, alerted by a new volley of abuse coming from the fort.

Already the short winter day was ending, fading to twilight. The fort was shrouded in gloom. The heads of the Franks showed as moving shadows on the ramparts, their distant voices like the bark of angry dogs.

Julian turned to us and shook his head. 'What fool abandons a fort without demolishing it? Little wonder the barbarians mock us, when we are besieging them in a fortress of our own making!'

Days passed. The weather stayed cold and grey. We saw the Franks staring out across the river, searching north over the forest line for the approach of their barbarian tribesfolk. Each day, Julian called on them to surrender. Each day, in answer, they roared insults at the herald, and pelted him with rocks.

But we did not sit idle. We sent sappers shielded under a housing of wicker and ox-hide to undermine the wall by the gate, where it looked weakest and had been shored up from within. But the foundations ran deep – our military architects had known their work – and the work progressed only slowly. Florentius came to observe, saying nothing, looking pleased with himself, making sure his silent presence was noted.

We began work on a siege-tower, and there was a lull while the troops felled trees, and the carpenters set to work with their axes and planes. One day, during this time, Oribasius came calling at our tent. He asked if we would go out riding with him and Julian next morning.

'Why, yes,' I said. 'Of course. Who else is coming?'

'Only you and Marcellus. Let us meet at dawn at the horse-paddocks.' And with that he bade us farewell and went off, with his heavy cloak pulled up against the damp.

'What do you suppose he wants?' asked Marcellus.

I shrugged. There was some purpose behind it, I said. It was not like Julian to go off on pleasure rides.

Overnight the wind shifted, and by dawn the low cloud and fine, ceaseless rain had gone, replaced by sunlight and a sky like blue crystal. We rode out eastwards, following the tracks through marsh-grass white with frost, along the line of an old watercourse.

In time the frozen marsh gave way to firmer ground; ahead, in the middle distance, I saw a wide, low plateau, with a circle of tall pines. They dominated the flatland all around, like massive standing-stones.

'This is the place,' said Julian, who had scarcely spoken. He urged his horse on.

We climbed the path to the top and dismounted. I turned and looked out over the land. To the east, the low sun shone white and cold. The frozen marshes glittered; and far off a solitary hawk balanced motionless in the air. We tethered our horses; and then Oribasius opened his saddle-bag and took out a small folded tripod, and a handful of tinder bound with straw. He stepped away, and set the tripod down in the middle of the circle of trees, and began kindling a fire. Julian said, 'This day is sacred to Apollo, Bringer of Light. Did you know?'

I hesitated. I knew my own mind well enough; but I remembered that for all his friendliness Julian was still the cousin of Constantius, who had closed the temples and forbidden sacrifice on pain of death. Nowadays, even a tripod was suspect. In Britain, under the notary Paulus, men had been dragged to their deaths for less. I asked myself again why we were here. Was this a test?

Carefully I answered, 'I have heard it said.'

He gave me a searching look; and I looked back at him.

But then, from behind, Oribasius spoke out. 'Julian, you are being unjust to keep them waiting. You brought them here. You must tell them, or stay silent.'

Julian frowned and nodded. 'I knew,' he said, 'from the first day that you were one of us, when I saw you pray to the god in the temple. I was ashamed to watch you when you did not know I was there; but perhaps the god intended it, for it showed me who you truly were. Such things are rarer than you might suppose.'

He stooped down and plucked a sprig of heather, and began twisting it between his fingers. 'At first, Oribasius advised caution. Eutherius had spoken well of you; but we needed to know for ourselves that we could trust you.'

I said, 'You can trust me.'

'I know; I know. And that is why I brought you here. I suppose you have been wondering. Though you did not mean to, you let me see the truth in your heart. It is time that I did the same.'

He turned and swept his outstretched arm about him, encompassing the circle of pines that stood around us like sentinels.

'I saw this place when we passed with the army, and vowed then to return. These trees were planted by men, long ago; see how they stand, just so? Whoever planted them knew it was holy ground; there are men who can sense such things, like people who divine hidden water below the earth. But first one must be open to what is there.'

He crossed to his horse, and took up a small leather pouch. Then he went to where Oribasius was standing beside the tripod. He unstrung the pouch and from it sprinkled tiny grains of myrrh over the burning tinder. They spluttered and hissed, and a line of purple smoke curled upwards, diffusing against the cobalt sky.

'For Apollo Helios,' he said. 'Small return for a great gift.' He met my eye and nodded. 'So now you know. The emperor would kill me if he found out. He is a Christian beyond all reason.'

He fell silent, and stared out east across the plain towards the pale sun. Then, turning, he scattered the last of the myrrh.

'The sun is a fitting image, don't you think? For what is God if not the light that throws everything else into its proper relief? When I was a boy the priests and bishops told me the old gods were lies and foolish myth. They mocked them, asking, "Do the gods smell the flowers we offer them in springtime? Is High-Thundering Zeus pleased with his hecatomb, and does Helios smell the sweet smell of frankincense?" I do not know the answer to those questions; but this I know: by honouring something greater than ourselves, we tread the high path that leads to the Good.'

He paused, then turning to me said, 'Constantius murdered my father. Did you know?'

I nodded and said I had heard. I had also heard how, all through his childhood, the emperor had kept him exiled on a remote estate in Asia, cut off from the world. Now he told us the rest.

'I was raised as a Christian, on Constantius's orders. I believed everything my priest-teachers told me, drinking it in like a child at its mother's breast. How could I not? I knew nothing other. But then, as I grew older and read a little, I began to question. I asked them why it was that if a man is jealous they think him blameworthy, but if their God is jealous they call it divine. I asked why He looked on for myriads in silence while men served false idols, save only for that little tribe in Palestine. And if it is their God's will that none other shall be worshipped, why do they worship his son also?' He gave a laugh, remembering. 'A child's questions, of course; but because they could not answer, or perhaps because I dared to ask at all, they beat me, and threatened to report my disobedience to the emperor. So I ceased to ask. But I did not cease to think. I kept my own counsel. I told them "yes" when they wanted yes, and "no" when they wanted no, like the slave of some cruel master.'

He paused, and looked up at the soaring pines. The pain of memory was etched on his face. I wondered how many others he had told, and remembered what Marcellus had said: that Julian was like a man who has kept a secret for too long, and needed it out.

He drew his breath and continued.

'One day, long after, I was permitted to go to the city – closely guarded by one of my pedagogues. But when he went to relieve himself I slipped away, and went off wandering among the columned streets and porticoes. By chance I came upon a group of men, sitting under an olive tree, talking. They were philosophers, though in those days I scarcely knew what a philosopher was. But to hear their words was like water after long drought. I knew at once that I had found what my soul yearned for, and in the years that followed I began to understand what the priests had tried to keep from me. For them philosophy is the enemy, because it sets men free. But there is no freedom without knowledge, only slavery and the endless cycle of unknowing . . . And so,' he said, 'I ceased to be a Christian.'

He fell silent. After a short pause Marcellus said, 'Yet

you attended the Christian church with the bishop of Paris.'

'Do you suppose I am my own man? All this fawning, all this "Yes, lord Caesar" and "No, lord Caesar" counts for nothing. I went because I must. Everything is reported to Constantius. Even my friends are looked into and examined.'

He tossed the sprig of heather into the dying fire and stared at it as it crisped and burned. 'Did you know, after I defeated the German high-king at Strasburg, Constantius sent out laurel-wreathed letters to the provinces praising *his* victory, declaring that he himself had fought in the front rank, had draw up the battle order and had routed the barbarians? There was not one mention of me, who was there, when he was forty days' march away. The victories are all his; but the defeats are mine alone. And so, you see, I can only ever fail; that is their scheme; that is what my enemies at court are waiting for . . . and then they will destroy me.'

In the days that followed, the wind turned to the north, bringing first rain, then bitter cold. I woke one morning to the sound of hacking at the ice on the water urn outside. It was Marcellus. He had gone out to wash.

'It's no good,' he said, putting his head in at the tent flap, 'it's frozen through. I'm going down to the river.'

I groaned and buried my head in the blankets. Then suddenly he was back, calling, 'Get up quickly, Drusus! There's something happening at the fort.'

I pulled on my clothes and hurried out. A covering of

heavy frost lay over the camp. It was early still. The first glimmer of dawn showed as a blood-red strip on the horizon. But at the river the fort was silent. The gate was still barricaded shut with whatever rubble the Franks had been able to find. The sappers' earthworks lay about. No faces showed from the ramparts.

'What are you talking about?' I said, rubbing the sleep from my eyes and peering up at the walls. 'Everything is quiet here.'

'Listen!' he said. He took my arm and drew me down the slope to the river. The long frozen grass crunched and snapped underfoot. I was about to accuse him of playing the fool, but then I heard it, the far-off sound of scraping, and the muffled tap of brick being placed upon brick.

'But what are they doing? Raising the walls?'

'No, not raising them; breaking them down. Come here, you'll see what I mean.'

We edged down to where the side of the fort dropped sheer to the water, keeping a careful eye on the battlements. From where we were, a well-hurled stone would break a man's head. Close up, the sound was clearer. Marcellus placed his hand on my shoulder and directed my eyes along the line of the river. And then at last I saw. The Franks were breaking open the sealed-up riverside postern, scratching out the old mortar and lifting away the bricks, carefully, one by one. The postern opened onto the river, and nowhere else.

I turned to Marcellus. 'But where will they go? They have no boats.'

'You are still asleep, Drusus! Look! They have no need for boats.'

I looked, and then I stared. The surface of the river was motionless, like dull grey glass, frozen hard.

'You see?' said Marcellus, crouching down and tapping the ice. 'They're going to walk across.'

'So that's it,' said Julian. He was standing with us on the bank shortly afterwards. Severus was beside him, and as we waited, Arintheus and Victor came hurrying from the camp.

'Are we going to let them escape?' asked Victor angrily. 'They will return as soon as we are gone. I'll go and rouse the men. We can cut them off before they reach the forest.'

Julian, who had been frowning to himself, said, 'No, wait.' He stooped down, and picked up a heavy terracotta roof-tile that lay at his feet. For a moment he turned it in his hand, gauging its weight; then, with a swing of his arm, he cast it out like a discus into the river.

It soared, landed with a dull thud, and glided over the frozen surface, finally coming to rest in midstream.

We watched in silence, our breath steaming from us in the bitter cold. Severus began to speak; but Julian raised his hand, silencing him.

At first there was nothing. Then came a sound like the snap of a falling branch. The river-ice groaned, the slab of tile shifted. It tilted, and then with a gentle splash it vanished beneath the surface.

Julian brushed the snow from his palms and turned to us. 'It seems,' he said smiling, 'that they have shown their hand too soon. Victor, send word for the boats.'

All morning we worked with axes and pikes, breaking up the frozen surface from our few flat-bottomed riverboats. The Franks crowded along the rampart, staring grimly down at us; and for once they were silent. Before sundown they had asked to parley. They were warriors, they said. They would not be slaves. If the Caesar treated them with honour they would surrender. If not, then they would die fighting, to the last man.

Julian, who would have done no less anyway, agreed. They would be treated as befitted fighting men; he would send them east, to serve in the army of the emperor, where other Frankish tribes had already enlisted. This satisfied them, and shortly after they filed out, clad in their rancid furs, tall men, with long yellow hair tied up like twine behind their shoulders.

Afterwards we restored the fort, and manned it with Romans. From the opposite bank of the Meuse, among the shadows of the dense forest, we saw fair-haired men observing us. Whatever they had planned, they now abandoned. They remained half a day, silently watching as their comrades were led away; then they vanished again into the boundless forest.

But while they were there, Florentius came to look from the rampart.

'This time,' he observed loudly to his servant, 'the Caesar has been fortunate.'

Julian was elsewhere. Perhaps I should have held my tongue. But his words seemed so mean and carping that I could not hold back from calling out in answer, 'I suppose, sir, it is beginner's luck again.' And at this a chuckle sounded from the men around me who were working on the fort.

Florentius looked sharply round, then stepped up close, and in a low voice muttered, 'Save your wit, Drusus. New wood makes a hot fire. He has had a small success against a band of raiders. He is reckless, and he will stumble yet.'

Eutherius returned to Paris from his mission to the emperor. I was with Julian when it was announced.

We were in Julian's study. He had been showing me his books. It was not a great library such as Marcellus's grandfather had owned in Britain, but favourites he would not be parted from – the Life of Alexander, which he read, he said, to remind him of greatness; Caesar's Conquest of Gaul, for tactics; Plato on law and love of wisdom; and a well-worn copy of Homer he had bought in Athens during his student days, which he kept in a brown leather scroll-case so he could always have it with him, even on campaign.

Now he set the books aside, called for warmed wine and honey-cakes, and sent the steward to find Oribasius. He was eager as a boy, fidgeting and pacing about. I told him I would leave him to his business; but he said, 'No, stay. There is nothing you cannot hear.'

Eutherius arrived fresh from his bath, looking as bright as flowers after rain, and smelling of scent of lilies.

He greeted Julian, then turning to me he spread his hands in a theatrical gesture and cried, 'Drusus! It is a joy to see you here.' He took my arm and enquired after Marcellus – he knew what mattered most to a man, and for all my reticence in such matters I believe he read me like an open book. The cakes and wine arrived; and then Julian asked, 'But what news?'

Eutherius eased himself down onto the couch and arranged his robe of jade-green silk about him. He reached for a honey-cake, dipped it into his wine, tasted it with evident pleasure, and then began.

When he arrived at the court at Sirmium, he said, after a most tedious journey, the grand chamberlain Eusebius had contrived to deny him an audience for a week. 'You know how it is, the usual petty spite concealed beneath a shallow patina of civility. No doubt he wanted to remind me of my place. But on the eighth day, after the intervention of certain of my old friends, I was finally admitted into the Presence and permitted to kiss the purple.'

After what Eutherius described as the ritual insincerities, the chamberlain had examined him with a barrage of questions about Barbatio – the Master of Infantry whom Julian had dismissed for incompetence – while Constantius sat motionless and silent, like a statue on a jewelled throne. Barbatio had accused Julian of exceeding his authority in Gaul. What, the chamberlain wanted to know, was Eutherius's answer to such a grave charge?

'What did you tell him?' asked Julian.

'I told him it was nonsense. Furthermore, since the range of your authority had not been defined, it was not possible for Barbatio or anyone else to know you were exceeding it. I said that in my view you were doing what was necessary to bring about the emperor's policy of restoring Gaul to order.'

'And was he satisfied?'

Eutherius rolled his eyes at the painted ceiling with its carved wood beams and old, faded gilding. 'Have you ever known the emperor say what he thinks? One struggles to know what passes through his mind. He listened with a face like alabaster. In the end, when there was really nothing more to say, he fluttered his finger for silence and declared in that odd voice he uses on such occasions: "Barbatio's dismissal is acceptable." So there it is. One must suppose he meant it, since no one from the court came to me afterwards, as is usually the case when the emperor has deliberately said what he did not mean.'

Julian shook his head, then paced across the room and gazed out at the plum-tree court.

'It is just as well, then,' he said, after a pause. 'Good men died because of Barbatio. I would not take him back. I owe the men more than that.'

Oribasius said, 'You have what you wanted, Julian. You are free of Barbatio.'

Julian nodded. 'Yes . . . thank you, Eutherius. Constantius would not have listened to anyone else.' But then he said, 'There was something more, wasn't there? I can see it in your face. What else did he say?'

Eutherius gave a resigned sigh. 'Only that there had been "adverse reports" . . .'

'"Adverse reports"!' cried Julian, snorting in derision at the phrase. 'Adverse reports from Barbatio, no doubt. What do they expect? Don't they see he is protecting himself?'

'The emperor is guided by his chamberlain in all things. Naturally he did not say where these reports came from, and, well, one does not question the emperor. But he did ask about the prefect, and said he wished you to take proper note of his advice.'

'So Florentius has been running to him too! Well, I should have guessed. I wonder I manage to fight the German tribes at all, with such enemies at my back. Tell me, has Constantius received the prisoners I sent from Strasburg? Did he find time, in all these complaints, to notice my victories?' He sounded hurt, even wounded.

'The matter came up – but do sit, my dear Julian; you are exhausting me with all this marching to and fro.'

Julian planted himself reluctantly on the far edge of the couch, sitting like a cat about to spring.

'Well? What did he say?'

Eutherius hesitated; then, with a weary motion of his large hand, he said, 'The emperor remarked that he was growing tired of the subject.'

Julian stared at him. It was seldom he showed anger – it was something he worked to control, thinking it unbecoming in a man whose goal was virtue. But now he cried, 'What! I have delivered Gaul from the barbarians; I have sent Constantius the German high-king in chains; I have dispatched hordes of recruits for his armies; and he *tires* of my victories?' He sprang to his feet once more. 'By the gods, Eutherius, *you* know I did not ask him to appoint me Caesar! But what choice did he give me? He sent me here without enough men, and with incompetent generals, and when I succeed in spite of that he "tires of my victories".'

Eutherius watched him with his dark, patient eyes; and

when Julian had finished he said gently, 'Come now, why be surprised? You know the man as well as anyone. I considered not telling you at all; but it is surely better to have the knowledge and use it to your advantage, than to dwell in ignorance. That, at any rate, is what I should prefer.'

He reached out, took Julian's hand as he passed, and sat him down. 'And what does the safety of the frontiers matter to the chamberlain and his army of clerks? Each is full of his own ambition – a move to improved quarters; a requisition for new tapestries and furniture; the provision of an extra house-boy, or a mistress, or a doe-eyed Ganymede. Such are the concerns of the court. What are the frontiers compared with that?'

Julian swallowed, shook his head, and, in spite of himself, smiled at Eutherius's words. I had been starting to wonder if he regretted asking me to stay. But now he turned to me.

'You see how it is, Drusus? He distrusts even my victories. Those, at least, I thought would please him.'

'Well, the court is the court,' said Eutherius, 'and the emperor is the emperor. But listen to this: at every town on my journey, you were on the people's lips; *they* have not tired of your victories, and Constantius knows it. Do you understand now why he is irked?'

'He claims my successes as his own. Is that not enough?'

'A man may lie to others; but he cannot lie to himself. Constantius needs a victory of his own. He does not care to have the moon outshine the sun.'

He sat back and sipped at his spiced wine. 'At court, I took the chance to speak to some old friends. It seems

PAUL WATERS

there is a new faction, led by the chamberlain. Whatever Constantius's view might be – and who can tell? – we can be sure the chamberlain knows the truth of your success, which is far more dangerous to us.'

'Have I not done as I was asked?'

'You never were a politician, my dear. The chamberlain sent you here not to succeed, but to fail. And now he sees his plans undone. He sees instead that you become popular, a hero in the people's eyes, while Constantius languishes in his palace, achieving nothing.'

Oribasius, from his stool beside the bookcase, said, 'What else can we do? Allow ourselves to be defeated, merely to please the chamberlain?'

Eutherius gestured, spreading his open palm at him. 'And there,' he said, 'is the paradox: the chamberlain thought he was sending a naive student to Gaul to meet his death. Now, instead, he finds a victorious warrior. He must be spitting blood. And as for Constantius, well, everyone knows the emperor hates heroes.'

86

FOUR

EARLY THE FOLLOWING SPRING, a new official appeared at the palace. His name was Gaudentius, and it was put out – it was never clear by whom – that he was attached to the office of Florentius. But no one ever saw him do any work at the prefect's offices, and he had a habit of lurking about in places where normal business would not take him.

Before long, everyone assumed he was a spy of Florentius's, but even so it was hard to take him with much seriousness. He came from Dacia or Thrace; and had a Thracian's ruddy hair, which stood up straight on his forehead in an unwieldy brush. This, together with his protuberant pale eyes, his thick lips and his habit of breathing through his open mouth, made him look like a comedy mask in the theatre. Apart from the jokes, I daresay I should not have taken much heed of him, except that he started following Marcellus, waylaying him in the corridors and courts, finding excuses to converse with him as if they were long-lost friends.

Marcellus, never quick to recognize guile in others, supposed he had picked up an admirer. I smiled at his innocence, and reminded him not to say anything in Gaudentius's hearing which he did not want to get back to the prefect.

I think, at first, he thought this over-cautious of me. But then one day, when we were walking together to the stables, he asked, 'Has Gaudentius said anything to you lately?'

'No, nothing.' And I added with a laugh, for it had become something of a joke between us, 'He has eyes only for you.'

He gave me a shove. 'Drusus, I'm serious.'

'Then no. He has sense enough to tell I don't like him and keeps away from me. But why? What has happened?'

'He's been asking questions about Julian again. It's not the first time.'

I asked what he had said.

Marcellus furrowed his brow. 'Oh, he doesn't come out with it directly, it's all hints and unfinished sentences, nothing you can nail down. This morning, for instance, he came to see my new mare, or so he claimed. He pretended to be interested for a while – though you can tell he knows nothing about horses. Then, suddenly, in the middle of his chatter, he made a ridiculous show of glancing over the stable-pens to make sure no one was listening, then lowering his voice asked if I had heard any of the tribunes complaining about Julian. He even asked if you had said anything.'

'What did you tell him?'

'I told him to go and ask the tribunes himself.'

He frowned up at the sky with its fast-moving clouds coming in from the west. Irritably he pushed his hand through his hair. He hated subterfuge.

'It will rain later,' he said absently. And then, 'I suppose I was quite sharp with him. Anyway, afterwards he grew angry, saying he had only been trying to do me a favour. He said that Julian was heading for a fall, and I had better keep my distance if I knew what was good for me.'

'I told you before, he is Florentius's crony. And no one needs a spy to know what *he* thinks of Julian.'

'Yes, well you were right about him. In any case, I expect he'll leave me alone now.'

We said no more on the matter, for just then young Rufus the squadron trumpeter appeared under the arch of the stable yard, leading a sleek chestnut mare. He waved and came over, and after that all the talk was of horses.

In the time since we returned from the Meuse, Marcellus had been working hard to get the cavalry recruits into shape. He had taken them out to the open country around Paris, where they could practise jumping ditches, clearing walls and leaping banks; where horse could bond with rider, and riders with one another. Marcellus was well liked, and Rufus had attached himself to him like a trusting dog. He was a good-natured, fine-looking youth of eighteen, with black hair, a fresh face, and striking bright eyes. His father was a horse-dealer in Marseilles, and Rufus had grown up with horses. He looked young for his age, and was teased about it. But he was a natural horseman.

'Well, what do you think of her, Drusus?' he asked smiling.

I smiled back, complimented him on the creature, and listened while he told me how he had spent the morning helping the groom. It was impossible to dislike the boy, and there was something moving in his tender love of horses, a kind of innocence that most men would try to conceal. I could understand why Marcellus had taken him under his wing.

But Gaudentius and his clumsy spying stayed on my mind, and when next I saw Eutherius I mentioned what had happened.

I made light of it, half-expecting him to laugh it off, for he was used to intrigue of all sorts, and regarded Florentius as something of an amateur. But instead he looked sharply and asked me to describe Gaudentius, whom he had not seen.

When I had finished he nodded and said, 'Yes, I know him. He is one of Constantius's agents.'

'So he is not working for Florentius after all?'

'The emperor's agents do not leave their employment, especially not for a demotion such as that.' He lifted a fig from a bowl of dried fruits and squinted at it. 'He will be reporting back to someone at court; the chamberlain, I expect.'

'He seems harmless enough – a bit of a fool, really.'

'Oh he is an incompetent buffoon,' said Eutherius, 'and clearly it was intended that he should be noticed. Nevertheless, men have died because of him. You should not underestimate his capacity for mischief.'

All through winter, Julian had worked on his strategy, consulting with the commanders and scouts, poring over maps of the frontier regions, studying each pass and plain and river crossing. In his first campaigns, when barbarians were ranging all over Gaul, he had done no more than drive them back wherever he found them, like a man stopping up leaks in a cistern. But now his plans had firmed: he wanted to bring about a lasting peace.

There had been a time, he said, when the frontier was a defensible line extending from where the Rhine flowed into the northern sea, all the way eastwards past Strasburg to the great barrier mountains of Raetia in the south. But in our weakness we had permitted Alamans and Franks and other itinerant German tribes to settle on Roman land; and now they had occupied it for so long they considered it their own.

At first, like beggars grateful for what they are given, these settlers had promised to respect Roman laws and live in peace. But German barbarians are naturally proud, and have not learned to temper their pride with reason. When they learned they could attack their undefended neighbours with impunity, they abandoned farming and turned to banditry instead. They stole crops; they burned settlements; they seized the helpless citizens and used them as their slaves. Such behaviour, since it had been so long tolerated, the barbarians had come to regard as their due. 'Yet why do we permit it?' Julian asked. 'Do we fear them? Or is it that we have lost faith in ourselves?'

He returned his attention to the great parchment map on the table. 'We must restore the frontiers,' he said. 'We must drive them back across the Rhine from east to west; or, one day, when our attention is elsewhere, they will sweep down through the passes into the plains of Gaul; and after Gaul then Spain, and Italy, and Rome itself.'

At this, the quaestors and tribunes around the table looked sideways at one another and exchanged private glances. The Caesar liked to exaggerate such things. But to say that Rome itself might fall, well that was taking credulity too far.

But Julian was still intent on the map. He did not see their knowing smiles. 'We must not allow it,' he declared. His finger stabbed at the curving line of the Rhine. 'It is *here*,' he said, 'that we must hold them!'

He waited impatiently for the long northern winter to pass. When the first blossom showed on the plum trees in the courtyard, and the yellow crocuses appeared on the riverbank, he ordered the army to make ready. Only then did Florentius come to him and say the supplies had not yet arrived from Aquitaine.

'Then where are they?' demanded Julian. 'You knew of my plans; you have had all winter to prepare.'

Florentius gave one of his astringent smiles and explained as if he were speaking to a fool that the progress of imperial convoys was hard to predict, especially in winter; furthermore there had been sickness in the requisitions office, causing unavoidable delays; orders had to be approved and reviewed and then passed up for higher consideration; surely a man in the Caesar's position understood such matters? He talked on, outlining in detail each difficulty, his voice monotonous and complacent.

Julian stared at him, the line of his mouth hardening.

'Then when,' he said, finally interrupting, 'will I have my supplies?'

'Perhaps in a month; possibly longer. I cannot say for sure, as I have just explained.'

'The convoy will be somewhere, will it not?'

'Of course.'

'Then dispatch one of your people to find it. Will that be possible, Prefect? Or must I go myself?'

'That will not be necessary,' began Florentius smoothly; but Julian broke in with, 'Good; then I await your answer. And now, it seems, we both have work to do.'

And with that he turned and left the room, not trusting himself, I believe, to remain.

But I was still there, and now the prefect turned to me and glared. The Caesar needed to understand, he said coldly, that there were procedures which had to be followed; and in all truth he should have considered these matters the previous year, or even the year before. If he now found himself in difficulties he had only his own reckless temperament to blame.

If Florentius thought he was addressing an ally, he was mistaken. I heard him out, then said, 'Our enemies, sir, have not yet learned to wait on the convenience of administrators and bureaucrats.' And then I too excused myself and left him.

Time passed. Days became weeks, and still the supply train did not arrive.

Julian complained he was losing all the advantage of surprise. Each day of delay would cost Roman lives. He waited a month; then, one early morning, he said, 'Come up to the camp with me, Drusus. I want to inspect the granaries.'

We rode up to the fort, and with the quartermaster standing beside us we peered into the dark timber-floored chambers at the remains of the winter barley ration.

Julian picked up a handful and sifted it through his fingers. 'It will do for twenty days,' he said. He ordered the quartermaster to have it baked into biscuit. Then, turning to me, he said with the hint of a smile, 'I wonder how long it will be before the prefect comes to see me.'

We did not have long to wait. Before the day was out, Florentius came bursting into Julian's study, attended by a train of pinch-faced officials. He ignored Oribasius and me, and cried, 'The Caesar jokes! You cannot propose to march with only twenty days' ration.'

Julian raised a quizzical brow. 'I do not joke, Prefect.'

'I cannot assure the supplies you need.'

'As you have said. But there is a task to be done. I shall not wait any longer for your department to catch up. Twenty days ought to suffice for you to deliver what is needed. If not, the army will go hungry, and we can both explain it to the emperor.'

Florentius was not lacking in intelligence; no man who is wholly foolish can rise so high. But perhaps comfort, and prosperity, and the habit of being obeyed without question, had formed on his character a husk of insensitivity, like the crust on the surface of rich, unstirred cream.

Whatever the cause, four days later, when Julian was touring the camp, making final preparations to march, we strode into the main courtyard and saw in the middle a pair of part-loaded wagons and a group of Florentius's liveried officials clustered about them.

'What is this?' asked Julian, turning to the nearest trooper.

'It is the prefect's luggage, sir.'

Just then, from the other side of the wagon, Florentius's chief steward appeared. He was a crass, self-important man who had learned his officiousness from his master.

'Can I help you?' he enquired in a loud, cold voice.

'Tell me,' asked Julian, 'is the prefect going somewhere?'

'Why, he is accompanying the army, of course.'

'Is he now?' Julian nodded slowly, then glanced round to where a detachment of men was passing. He beckoned to the captain. 'Offload all this,' he ordered.

'But sir—!' protested the steward.

'You may tell the prefect,' said Julian, raising his voice to silence him, 'that he shall remain here; and perhaps, if we are fortunate, he will manage to locate our supplies. Then, if he wishes, he may join us, bringing the supplies with him. But until that time, we have no need of him.'

He turned and strode away, leaving the astonished servant staring, while the troops, grinning to one another, heaved down Florentius's bronze-bound chests and ornate boxes, and flung them into a pile in the middle of the fortress yard.

*

We marched next day, in bright, cool spring weather. Where we encountered pockets of barbarians, we engaged them. But mostly they just slipped off at our approach, like grass-snakes at the sound of footfalls.

Then, near Tongres, envoys arrived from the Franks, demanding to see the Caesar.

'Very well,' said Julian. 'Let us hear what they have to say.'

We arranged to meet in the stone barn of a ruined farmstead. Eventually, after a long wait, the Frankish ambassador came swaggering in. He was tall, like all Germans, clad in heavy furs clustered with brooches inlaid with precious stones. His long yellow hair was tied back in intricate knots, a labour as fine as any Keltic bronzework.

He paused at the line of officers, inspecting us – Marcellus and me; then Severus, Arintheus, Victor, Valentinian and others – all of us dressed in our best uniforms with our plumed helmets and polished breastplates and scarlet cloaks. He cast his eyes disdainfully over us as if we were the dregs of cattle, gave a scornful bark, and then, at his own desultory pace, like a fat man taking a summer stroll in his pleasure garden, he advanced to the dais where Julian stood waiting. Our display of might, as old Severus commented later, would once have impressed the barbarians into respect. But no longer. They had learned that the mailed glove concealed nothing but a trembling hand.

At the makeshift dais he halted and made a show of looking about him, as if the young lean soldier before him could not possibly be the Caesar. But he knew well enough who Julian was. Then at last he spoke, in rough accented

Latin. What was the meaning, he wished to know, of bringing our army so close to Frankish lands? Our closeness was a threat, a provocation. He demanded that we withdraw.

All this took some time, for it was more of a harangue than an ordered speech, and every so often he broke off to make comments in his Frankish tongue to the fur-clad lieutenants who stood beside him. But when at length he was finished, and was standing with his broad hands on his hips, Julian replied pleasantly that he had received reports of brigands in the area, marauding upon Roman land; he was sure the ambassador's own people had nothing to do with these criminals, and so they had nothing to fear.

The ambassador laughed. His lieutenants, taking his lead, laughed too. Then, as suddenly as a sword-blade slicing through rope, he broke off. Jutting his great blond-bearded chin at Julian he cried, 'We know nothing of these brigands you speak of. Romans have not disturbed us for many years. Do you wish for war?'

'We wish for peace,' said Julian. He paused, took a step forward, and fixed the ambassador with his eye. 'We wish for peace, and we shall make sure that we have it. You may go and tell that to your chief.'

He sent the envoys off, and we continued north, pausing to restore abandoned forts wherever we found them. Still there was no word from Paris. Mindful of our rations, Julian sent out troops of men to hunt for boar and deer. The forts had to be garrisoned, and the garrisons fed.

Julian supplied them by dividing the men's biscuit

rations. The men grumbled; but there was no other way. And here Julian made a mistake, for he promised to make up what they lacked by requisitioning crops along the way, and that the supplies from Aquitaine should soon arrive – a dangerous promise, since it was not his to deliver. The men believed him, because he had never failed them. But after he had finished his address and they were dispersing, I saw long faces in the crowd. I shrugged it off as nothing. I too was taken up in the dream he had woven.

And meanwhile we continued to advance.

Sometimes we fought minor skirmishes; but mostly the enemy declined to fight. Though they are fearsome when they gather into a horde, barbarians quickly fall to squabbling among themselves, lacking the discipline and order to forge themselves into a great army. So each small tribe, looking to itself, made its own peace with us, swearing solemn promises of submission and loyalty.

But when Julian asked for corn they pointed to the still-green shoots in their fields and said they had nothing to give.

Day by day, the ration of biscuit dwindled, and the men grew uneasy.

One evening, I was sitting with Marcellus and his cavalry friends around the fire, drinking watered wine. The night was cool; above us the sky was speckled with glinting stars. We had been talking of Julian's early campaigns, from the time before Marcellus and I arrived at Paris. Now there was a pause. One, whose name was Plancus, shook his head and said, 'Yet how soon the men forget what he has done for them.'

'Not so, Plancus,' said young bright-eyed Rufus who was sitting beside him. 'They would not have followed another as they have followed him – and all of it without pay.'

'Without pay?' I said, looking up.

'Oh, didn't you know, Drusus? They've had nothing since before Strasburg. The emperor will not authorize the funds.'

'Well they can't blame Julian for that!' said another.

'They don't,' said Plancus. 'But if you leave a man with an empty purse, then best make sure his belly is full.'

A third, who liked to joke, said, 'Anyway, Plancus, you look well enough fed.' Comically he began caressing Plancus's belly with his hand. 'What is your secret? Have you found some barbarian girl to slip you a fine meal each night? And what does she get in return?' He made a face, and pulled at Plancus's kilt to show what he meant. There was laughter.

Plancus pushed him off. 'Very funny, Maudio. But listen to this. When I was down at the horse-pens today, I heard some ugly talk.'

The laughter died. 'What talk?'

'Mutiny talk, if you ask me. If my horse wasn't lame I shouldn't have been there at all. I heard the men across the wall, where the latrines are. They were complaining about Julian, calling him a foolish Greek and saying he had led them on, that he should have stuck to his books and left generalship to those that know it . . . Like I said, they have short memories.'

'Well, every trooper loves to complain. Serves you right for pressing your ear to the shithouse door.'

'Ha! ha! Go ahead and laugh. But mark my words: something is afoot.'

In the two days that followed the men grew less careful with their grumbling. Julian took it hard. He never pandered to a crowd, but he liked to be liked, all the same. Ever since his first victories the troops had adored him. They were local men, recruited from Gaul; he had fought beside them to save their homes and families. And now they wanted to turn back.

I asked Marcellus if Severus was of the same mind, for he was an old hand with soldiers and knew their moods better than anyone.

'He says march on; we have no choice now. If we turn back, the Frankish tribes will rise up behind us. They can smell weakness like a pig rooting out truffles. We would not get out alive.'

Somewhere in the camp there began the clangour of hammer on metal. Marcellus's head went up.

'It's only one of the farriers at his anvil,' I said, placing my hand on his shoulder.

He listened; then nodded. 'So it is. I'm as tense as a bowstring today.'

We all were. A stillness had settled on the camp. It was not the quiet of happy men; it was the bristling calm before the tempest, when the leaves hang limp on the trees, and even the birds fall silent. One ends up wishing it to break, so it may be over.

That evening, shortly before sundown, I was with Julian and the others, going over the next day's march. He had been about to speak, but in the pause there came from across the camp the sound of men's voices raised in anger. Julian glanced up frowning. No one needed to tell him what it meant.

He said, 'I shall go to them.' And before anyone thought to stop him, he had ducked out under the tent flap.

We all looked at one another, open-mouthed; then rushed out after him, among the makeshift huts and tents and smouldering cook-fires. The fires stood abandoned. There was an eerie quiet everywhere, except from the middle of the camp, where the assembly-ground was. 'By God!' cried Severus, 'he must not go there alone.' And then we ran.

Eventually we saw him, about forty paces ahead. Already the crowd of men was closing around him. I could hear his voice, speaking in his careful Greek-speaker's Latin, trying to make himself heard over the din. Pent-up violence hung in the air. But now there was confusion too. The men had not expected him to come alone.

He was talking on, reasonable and measured, trying to make them understand. Maybe those closest to him could follow his words – if they cared to. But he was losing the rest. I saw them looking about, speaking to one another and shaking their heads.

Then, just as we drew near, a surge of men came running from the avenue of tents on the far side. They poured in among the rest like a river into a lake. Something had already fired their spirits, like men who arrive at the games drunk and spoiling for a fight. They started whistling and calling, saying that Julian was a deceiver and a Greek amateur who should leave war to those who knew it.

Still Julian was trying to reason with them. I saw Severus shake his short-cropped, grizzled head: one does not reason with a mob. To the common soldier a general should be incapable of error. They do not want to hear excuses. Just then, close by, a different sound caught my ear. There was something not quite right, something all of a sudden rehearsed and staged in the jeering. But I had no time to reflect on it. We were quickly being encircled as the men pressed round. Soon there would be no way out.

I glanced about, quickly taking my bearings. Marcellus was close by. Rufus was beside him, his young face alert and full of moment. I do not think he had quite grasped the danger. But Marcellus knew, and was keeping the boy close. He nodded at me, and gave a private sign of acknowledgement. Two paces off, Severus stood poised, like a solid warhorse, with one hand at his sword-belt, and the other held out as a signal for us to wait upon his word. As a hunt-dog sniffs the air, he was gauging the shifting mood of the crowd. It was not yet mutiny – not quite. But to move too soon would provoke it.

Suddenly Julian's voice rang out, clear and sharp. His tone had changed. He was losing the men. He had realized his mistake.

'What is all this?' he cried. 'Look at you all! You put me in mind of a parcel of women, who stand clucking at the bread-shop door when the baker is late. Have you grown afraid of your own shadows? Where are the men that served me at Strasburg? There the danger was real, and yet we prevailed. Have you forgotten what you are capable of?'

All around the voices began to fall silent.

'You are in enemy country. If we turn back now, what will the barbarians think? They will cast their treaties into the river and fall upon us. I have not come this far, and endured such hardship, to turn back now, when victory is within my grasp. I am going to finish what I have begun. But leave, if you wish. I shall not compel unwilling men. Go to your wives and children! I shall not stop you. I will defend your homes without you.'

There was a pause, a faltering. And then, from within the crowd, different, quieter voices spoke up, assenting, remembering their past glories. Someone even ventured a cheer; it rose and died; but after a moment was picked up by those around him.

Julian had shamed them.

I saw the muscles in Severus's back and shoulders ease. His hand moved away from his sword-hilt. He stepped forward, his soldier's horse-sense telling him it was time for the men to remember their duty.

'Dismiss!' he barked out in his loudest parade-ground voice.

The men's backs straightened; slowly they began to disperse. I felt a touch on my arm. It was Marcellus.

'See who's here?' he said, nodding at the crowd.

I looked. The man was stumbling away, ducking down, trying to conceal himself between the tents. He had his back to us. But even at a distance, no one could mistake the brush of red hair that stuck up from under his pulled-up hood.

'Gaudentius!' I said, watching with disdain as he scuttled

away. 'But why? How can it benefit him to stir up a mutiny?'

But even as I spoke, I thought again of Eutherius's words, and remembered the jeering and the catcalls. Understanding dawned, like a sickness in my belly. I swallowed, and looked at Marcellus.

'This was not unprompted,' I said bitterly. 'The men have been worked on. Someone is seeking to undermine Julian, and whoever it is doesn't care what it costs.'

At first light next morning Julian called for his horse. He would brook no discussion. His mind was set. He rode straight to the nearest Frankish settlement – one of those that had recently promised peace and sworn a treaty – pulled up in the muddy open ground, and demanded to see the chief.

There was only a small band of us with him – Severus, Marcellus and I, and two others. The rest, at Julian's insistence, had remained at the camp. He would do this alone.

There was an uneasy wait. Outside the huts, tall fierce-looking Frankish wives and their yellow-haired children left off what they were doing and glared. Eventually, from within the long thatched building that was the chief's house, there was a stirring, and an ancient white-haired man emerged, leaning on a heavy oak pole carved with whorls and dragon-heads. Six young men stepped out beside him, dressed in heavy leather and armed with swords.

'I have come for corn,' declared Julian, 'in accordance with our treaty.'

The chief shook his head. Whether it was in refusal, or because he did not understand, I could not tell.

But Julian was in no mood for games. He strode to where a woman was sitting on a low rough-wood stool beside a quern-stone. 'This!' he cried, grabbing at the wheat in the basket and letting it pour out through his fingers.

From the surrounding huts, armed men had begun to emerge. They stood silent and threatening, their swords ready in their hands – old Roman swords, I noticed. The white-haired chieftain made a slight gesture; and at this the men paused, like well-trained dogs waiting for a word from their master. The chieftain peered at Julian with sharp cobalt-blue eyes, then loudly cleared his throat, moved his mouth, and spat into the mud.

'What shall we eat, Roman, if you take our corn?'

'I ask only for a part of what you have; I shall repay double what I take. In corn or in gold. You have my word.'

Murmurs arose from the men standing about. They could understand Latin when they wished.

The chief looked at us. There was nothing foolish about him. He must have guessed we were alone, and outnumbered. Perhaps he was weighing up the benefit of taking us hostage against the revenge that would be sure to follow. Or perhaps, as is told, the Germans respect individual courage above all else.

But he was master of his features, and gave nothing away.

'We cannot eat gold,' he said.

'Then you shall have corn.'

'And when you are gone, will you remember our corn? I think not.'

'I shall remember.'

The chief eyed Julian carefully, studying his face as a man might try to spy a still fish at the bottom of a murky pool. And Julian looked steadily back at him. There was a long, tense pause. Then, with sudden force, he raised the carved oak stave in his hand and pointing to the sky spoke out to the others in his guttural tongue. There were discontented mutterings from the young men, silenced by a cutting sweep of the chief's arm.

Then he turned to Julian. He did not smile. But there was the hint of laughter under his heavy white brow.

'You shall have your corn,' he said.

A steady rain was falling by the time we returned to the camp. Word had got round, and a shamefaced deputation of common soldiers had gathered outside Julian's tent.

There were too many to fit within, so he received them outside, standing with them in the rain. He ought to have taken them with him, they said, chiding; he had risked his life for them. How could he go into such danger and leave them behind?

There were tears, and embraces; and afterwards he gave each man in turn a coin from the little he had. It was no more than a token; but as the men turned to leave, wiping their eyes and casting affectionate backward looks, there was a sudden shifting from the back of the crowd and Gaudentius pushed forward. In a loud, officious voice he declared, 'It is against the law for a Caesar to pay a donative to the troops.'

Julian turned, his eyes widening. Across the rain-soaked, muddy square the band of retreating men paused and stared. Anyone else would have had Gaudentius dragged off; but Julian was so lacking in the usual arrogance of power that I doubt it even occurred to him.

'Donative?' he asked. 'What are you talking about? It was barely enough for a shave.' He spoke mildly, trying to make light of it. But Gaudentius, fool that he was, pressed on, saying the amount was immaterial, that he was obliged to take the money back.

'A man does not take back a gift,' cried Julian, his voice rising, 'have you lost your mind?'

Gaudentius, possessed of I know not what insane self-confidence, even began to answer this, quoting some rule or statute at him. But Julian cut him short. 'Who are you, by Hades, to interfere? Do you think I need some bar-rack-room lawyer to tell me my work?' He narrowed his eyes. 'But wait, I know you, I have seen you at Paris . . . You are Florentius's man, are you not? Then what are you doing here?' And when Gaudentius made to speak, Julian cried, 'Be silent! Florentius cannot do his own job; I will not have him – or you – instruct me in mine!'

He turned away. The little ceremony of reconciliation, under the drizzle, in that muddy patch of northern Gaul, had been spoiled; yet even now Julian left the matter. But as he moved off Gaudentius called out, 'You have no authority. The money must be returned.'

Julian froze in his step. Everyone was staring, even old Severus, whom little surprised.

Slowly Julian turned. His eyes moved to the group of

soldiers he had rewarded, who were standing now in one corner, open-mouthed.

'Remove this man,' he ordered. 'Give him a horse and send him back to his master. But see he leaves today – by the point of a sword if necessary.'

Then, grim-faced, he strode to his tent, slapping the leather flap aside as he entered.

We proceeded to the great barrier of the Rhine, and here the supply train arrived at last, escorted personally by Florentius.

He was received by me, Julian having ridden out that morning to inspect the boat-bridge he was building to carry us over the river. I dispatched a messenger, and waited with the prefect in the abandoned farmhouse, which just then Julian was using as his quarters.

Florentius stood in silence, long-faced, tapping his calf-skin boot impatiently on the stone slab. Somehow, I noticed, he had found time to have his hair curled and prepared. To be civil, I tried to speak to him, asking him about his journey and such things. But he answered shortly, as if I were one of his slaves, and soon I gave up and relapsed into awkward silence. By now, I knew, Gaudentius would have reported back to him; and, if I was any judge of Gaudentius, the story would have been embellished in the telling. At last, voices sounded outside. Julian came clattering in at the door, accompanied by the chief engineer, and by Oribasius and Severus. His boots and cloak were mud-spattered, and there was a smear across his brow where he had wiped it. He looked as if he had been clambering all over the riverbank, as I daresay he had, for he was not one to leave the dirty work to others. He was a little out of breath, and the glow of enthusiasm still showed in his face. He even smiled.

'You have come yourself,' he said pleasantly.

Florentius returned his smile with an icy stare. 'How not? The matter was pressing, so I was told.'

'Yes, well, that is true. Even so, I thank you for your trouble.'

There was a difficult pause. Julian coughed and glanced at me. 'Nevertheless,' he said, and then went on to ask after particular items he had been waiting for – cured meat and biscuit for the men, amphoras of oil and wine, a consignment of armour from the military factories, and various building supplies.

'I cannot possibly tell you about any of these things,' broke in Florentius in a hard voice, 'you will have to ask the quartermaster. I do not concern myself with minor details. What does concern me, however, is that I am told you propose to cross the Rhine into German territory. I hope these reports are mistaken. I fear they are not.'

'They are not. The German tribes have been plundering our river traffic. They have made the Rhine impassable.'

Florentius gave a loud sigh, like a man who is forced to repeat himself to a fool. 'You are new to Gaul, Caesar, so perhaps you are unaware, but it is our policy to pay a subsidy to the barbarians, and in return they permit unhindered passage for our ships.'

Julian stared at him. 'A subsidy? We pay them a *subsidy*?'

'Why, yes. I should consider, ah, let us say two thousand pounds of silver as sufficient, though of course each year they expect more than before; but, as I say, two thousand pounds is reasonable.'

'Two thousand pounds, you say?'

'I believe that will prove acceptable. If they want more, they will tell us.'

Julian drew his breath and scanned the room, with a look that said: save me from this man. 'And yet,' he said slowly, 'when I ask you for funds to pay my troops, you tell me there is nothing.'

'That is a different matter entirely, a different account, which I—'

'No, wait; let me be clear. My men go hungry for lack of pay or supplies, and you talk of handing a ransom to barbarians? The same barbarians I am in the midst of making war upon so that we may traverse our own territory?'

'It is the custom.'

'The custom,' repeated Julian flatly. 'We hand out money to our enemies, because it is the *custom*.'

Their eyes locked. Florentius said, 'I have been here for some time, Caesar. I know how to manage matters. To stir up the German tribes is rash – reckless even. The emperor should be consulted.'

'That will take months – you know it will. The barbarians are in disarray; if we strike now, we shall secure the frontiers for a generation.'

'So you suppose. But the risk is too great. I cannot agree to it.'

There was a pause; both men looked at one another in silent incomprehension. Somewhere outside I could hear the quartermaster shouting out orders as the wagon-train was unloaded, and the sounds of moving baggage.

'Very well,' said Julian, 'you have made your opinion clear. No blame can attach to you. You may have that in writing if you wish. Now was there anything else, Prefect? If not, I have work to do.'

Florentius hesitated; his expression tightened. He had not expected to be overruled. He dwelt in an ordered world of fawning bureaucrats where his instructions were followed without question. It was as if one of his servants had suddenly slapped him in the face. Now his eyes swept over the rest of us for the first time, and over the crude little peasant's room that was Julian's quarters, with its muddy stone floor and bare walls and cracked windows. He was wondering whether to feel humiliated, whether he could read it in our faces. But everyone was keeping his expression as wooden as the prefect's, giving nothing away.

'There is another matter,' he said coldly. 'But it would be better, I think, if I spoke to you in private.'

If some goodwill had existed between the two men, I daresay Julian would have led him off by the arm, or asked us to step outside. But instead he replied that whatever the prefect wished to say could be said openly in front of his friends. I suppose he expected some private threat from the emperor, or a complaint about how Gaudentius was ejected from the camp.

'Very well,' he went on coldly, 'as the Caesar wishes. I

bring news of your wife. She has given birth to a son. The child was stillborn.'

There was an astounded silence. The young orderly in the small open room beyond dropped his pen. I heard it clatter and roll on the stone floor. Julian drew in his breath, and for a moment stared at the window. His colour scarcely changed.

'Thank you, Prefect. Was there anything more?'

Florentius shook his head. The self-satisfied curl on his lips had melted away. I think even he realized he had gone too far.

'In that case,' said Julian, 'I believe this meeting is over, so you will excuse me.' He turned to the chief engineer, who was standing against the wall, looking appalled. With hardly a pause he went on, 'We were in the middle of inspecting the rope bindings on the bridge, were we not? Let us go and finish, then, while there is still daylight.'

And he stepped out of the door, and after a moment the engineer remembered to hurry after him.

For all my closeness to Julian, it had taken some time before I discovered that he had a wife. Even then it was from another that I heard it, for he himself had not spoken of her.

She was a woman many years his senior, whom he had been compelled to marry when he was appointed Caesar. Her name was Helena. She was the sister of Constantius. Once, in Paris, I had caught a glimpse of her as she hurried along the colonnade towards her apartments; a stocky lumbering woman with straight brown hair and short legs.

I do not think there was even the pretence of love between them. Little wonder, for if she resembled anyone at all it was her brother the emperor, a fact that was sure to chill the marriage bed.

But one never heard of women being taken to his room, or boys either. A saying he had picked up from his philosopher teachers in Athens was that a wise man is the master of his passions. He despised grossness in all things, and prided himself on controlling his appetites. Yet I suspect, in the end, his reticence had as much to do with shyness, and not considering himself attractive. He hated the thought of forcing himself on anyone. He had seen too much abuse of power, and would not have men accuse him of it.

That evening, after supper, I walked down to the river with Marcellus. A mist was rising from the water; the air smelled of wet leaves and river mud. Torches illuminated the hulls of the boat-bridge, and the ramp of the causeway, and the guards' hut by the water. We strolled down the slope to look. Hawsers bound each boat one to the other, and already the causeway across the hulls was almost complete. We greeted the guards and walked on, talking quietly.

Presently Marcellus broke off. 'See there,' he said, nodding into the mist.

I looked up. Ahead, a solitary figure stood gazing out across the water. I recognized the square shoulders under the shabby army-issue cloak. Touching Marcellus's arm I said, 'We should leave him. I expect he wants to be alone, after today.'

But as we veered off he raised his arm, and called to us to join him.

For a while he stood in silence, gazing out across the Rhine at the mist-shrouded line of forest. Then, in a voice laden with melancholy, he said, 'Always the night comes on. They are out there somewhere, watching us, like wolves in the dark, waiting for us to falter.'

Wanting to dispel a little of his pain, I said, 'The word has spread of your victories. They will think twice now. Already you have done more than anyone thought possible.'

He nodded, frowning, and pulled the cloak around him.

'Yet there is so much more. Standing here at the limit of civilization, with nothing but endless waste beyond, a man feels his responsibility. Death comes to us all, for that is in our nature; but we are the slaves of Fate only if we choose it.'

He fell quiet. Presently he said, 'I loved my life in Athens, where no question was forbidden, no subject avoided out of fear of heresy. I wept when I was called away; I wept for the end of my happiness. And now I am here, a soldier making war. But I fight so that those men in Athens may live on in freedom, speaking their minds, and dispelling a little of the darkness.' He gestured towards the forest. 'Where are *their* philosophers? Where are *their* great libraries and cities? They do not want to possess what we have; they want only to destroy it. They would cut down the philosophers along with the rest, if once we let them in.'

The wind stirred, sighing and eddying in the trees.

Behind, on the high ground of the camp, the lights on the palisade flickered, and disembodied sounds of laughing voices came drifting down.

Julian turned and looked, the distant torchlight shining in his dark eyes.

'But I have learned something here in Gaul; I have learned that a man must engage with the world, for only then can he know his true self, and bring it under the rule of reason. Those priests of my childhood feared the greatness in man, and so they denied it. The age of heroes was finished; the best of men were no more than the worst, serfs to their jealous god. Such is their truth, and they would make us in their image. How they would have laughed if I had told them I should drive the barbarians from Gaul. Yet here I stand, and up there the men make merry, knowing their homes and wives and children are safe tonight. I am my own proof that men can be more than they know. But first must come the vision. Without that there is nothing.'

FIVE

THE WEATHER TURNED COOL and clear, good
marching weather. Shortly before the army crossed the
Rhine, I was passing through the camp when someone
called my name.

Dawn was breaking, and turning I was dazzled by the
low sun rising over the palisade. I shaded my eyes with
my hand. A figure was standing in the path of light, some
paces off. His hood was up; but as I turned he pulled it
from his head, and then I saw his face.

He had aged, and there was an old livid scar running
from his right temple to his cheek, ruining the handsome
features I had once known so well. But his blue-crystal
eyes and his strong, serious mouth were the same.

'Durano!' I cried.

His call had been uncertain. But now, seeing my smile,
he strode forward and we fell into a laughing embrace.

'Come on,' he said, throwing his arm about my shoulder

just as he had always done, 'I was on my way to break-fast.' And as we walked he told me how he had recently arrived, coming up from the south with the baggage-train.

At his tent, a lean, olive-skinned girl was crouching, kindling a fire. He spoke a few brisk words to her in some barbarian tongue I could not follow, and at this she went off and brought bread and cheese and wine. We sat on the low timber bench and ate, and as I pulled at the rough army-issue loaf and dipped it into my earthen cup of wine, I asked Durano about his comrades I had known in London – Tascus, Romulus and Equitius.

He frowned as he chewed on his food. Tascus, he said, had picked one fight too many when he was drunk, and got himself stabbed in the neck in a tavern brawl. As for Romulus, he had fallen in the battle at Strasburg.

'And Equitius?' I asked.

'He was with Magnentius at Mursa. After that I don't know. Maybe he made it; many did not.'

We spoke for a while of the great battle of Mursa, and the war between Magnentius and the emperor Constantius. I had been a youth in London at the time. The war had bled away the strength of the West; it had torn apart the imperial family, and eventually, in the exhaustion that followed, had let in the terrors of the scavenging barbarians and – far worse – the horrifying, corrupt treason inquisitions of the emperor's agent, the notary Paulus.

It was true, too, I reflected, that, but for the war, I should not have met Durano; for it had brought him to London. And without that, my life would have taken some other course. I shrugged. I am what I am, I thought. All

I can do is make the best of it. It is no use unpicking the past.

Durano, too, had fallen silent. When I looked round he had shaken the cloak from his shoulders, exposing the insignia on his tunic.

'You're a centurion then,' I said.

'First rank too. I was promoted two years ago.'

So we talked of that, and then of our lives, skirting around what was painful to remember. And as we talked I remembered the unsure youth I had once been, orphaned and alone, whom he had befriended. He had taught me to fight, and opened my heart to love, when I had supposed I should never be fit for either.

I sensed, behind his easy talk, that he was remembering it too. Wounds heal, I thought; yet the scars remain. He was a tough weathered soldier now. But I had known a younger, tender Durano, who had given much, and taken little in return; and in my youthful folly I had hurt him.

In front of us the servant-girl was going about her tasks. She had fetched a pile of dry twigs and, kneeling down, was carefully adding them in little bunches to the fire, pressing them into the small flame with her fingers. Her black hair was cropped short, so that she looked almost like a young recruit; and round her neck she wore some kind of charm, a plaited torque fashioned in bronze, with a dragon's head wrought at each end. She caught me looking. I smiled and she looked away. She had a lithe body under her loose homespun clothing, like a young runner's; but her eyes were not childlike: they were dark and thoughtful, and spoke of old suffering.

Durano, seeing my glance, said, 'The Germans took her. They kept her as a slave, but she escaped. I found her wandering in the forest.'

I asked him if he owned her.

'No, I don't own her. She had enough of that from them. She stays because she wishes.' He spat on the grass and twisted the fleck of white spittle into the ground with his foot. 'She won't speak of what they did to her; but even now she starts awake at night. She hates them, and would fight them herself if she could.'

We sipped at our wine, and for a while we talked of military matters – the coming campaign across the Rhine; his own troop; everyday camp gossip. Then he said, as if the thought had only just come to him, 'You have a friend in the cavalry. He is crossing to Germany with us, and you are staying behind.'

I turned and met his eye. 'Yes,' I said. And then, 'So you knew I was here.'

He laughed lightly, self-consciously, making the weathered lines crease in his face. 'I knew,' he said. 'But time passes.'

I understood. He had his pride, after all. It would not have done for him to come seeking me out, only to find I did not know him, or did not wish to.

I toyed at the fire with a twig and for a short while did not speak.

Presently I sighed and said, 'I was young, Durano. I did not know myself. But I owed you better. I should have been killed long ago, but for the things you taught me.'

He made a gesture that I was making much of little.

But when I looked at him I could see in his face that he was pleased. At least, I thought, I am no longer the tongue-tied boy I was, who dared not speak what he felt. I reached out and touched my finger to the scar on his temple. The wound had long since healed, but there was a dark furrow where the flesh had knitted.

After a moment he took my hand, and brought it gently down, holding it in his, looking into my open palm.

'That was a German sword,' he said. 'I got it at Strasburg. It was the same day Romulus died.'

'I am sorry,' I said.

He released my hand and shrugged. 'It is war. Men die.' And then, after a moment, 'Why don't you fight beside your friend?'

I drew my breath and frowned at the pale morning. It was something Marcellus and I had spoken of often, and it troubled me.

I said, 'He is in the cavalry; I am not.'

But Durano carried on looking at me, knowing as well as I that this was not a proper answer. And so I added, 'He is a better horseman. He would always be looking out for me, and not for himself. That is what he says.'

He nodded slowly. 'Then you are right to keep away. Each to his own strength. The men speak well of him. They say he's quite a warrior: he fights from the front.'

'So I have heard.' And it was true that one or two friends, thinking they were doing me a kindness, had praised his bravery in battle, giving me blow-by-blow accounts of how he risked himself. To this I had listened and said what was expected. In truth I had rather not have known.

Then, like an arrow coming unseen from the sky, he said, 'Do you love him, Drusus?'

I looked at him, to see if he was laughing at me. But his rugged face was serious, and his blue eyes returned my gaze without mockery.

So I answered, 'Yes, I love him. But I cannot do his fighting for him, nor stop him fighting. Some things a man must leave alone, or they break at his touch. I know that now.'

He nodded, and studied my face without speaking. He had never been much of a talker, when it came to what mattered. It was a thing I liked about him.

After a pause he said, 'It is with the gods; it is better thus.'

Then he drew himself up and stretched, like a man rising from his bed, spreading his tanned arms with their hard muscle and old sword wounds.

Around us the camp was stirring. We finished the bread, mopping up the crumbled cheese from the dish, and drank the wine, and soon afterwards I took my leave, promising to see him beyond the Rhine, when the rest of the army met up with the vanguard.

As we clasped each other's arms in farewell, he caught me back and said he had a favour to ask.

'Then ask,' I said.

He tipped his head to where the barbarian girl was sitting close by, busy with some sewing work. 'She has looked after me well, and for little reward. She has suffered enough from men. Find her something, will you, if I don't return?'

I promised I should, and made a sign against ill omen. He laughed at that; and then we parted.

But before I rounded the corner something made me glance back. Durano had already gone; but the girl was still there, sitting on her low stool outside the tent. Her sewing – a scarlet tunic of Durano's – lay on her lap. Yet her eyes were not downcast. She was watching me as I went, cool and bold and appraising.

Two days later, the vanguard of the army crossed the Rhine.

I stood watching from the western bank, with Oribasius at my side, while in front of us the army advanced over the boat-bridge, in single file, breaking their step to reduce the swaying of the floating causeway. The causeway – a continuous road linking one boat to the boat beside it – extended now from the west bank of the great Rhine river to the east. On the far side, in the clearing beside the forest, those who had crossed were waiting, formed into defensive lines. Already advance scouts had reported the area by the bridgehead clear; but a river crossing is a dangerous time, and the men were unnerved by the vast German forest, which is full of terrors.

By noon they had all crossed; then there was a lull as the companies re-formed and prepared to march.

I had been looking for Marcellus, and now I caught sight of him, looking fine and straight-backed on his chestnut mare, riding up the line to the head of his squadron.

Young Rufus was beside him, talking and pointing, full of happy expectation. I smiled to myself. I might almost have been jealous, for the boy was in love, if only he had known it. For the past days, whenever I had seen him, he had talked of little else but the campaign, and of Marcellus, who would be with him. One night in bed I had even teased Marcellus about it. But there was nothing in the boy's open simplicity to distrust.

There was a stirring. Severus, seated on his horse at the front, raised his arm and gave the signal, and then the trumpeters sounded the order to advance.

I glanced across at Julian. He was standing a little apart from the rest, frowning silently out at the army on the far bank, watching it move off under the forest canopy. He hated not being in the front line. He would have led them himself, if Severus had not dissuaded him, telling him bluntly how much he risked if he fell.

The land opposite was held by a Suomar, the chieftain of the German Alaman tribe. As the boat-bridge had neared completion and he saw we were in earnest, he had presented himself to Julian and asked for a treaty of peace, which Julian granted on condition that he allowed safe passage for the advancing troops, and handed back the Roman captives he held as slaves. This Suomar agreed to, and the treaty was sworn. Afterwards, with every appearance of friendliness, he had offered us scouts, two of his young warriors, who knew the pathless forest and would guide us.

I could see them now, at the head of the line, close to Severus – two blond youths in barbarian trousers. Severus had not wanted them, saying they could not be trusted, that they could lead our men anywhere. But the season for campaigning was drawing on, and in the end, reluctantly, he had agreed.

With the army gone, Julian did not sit idle. All that year, he had been making plans to restore the towns and forts along the Rhine, summoning artisans from every city in Gaul: surveyors and architects, carpenters, metalworkers and masons. But fewer had come than he expected, and we were short: there had been no need of their skills for so long that old masters had ceased to pass on what they knew to their apprentices, and the knowledge was being forgotten. Sometimes we searched far and wide to find a man who could build an arch, or a colonnade, or a well-set roof in the old confident style of the past.

To those citizens willing to return, or others who wished to start a new life on the frontier, Julian made grants of land on the fertile river plain, and built pleasant, spacious houses for them to live in. He was full of hope. Within a generation, he said, the borderlands would thrive as once they had before, and with the line of towns and forts complete, the frontier and all of Gaul behind would be secure.

Next he set about clearing the river of pirates, restoring the important trade route that ran from Britain to the towns along the Rhine. Britain, which had been spared the ravages of the German invasions, produced a surplus; the restored towns needed food – Britain would supply them.

Though he was only one man among so many, Julian's

enthusiasm spread like fire in tinder. Men who had grown used to defeat strove with a new vigour, each drawing strength from the vision Julian had placed before their eyes. If he allowed himself a little praise for it, I was not the one to begrudge him. A man knows his powers by what he achieves; and already he had achieved what others said could not be done.

Certainly no encouragement came from Paris, from where Florentius sent a steady stream of carping officials.

One evening, having wasted yet another afternoon with a deputation of them, Julian said bitterly, 'If you ask me, Drusus, he would gladly see Gaul overrun, provided only that his regulations and procedures were met.' We were dining in his quarters – a sparing meal of river trout and lentils. 'I've never met such blind arrogance, and by the gods there were enough petty puffed-up men at court. You know, I called at his house in Paris once. Have you seen it? You can scarcely move for hangings and bronzes and precious furniture.'

We laughed. Everyone knew how Florentius had grown rich from his office. His Paris apartments were sumptuous enough; but they were only a small part of what he had acquired. In addition, he kept a magnificent villa at Vienne, where his wife, who hated the northern cold, lived with his children. It was said too that he owned a house in Rome, as close to the Palatine as one could buy.

Julian nodded at our smiles and bit into an apple.

'I don't expect,' he said as he chewed, 'we should find requisitions for *those* in the public accounts.'

Our conversation moved to other matters, and for a

while we talked of the building work in the frontier towns.

But later, when the slaves had cleared away the tables, and we were sitting with our wine-cups around a single flickering lamp, Julian, who had remained a long time silent, suddenly said, 'I shall not let men like Florentius thwart me!'

Florentius, however, was a master of obstruction, and he had been busy at his art. Shortly after, an imperial courier arrived with a letter from Constantius, who at that time was at Sirmium in Illyricum.

That evening Julian showed me the letter. His eternity the emperor was disappointed to hear that his Caesar had found cause to disagree with the prefect on the matter of a payment to the barbarians. He should bear in mind that Florentius was experienced in such questions; he would be wise to defer to his judgement.

I read the words, and looked at the mighty seal, and then set the letter aside.

Julian said, 'So he went complaining to Constantius; it did not take him long.' He gave a shrug. 'No matter; the horse has fled the stable. I shall reply and tell Constantius he can save his money for something worthy. The Franks have submitted, our army is pacifying the far side of the Rhine, and soon the grain-barges will be on the water . . .' He broke off, interrupted by raised voices beyond the door. 'What now?' he said, looking up. I heard the rapid approach of boots on stone; then the door flew open and a cloaked tribune came clattering in.

'Yes Dagalaif, what on earth is the matter?'

'Sir,' he cried, catching his breath. 'It is Maudio, back from the German forest. There has been an ambush.'

We ran out. Maudio and a group of cavalrymen were waiting in the courtyard. Their uniforms were filthy; their faces were streaked with mud and sweat. I knew Maudio – he was one of Marcellus's friends. I looked for Marcellus. He was not there.

'What has happened?' cried Julian. 'Where are your men?'

At his words they all began to answer at once.

'No; wait,' said Julian, silencing them. 'Maudio. You speak.'

He began. His voice was flat with exhaustion. As he took a step forward, I saw that his right arm was grazed and bloody. They had been advancing through the forest, he said, when late in the day they came to a narrow defile, and a barrier of felled trees, blocking their path.

'What of the scouts?'

Maudio stood staring, like a man woken from his sleep.

'The scouts, Maudio! The German scouts. Did they lead you there?'

'The scouts? Oh, they were as surprised as anyone, sir.'

'I see. What then?'

Immediately Severus had given the order to close into defensive formation. Then one of the scouts had spoken up, saying he knew another route which skirted the pass, taking them above and behind. But sensing a trap, and reluctant to trust the scout's word, Severus had decided instead to clear a passage through the barrier and ride on with a small detachment, to see what lay ahead.

'When he did not return, some of us were for going after him. By then night was falling, and the men were growing uneasy.'

Julian frowned at this, then asked, 'Who was left in command, with Severus gone?'

'Jovinus, sir, for the cavalry; and for the infantry, Cella.'

'Two commanders.' Julian shook his head. 'Could they not agree on one? Where was Marcellus?'

'With Severus, sir, along with—' And he gave a list of names. I recognized many of them: they were from Marcellus's unit. I took a deep breath, and felt a creeping chill about my heart.

I listened on. Of the two commanders, Jovinus had wanted the army to advance at once through the forest in search of Severus. But Cella had insisted on waiting, saying that to follow in darkness would endanger them all. They had argued, but it was no time for generals to dispute in front of the men. In the end it was agreed that Jovinus and a small force would go ahead that evening, just to investigate, while there was still twilight to see.

'I went with him, sir,' said Maudio.

They did not have to go far. After a mile, in a place of deep shade, they came across a trench. It was partly covered still, with a concealing lattice of sticks and bracken. At the bottom had been laid ranks of sharpened upturned stakes.

Maudio sniffed and wiped his eyes with his forearm, smearing blood across his brow. 'If we had been going any faster, we'd have ridden straight in too. But we were walking the horses and on our guard, going slowly—' He choked and broke off.

The man beside him, Decimus, carried on. 'Severus lay at the bottom, sir. He was dead, still on his horse. He must have ridden straight into the pit.'

'And the others?' whispered Julian.

'Another horse – Rufus's, I think; or maybe Marcellus's chestnut . . .' He stole a glace at me and added quickly, 'But no more bodies . . . Severus always rode at the front. Jovinus thinks the others must have been taken.'

I became aware of a hand gripping my arm. It was Oribasius, and when I looked his eyes were full of concern. It was just like him to think of others' feelings, even at such a time. Julian was talking again, questioning Maudio. I forced myself to attend. Had the infantry been attacked? Where were they now? How long would it take to reach them?

Maudio, his eyes wet and his voice breaking, replied that the main body of troops was unharmed. They had withdrawn to safer ground and made camp. 'After that, sir, Jovinus sent us here, and I know no more.'

Julian turned to Dagalaif. 'Give word, we leave at dawn. Maudio, Decimus, I need you to come with me. I need men who know the place.'

'Yes, Julian,' they said together.

'Good. Now have the surgeon see to that arm, and then get some rest.'

He turned to go. I said, 'I too will come.'

'No, I need you here.'

But then he paused and looked at me.

'Yes, come, Drusus; of course. How could you not?'

*

We crossed the boat-bridge next day, in the first grey light of dawn.

I had known forest before, in Britain. But mostly, there, it has been thinned by centuries of cultivation, and traversed by roads or tracks, so that the woodland places seemed like islands surrounded by the works of man.

Here, though, the forest seemed to go on without end, dense and twisting and interlocking, vast limitless tracts where no man had ever passed, under a high canopy of oak- and beech-branches which shut out the light, making even full day seem like dusk. Innocent sounds – of leaves underfoot, or groaning boughs – made the dread creep in my hair, as if the trees themselves resented our presence.

But I had no time for fear, and pushed the brooding tree-gods from my mind. I had Marcellus to think of. I had seen the stolen looks of pity; but only Oribasius had spoken of it, coming to my room the night before and saying, 'There was no body, Drusus; remember that. There is hope yet.'

'Yes, Oribasius. He is not dead. I know it. I will find him, whatever it takes.'

I had thanked him for coming, and for his kindness. The rest I kept to myself. I could not conceive of life without Marcellus. I felt like a man on the edge of a precipice.

Late on the second day we reached the army, encamped on a knoll fortified by a hastily erected palisade. The men were hushed and nervous. At once Julian summoned Jovinus and Cella, and called for the German scouts to be brought to him.

The scouts had been fettered; they stumbled up with

fear in their eyes, expecting death. Using a German-speaking tribune as translator, Julian questioned them. Whose territory was this? What people lived here – Alamans or Burgundians, or some other German tribe? How many were they? Where were their settlements?

I watched their faces as they answered. Julian was angry. He would have put them to the sword at once if he had sensed deceit. But he spared them. Germans are not skilled in hiding their true thoughts, and their faces under their youthful blond beards showed they spoke the truth. They had been as surprised as the rest of us.

I was walking off after this, deep in my own concerns, when someone caught my arm. I turned in surprise, and saw it was Durano.

'Listen, Drusus,' he said, pulling me to one side, 'you must speak to Julian. That fool Cella wants to go blundering through the forest with the whole army, like a pack of dogs after a hare.'

'What of it? We shall find them thus.'

He shook his head. 'No, you will not. As soon as he approaches, the Germans will vanish into the forest, taking their prisoners with them . . . or killing them. They will not give Cella the pleasure of the battle he wants. That is not their way.'

'Then what, Durano?' I said a little crossly, 'How else shall we find them?'

'Persuade Julian to let me go after them tonight. Me and three men. That is all I need.'

I paused, seeing the sense in his words. Then I fixed his eye.

'And me,' I said. 'I will go too.'

He gave me a long look; then said, 'You may die.'

'Do you think I care about that? They have Marcellus, or he is dead already.'

He nodded slowly. 'Then speak to Julian. He trusts you, and does not know me from any other common soldier. Make him see the sense in what I say. And be quick. Already night is falling.'

And so it was that we set out into the twilight, soon after – Durano and his men, one of the German scouts, and me.

On Durano's insistence, we had left our armour and heavy weapons behind, and were dressed only in our leather military tunics and armed with daggers. Armour would only slow us down: what mattered was speed, and surprise.

The grey cloud that had sat over the forest since we crossed the Rhine had partially cleared, blown off by a freshening easterly wind. The scout, speaking in simple broken Latin, said he had seen a rill of water close to where Severus had fallen. If we followed it, there would be a stream; and somewhere along its course, he supposed, we should find a settlement.

We moved on, treading carefully, staring warily about. Presently the young scout paused, stilling us with a wave of his hand. Silently he gazed along the dark ground, like a dog on a scent. Then, with a nod to himself, he led us off the woodland track and up an incline between the trees. Soon we came to a rocky, bracken-covered outcrop. The scout paused, then scrambled up to the low peak, parted the undergrowth, and beckoned at the bubbling spring that lay concealed there.

After that, we traced the water's course downhill for about half a mile, to a place where it fell into a shallow, stony brook. Then we turned east, following the line of the brook along the base of a ravine.

I did not know Durano's men, and in the hurry before we set out there had been time only for a brief, rather cool introduction. There were three of them: Gereon, Pallas and Phormio; a tight-knit band of young men who had fought many times together. I was the stranger, and they regarded me warily, accepting me only because they trusted Durano. This I understood. At such times, when their lives depend on their comrades, soldiers want to stick with those they know. In other circumstances I daresay I should have withdrawn and left them to their mission. But I was seized by a kind of madness at that time – or perhaps it was some god that drew me on. Whatever it was, I was in no mood to give it thought. All I knew was that I would not be turned away.

The night hours passed. The moon rose and traversed the sky, sending shafts of cold blue light down through the partings in the forest canopy.

Little by little the watercourse we were following grew wider, fed and increased by small tributaries no bigger than a man's pace. After a while the terrain began to change, and we saw the first signs of the activity of men – a tree stump with old saw marks; a track indented with mule traces; and then, ahead on a hillside between the trees, a strip of field planted with corn.

We stepped up to the edge of the open ground, crouching in the shadows of the tree line. The scout muttered something in German to Gereon.

'What is it?' asked Durano from behind.

'Wood-smoke,' said Gereon. 'He smells wood-smoke.'

I sniffed at the air. At first I could smell nothing except leather and men's sweat. But then the breeze stirred and I too caught the tang of burning wood in the air. An owl hooted. Somewhere in the distance a dog began barking and howling into the night. We froze, listening. Durano whispered, 'It's not us, we're downwind; it has probably smelt a fox. Go carefully now. The settlement must be close.'

We edged forward. Beyond the ridge the land dropped steeply away into a hollow of coppiced hazel. At the bottom of the dip there was a wood kiln, gently smouldering; and next to it a watchman's hut.

'Stay down!' muttered Durano. He waved Pallas and Phormio ahead to investigate, and they went stalking down the slope, keeping out of view of the hut door. At the bottom they paused for a moment, drew their knives, and crept up from behind, edging round the cracked wooden walls, one each side, until they could see within. Then Phormio turned and raised his arm, beckoning us down. The hut was empty.

As I descended I stepped on something, and stooping picked up an apple core. It was brown – but not yet rotten. 'Come on,' said Durano, peering at it, then glancing uneasily at the star-speckled sky.

We took the track up the opposite side of the hollow

and followed it along a wooded ridge. Somewhere below, out of sight through the trees, I could hear the sound of running water. Then the path veered and descended, and we came out once more at the stream. It was wider now, with a row of stepping-stones laid across.

Gereon touched Durano on the shoulder and pointed. 'See there!' he said.

Ahead, looming dark against the night, lay a hamlet of squat mud-and-thatch houses, with rough animal enclosures in between. On the far side, apart from the others, there was a taller building, built in a ham-fisted imitation of the Roman style.

'The headman's house,' said Durano, after he had gazed at it for a while. 'Keep away from there. That is where the warriors will be.'

The moon had set. Venus shone in the eastern sky, and already the first dawn birds were stirring. 'This way,' he said, 'it's time we got off the track.'

We turned aside, into an expanse of shrub and tall grass that grew up in an area of low wet ground between the forest and the settlement. Pallas, a lean, fine-boned Greek from south Gaul, went ahead to check the way. 'Well?' whispered Durano, when he came stepping back.

'See that fir tree there, the one standing on its own? There is a man bound up against it.'

'What about guards?'

'None that I can see.'

We advanced, wading through the tall grass, keeping the settlement on our left. Then we climbed a low bank and came out into well-trodden open ground; it was a kind of village square, between the animal enclosures. Ahead, in the place where Pallas had said, a figure sat tethered to a tree trunk. He was seated on the ground, slumped and motionless. I could not tell if he was asleep or dead.

We darted across the open ground, ducking between the enclosures. The tethered man lay directly ahead now, dark and still against the greying sky. I paused, crouching down.

On one side of me, in a withy pen, a heavy she-pig lay on her side snoring, with her bald pink babies arranged in a sleeping row around her dugs. Durano came up beside me, followed by Gereon and the others. Then, just as we drew near, the bound man jerked his head up with a start. I heard him draw his breath to shout; but before he could make a sound I leaped forward and clapped my hand over his mouth, and made a sign for him to hush. Then I looked him in the face. It was not Marcellus – I knew that already. But I recognized him all the same. It was young Rufus.

'Are you the only one?' I asked.

He looked at me, dazed and blinking. He had been badly beaten.

'There were five of us,' he murmured through parched and broken lips. 'They took the others to the forest and killed them, one after the other. I heard their cries.'

I lifted my flask to his lips. He drank in great gulps, spilling the water down his bloodied tunic. I wiped his chin, and had it in my mind to ask why he alone had been spared. But then something made me look again at his torn kilt, and the blood and scratches on his half-naked buttock. And then I realized what they had kept him for, and what they had done to him.

He met my eye, imploring, his face full of shame. Silently I nodded, and tried to smile; and my eyes filled with tears of grief and rage.

I let him drink, and gently covered his kilt where it exposed him. He had possessed, after all, a fresh-faced, vulnerable childlike innocence; the very kind that a barbaric lust, loosed of all decency or restraint, would want to defile.

Around me the others had not noticed. They were speaking in urgent whispers, but I was only attending with part of my mind. There was a ringing in my ears, like a man who has been beaten about the head. Rufus coughed. 'Wait, Drusus,' he said, peering at me. 'Marcellus . . . Marcellus wasn't with the others; they took him apart, to the headman's house.'

The madness, which I had kept scarcely controlled, seized me then. I sprang up like a wild scalded thing and began to move. Someone grabbed me hard by the arm and jerked me back. It was Durano.

'Wait! Be still. The warriors will be sleeping in the headman's house. That is where they all go.'

I tried to snatch myself free of him, but he held me firm, his blue eyes locking onto mine. 'Think, Drusus! Remember what I taught you – now more than ever, if you want to save him.'

'Live or die, I will not leave him.' I spoke, but at first it seemed my voice was far away, as if it were not my own. But now my mind came back to me. I drew a deep breath and nodded, and said, 'Yes, I will remember.'

Meanwhile the others had cut Rufus free. He was standing unsurely, looking wretched. Turning to him, Durano said, 'They took him inside? Are you sure of it?'

Rufus frowned and shook his head. 'Maybe not inside. I could not tell.'

Durano turned, and saw my eyes on his face. 'Yes, go then,' he said, 'and see what you can find. Be quick, Drusus; it will soon be daylight.'

I left him, and hurried off between the enclosures. As I passed a hen coop a cock crew, loud and indignant, and I heard hens scurrying and clucking in alarm. I cursed under my breath. There was a house behind; anyone inside would surely have heard.

The hens settled. I went on more carefully. Behind me I heard footfalls and I swung round; but it was only Gereon, coming up behind. He nodded an acknowledgement and matched my pace, and we advanced together.

The headman's house stood in its own grassy clearing, between the settlement and the encircling forest. At the front, extending along the whole length, there was a raised overhanging porch, like a colonnade, with pillars of rough-hewn wood.

We crept to the corner, then paused and listened. All was quiet within. I stuck my head forward.

'Can you see anything?' whispered Gereon.

I shook my head. Tall wicker baskets, piled up near the door, obscured my view. I said, 'Wait here and watch for me. I need to get closer.'

'It's too dangerous, Drusus. I don't think anyone's there. Your friend is probably dead already. You heard what the boy said.'

I looked him in the face.

He looked back at me, and after a moment shrugged. 'He may be inside. What then?'

'I don't know; but I have to do this. That is how it is between him and me. Go back to the others if you want.'

'No,' he said firmly, 'I stay. Be careful.'

I stepped out and scurried along the exposed open ground, keeping my head low. Then I followed the line of the porch, to where I could get a proper view.

Beyond the pile of baskets was the great door of the chief's house, old black oak, carved with whorls and fearsome animal heads. I glanced about. At first I could see nothing but baskets and pots and other clutter. Then, at the end of the porch, near the great door, I noticed a shape, deep in twilight shadow, lying curled up against the post. I stared, narrowing my eyes, remembering the barking dog. But it was no dog that lay before me; it was a man's body.

I took a breath, and listened, forcing myself not to rush forward. The dawn birds were calling loudly, but I could hear no other sound, except my own heart beating. I crept up, moving on my hands and knees as I passed the door, expecting at any moment a band of sword-wielding warriors to fall upon me.

Then, closer now, at the edge of the shadow, I saw the broad hand I knew so well and, on the wrist, the tan leather strap that Marcellus had worn since he was a boy.

He was bound with a rope to the supporting post. Like

Rufus, he had been beaten about the face, though not so badly. They had stripped him of his belt and leather outer tunic, leaving only the thin red linen garment beneath. Through it I saw his sides stir gently with his breathing, and I allowed myself to live again.

Softly I touched his shoulder. His eyes flashed open, and I signalled for him to make no sound. Then I took my knife, and began cutting at the tether.

It was tough plaited hide; the knife slipped and slid and would not bite. I braced myself and pulled it taut, and pressed down hard with the blade. Marcellus pulled too. Then suddenly, with a loud snap, the tether parted, sending me falling heavily back on my haunches.

I froze, startled at the noise, looking up at the house.

The sound had echoed up the wooden post like the beat of a drum. At first there was nothing. Marcellus began to speak, saying something about how the Germans had been up half the night at their wine, and it would take a kick to the head to wake them. I almost laughed. But then, just as I thought we were safe, it began, a furious grating of animal claws scrambling violently on wood, followed by frenzied barking.

We leaped from the stoop and ran to where Gereon was waiting, tense and wide-eyed. Behind me urgent voices were already shouting from within the headman's house. Then I heard the heavy door-bolts shifting.

We raced down the track. Ahead the others were urging the horses out of the paddock. As I passed the pigsty, I heaved open the gate, and yelled and waved my arms, rousing the she-pig and scattering the squealing piglets into the path. The dogs had been loosed from the house. I could see them behind me, coursing across the open ground; they were closing fast.

'This way,' I cried, pulling Marcellus with me.

We veered off the track into the tall grass and ran on, stumbling over concealed runnels and boggy pools. It slowed us, but – as I had hoped – it put the dogs off our scent. We were almost through, where the grass met the forest and the stream, and the others were waiting. But then, ten paces behind, Gereon suddenly cried out and fell. I stopped and turned. A dog was upon him, snarling and biting. I shouted for Marcellus to go on. Then I turned, drawing my dagger.

Gereon was struggling to keep the creature off. It stood over him, tearing at his forearms, trying to reach his throat. Then, as I moved, its head jerked round: it must have sensed me coming. It growled and drew back, ready to spring, baring its bloodied fangs. Carefully I advanced, stepping sideways, using a wrestling feint I knew; and at this, as I had intended, the creature abandoned Gereon and leaped at me.

It was powerful and quick, with huge strong jaws. Yet I was quicker. I twisted round, ducked down, and sank the knife into its side. The dog gave a furious howl, but the blow was not mortal and whipping round it lunged at me again, snapping at my face. But Gereon, his hands now free, had found his own dagger. He stumbled forward and thrust it into the dog's throat. There was a gurgling hiss of air; the beast shuddered and choked, and then fell lifeless between us.

There was no time to talk. We ran on, panting for air. Gereon's left arm was bleeding, and when we reached the others I sat him down by the stream, and helped him clean it. All over the barbarian village there was shouting now. 'Time to go,' said Durano.

We moved off, splashing through the chill shallow water to hide our scent, and soon we were back under the deep concealing shade of the forest. We followed a narrow gully, where the stream flowed clear on a pebbled bed, through a tunnel of overhanging branches. I was last, with the rest some paces ahead. The stream changed course at a great smooth rock, and as our advancing line moved around it, I lost sight of the others.

I saw the shaggy creature in the instant before it struck. For a moment I thought it was a bear, or some other wild thing of the forest. Only as I fell did I see the iron belt-studs in the animal furs; and then I knew it was a man. He must have come over the ridge by a shorter path, or lain in wait behind the rock, among the osiers and tall ferns. I had no time even to reach for my knife. He held me pinned with his great bulk beneath the surface of the water, pressing my face down, suffocating me. I sensed his body shift, and through the water I saw his arm rise above me for the fatal blow.

With the last of my strength I kicked out hard and twisted. He seemed to hesitate. My head broke the surface and I hauled the air into my lungs. I saw then why he had paused. Marcellus was on his back, clinging on like a child on a bucking horse, while the barbarian roared and swung at him with his dagger. I reached down to my belt, but my knife was gone: I must have lost it when I fell. I began searching wildly in the stream-bed with my fingers, but all I felt were pebbles and sand. But then, turning my head, I saw the blue-silver blade in the stirred-up water, two paces away, at the furthest edge of my reach.

I lunged out. For a moment I felt nothing but yielding sand, and could stretch no further. Then, at last, my fingers touched the familiar cord-bound hilt. I snatched at it, and with a great yell rose up and buried the blade in the struggling mass of wet furs above me. I heard Marcellus fall; then Gereon and Durano were there. I struck again. My attacker wheeled round with a bellowing roar. For an instant his eyes above his beard met mine; then he staggered, toppled into the blood-smoked water, and was still.

I climbed to my feet, and stood fighting for my breath, with my hands on my knees. My leg was bleeding, but the wound was not deep. Beside me Durano kicked the body and cursed. Then I looked up and saw Marcellus clutching at his side.

'It's nothing, a graze . . .' he said, meeting my eye. But his face betrayed him, and looking down I saw blood welling between his fingers, spreading over the side of his tunic and dropping into the water like great red tears.

I ran forward. 'Don't be a fool, let me see.' I took his hand away and pulled up his tunic, exposing the bare flesh. There was a deep gash in his side, along the line of his ribs. Pulses of blood surged from it each time he took his breath.

I sat him down. 'You're shaking.'

'I got wet. The water's cold.' He tried to smile. But instead he gasped and coughed, and when he looked up again I saw blood on his lips.

Durano had gone scrambling up the bank to make sure the warrior had been alone. He returned while I was binding Marcellus with a strip torn from my tunic. He crouched, and inspected the wound, and helped me pull the bandage tight. 'We must continue,' he said frowning. 'The rest will not be far behind.'

We pushed on through the forest, following the stream. Marcellus could walk, but his face was ash-grey, and every few steps I heard him catch his breath, though he tried to hide it. The day came on, and slanting threads of light pierced the canopy of forest.

Presently I saw Gereon pause. He was with the German scout, about a spear's throw ahead. The scout touched Gereon on the shoulder and directed his attention into the distance. I looked, following their gaze. At first I saw nothing; but then, beyond a thicket, I noticed a slight movement in the dappled light, and saw in a bright clearing a grey stallion, wearing a Roman headstall, calmly chewing at the grass.

Marcellus said, 'That's Plancus's horse. It bolted when we were taken.'

He climbed up the bank and went to it. The creature, knowing him, tossed its head and nuzzled its face against his hand.

'What happened to Plancus?' asked Gereon.

'They took him into the forest with the others. He did

not beg for his life; but I knew when they killed him. He cried out his father's name.'

Gereon frowned and looked down. Durano muttered some curse, then said, 'You are hurt, Marcellus. Can you stay on a horse?'

'I can ride asleep,' said Marcellus, making light of it.

And so together we eased him up. By now he could no longer hide the lines of pain in his face. His breath came shallow; and after he was mounted I saw his midriff soaked with new red blood.

But Durano was bright with him, saying, 'There! You will travel better so. Some horse-god must be watching over you.'

He laughed and patted the horse's flank; but as he turned away, I saw the smile fall too quickly from his face.

'What, Durano?' I whispered, going after him. 'Is he dying?'

He turned and looked at me. Dark night-stubble showed on his jaw, and there were blue lines under his eyes.

He put his hand on my shoulder and let out his breath. 'He has the horse to carry him now. He may yet live, but he is worse than he pretends. Stay with him, Drusus, and see he does not fall.'

The army advanced across a wide swathe of forest, like men on a hunt who beat the scrub to flush out their quarry. They put the German settlement to the torch; but just as Durano had predicted, the inhabitants had already fled. Those few they caught they put to death. The men were in no mood for mercy, after they discovered what remained of their comrades in the grove beside the village.

All this I heard later. At the time my only thought was for Marcellus.

He had long since fallen unconscious. The doctor, an old sharp-faced Gaul from Metz, mumbled and clucked and shook his head, while his pallid assistant applied some ill-smelling concoction to the wound from a steaming earthenware bowl, with the air of some ham-fisted slave whitewashing a wall.

I stood and glared. The return through the forest had been taken up with survival, and keeping Marcellus on his horse. Now, the shock of battle having passed and being suddenly at leisure to reflect, I saw his life ebbing away before me, and I had no resources. Yet the doctor treated me as if Marcellus's life or death were a matter of indifference, and spoke like some bored cattle-healer discoursing to a farmer about a creature in his herd.

Finally, when I could take no more, I lost my temper and spoke sharply, demanding to know what more could be done. He turned his solemn face to me, and for some moments did not answer – he was the sort of man who delights in drawing out bad news. He might have done something, he said, pursing his lips, if he had been summoned sooner, and when I protested he said, 'Yes, I understand you were not here. It is unfortunate . . .' His voice drifted into silence and he gazed at Marcellus lying on the bed, still and grey as a corpse. I stared, horror-struck, scarcely able to draw my breath. 'In any event,' he went on after a pause, 'you should find someone who will stay with him, though I cannot think it will greatly affect the case.'

'I will stay. What else does he need? Tell me and I shall bring it.'

He shrugged, as if to say the patient was beyond all help. I could almost have struck him.

'You might pray,' he said eventually, with an amused smile, 'if you believe in such things. And send for me if there is any change. Otherwise I shall return tomorrow.'

He made to go; but instead of leaving he paused at the door and gave a significant cough. I looked at him; then, realizing what he was waiting for I snatched a coin from my purse and pressed it into his waiting palm. 'Just so,' he said. 'I thank you.' And then he went away.

That night I lay with the lamp burning, staring across at Marcellus on the bed opposite, willing him to live. In the end I must have dozed, for I woke with a start to the grey dawn, and the sound of scratching on the door. I leaped up, thinking the doctor had returned. But when I threw open the door it was Durano's dark-haired girl, standing silent on the threshold.

I suppose, in my confusion, I stood open-mouthed. She looked back at me, said something in her own tongue, and after a moment, when I did not move, eased past me, pulled up the stool, and sat herself down beside Marcellus's bed.

She watched him for a moment, then touched his brow, and straightened his tousled hair.

'What are you doing?' I cried, staring. Then I realized I was still naked, and grabbed at my bedding.

She stayed, tending to Marcellus, sitting all day beside him, now and then intoning strange, charm-like words under her breath. That night, like a guard dog, she slept on a mat at the foot of his bed.

For five days he lay at the threshold of death, and still she remained. One day I went to a stall-holder at the camp and bought a cock, and that night offered it to Luna and the Great Mother, not caring who might see and report me for conducting a banned sacrifice. Julian came to visit. He talked of the gods, and of Fate; but just then I was in no mood for philosophy, and soon he left, insisting I must come to him if I needed anything. Later Oribasius, who was away in Paris, wrote with detailed instructions for the doctor. Julian must have sent a courier.

It was on the night I sacrificed to Luna that the girl came to my bed.

I had crept out after dark, carrying the bird in a withy cage to a secluded wooded bluff I knew, a place overlooking the river where the wind whispered in the alders and the ground smelled of damp earth. The lamp in the window was out when I returned, and the girl lay sleeping on her mat. I pulled off my clothes and climbed into my bed. I felt restless from the sacrifice, and lay staring up into the darkness.

Presently I heard the girl stir, and glancing round I saw her shadow against the moonlight. Silently she lifted the coverlet of my bed, and silently I let her in. She smelt of lavender and cedar oil, and of Marcellus.

Every camp has its courtesans. They follow the army from place to place, along with the wine-sellers, soothsayers, farriers, cobblers and all the other trades that supply the needs of men. There were ladies of some style, painted and urbane, who travelled in closed wagons hung with brightly coloured silks; there were rough dishevelled trulls, coarse and gap-toothed, and there were many in between. I felt a deep-seated distaste for what they had to sell, which I could not account for; and they, with their sharp-witted business-sense, had quickly learned to leave me be.

But this barbarian girl, whose name I did not know, took me by surprise. She had given me no time to consider; and in the midst of my grief her touch was like the warmth of fire in winter. What she gave, she gave willingly, with true delight. I felt her pride like something physical, pride for pride, a meeting of equals.

Later she lay close and silent, her hand tracing the hard contours of my chest. I drifted into sleep, and dreamed sunlit images of my childhood, and of the Virgin Huntress with her hounds, and of my mother I had never known.

Next day, returning from the bath-house, I found Marcellus propped up against his pillow, while she spooned him chicken broth. I cried out from the door.

'Hello!' he said brightly, as if he had just woken from a long night's sleep. The girl turned and smiled, and then I went running through the camp to find the doctor.

Six

WE RETURNED TO PARIS for the winter with the Rhine frontier secure. In the spring that followed, the emperor sent out a new Master of Cavalry to replace Severus. His name was Lupicinus.

Julian, in his quiet way, had mourned blunt-speaking Severus, who had sworn and argued with him, but was never false. Like it or not, with Severus one always knew what one was getting, and if he disagreed he said so.

Not so with Lupicinus. He had made his name in the army of the East and had moved his household from Illyricum to fashionable Constantinople, where he would be noticed. He had a hard, self-assured face, yet spoke with a veiled, affected air, so that one was always left with the impression of never quite knowing what he had intended to say – which, I believe, was his aim, for it allowed him to disavow responsibility for anything that went wrong.

Marcellus, being in the cavalry, was forced to spend more time with Lupicinus than I, and disliked him from the first day, when he had gone with the other cavalry officers to pay his respects. An elderly steward had been there, quietly unpacking in the corner. Nervous of his new master, the steward had let slip a glass platter from his hand, breaking it. Lupicinus, in the midst of speaking to his new officers, and without any sign of emotion, had broken off, calmly walked to his table, and had taken up the baton that lay there. Then, crossing to the cowering servant, he had beaten him with such ferocity that he drew blood; after which he resumed his conversation as if he had done no more than swat a troublesome fly.

'Grandfather always told me,' said Marcellus, relating this to me later, 'that one gets the mark of a man from how he treats those he has power over. Such brutality would be shameful even on the field of battle.'

With Julian, Lupicinus was correct and distant and non-committal. It was a great loss, after the open frankness of Severus. Even Julian, who was slow to pick up on intrigue, was politician enough to see he could not afford to quarrel with his Master of Cavalry as well as the prefect; and just then he and Florentius were at loggerheads, in a conflict that was to be final.

Everyone knew that Florentius was corrupt. But that year the citizens of Gaul, who trusted Julian, began to bring him their complaints. They told him how the prefect abused his power in order to acquire property and land, how he promoted his friends and extorted money for favours; how he enriched himself from the general distress.

At first Julian tried to intervene discreetly. He dropped hints; he sent word through others that it would be better for the abuses to stop, whoever was responsible, and hoped the prefect would find time to look into it. But the whole matter depressed him, and while we were campaigning against the Germans he pushed it from his mind.

Then, during the winter, a deputation of provincials laid a formal charge, backed by firm evidence. Florentius had overreached himself. He had outraged too many people, and in spite of his bullying, the plaintiffs pressed their case.

The whole ugly business took some weeks to unravel. But eventually, when Florentius had exhausted all his usual bureaucratic ploys in an attempt to cause the case to be withdrawn, or cause the papers inexplicably to be lost, he came to Julian with the outraged air of an innocent man wronged, and demanded that Julian use his authority to dismiss the matter before it came to court.

'But, Prefect,' said Julian smoothly, 'I thought you told me none of it was true.'

'Quite so,' responded Florentius, 'it is not.'

'In that case you have nothing to fear. It is surely better for a public figure of your honour and standing to be shown to be innocent, and for these lies to be exposed for all to see. Or do you not think so?'

'You will only provoke him,' said Oribasius later, when we were all together and Julian retold this tale to his friends.

'I expect you are right. But God knows I have kept silent long enough in the face of his abuses. Now he wants me to connive in them. That is asking too much.'

Oribasius was right. Before long, Florentius attacked.

The first Julian heard of it was when his friend the quaestor Salutius, with whom he was close, was suddenly ordered back to court. It was a cruel blow, designed to hurt. All through his life, from the time he had been permitted to have them, Julian's friends mattered greatly to him. Salutius had been one of the few he had been allowed to bring to Paris; and he felt the loss keenly. At the same time, a letter arrived from Constantius instructing him in cold terms not to undermine the prefect's authority. Florentius was showing he could strike at Julian whenever he chose.

Then, one day soon after, I too was singled out.

I was with Julian in his study, helping him unpack a consignment of books newly arrived from the empress Eusebia. The empress, although she was Constantius's wife, had been a friend to Julian at court. She possessed a fine library and was, he told me, an intelligent, cultured woman, who shared his love of learning.

While we were busy with this, talking easily with each other, pausing now and then as Julian discovered some new delight among the books, a steward scratched at the door and announced that the bishop of Paris was waiting.

Julian cast a wistful look at the new bound volumes and honey-coloured scrolls. With a sigh he said, 'Very well; send him in.' And to me, when the steward had gone, 'Now what does *he* want, I wonder.'

The bishop of Paris was not a man I had spent any time with; though, in fairness, he was not the base, scheming creature the bishop of London was. He was shy and thin and sickly-looking, and spent his time – as I was told – ministering to the city poor.

This Julian admired, even if he distrusted the motive. By now, Julian's reverence for the old gods had become something of an open secret among those that cared to know. For such things show, to the curious, or the suspicious. Even so, he watched his words, and was always careful to keep the Christian festivals – which otherwise would have been reported to Constantius. The bishop, in his turn, did not to enquire too deeply into the Caesar's faith, or comment on the rumours he had heard; and thus they got along, being civil to one another, and keeping out of each other's way.

The steward returned, escorting the bishop. As soon as he entered, his eyes darted to where I was standing, and a stricken look flashed across his gaunt features. I wondered why; he hardly knew me, and I had never given him cause for dislike.

Meanwhile Julian, who had not noticed, greeted him, and reminded him who I was, and said something about the books which lay scattered about. To this the bishop made some civil answer, eyeing the books as if they were demons. Then there was a pause.

'But you wished to see me?' asked Julian.

The bishop shifted on his feet, and bit his lip. He had not realized, he said, that the Caesar had company. His business could wait. Another time would be more suitable.

'Oh no, you may speak,' said Julian, smiling to put the man at his ease. 'Is it a matter of the corn dole again?'

But the bishop coughed and hesitated, and kept glancing my way. Eventually Julian perceived this. His face darkened. 'What is it, Bishop?' he said, more sharply.

'It can wait. I shall return another time.'

By now it was clear enough that my presence was embarrassing him, and so I said, 'I was just leaving,' and mentioned some matter I had to attend to.

'Yes, very well, Drusus,' said Julian. He let me go, and turned frowning to the bishop, sensing intrigue. Later he came to find me.

'Walk with me in the garden,' he said.

The plum trees were in flower, dense with speckled white blossom. It had rained. Sharp clean sunlight glanced off the wet marble paving. We sat down on a bench, under the enclosure wall, a place hidden from the palace windows by the row of trees. 'He brought this,' said Julian, pulling a letter from his cloak and passing it to me.

I unfolded the parchment and peered at it, then drew my breath. I suppose I was expecting something from the court, another cold instruction from Constantius. My mouth went dry. I looked quickly up again. It was from my enemy, the bishop of London, Bishop Pulcher, and it was addressed to the bishop of Paris.

'No, read it,' said Julian, with a nod.

And so I read.

The bishop sent greetings to his dear brother and colleague in Paris, and hoped, with God's grace, that he was in good health.

I hurried on through the salutations and empty chatter,

silently mouthing the words, and hearing in my head the smooth, unctuous tones of the bishop.

Soon, as I knew he would, he came to me. He had heard, he said, with fear and concern, that a certain Drusus, son of the executed traitor Appius Gallienus, having escaped from the custody of the notary Paulus, had by deception gained a position as an intimate of the most honourable Caesar Julian. The Caesar's life was thus in great danger, and it was the bishop's duty to warn him. There followed a list of crimes I was supposed to have committed – murder, apostasy, treason, immorality – with details of each. I forced myself to read them through to the end. Then, at last, I looked up.

I knew my colour had risen. 'Do you believe it?' I asked, and my own voice sounded tight and constrained. I had long ago told Julian the truth of what happened in Britain – but that was nothing against the bishop's web of lies.

To my surprise he laughed.

'Of course I don't. I showed you so you can see what lengths they will go to.'

I looked at him frowning, failing to understand.

'No wonder,' he went on, 'our friend the bishop of Paris was so nervous. He had come to tell tales about you. He could hardly do it with you standing there – or not this particular bishop anyway; he is a kindly man at heart, even if he is another's cat's-paw.'

I drew a breath and asked what he had said.

'Oh, the usual mumblings about doing his duty, loyalty to the imperial family, that sort of thing. One always knows something is up when a person starts with that. I told him Pulcher had his facts wrong, and to think no more of it. The poor man is in too deep, if only he knew.' He glanced round. 'But good, here comes Eutherius. I asked him to join us.'

I turned on the bench to look. Eutherius had appeared from under the colonnade and was treading warily over the fallen plum blossom in his doe-skin slippers. 'Dear friends,' he said with a smile. He cast his eyes over the damp stone bench where we were sitting, pursed his lips, and decided to stand.

'Look at this,' said Julian, handing him the letter.

Eutherius read, and when he had finished he cast it aside with a snort of amused contempt.

'Amateurish! A crude, ugly piece. The sort of scurrilous nonsense Constantius thrives on, except this is so obvious it fools no one. Really, can they do no better? But I thought soup-kitchens was more the bishop of Paris's line.'

'It is. The old man was put up to it.'

I said, 'By Bishop Pulcher.'

'Oh, no,' said Eutherius, with a kindly smile at my naivety. 'Your London bishop is insignificant.'

I stared down at the letter as if it were some biting creature. It seemed to me that Bishop Pulcher had gone to a lot of work. He had taken flecks of truth and twisted them into base and monstrous lies. I felt I had looked into a mirror and seen something deformed and evil looking back at me.

'You can be sure,' continued Eutherius, divining perhaps my thoughts, 'that somebody or other will have delved into your background long ago. There will be a file on you at court. Do not let it trouble you, Drusus. You are a friend of Julian's, after all.'

A gust of wind stirred the plum trees, shaking water from the branches above us. A cold runnel crept down my back. I shivered, and thought of poisoned wine, and daggers in the night. And then I remembered that Julian had lived with such fears all his life.

I looked up. Julian met my eye. 'A few days ago,' he said, 'Oribasius told me someone had visited his rooms. Nothing was stolen. But they had been through his medical books, taking care not to hide it – a book left open, a chair out of place, an upset pen-pot; that kind of thing.'

'But why? What were they looking for?'

'Nothing,' said Eutherius. 'What use is a threat, if your enemy does not know of it?'

'First Salutius,' said Julian, 'then Oribasius; and now you . . . Florentius is warning me not to cross him.' He stood up, and began pacing the wet flagstones, with their scattering of white blossom. 'He wants me to stop the prosecution, of course; tell me,' he said, turning to Eutherius, 'is it fitting for a man who loves philosophy to look on at injustice and do nothing?'

'You do not need me to give you the answer, my dear Julian. But remember, all things have a price. Even virtue – perhaps virtue most of all.'

Julian frowned up at the high enclosing wall – old red brick, and the remains of some forgotten climbing plant, cut off at the root. After a long pause he said, 'The people are robbed and cheated. I shall not ignore it. What good are all my books to me if now, when the time comes, I

158

choose only what is expedient? Better for Constantius to recall me; better to suffer wrong than to do it.'

When later I told Marcellus, he banged the table with his fist and cried, 'Pulcher! Has he no shame at all? We should have finished him off when we could.'

I shrugged. 'I thought that too, when I read his letter. But my head is clearer now. What we decided at the time was right: that, living, he is his own testament. A quick death would have been too easy. His followers would have called him a martyr and a saint.'

'As for Florentius,' Marcellus went on, 'everyone knows he's guilty. If only Julian would dismiss him and have done with it.'

'He cannot. Constantius stands behind him, and Florentius knows it. But Julian will not stop the prosecution.'

'Then good,' he said crossly, 'let him be prosecuted, at least. This is what comes of leaving men to rule who cannot even rule themselves. That is what Grandfather would have said.' He pushed his hand through his hair, then winced. His wound still caught him when he stretched. Though the flesh had healed cleanly, the scar would be with him always. Each time I saw him naked it reminded me of how nearly I had lost him.

The barbarian girl had left our hut on the day Marcellus had woken, departing as suddenly as she had arrived. At that time the army was preparing to leave the German frontier and disperse to winter quarters, and all the camp was like a town being hurriedly abandoned, as tents, wooden shacks, animal pens, and the surrounding palisade were dismantled.

With Marcellus safe, I had gone to find Durano. I had not told anyone of the night with the girl. At times, indeed, during my waking day, it almost seemed it had never happened.

Yet knowledge cannot be unlearned; nor did I wish it so. I found, as I walked, that she was in my thoughts, and as I drew near to Durano's tent my heart quickened to see her there. She was sitting on the verge, dressed in her simple loose-fitting tunic, waxing the leather straps of his corselet, which lay spread out on the grass.

I crouched beside her on my haunches, feeling suddenly awkward. She glanced up, and seeing the blush in my face her stern features softened into a small smile. I thanked her then for tending to Marcellus, using a mix of words and hand-signs. And my thanks were heartfelt, for it seemed to me she was the only one who had done him any good.

I do not know how much she understood. But when I had finished she touched me gently on the arm, and for a moment let her hand rest there. Close by, over the smell of wax and leather, I caught from her body the sharp-sweet fragrance of cedar oil; and suddenly, disconcertingly, I felt my blood race, and desire surge in my loins.

Sensing this she looked amused; and through my awkwardness I laughed, and made some joke. Then I heard Durano's voice, approaching from among the wagons and piled-up tent-hides.

Pallas and Gereon were with him; we greeted one another with the warmness of men who have faced death together. And when next I turned, the girl was gone, leaving the corselet laid out on the ground.

Durano, seeing me look, said, 'People tell me she has a healing way. She knows how to summon the spirits that make men well.'

I agreed, and thanked him for sending her.

'Oh, but I did not send her. She went of her own accord. How is Marcellus?'

'Ready to fight, or so he says. You saved his life, Durano. Perhaps she did too. I shall never forget.'

He smiled, and clapped his hand on my shoulder. He was being posted, he said, to one of the newly fortified towns overlooking the Rhine, so it was time to say farewell.

And so we went off with the others, down the long thoroughfare of the camp, to find some wine to toast our parting.

With the next courier from the East came the news that Julian's friend the empress Eusebia had died.

It struck Julian deeply. On the day he heard, not wishing to put his grief on public display, he kept to his private rooms, among the books she had so recently sent him. It was not, as Eutherius told me, only her gifts of books that he would miss. She alone had spoken up for him at court, and without her there was no one left to counter the insidious work of Constantius's grand chamberlain.

Eutherius told me about the time that Julian had first been summoned from his studies in Athens and ordered to the court. For weeks he had been held a virtual prisoner at the imperial palace, while the courtiers disputed whether he should be elevated to the rank of Caesar, or put to death as a dangerous threat. The emperor could not make up his mind. The chamberlain had argued for execution; it was the empress who had intervened on Julian's behalf and, as Julian himself thought, saved his life.

Now, with the moderate, educated influence of the empress gone, Constantius's only advisers would be flatterers and sycophants – led by the chamberlain, who controlled all access to the imperial presence.

'The word at court,' Eutherius said, taking my arm as we walked in the garden, and giving me one of his dry, amused glances, 'is that Constantius is fortunate to possess some influence with his chamberlain.'

He rolled his eyes, and waited for me to see the joke.

Meanwhile, the conflict with Florentius continued. Word came that the plaintiffs who had brought the charge against him had suddenly withdrawn it. Julian made no comment. But then Florentius announced he intended to raise an extraordinary tax levy on the citizens of Gaul, saying that the usual revenues for that year would not be sufficient.

He did not trouble to tell Julian himself; he sent a subordinate. I doubt he would have done even this, were it not that the levy, being extraordinary, required the Caesar's signature.

Julian met the official in the citadel's great audience chamber, with its echoing barrel-vaulted roof, squat stone columns and heavy faded tapestries. He preferred his study, but on this day he had chosen the cold ill-lit chamber on purpose, knowing that in the aisles behind the limp hangings there would be listening ears, informers waiting to relay everything they heard to their paymasters.

'Ask the prefect to reconsider,' Julian said carefully – and loudly. 'The provincials can scarcely feed themselves. I have spent the past three years securing the borders and resettling the frontier. Advise the prefect that a prudent farmer does not harvest the crop until it is grown. Tell him to come to me himself, and we shall speak of it privately.'

But Florentius did not come. Then, one morning a few days later, he submitted the order for signature, arriving this time in person, accompanied by a crowd of his bustling liveried clerks. It was a heavy formal document, prepared by scribes, intended for the archive records.

'What is this?' asked Julian.

With his usual haughtiness, Florentius replied that it was the authority for the levy, as the Caesar had been told.

Up to now, Julian had always treated the prefect with cool civility. But now his patience ended. With an angry cry he snatched the document from the hands of the clerk and cast it down on the ground.

'Do you take me for a fool?' he cried. 'The provincials charge you with extortion, and you respond with this new assessment. They cannot pay, I tell you!'

Florentius's face tensed. Dangerous pools of red appeared on his pale cheeks. For all his scheming and goading, this outburst had caught him by surprise. To be addressed in such a way, in front of his own officials, was an outrage beyond the scope of his routine mind.

'The levy,' he said in a quiet, icy voice, 'is a separate matter, and may I remind the Caesar that the case brought against me was vexatious, and was dropped for lack of evidence.'

'Lack of evidence?' cried Julian. 'Lack of evidence indeed! Only when the plaintiffs, having prepared a detailed charge against you, discovered to their surprise that they were mistaken in the very evidence that they themselves had prepared. This after they had all become – suddenly and mysteriously – enriched. They have made themselves a laughing-stock, and you must take me for as big a fool as they!'

The crowd of clerks who stood gathered behind the prefect stared at the floor, horror-struck. Florentius, his brittle voice rising, said, 'You have no right to question my authority. The emperor has appointed me to conduct the financial affairs of Gaul at my discretion, yet you persist in interfering. I will not tolerate it.'

'And did the emperor also instruct you to sell exemptions?' demanded Julian. This was a long-standing abuse: the revenue collectors, who were landowners and rich decurions, collected taxes from the rural poor; then, having collected the taxes, they sought exemptions on the grounds that the taxes could not be raised, and kept the funds for themselves.

Florentius glared, momentarily at a loss. I do not think he had realized Julian knew of this.

'No, indeed,' continued Julian, 'I will not accept this levy of yours. I will not sign it. I have said so often enough. Have your spies not told you? By all the gods, you have enough of them!'

With a chill rictus of a smile Florentius said, 'In that case, Caesar, perhaps you would like to explain to the emperor how you propose to cover the deficit in the provincial finances.'

There was a pause. Julian's eyes dropped to the floor with its bands of red and yellow marble, and the scattered pages of the levy-document. A look of satisfaction formed on Florentius's face; though I could have told him how Julian would have responded to such a challenge. The clerks looked up, their curiosity getting the better of their fear.

Julian said, 'I shall do more than that, Prefect. I shall conduct the assessment myself. I will bring in the funds without recourse to your levy; and if I cannot, I shall sign your order.'

Florentius glanced at his secretary – the man who had once ejected me and Marcellus from the citadel – then looked back at Julian with an incredulous sneer.

'You will bring in the funds?' He almost smiled. 'Very well . . . then let us see it. But if you fail, be in no doubt, sir, that you shall answer to the emperor.'

'And if I succeed, what will you tell Constantius then?'

To this, Florentius merely snorted down his nose in derision. 'You will excuse me, Caesar,' he said, with a rigid, unpleasant smile, 'if I do not engage in idle talk; but clearly you have much work to do.' And then he turned on his heels and left. And the clerks, after a gaping moment, hurried after, like a timid line of duck-chicks behind their mother.

When they had gone, Julian turned to me. I daresay I had turned as pale as the others.

'And now,' he said, 'I had better make sure I can do it.'

Next day Florentius sent a band of financial clerks to Julian, bearing tomes of figures for him to review. Julian took one look at them, realized what the prefect was trying to do, and told the clerks to take the pile of books away. Overnight he had been doing some thinking. Now he announced that not only would no additional levy take place, but that the existing tax would be halved.

Florentius's chief actuary, when he heard, came rushing across the palace courtyard, ashen-faced, clucking disapproval. What could the Caesar be thinking? He would bring down disaster upon them. It was not too late to reverse the proclamation; they would find some way of explaining it as a mistake, a clerical error, the fault of some minor bookkeeper.

'I do not wish to reverse it,' Julian told him. 'If the tax is less onerous, more people will pay it.'

The actuary went away appalled, making little tutting noises and shaking his head.

But Julian had not finished. Next he announced an end to the tax exemptions. The rich estate-owners were outraged. They sent deputations to Paris, pleading poverty; but Julian cast his eyes over their well-wrought polished gigs, their thoroughbred, bedizened horses and their expensive Italian clothes, and sent them away. He said he preferred to listen to the rural smallholders who sold at market, and to the city artisans – the bakers and basket-weavers, potters and fullers and dyers – all men who lacked great fortunes, who were unable to buy influence, and always had to pay their tax on the nail – men that Florentius would never have lowered himself to consider, let alone speak to. But Julian knew them. It was the sons of these men who served in the army; it was their homes the invaders would burn first, if once they were let in.

The people heard him, and they responded. They liked the bright young Caesar, who had saved them from the barbarians and now had spared them the abuses of the rich landowners. They paid their taxes, even before they were due. The revenues poured in.

Florentius's officials, for all their pettifogging, remembered enough goodness of spirit to mumble congratulations and concede they had been wrong. His conquests had meant little to them; but for this young stubble-faced Greekling to halve the tax and increase the revenue was a feat that truly commanded their respect.

Florentius, however, said nothing. And, shortly after, he departed south for Vienne, saying he wished to supervise the distribution of corn.

One late afternoon, during that winter in Paris, Marcellus returned to our room in the palace and said, 'Rufus came to me today. He wants to join Nevitta's squadron.'

I glanced at him, surprised. He was looking down, sitting on the edge of his bed, unstringing his boots.

'What did you tell him?'

'I asked him why Nevitta; but he did not want to talk about it. He said he wanted a change, that's all, and would I let him go or not? So I let him go. There's no point keeping him, if that's what he wants.' He shrugged, then added, 'Perhaps it will do him some good.'

I frowned. Since his captivity in the German forest, Rufus had become sullen and brooding. The light had gone from his eyes. It was as if something fine and delicate, which needed gentle nurturing, had been ripped from him and trampled.

Marcellus, who saw more of Rufus than I, supposed it was the shock of what had happened to his comrades that had changed him; and I had agreed that this must be so. I had not confided, even to him, what more I knew. It seemed the least I could do for the boy.

Once or twice, I had tried to speak to him myself, in private. He had been civil enough, but brisk and remote, and it was clear he did not wish to talk.

So now all I said was, 'Nevitta seems an odd choice, if you ask me.'

'That's what I thought too.'

Neither of us much cared for Nevitta. He was a cavalryman of barbarian birth who had distinguished himself at Strasburg. Julian liked him for his bluntness, and had promoted him. Since then, he was always finding cause to be around Julian, and had something to say on everything, whether he knew about it or not. He was able enough; but beneath all his noise and boasting he had a veiled, suspicious air I did not trust. He put me in mind of an escaped convict.

Yet the greater evil obscures the lesser, and soon there was no time to think of such matters. One clear morning in January, when Marcellus and I were in the stable yard at the fort, preparing to go out riding along the Seine, a courier came clattering through the gate, his relay-horse steaming in the cold winter air.

'What news?' someone shouted brightly.

'Nothing to smile about,' the courier called back. He jumped down from his horse and took out the dispatch from his saddle-bag. 'There's trouble in Britain, if you want to know. A disaster, they say, and Julian's going to have his hands full with it.'

He gave his bound-up packet to a runner, who would take it to the citadel. Marcellus turned to me. 'We had better go and find Julian,' he said.

By the time we reached his study, the dispatch lay open on the table, and a map of Britain next to it.

Lupicinus, the new Master of Cavalry, was there; and other officers of the corps – Victor, Arintheus and Valentinian. Eutherius was seated on a low stool beside the stove, warming his hands, dressed in a heavy winter robe of Gallic wool with a fox-fur collar. Oribasius, in his simple, dark cloak, was waiting apart, beside the window.

'Ah, Drusus, Marcellus,' said Julian, turning from the map. 'Come and look. You know Britain better than anyone.'

Then he told us what had happened.

Two barbarian British tribes, one known as Picts and the other Scots, who live an existence beyond the Northern Wall untouched by civilization, had broken their treaty and overrun the frontier. They had sailed boats around the coast, avoiding the Wall, while others had assaulted the Wall itself. Border forts had been put to the torch, or abandoned by the panicked frontier guards. 'The city of Chester is threatened; the governor in London – his name is Alypius, I know him, he is a good man – supposes that by the time this letter reaches us, York itself may be under siege. He says the attack is no mere raid: it has been planned, by someone who knows how to plan such things.'

'Planned?' Lupicinus asked sharply. 'Whatever does the man mean? Planned by whom?'

Julian paused and gave him a careful, appraising look before he answered. They had never fought a campaign together. Neither man had the true measure of the other.

'Alypius says he does not know.'

'Yet he claims to know it was planned?'

'These are tribes that normally squabble between one another like dogs in a yard; they are little more than cattle-raiders. Yet suddenly they have united. They have struck in the middle of winter, when defences are weakest; and our usual spies, who keep an eye out for trouble, somehow missed it all. There was mind behind it; that is Alypius's opinion. You are not obliged to accept it.'

Julian paused, in case Lupicinus had more to say. He did not. The Master of Cavalry was holding a polished military baton, cherry red, with gilding and victory wreaths carved in ivory. He tapped it impatiently in his palm. Julian returned his eyes to the map.

'We cannot repel them with the British garrison alone,' he continued. 'How soon can we march?'

'Why, Caesar,' cried Valentinian, 'surely you will not risk a crossing in winter!'

'You are too timid,' said Lupicinus dryly.

Valentinian gave him an angry look and drew his breath. But before he could fire back an answer, Julian cut in, saying, 'That, anyway, is what our enemies suppose. These Picts and Scots will not be expecting us until the spring. Well, we shall surprise them.'

Eutherius coughed. Julian turned to him.

'Eutherius?'

'If indeed there is mind in these attacks,' he said from his comfortable place by the bronze stove, 'then we should ask ourselves whom it would benefit, and what reaction they would expect from us.'

'What are you talking about?' cried Lupicinus, turning impatiently. 'They benefit themselves, of course, or think they do. They must be taught a lesson, and swiftly. There is no more to it than that. They must be crushed. Julian must march at once.'

Eutherius waited for him to finish, with a patient expression on his large face. As I stood listening, it came to me that Eutherius was leading somewhere, drawing Lupicinus on, as a hunter entices the rabbit from his hole.

'Quite so, Master of Cavalry,' he said. 'Yet let us suppose Alypius is correct.'

'Well?'

'Well, we can believe it would benefit the German tribes, for one, if Julian were to leave Gaul. He has caused them enough trouble, after all, and no doubt his absence would be welcome. It would give them a free hand.'

He paused. His eyes moved from Lupicinus and settled on Julian's face. Then, with a short pause, and the merest hint of a nod, he added, 'It would give all of our enemies a free hand.'

Perhaps it was no more than the poison of intrigue, which swirled about the citadel like a mist; but I was sure I felt an undercurrent of private meaning. I remembered how Constantius, during his civil war with Magnentius, had stirred up the barbarians and sent them raiding into Roman lands, not caring what damage he caused, so long as he secured his own ends. Was this what Eutherius was hinting at? Did someone want Julian out of the way? I could not be sure. Whatever it was, he did not wish to say it openly.

I pushed the thought from my mind, telling myself I was seeing conspiracy everywhere.

'There is no question,' Eutherius continued, looking pointedly at Julian, 'but you must remain in Gaul. Someone else must go to Britain.'

'Yet surely it is the Caesar's place to go,' said Lupicinus. 'It is his duty, and his wish too, as you have heard. So why all this talk? Besides, who else is there?'

'You have fought in the East,' said Eutherius with a smile, 'to great renown, so it is said. A few Keltic ruffians will be nothing after the Persians.'

And it was true that Lupicinus, whatever Marcellus and I thought of him as a man, was an experienced and successful soldier. Yet now, to my surprise, he seemed to demur, wrapping it up in questions of logistics. He began wondering whether sending a few reinforcements would after all suffice, whether it would not be better for a man of his ability to stay in Gaul in case of trouble, for the

Germans were unpredictable. He questioned the wisdom of a winter crossing, when storms were so frequent, and troop transports could so easily be overwhelmed.

He went on, and everyone – particularly Valentinian, who had not liked being called timid – looked at him with surprise, until eventually Julian broke in: 'Well, one of us must go. Delay will be taken as weakness. Is that not your opinion too?'

'It is,' said Lupicinus, irritably.

Julian paused and nodded. His eyes moved back to the bronze stove, with its turned finials and little embossed garlands; and to Eutherius beside it, who was warming his hands, and wearing a face that gave nothing away.

'Then I shall remain, if you advise it, Eutherius. We must not risk all that we have achieved. We will keep back enough men to protect our flank against the Germans.'

He considered for a moment, rubbing his chin. Then turning to Lupicinus he said, 'Take the Herulians and Batavians. They are good, keen fighting men; and it will leave us enough in reserve to guard the Rhine.'

So in the end, Lupicinus set out for Britain.

He embarked at Boulogne, and, soon after, word came that he was in London. Then the weather closed in and we waited, cheering ourselves with the story that was doing the rounds, of how Lupicinus, after he had offered prayers at the Christian church, had discreetly sent for an old priest and asked him to offer incense on the altar of Neptune for a safe crossing.

It was shortly after, late in January, that an imperial

notary arrived. A captain of the palace guard announced him.

'A notary?' said Julian. 'Has he come from Florentius?' For we had heard nothing from Florentius since his hurried departure for Vienne.

'No, sir. He says he has come from the emperor himself. His name is Decentius. He asked first for the prefect Florentius; but when I said the prefect was away in Vienne, he asked to see Lupicinus.'

'. . . And Lupicinus is in Britain.'

'That's what I told him, sir. And then he ordered me to . . . ah . . . summon you.'

'Summon?' said Julian, raising his brows in amusement. 'He told you to *summon* me?'

The captain, a young Gaul, newly promoted, looked uncomfortable. 'Yes, sir. That was the word.'

'In that case,' said Julian, 'we had better not keep him waiting.'

The captain was too nervous to acknowledge the sarcasm. But on his way out he paused at the door and turned.

'What is it?' said Julian.

'One thing, sir. He told me, after I had seen you, to find Sintula and bring him too.'

'I wonder,' said Julian, when he had gone, 'what he wants with Sintula.'

I knew Sintula. He was an ambitious officer of the palace guard, whose main concern was furthering his own career. It was well known that he was part of Florentius's clique. Clearly the guard captain too had found it odd that he should be summoned to the same meeting, for political matters were none of Sintula's concern.

Sintula, however, had wasted no time. He was already waiting in the great audience chamber by the time we arrived, looking pleased with himself, like a child with a secret. Beside him was a man with a black bob of hair and a small, mean mouth, dressed in the dark garb of an imperial notary.

As Julian strode in the notary declared in a curt, loud voice, 'I had hoped to find the honourable Lupicinus here; but it appears you have sent him away.'

'Lupicinus is in Britain—' began Julian.

'So I am informed,' said the man, cutting him off.

Julian's expression hardened. He did not care for ceremony; but he could tell the difference between familiarity and insolence. The corps of notaries – Constantius's private agents – were hated across the empire, and for good reason. They were above the law, or supposed they were; they were haughty and dangerous; they abused their power, which anyway was never quite defined; and to the emperor they could do no wrong.

Now, ignoring Julian's expression, he continued in the same tone, 'The orders I bring were intended for the Master of Cavalry, Lupicinus. In his absence I was to speak to the prefect Florentius. And now I find that he too is away.'

'He is in Vienne.'

'Yes. It is unfortunate.'

Coldly Julian said, 'You asked to see me. Well, I am here. What do you want?'

The notary sighed, then snapped his fingers and made a little beckoning motion with his hand.

A clerk stepped forward with a scroll. Upon it, in the flickering light of the wall-cresset, I could see the great imperial seal.

'You know its contents?' Julian asked.

'Indeed I do,' responded the notary. 'And I am here to ensure the instructions are carried out.'

Julian narrowed his eyes. 'Well?' he said slowly, 'What does he want?'

'You are required to send troops from the Gallic army, which the emperor has need of in his war with the Persians. You shall send the following legions: the Herulians; the Batavians; and from the auxiliaries the Keltic regiment and the Petulantes; in addition three hundred men from each of the remaining units, and a detachment from the palace guard of Paris.'

He ceased. Quietly Julian said, 'Do you realize you are demanding more than half my army?'

The notary gave a thin smile. 'I am not a military man, Caesar. I am here to carry out the emperor's orders. I am instructed also to tell you not to interfere. These orders are for the emperor's agents in Gaul: the Master of Cavalry Lupicinus, and the prefect Florentius. I communicate them to you only in their absence, as a courtesy. The tribune here' – with a knowing nod at Sintula – 'is charged with selecting the three hundred from each unit, ensuring the best are taken. He is then required to lead the men of the palace guard east.'

Julian's eyes moved to Sintula, who knew, even if this

notary Decentius did not, that to take so much of his army would render him helpless. Sintula shifted on his feet, and studied the floor.

Oribasius and Eutherius had remained upstairs in the study, but I was with Julian, and Marcellus was beside me. For a moment he glanced at us, and I saw the tension in his face. I knew what he was thinking: that his enemies at court had finally defeated him. For an instant he looked hopeless. But then he drew himself up; he would not let this arrogant notary see his pain.

Turning to him, he said, 'As the emperor wishes.'

The notary raised his brow. 'How not?' He motioned to the clerk. But Julian had not finished.

'Yet the legions you demand, the Herulians and Batavians, are away in Britain with the Master of Cavalry; and the prefect Florentius, who must arrange supplies and transports, has taken himself off to Vienne. So I fear you will have to wait. In the meantime, Sintula will do his best to make your stay in Paris comfortable.'

He turned to Marcellus and me. 'But come,' he said, in a taut, formal voice, 'these men have much to do, to strip the province of its defences, which we have done so much to build. We had better leave them to their work.'

Then, before anyone could speak further, he strode away, across the echoing flagstones of the audience chamber, leaving the notary with a conceited look of unconcern on his face, and Sintula doing his best to look important, but forgetting to keep his mouth closed.

*

'A fool could see what he is about!' cried Julian, back in his study. 'He intends to take away my troops; and then he will send a warrant for my arrest. And what is my crime? That I have done what I was asked and freed Gaul?'

He had been speaking to Eutherius, pacing to and fro as he spoke, motioning angrily with his arms. But now he turned to Marcellus and me.

'Thus it turns, the Wheel of Fortune,' he said bitterly, 'yet still men envy high office, and waste their lives in its pursuit. You have been loyal friends, but I cannot bind you to this, now I see clearly where it must lead. You must leave before I am arrested, or you too will be caught up in the net.'

'We stay!' said Marcellus, without a moment of hesitation.

In his usual self-possessed voice Eutherius said, 'Let us be calm . . . My dear Julian, do keep still. Why don't you sit down?'

Julian threw himself into the high-backed ebony chair that stood against the wall. He rubbed his face with his hand, then looked at Eutherius.

'What now?' he said.

'These are old tactics. The hunted hare runs always into the net; but men possess the gift of reason. Your enemies at court are trying to push you into a trap. See it for what it is, and do not give them the cause they seek. For now, do all that is proper.'

Eutherius gave his advice; and Julian listened. And afterwards he sent an urgent dispatch by imperial relay to Vienne, telling Florentius he was required in Paris, that he needed to consult with him on state business. Meanwhile, the notary Decentius sent Sintula among the household troops, to pick out the men he would take.

On the day this work began, Marcellus, returning from the barracks, said wryly, 'He is having a harder time of it than he expected. The men don't want to go. They say they have received no orders from Julian. They don't like Sintula. They think he's arrogant.'

Soon Sintula came complaining to Julian, bringing Decentius with him, and also his new ally Pentadius, who was one of Florentius's creatures and a man Julian disliked.

'The men do not want to go,' he protested. 'They claim you promised they should not have to serve beyond the Alps.'

'So I did. You were there, Sintula; or have you forgotten? I told them they would never be forced to leave Gaul. I told them they were fighting for their homes and families. How else would they have followed us, when the emperor could not find funds to pay them? I recall you agreed with me at the time.'

'I was following orders.'

'And now you are following orders again. No doubt you can explain that to the men.'

Decentius said, 'You are not cooperating.'

'I gave my word to those men.'

'You should not have made such a promise. You had no authority.'

'The emperor,' said Julian, 'required me to safeguard the province. That was my authority. If Constantius now wishes to replace me he may do so. I am ready to leave.'

'At least,' cried Florentius's lackey Pentadius, 'let us say to the men that you have no objection.'

Julian turned to him and regarded him with distaste. Pentadius was one of those men who have learned so little of philosophy that they would be better off having learned none at all. He had picked up, somewhere, that the middle way is always best, without understanding why or how. Now he saw himself as a conciliator, blinded to the truth that he was merely furthering his career in the imperial bureaucracy, as he had always done.

'You may tell them I have no objection, if you wish,' replied Julian. He paced to the shelf of books beside his work-table, gazed at the untidy pile of scrolls with their labels and wooden spindles, and then turned. 'But do not be surprised, next time you seek to recruit men in Gaul, if there are no volunteers.'

Days passed. From Florentius in Vienne there came no reply. Julian sent a second dispatch. The province was about to be stripped of troops; he needed Florentius in Paris. It was the prefect's duty to manage the supplies and transport for the departing troops.

'He will not come,' said Julian later.

'He knows you suspect him,' said Oribasius.

Julian looked out of the window. It was raining. 'Well, I have good cause; his absence is too convenient.' He shook his head. 'Even so, he has his work to do. What is it, does he fear for his life? He knows me better than that.'

During those grey, lightless days of winter we all tried, in different ways, to intervene with the notary Decentius, urging him to delay and send for fresh instructions.

Returning from one such unpleasant meeting – for the man was impervious to reason and aggressively stubborn – I ran into Eutherius as he was passing through the garden colonnade.

He took me by the arm and invited me to drink a cup of wine with him; and when we were seated in his warm, sweet-scented quarters with their coloured silk hangings, and Agatho had brought us our wine, I said, 'It is no good; he will not listen. One might as well discuss the matter with a stone.'

'Yes, Drusus, but we can hardly be surprised. Now here, take one of these charming cinnamon-cakes and don't look so glum.'

I took a cake from the little tapered dish of red glass. He always had an assortment of such snacks waiting in his room.

'It is clear that Decentius has no intention of heeding anything we tell him. He has not come here to listen, but to instruct. And yet,' he said, chewing thoughtfully, 'have you noticed, beneath his pompous act, he is not as sure of himself as he likes to pretend?'

'I suppose,' I said, 'he expected to give his orders to Lupicinus and be done with it.'

'I daresay. And now he is forced to take charge himself. Though he will not admit it, it is beyond him.'

'A bureaucrat,' I said bitterly, 'doing a soldier's work.'

Eutherius nodded.

'And,' he said, 'he will make a mistake. We need only wait.'

SEVEN

SOME DAYS LATER, SINTULA made ready to depart from Paris, leading the troops he had picked from the palace guard. Decentius had instructed Julian to keep to his quarters, out of view; but the men were not so easily deceived. Word had got out that Julian was unhappy. The men were ill-tempered and suspicious, and an atmosphere of resentment hung over the city.

On the morning of their departure, Marcellus and I went down to the Paris forum to watch. It was a day of low grey cloud, and with the dawn a fine drizzle had begun to fall. We walked with our hoods up, not wishing to be recognized; and when we reached the forum we went to a tavern we knew, a discreet, small place tucked into a corner of the colonnade, on one side of a baker's shop. The serving-boy brought watered wine, and bread, and a dish of smoked meat and cheese; and with these set on the table before us we waited for the troops to pass.

It was early still. Now and then a house-slave called at the baker's, collecting loaves for the morning. We sipped our wine in silence, and ate, and watched the few rain-bedraggled figures as they passed across the paved square in front of us.

Presently Marcellus set down his cup, turned his head this way and that, and peered along the colonnade.

'Have you noticed,' he said, frowning, 'none of the other shops has opened?'

I looked. Except for the baker's shop, everything remained closed.

'I expect,' I said, 'they're waiting till the men have passed.' But after that I began to keep my wits about me.

On the far side of the forum, under the pillared porch of an old abandoned temple, a group of town women in shawls were sheltering from the rain, waiting, I supposed, for the market-traders. Turning, I saw others too, gathering under the high doorway of the basilica. Perhaps it was their silence, or a look in their stolid faces; but something, some soldier's instinct, made me look over my shoulder into the back of the tavern, checking for a second exit, in case we should need it.

Then, from somewhere out of sight, distant at first, came the regular drum-like beat of marching men, their boots sounding in unison on the cobbles and echoing down the street. We turned our heads towards the north-east side of the forum, where they would enter under the triumphal arch.

Sintula appeared first, straight-backed on a grey dappled horse, dressed in his best uniform, with a fine, plumed helmet that shone even in the grey light. Next, a few paces behind, came the first ranks of men, marching five abreast, stern-faced, with their packs strapped to their backs. They entered the wide, open square of the forum, heading for the gateway on the opposite side, where the road led off to the south.

At first the only sound was that of marching men, hard and powerful, yet familiar too. I reached for the wine jug, thinking my uneasiness had been overdone. But then, like some terrible effect in the theatre, there arose from nowhere and from everywhere a high-pitched keening animal cry that lifted the hair on my head and made me start from my seat. I looked about, astonished. And then I perceived the cause.

Bands of women had begun pouring like Furies from the side-alleys and doorways and sheltered porticoes, their shawls and cloaks streaming as they ran, carrying babies, or pulling young children with them. They were screaming out and crying, proffering swaddled bundles, calling to their menfolk, each by his name, imploring them to consider their sons and daughters whom they were abandoning to their fate.

Sintula's horse shied and recoiled; Sintula, shaken from his wooden expression of authority, turned with a look of horror on his youthful face.

By now the women had reached the line, and were thrusting their infant children into the faces of their husbands. The pace of the march faltered; the men began calling out to their women and children, their hard soldier faces wet with tears.

Marcellus turned to me with a look of amazement; and indeed it was a strange thing to see an army set upon by a mob of women. Even then I think the men would have continued; but at that moment an uneasy murmur ran down the line from the front. At the far side of the forum, clustered about the opposite gate, another group had gathered, linking arms and blocking the way.

Sintula gaped at them, then looked back, his confusion clear. The line was beginning to bulge and break as the men in front, perceiving the human barrier of wives and children ahead of them, slowed their pace.

'By God!' cried Marcellus, starting up from his chair, 'He'd better order them to stop!'

I said nothing. I was watching Sintula's face as he weighed up the price of his dignity.

His mouth firmed into a hard, stubborn line. Ahead, the women stood fast – fierce, red-haired Gallic women, standing in determined silence.

'Make way!' cried Sintula.

They glared silently back at him. Already others were joining them, streaming in from behind, an unyielding barrier of human flesh.

Sintula's horse jerked its head and strained at the bridle. Angrily he urged it on. The horse resisted, and whinnied in protest. He barked out a curse; the horse proceeded a few more steps, then shied again. And then Sintula grew suddenly still.

For a moment he stared ahead, his jaw tense with fury. Then, with a sudden violent movement of his arm, he gave the signal to halt; and all about him the women began clamouring and jeering, surging forward, surrounding his horse, pushing in between the now broken line of their weeping menfolk.

Rumour, swifter than the wind, had reached the citadel before us. When we arrived at the gate, the guard asked with glowing eyes if it was true that Sintula had been put to flight by a pack of women. Then, passing through the colonnade on our way to the inner court, we came upon Oribasius.

'You have heard, I take it?' he said.

'We were there,' answered Marcellus.

'You were there?' He looked at us, impressed; for a moment his fine-boned, solemn, almost feminine features moved in a half-smile. 'Well, Julian warned them. Even so, it is he who will be blamed. He is with them now in his study. He asked for you.'

I heard raised voices even from the stairway. As we entered, a row of grim faces snapped round and stared, as if at any moment they expected a band of mutinous soldiers to burst in and butcher them – Decentius the notary, his air of self-consequence gone, replaced by a tense, hunted look; Pentadius, looking shocked; and with him another of Florentius's people, the quaestor Nebridius, whom they had co-opted for their work.

Seeing who it was, they returned their attention to where Sintula stood by the window, looking ashen-faced, still dressed in his riding-cloak. He must have abandoned the men and hurried straight back.

'It seems,' said Julian, catching my eye and for an instant

allowing his amusement to show, 'that our friends have a problem. Perhaps, Drusus, you will give them your opinion of what can be done – for my own opinion, it seems, does not suit them.'

So I repeated what had been said many times already: that the men's loyalty was to Gaul, where they had been born, and where their families were; that over the past years, with Julian's help, they had fought against all odds to protect what was theirs; that they were loath to leave it.

'Their loyalty,' snapped Decentius, raising his voice to silence me, 'is to the emperor.'

'And what of military discipline?' added Sintula.

'They feel betrayed. They were given a promise.'

Decentius snorted. 'That promise should never have been given. I will hear no more of promises.' Suddenly he rounded on Sintula. 'Why did you not proceed? Do you expect me to believe you were unable to face down a clutch of women?'

Sintula's face reddened. 'But sir! It was not like that. The men would have mutinied!'

'He is right,' I said. 'There would have been a rebellion.' I did not care for Sintula: he sacrificed too much to ambition. But he was soldier enough to know what would have ensued if he had marched on. Decentius, on the other hand, had all the courage of a man who has never seen a battlefield.

The quaestor Nebridius, who so far had not spoken, said in a calmer voice, 'What now?'

A silence fell. Eyes turned to Julian. Decentius, seeing

this, cried, 'Surely you cannot expect an answer from *him*!'

'Have you a better idea?' Nebridius asked him.

Decentius gave him a furious glare. One did not answer back to one of the emperor's personal agents, unless one loved death. But Marcellus, who loathed such men and did not care, said, 'Julian knows the men. You, sir, do not.'

Like a vicious, cornered dog, Decentius's face snapped round. Marcellus looked blandly back at him. Then Julian said, 'Here is what you must do, Notary: you must allow the men to take their wives and children. That is the only way.'

'Why, that is absurd!'

'Then do as you please. The difficulty is of your own making. Have you any idea what nearly happened today? I suggest you think on it.'

Julian turned to Nebridius, who had more sense.

'The quartermaster,' he said, 'will give you wagons for the women. You had better get them away from Paris, before the other units arrive.'

Two days later the troops of the palace guard finally departed from the citadel, a sullen band of demoralized soldiers followed by carts of ragged womenfolk wrapped against the cold, led by a hangdog tribune.

While the arrangements were being made, Decentius had kept to his rooms in the citadel; but now, with the troops departed, he emerged once more, wholly un-daunted, full of foolish confidence, strutting about with Pentadius as though he had won some sort of victory. He complained to Julian that still there had been no word from Lupicinus in Britain, whose legions – the Herulians and the Batavians – he required. And why, he demanded, had the prefect Florentius not come? The remaining troops were still in their outlying winter quarters; he could wait no longer; Julian himself must issue the order for them to assemble in Paris.

No one but Julian was present at this exchange. When later he recounted it to Oribasius and me, he said, 'He complains I am not cooperating; he blames me for the trouble with the women, and says it will be better for me if I show the emperor my good faith. He does not even trouble to conceal the threat.'

He let out his breath, and made a small, hopeless gesture. He looked suddenly very young, I thought, like an unhappy boy. 'It was just the same,' he said, 'with Gallus.'

Gallus was his elder brother. He too had grown up in isolation, kept on the same remote estate in Asia – until Constantius decided he had need of him. Then, though he had no education in ruling, the emperor had promoted him to the rank of Caesar, just as he had later done with Julian. But that was where the similarity between the two brothers ended. Gallus's character was not honed and tempered by learning, as Julian's was. Having been taught nothing of moderation, he had grown drunk on power, until in the end Constantius had removed him, first of all summoning away his troops, then ordering him to court for 'consultations'. The consultations were a lie. On the way he was arrested, summarily condemned without a trial, and beheaded.

Julian seldom mentioned him. I suppose he was ashamed. But they were brothers, all the same – and Gallus, for all his faults, had been the last of his family.

Switching from Latin to Greek, he said quietly, 'And purple death and mighty fate overwhelmed him.'

'So Homer says,' said Oribasius. 'But that is not your destiny, unless you choose it.'

Julian heard him, but did not speak. He stood for a long time silent, looking out at the courtyard with its row of leafless fruit trees. Beyond, from the west, from the direction of the boundless ocean, the air was stirring, driving off the rain. Spreading bands of golden light were shafting across the land.

He watched for a while; but his mind was elsewhere, deep in his thoughts. Then, with an almost imperceptible nod, he turned back to the room and glanced down at the table. The map of the Rhine frontier lay there, forgotten. He regarded it for a moment, with the expression of an old man who recalls his youth.

'It will soon be spring,' he said. 'I had great plans.'

Oribasius made to speak; but Julian raised his hand.

'No, my friend; I know what you think. Let it not be spoken. We have acted as we must; and we both know that to refuse the emperor will be treason. Better to suffer wrong than to do it.'

Not long after this, returning from some business of my own, I saw Marcellus in the citadel yard. Rufus was with him.

I had scarcely set eyes on Rufus since he joined Nevitta's

company; now I was struck by the change in him. Nevitta's set were loud and swaggering, and he had picked up their brash manner. It ill suited him. And from his face, which was pale and unslept, I guessed he had been drawn into their habit of all-night drinking too. His bloom was gone. His curling black hair had lost its sheen.

Marcellus had his back to me. It was Rufus who saw me first.

'Oh, there you are, Drusus,' he called out across the yard. 'Have you heard? I was just telling Marcellus. Julian has summoned the men from winter quarters.'

'Is that so?' I answered cautiously.

'Yes indeed; and there's more too. Listen to this: that stupid notary – what's his name? Decentius? – has told Julian the troops must assemble at Paris. There will be trouble. That's what Nevitta thinks.' He laughed out loud, as if this were some barrack-room joke; then went on, 'Nevitta says Julian is opposed to it, but the notary will not listen to him. Is it true?'

Across the yard some passing clerk had paused to look. I frowned, wishing Rufus would think to lower his voice. Did he not know what a nest of intrigue the citadel had become? Anyone might be listening, concealing themselves behind the columns or the shuttered windows. I caught Marcellus's eye. Even to name these agents of the emperor in such a tone was dangerous. Did the boy not realize?

I gave him some vague answer, and told him not to listen to rumours. Then, to change the subject, I quickly asked him about his new silver mare. Nevitta liked all his troop to ride horses of the same colour – it seemed to me a showy affectation typical of Nevitta – but I wanted to get Rufus onto safer ground. In the far colonnade, the clerk had paused again, and was pretending to inspect the bundle of papers he was carrying.

There was a time when Rufus's eyes would have shone with joy and love at the mention of his horse. But now he merely shrugged, and commented without interest that the creature was skittish and ill-behaved. His eyes wandered, and soon he made an excuse and hurried off, more concerned, it seemed, with spreading his dangerous gossip.

Marcellus, who had understood my mind, watched him go, and turned to me with a shake of his head.

'Let's walk,' I said.

We did not speak again until we had passed under the arch and through to the plum-tree garden, where we should not be overheard.

'Has Decentius lost his mind?' he said. 'He knows what happened with the palace guard. Does he see nothing?'

Julian had spent the past two days trying to persuade Decentius to bring the men together elsewhere, in smaller, scattered groups, where their discontent would be less likely to spread. The last I had heard was that Decentius had finally seen the sense in it. He must have changed his mind; and Nevitta, hearing of it, had shared it with his drinking friends.

'Decentius does not like to take advice from anyone,' I said. 'He thinks Julian is merely trying to thwart him.'

'A fool could see it is the wrong thing to do.'

'But not Decentius. He suspects Julian is up to something. He thinks he has outwitted him.'

Marcellus tapped his fist slowly against the dark bark of the fruit tree beside him, and muttered a curse.

'I know,' I said, meeting his eye. 'He is casting fire into tinder.'

Soon the units of the army began to arrive; the Petulantes first; then the Keltic auxiliaries and the cohorts from the other legions. All except the Herulians and Batavians, who were still in Britain with Lupicinus.

Being too many for the military fort on the hill, they bivouacked outside the walls, on the low slopes beyond the river. Julian greeted old comrades; he remembered with the men their brave deeds; and, when they complained at being ordered east, he reminded them that there were many victories to be won, and that they were sure to meet with success and riches. To this the men listened in respectful silence, because they liked him. But their faces told they were not persuaded.

Decentius protested to Julian that he was making an exhibition of himself. But I was there. If he had broken with custom and not shown himself, the men would at once have grown suspicious. Already they had heard dark rumours; they were ready to believe any bad news they heard.

Then, one bleak winter morning, when all the troops were assembled and ready to depart, I was on my way to Julian when I passed Decentius strutting angrily through the inner court from the direction of his study. Pentadius and the quaestor Nebridius were with him. When I saw Julian he said, 'Decentius has just been here. He has decided to bring forward the day of departure.' He took up a sheet from his table and said, 'Look at this. He says he found it circulating among the Petulantes.'

I read. Upon the sheet, written in a rough unschooled hand, were the same familiar complaints: that the men were being driven from their homes; that promises were being broken; that as soon as they were gone the barbarians would return.

'Do you know who wrote it?' I asked, passing it back.

'Decentius accuses me.'

Our eyes met. After a moment Julian shrugged and looked away. 'I am blamed even when I do nothing. Now he is demanding that I sound out the officers myself, to find out how far this has spread. No one will speak to *him*, of course . . . So I have asked all the officers to dinner tonight. You come too, and tell Marcellus.'

The Petulantes and the Kelts were regiments of men recruited from Gaul, mixed with an assortment of barbarian volunteers. Some were accustomed to Roman ways; others, especially the Petulantes, were less so, and they kept to their own traditions. To please them, Julian assembled a feast worthy of any barbarian chieftain: great dishes of roasted meats with heavy spiced sauces; and strong red Gallic wine, served from a massive silver krater – a fine piece embossed with prancing stags – which was large enough to contain a crouching man.

I daresay the piles of rich food appalled his austere palate. But he knew how to entertain when he had to, and he cleared his bowl, with the help of the grateful brighteyed dogs that sat around in the long shadows beneath the couches.

After the heavy platters had been carried off, he called for the wine-cups to be filled once more and sent the servants off to bed. Only then did he ask about the morale of the men.

As fast as lead through water, the laughter and noise fell away. Each officer glanced at his neighbour, not wishing to be the first to speak.

'There is a rumour,' said Julian, 'that the men are unhappy.'

At this, Dagalaif, the burly German-born commander of the Petulantes, let out a harsh laugh and slapped his thigh. He was one of Nevitta's friends. Like Nevitta beside him, he had drunk a good deal that night.

'Unhappy!' he cried, surveying the rest of us with an ironic look. He was about to go on; but then, last of all, his gaze fell on Nevitta and he closed his mouth on his words. I glanced at Nevitta. His shrewd, weaselish face had assumed a look of bland vacancy. Nevitta may have been gross, but he was calculating with it. He was not a man who steps out first onto uncertain ice.

How much of this occurred to Dagalaif I could not tell. I guessed that some, at least, must have penetrated; for then, in a quieter, uneasy voice he went on, 'But I can speak only for my own men.'

'Then speak,' said Julian.

Dagalaif frowned and looked about, and was met with closed faces and averted eyes. He set down his heavy silver wine-cup, and slowly wiped his mouth with the back of his hairy forearm. 'Morale is low. If you want the truth of it, I have never seen it lower. Not even after Mount

Seleucus, and that was the worst I have known – before this.'

From among the shadowy couches there arose murmurs of agreement. Encouraged by this, Dagalaif went on, 'They are good honest men, sir; salt of the earth and not afraid of a fight. You know that. But they do not like it that they are called away. A promise is a promise.'

There was a pause. Then the floodgates opened and suddenly everyone was calling out. All the regiments were complaining, they cried; the men were saying they were being treated like criminals, taken far from their native land to the very ends of the earth; and was it for this that they had risked their lives in battle? Julian was their commander, not Constantius. The men wanted to stay with him. Let Constantius fight his own wars with his own armies.

I glanced across at Marcellus. Like me, he had been sparing with the potent, dark wine, knowing what was coming. I thought to myself, 'It is as well he sent the servants out.' This was not something for the emperor's ears.

The complaining and lamenting went on for some time. Julian listened without comment, turning his head this way and that as the men called out, his eyes shining in the lamplight.

Eventually, when all had been said and repeated, the voices died away, and the officers waited with parted lips for him to speak.

He wanted them to know, he said carefully, measuring each word, that the order to march east had not been his wish. Like them, he had to obey orders. He told them of

Constantius's demands. He could only suppose, he said, that the emperor had genuine need of the Gallic army. He wanted the troops to know he was powerless to intervene. They had served him well; but now they must do their duty.

It was a simple speech, full of emotion, seemingly without rhetoric. But I found myself thinking that it was not for nothing that he had studied with the finest minds of Athens.

Afterwards there were glistening eyes and wet cheeks everywhere; and soon after, the officers went off, embracing one another, lit by torches into the dark night.

When they were gone, and Marcellus and I were alone with him, Julian surveyed the empty krater and scattered cups and chewed-over bones and said, 'I have done nothing I am ashamed of. Yet there is something I overlooked.'

Marcellus asked him what he meant.

'I called them together,' he said, 'to learn the feelings of each one of them.' He paused, trying to think. He was no drinker, and had drunk more than he was used to. 'I asked them, and they have told me. But, more than that, they have told one another too.'

Marcellus looked at him, frowning.

'Do you not see?' said Julian. 'Before tonight each could only guess at what the others thought. Now they know for certain. The knowledge has united them.'

Later, back in our room, Marcellus and I lay in bed, talking over what had passed. The palace was quiet; yet we both felt new dangers, unforeseen until that night.

I had been saying something about Nevitta. My dislike of him had increased, after what I had seen that evening. But now we had both fallen silent, and I was watching the lamp-shadows on the ceiling as my mind turned with my thoughts. I yawned and shifted. Suddenly Marcellus leaped up and went to the window.

'What is it?' I asked.

'Hush,' he said, 'listen!'

But already I was on my feet, for by now I too had heard. It was the roar of onset, like a charge in battle, a sea of angry men, approaching at the double, chanting and yelling.

Marcellus had opened the window. A cold gust blew in, extinguishing the lamp flame. I heard a shout. From somewhere below came the sound of running footsteps. 'Come on,' he said, pulling on his clothes and throwing mine to me.

At the bottom of the stairwell a terrified slave pushed past us, like a rabbit fleeing a burning field. Marcellus seized his arm, jerking him to a halt. 'Calm yourself!' he said sharply.

The slave stared at him wide-eyed, trying to pull away. 'Run!' he cried, 'the legions are coming. They are storming the palace!' He snatched his arm free and was gone.

I said, 'Then it has started. We had better find Julian.'

He was not in his rooms. The doors stood open. No guards were present. We found the steward craning out of the window; he told us Julian had gone to his wife's apartments; already he had sent a slave to fetch him, though by now he must surely have heard the din for himself. So we hurried on, emerging into the high-walled outer court. It was a mistake, for at that moment the first legionaries came streaming in at the gateway.

Marcellus grabbed my arm and pulled me into the corner, just as a great mass of yelling wild-faced men, their swords drawn, came surging into the square, filling the space between the high walls like a river in spate. Those at the front wore the dyed furs and insignia of the Petulantes; in their train followed Kelts and auxiliaries. The courtyard filled with far more than it could hold, and we were pressed hard against the wall, unable to move from where we stood.

Then the chanting began, led by the men at the front – 'Julian! Julian! Julian! Julian!' – louder and louder, each man picking up the cry from the other, spreading like fire in dry undergrowth, back through the crowd and out beyond the gates into the darkness: Julian's name, endlessly repeated like a challenge, echoing from the sheer stone walls and shuttered windows, shaking the ground and ringing in my ears. And still the men were pressing in, ever more of them, a whole army. The air reeked of wine and beer and soldiers' sweat. Then, from somewhere in the midst of them, a new rhythm started and was taken up by those about, mingled with cheers and wild battle-cries. At first I could not make it out; but then my hands went cold as I realized what they were saying: 'Julian *Augustus*, Julian *Augustus*, Julian *Augustus* . . .' on and on and on.

I looked at Marcellus. There was no need for words. Around us men were laughing and punching the air, crying out at the top of their voices the terrible formula that could never be retracted, proclaiming Julian as emperor, calling for him to show himself.

A trooper beside me yelled at his neighbour, 'Where is he? Why does he not come?' His comrade, a gap-toothed, battle-scarred Gaul, said laughing, 'Well he's not asleep, not now.' And on the chanting went. It was like the games, or the chariot races; noise and fervour that reach into a man's heart, like a madness, and make him one with the crowd, forming out of many souls one mighty beast with one single purpose.

It seemed the din went on for hours, rising and falling like a tempest; and we were trapped in its midst. Then, as the torches above the gateway dimmed, and the first glimmer of dawn streaked red across the sky, a great yell of victory broke out from the front. The postern in the great, studded doors had opened, and onto the balcony, above the high steps, appeared Julian.

The Petulantes being of German stock are tall men, and I struggled to see between their broad backs. But every so often, as the dense crowd surged and parted, I caught glimpses of him, raising his hands in an appeal for calm, trying to make himself heard over the roar. But the acclamations only mounted louder. I saw him shake his head and gesture for the men to listen; but after a while, seeing the futility of this, he dropped his arms to his sides and waited, until eventually the ones at the front started hushing the others behind. Then, at last, he could address them. His voice was hesitant, even shaken. It was hard to tell if it was from anger, or emotion, or fear.

They were good men, he said, who had served Rome well. They had shared victories and hardships together; they had fought the Franks, and Alamans, and other German tribes, and had driven them back beyond the frontiers. Now, when Gaul was once again secure, was not the time to spoil what they had gained. Their demands could be met, he was sure of it; but if they did not desist, they would only bring ruin upon them all.

He paused, his breath showing in the crisp air of the early dawn. The men looked at him sullenly. 'I give my word,' he said, 'that you will not be forced to leave your homes against your will. I shall intercede with the emperor; he will surely listen. But now you must return to your quarters.'

For a moment there was disappointed silence. Then they roared. It was not a cheer. It was a great defiant cry of 'No!'

A lone voice in the midst of the crowd resumed the chant, 'Julian Augustus! Julian Augustus!' Swiftly it was taken up by the rest. The cries rose, loud and furious and full of menace, like some wild and terrible music.

Up to now Julian had affected not to hear; hoping, I suppose, that if the men returned to their quarters it could somehow be forgotten. Everything else – their protests, their near-mutiny, their indiscipline and drunkenness – could be explained away and forgiven. But the acclamation, once report of it reached the ears of the emperor, would be fatal.

As the roar of voices rose once more, he abandoned his efforts to quieten them, and merely stood with his head bowed. The men around me were grinning and laughing to one another, showing their teeth and the reds of their mouths. But there was no joy in their laughter; it was a shared delight in their doomful power. It seemed that there could be no end. But then, as the last stars were fading in the sky, from the front there arose a cry, and suddenly the crowd surged forward, carrying us with them like leaves in the flood. I strained to see; and then I understood. For up on the step, Julian had extended his arms, palms open, in the timeless sign of acknowledgement, accepting at last the acclamation.

And then, everywhere, there was wild cheering.

Already men were scrambling up the steps to the small stone balcony where he stood, pushing one another as they vied to be first. They were all around him, mobbing him. He disappeared from view, among a seething tide of moving bodies. Then I saw him rise above their shoulders as they lifted him and bore him down. Somebody brought an infantry shield, blue on yellow, the colours of the Petulantes; they placed him upon it, and raised him high, all the time shouting at the top of their voices, 'Julian Augustus! Julian Augustus! Julian Augustus!'

'A diadem!' someone cried; and the call was taken up, 'A diadem! Where's a diadem? Bring a diadem!' Julian gestured that he did not have such a thing – and indeed how could he, for only the emperor wore the diadem.

'What about your wife?' someone shouted.

It would be an inauspicious start, he cried in answer, for him to wear a woman's trinket.

The men laughed. They would have laughed at anything. Then a standard-bearer, a man named Maurus, was pushed to the front. He took off his decorated collar of rank, and it was passed from hand to hand over the heads of the crowd, until someone planted it upon Julian's head. It was hardly befitting, but no one cared, and all around us the men cheered and whistled and roared approval.

After this there was something of a lull. Everyone looked at one another, unsure what came next. Julian, sensing his moment, spoke out. He thanked them for their love and loyalty, and promised each man a donative of five pieces of gold and a pound of silver. Then he told them to return to quarters.

This time they obeyed, withdrawing from the palace courtyard like a receding sea, leaving Marcellus and me alone in silence, under a blood-red angry dawn.

We found Julian in the audience chamber with its rows of squat stone pillars and ancient hangings. Decentius the notary was there, and Pentadius, and the quaestor Nebridius, all of them shouting at once. Further back, gathered beneath the flickering light of the cresset, a group of Florentius's liveried officials stood staring in silent terror, their carefully ordered world suddenly turned awry.

Decentius was shouting incoherently, pointing and waving his arms.

'Go to the camp yourself and tell them!' Julian shouted back at him.

'But you must retract! It is treason!'

'Do you think I do not know? I warned you what would happen.'

Suddenly, realizing that the absurd diadem was still on his head, he cast it angrily down. It landed at Decentius's feet. The notary backed away, and stared at it as if it were a serpent ready to strike him. 'Well?' said Julian. 'Now, at last, you have your rebellion. What are you going to do about it?'

But Decentius just opened his mouth, and then closed it again and shook his head. Julian, with a gesture of impatience, turned and strode off towards his quarters.

'Wait!' cried the notary, beginning to follow. But Marcellus stepped forward, blocking his path.

'No, Decentius,' he said. 'You have already done enough. Leave him to rest.'

'You too!' he spluttered.

'Don't be a fool. The men are gone. Let them sleep off their wine.' And then, looking at Pentadius and Nebridius, who were standing behind, gaping at him, 'We were there; Julian had no choice. They would have sacked the palace.'

The two men exchanged appalled looks. I think it was only then that they realized how close to death they had come.

Of them all, Nebridius was the only one who had some honour about him. He had assisted Decentius and Pentadius because they had demanded it; but he did so from duty, without pleasure or an air of triumph.

'Do you think,' he asked Marcellus, 'that they will come to their senses when they are sober?'

Marcellus shrugged. 'Perhaps they will. But they are angry and dangerous – and now they know the power

204

they possess. It is hard to tell, after this night, whether we are their masters or their prisoners.'

We left them with their clutch of officials, looking at one another in horror, and returned to our rooms.

Marcellus sat on the bed and looked at me. 'There is no going back now, Drusus, not for any of us. Whatever that fool Decentius says, such words cannot be retracted, and Julian knows it better than anyone.'

'Yes, Marcellus,' I said. And then, after a pause, 'But we chose our sides long ago, if it has come to that.'

I yawned and rubbed my eyes.

'Get some rest,' he said, pressing my shoulder.

'What, after all that has happened?'

But somehow I must have dozed off, for one minute my mind was racing, going over the events of the night; the next, it seemed, Marcellus was shaking me, saying, 'Up quickly, Drusus! They are back.'

I took up my sword-belt. Marcellus had pushed open the shutters and was leaning out. From somewhere beyond the gate I could hear the low grumble of men's voices. At least, I thought, as I buckled on my belt, it is not a riot this time.

Julian was back in the audience chamber; but this time he was ready for them. He was seated on the dais, in a high chair draped with white linen, wearing a cloak of imperial purple, with Oribasius and Eutherius at his side. Daylight flooded in through the rose-window behind him, casting brilliant dust-flecked shafts across the stone-flagged floor.

Before him stood a delegation from the men, a group

of twenty or thirty troops. Julian was saying to them that they had nothing to fear, assuring them that he was well and unthreatened. They listened gravely, and nodded, and stared, awed by the trappings of imperium. I found out later what had happened.

While Julian had been resting, Decentius, instead of leaving them to sober up and reflect on the night, had begun secretly to offer money to the lower-ranking officers of the Petulantes, trying to bribe them to return to the unguarded citadel and arrest Julian as a traitor. As usual he had miscalculated, not realizing that it was not gold that had first impelled them, but honour and fear and injured pride. They had not been bought by Julian; and gold would not now turn them.

Word of Decentius's plotting had soon got round; the rumour had spread through the camp that Julian was in danger, or had been arrested and was about to be put to death. At once the men had come rushing. They would not leave, they said, until they had seen Julian for themselves, and heard from his own mouth that he was safe.

After this, Decentius was summoned and could not be found; realizing he had been caught out he had gone into hiding. But Paris is too small a city, and Decentius – as one of the emperor's spies – was too much hated for him to hide for long. Within hours he was brought back to the palace.

'What will you do with him?' asked Nebridius.

'Do with him? Nothing. I imagine the men who found him gave him fright enough. He is fortunate they did not cut his throat and cast him into the river.'

'And now?'

'Let him leave, if that is what he wants. We do not need him here.'

Soon afterwards, the troops of the palace guard returned – the ones who had marched east with Sintula and their womenfolk. They had not travelled far, being miserable and reluctant; and as soon as they heard the news from Paris they hurried back. Sintula, to his credit, returned too, though he could easily have fled.

Then, when a measure of calm had returned, Julian called all the men to assembly.

He rode out to the open ground beyond the city, where the various units had made camp, and under a sky of towering clouds and fleeting springtime sunlight he addressed the men, reminding them of all they had been through together. Now, in the time of his need, he hoped they would stand by him.

They cheered him long and loud, raising their arms in salute and beating their spears against their shining shields. The sound rolled through the assembled ranks like thunder. They were Julian's to command.

Later he held a private dinner for his friends, and to us he confided his private fears. His position in Gaul was secure, he explained, but only while the emperor was occupied with the Persians on the eastern frontiers. 'Constantius must be made to understand: I did not choose this acclamation; I do not challenge him. The men were unwilling to leave Gaul and their homes, that is all. It is not rebellion against him.'

'That is not how Constantius will see it,' said Eutherius.

'Already he believes he sees traitors everywhere; and Decentius, when he arrives at court, will protect himself at your expense. So will Florentius. We already have the measure of those men.'

Julian considered for a while. A messenger had arrived the day before, bringing news that Florentius had fled from Vienne, abandoning his wife and children in his haste. Julian had sent orders that they and all their possessions were to be conveyed in safety to the East. Constantius would have seized them, and put the family to death.

'I have no wish for civil war,' he said, turning to Eutherius. 'I shall write to Constantius myself, and tell him how the men were driven to this. I shall offer troops, as he wished . . . not the Petulantes, who will not go; nor the Herulians, who are not here. But we can send—' And he named units he would dispatch east in their place. 'I shall invite Constantius to appoint a new prefect – whomever he wishes. But otherwise I must choose my own staff. We should have spared ourselves much trouble if he had allowed me to do that at the start. Let him make enquiries; he will see that all I tell him is true.'

'And from whom,' asked Eutherius, 'will he enquire? Decentius and Florentius? No, that will not do. Someone must go and speak for you.'

I said, 'I will go. I was there; I saw what happened.'

'Thank you, Drusus,' said Julian with a smile, 'but I would not send you into that vipers' nest. I have some-thing else to ask of you. No, there is only one man here Constantius will listen to.'

He looked over the tables and couches, to where

Eutherius was toying with a bowl of honeyed figs. Eutherius set down the bowl and sighed.

'Ah! Another winter journey. In that case, dear Julian, I suggest I take Pentadius with me.'

'Pentadius? – But why? Everyone knows he is one of Florentius's lackeys.'

'Which is why Constantius might listen to him.'

Pentadius, though he could have fled with Decentius, had chosen to stay. It seemed now he regretted his support for the notary, who had abandoned him, concerned only to save his own skin. Pentadius now saw he had been used, and then discarded.

Oribasius, who had been sitting silently, said, 'Whatever happens, you cannot surrender now. You know that.'

Julian nodded. His wine – in a cup of simple Gallic earthenware, embossed with grapes and vines – sat untouched before him.

'Constantius must let me keep what I hold,' he said eventually. 'Nothing else is possible.'

'Yes; but will he accept?'

'He has the Persians at his back,' said Eutherius. 'He may concede . . . if he sees no other way. But he will struggle like a netted cat first.'

'And still,' said Julian, turning to me, 'there is the problem of Lupicinus.'

Two of his best legions were still in Britain, under the command of Lupicinus. 'Constantius will order him to move against us. We must make sure that he does not.'

He would write, he said, recalling Lupicinus to Paris. This was the task he needed me for. Marcellus and I must go to Britain, bearing Julian's letter to the Master of Cavalry; Marcellus, being on Lupicinus's staff, would not arouse undue suspicion. 'You must do all you can to make sure Constantius does not succeed in getting word to him. I shall send trusted men to all the ports of Gaul and Spain – wherever a messenger might put out. But that may not be enough; you must do what you can from the other side.'

He said he was promoting me to the rank of count, which would ensure I possessed sufficient authority not to be hindered. 'And speak to Alypius in London. He is a friend. He can be trusted.'

For a while then we discussed details. But before we parted he turned to me and said, 'And now, Drusus, there is an injustice I have long wanted to rectify.'

He stood, and from the side-table picked up a letter sealed with wax. The light from the standard caught his face, and I saw that he was blushing.

'This,' he said, turning, 'declares your father free of any crime, and restores all your lands and properties.'

I took the folded bundle, and gazed down at the seal; but in my mind I was seeing the image of my father as I remembered him, standing tall against the windows of his sunlit study, on the day he sent me away. For all this time Julian must have known, without the power to act.

I looked up to thank him. But I found my throat tightened, and the words would not come.

'Tell me, Drusus, do you believe the gods speak to us in dreams, as it is often claimed?'

I swallowed, and thought.

'Yes,' I replied, after a pause, 'but it takes man's reason to know the meaning of what they tell. We are not mere playthings of the gods, like chaff in a torrent.'

He nodded and smiled.

'A good answer. Only the well-ordered soul sees rightly. Last night, I dreamed of a tall tree, and, about its roots, a sapling struggling to grow in its shadow. The tall tree had partly fallen, its roots torn from the soil. But as I drew nearer to see, Hermes touched me on the shoulder and said, "Look and take heart; the sapling remains bound to the earth; it will grow up strong, and the other will die away."'

He gave a shy self-conscious laugh.

I said, 'But what does it mean?'

He shrugged. 'Perhaps this. The tall tree is Constantius; and though I did not ask for it, yet God has given me the chance to put right many evils that Constantius has caused.' He nodded at the scroll in my hand. 'This is a beginning. As for the rest, I do not know where it will lead. But I sense the gods are with me. If I refuse what they proffer, there will be no second chance.'

EIGHT

WE CROSSED TO BRITAIN in a fast single-banked galley, on a spring day of scudding clouds, blown in on a westerly breeze that rocked and pitched the boat. At Richborough fort we picked up horses and a military escort, and then rode west through the dew-fresh pastures of the coastal plain, taking the road to London.

The road was familiar. The memories returned. In due course, at the turn-off to a southwards-leading pathway, I reined in my horse. The track was overgrown with brambles and whitethorn; violets and blue hyacinth showed on the grass bank. I pointed towards the tall avenue of limes in the middle-distance. 'The house is there behind,' I said to Marcellus. 'All this was my father's land.'

'And now it is restored to you. The riders need a break; we should go and look.'

I felt a pang of reluctance for which I had no easy words. But Marcellus had already dismissed the escort, telling them to ride on and wait in the next village. So shaking off my feeling I set off with him down the disused path.

Ivy and tangled honeysuckle had grown up over the high stone arch of the gateway. We rode on through, and dismounted. Within the enclosure, the walls of the house still stood; but the roof was gone, and fire-charred beams lay fallen on the atrium floor.

Inside, where there had once been a small square tiled pool, a rowan had taken root. Already it was tall as two men and branching out, taking possession. We stepped around it. The breeze stirred in an eddy around us. I paused, and rubbed the stirred-up soot from my eyes, and saw in the spangling darkness behind my eyelids the house as I remembered it, with its urns of trailing flowers, and painted walls, and marble inlaid floors. I scuffed at the floor with my toe. Below the layer of rubble the marble was still there: coloured strips of red and honey-white and serpentine.

'I had supposed,' I said, 'that someone else would be living here. The bishop took it all, and for what? A bequest to the Church from my father, so he claimed, though everyone knew it was a lie. But I was a boy; and who would gainsay him? And now it is a wasteland. A man should own nothing he cannot put to proper use. It makes me angry.' And I kicked hard at a blackened rafter.

'Yet perhaps,' said Marcellus, placing his hand on my shoulder, 'it is better so; for at least there is no stranger here, demanding to know your business in your own house. That would be worse.'

We walked on inside. The fire that had consumed the house had been set in my father's study. The once-bright frescoes were blackened and cracked; great swathes of plaster had parted from the wall, exposing the brick beneath. In one of the high alcoves where he had kept his books, a martin had built her nest.

Frowning and silent, I picked my way through the debris, pausing here and there to look. My father's great onyx table remained, in the place where it had always been, between the tall windows. No doubt it had been too heavy for the looters to shift. Absently I traced my finger across the blackened surface, leaving a line of white stone. There was a stirring, and the martin came fluttering in, and sat chirping indignantly on her shelf. I glanced around the ruin of the room where I had so often stood as a child, waiting to be punished or rebuked. Though my father had been a stranger to me, he had been just, and was brought low by lesser men than he. I understood such things better now. I used to think he hated me; but he had loved me in his austere way. I had not seen it while he lived.

I swallowed and turned. Marcellus's grey eyes were upon me.

'For years,' I said, 'this place has been in my dreams, somewhere forever lost. I never thought I should return; and in a way I wish I had not, for now it is this ruin I shall remember.'

I took a last look, drew my breath, and walked over to where he was waiting by the door.

'I am what I have become,' I said. 'There is no going

back.' And then, after a pause, 'Time and change turn everything to dust.'

He brought his hand up to my neck and easing me to him kissed my brow. It was something he seldom did.

'Some things are forever, Drusus; and I am still here. You belong with me now.'

We spoke no more. And presently we turned away, kicking through the black dust, to where the horses were waiting in the courtyard, chewing at the tall grass that grew up between the cracked untended pavings.

Next day we came to London. After the ravaged look of Gaul, everything seemed prosperous. The Saxons had come raiding when I was a boy, spreading their usual terror; but the danger had been forgotten, and the villas and farmsteads in the spreading open suburbs south of the Thames had been rebuilt and even extended.

Crossing the bridge I pointed to the barges tied two and three deep along the wharf and asked the escort nearest me, a good-looking black-haired Briton newly recruited and eager to please, why the port was so busy, seeing as it was still early spring.

'Oh, sir, this is nothing at all,' he cried. 'Just wait till the sea-roads open with the fine weather, and the ships from the Rhine return.'

I smiled to myself. Julian would be pleased to see his dream come real. I noted in my mind, to relate to him later, all the signs of activity and new wealth: the laden wagons beside the storehouses; the rows of amphoras and barrels and piled-up crates on the wharf; the lines of barges with their bright furled sails; and, everywhere, busy, well-dressed citizens hurrying about their business.

Only the city walls had been neglected; and when I mentioned this to the young escort he just gave a civil laugh and said that Romans had nothing to fear from primitive Saxons. I smiled at his innocent courage and said nothing. I had heard the same words before.

At the governor's palace we were met by the new governor Alypius, Julian's friend from Antioch. He was a middle-aged Greek with an intelligent, careworn face. We gave him letters from Paris, and told him something of what had occurred there. We were brief and discreet. It was not a time for too many words. When we had finished he frowned and said, 'It is a difficult, unpleasant matter, to be sure; but I am surprised to see you so soon after the other, for only two days ago there was a courier from Paris, and I might have supposed—'

'A courier, sir?' I said, breaking in. 'But what courier was this? No one was sent from Paris.'

Alypius looked at me. 'Are you quite sure? He was here only two days ago – an imperial messenger on his way to Lupicinus. How odd. He was from Paris – he *said* he had come from Paris – with urgent dispatches from the prefect Florentius.'

'Then forgive me, sir, but that cannot be: Florentius is not in Paris. He has been absent from there all winter.'

A deep frown settled on Alypius's face. 'I see; I see. Then I fear we have a problem. I did not meet the man myself, and so cannot give you my direct opinion; but the stable-master said he was oddly agitated when he learnt that

Lupicinus was not here in London. I thought little of it at the time; but, now that I reflect, it does seem rather strange, for it is surely known in Paris that Lupicinus left London long ago.'

'May we question the stable-master ourselves?' asked Marcellus.

'Why yes, of course.' He signalled to a steward and told him to conduct us to the stables. As we walked with him to the door he said in a low, confidential voice, 'I do hope Julian . . . I mean the Caesar – or rather the Augustus – will not think . . .'

'The man lied to you, sir,' I said. 'You were not to know. But now we must make haste; we must overtake this courier, whoever he is, before he reaches Lupicinus.'

We hurried outside and across the courtyard with its cascading Neptune fountain, where once, as an orphaned youth, I had sat and considered Gratian's offer of a place in the army. 'Yes,' said the stable-master, 'I remember the man well.' He described him, adding, 'He was not one of the usual relay-riders; I know them all. And he refused a relief-man, saying his orders were to deliver his message in person.'

By then the first lamps of evening were being kindled. We asked about the route and other such matters; and then, leaving orders for horses to be ready with the dawn, we went off to wash and eat.

Later, sitting at a tavern we knew, I said to Marcellus, 'We may be too late. If he reaches Lupicinus then our game is up.'

Marcellus nodded. 'Yet it could be he does not know

the message he carries. We may be able to persuade him.' He hesitated and looked me in the eye. 'But if we cannot, we shall have to kill him.'

'Yes,' I said.

I had thought of it already.

We set out at first light and rode hard, changing horses along the way. Finally, at a drab settlement called Letocetum, we caught up with our courier.

Rain had blown in from the west, and we arrived at the staging-inn cold and wet and aching. But there was work to do. I took care of arrangements with the inn-keeper, and Marcellus went off to make enquiries among the grooms at the stables.

At each stop along the way we had slowly gained on our quarry. We travelled without an escort, and had removed our signs of rank; for no one will pause and gossip with a tribune, but any idle drinker will kill time with a common soldier, especially one who stands him a pint of wine.

And thus it was that we discovered, over many a rancid cup, when we were dog-tired from riding and wanted nothing but our beds, that our man had a particular weakness, and indulged his pleasure in the small-town brothels along the way, at imperial expense.

We learned too that after his evening's entertainment, with no one to urge him on, he was allowing himself to sleep late; and each day we had gained on him. Even so, he had remained stubbornly ahead of us. But now, finally, at Letocetum, his horse had fallen lame, and there was no replacement.

From the chamber-girl we found out that he was not presently in his room. We went off to check at the small bath-house next door, but the attendant told us there had been a problem with the piping, and the baths were closed. Next we wandered up the main street, looking in at the taverns and cheap eating-houses, of which Letocetum has a great many. At the last of them, just when I was starting to think we should have to trawl the stews, Marcellus touched my arm and nodded into an unlit corner. 'There!' he murmured.

Casually, as if I were idly scanning the room, I turned my head and looked. In the shadows a figure in a heavy cloak was sitting alone at a table, with a cup and pitcher before him.

We took our wine and ambled across the sawdust-strewn floor, halting at his table. 'Greetings, friend!' I said with a wide smile. 'Have we not met before?'

The man looked up and regarded me suspiciously. He was a little older than I, thin-built with poor skin and a mean, dissatisfied face. One of his hands rested on the rough, drink-stained table; with the other he was clutching his cloak about him as if he were cold, though the stale air of the room was warm enough.

He shrugged. 'I doubt it,' he said, and looked away.

We sat down anyway, heartily setting down our wine-cups next to his, smiling and laughing like a pair of idiot party-goers. I shouted across to the tavern-keeper for another pitcher; Marcellus, improvising, began talking about horses, the frustrations of travel, and the poor state of entertainment in such a dull, rain-swept outpost.

'Yes indeed!' I said. 'What a place to be delayed! Already we are late, and our business with Lupicinus is urgent.' I laughed merrily. 'But enough of business! Here is the wine at last; let us drink, my friend, and enjoy the night – if such a thing is possible in this god-forsaken hole.' And I made a great fuss of filling all our cups from the new pitcher, like a man who takes his pleasures seriously.

'I'm Marcellus,' said Marcellus, grinning and putting out his hand. The man looked at his hand and did not take it.

'Firmus,' he said warily.

He had a gaunt, unfed look. His skin was grey and pocked, and there were blue lines about his bulging eyes. He had enough sense to realize there was nothing attractive about him; and he was clearly unused to the attention of friends.

Marcellus carried on talking and laughing, laying it on thick, as if every moment with this man were a rare pleasure. I thought at first Firmus had not noticed the hook we had dangled before him. But then, abruptly, he asked, 'Why are you going to Lupicinus?'

I paused and drew a breath, and made sure he saw me glancing at the neighbouring tables before I answered. Dropping my voice I said, 'We carry a message from the prefect – his name is Florentius – a very important person . . .' I tapped my nose with my finger, and then with a knowing nod went on, 'But a still tongue makes a wise head, as they say.'

I lifted the pitcher, intending to ply him with more of

the cheap wine. But he brought up his hand and blocked the top of his cup.

Then he leant forward and murmured, 'I too carry a letter from the prefect.'

'Is that so? . . . Well, what a thing! Then it seems we have more in common than I thought.'

Not wanting to show too much interest, I filled my own wine-cup and, to change the subject, fell to talking some nonsense with Marcellus about the serving-girl; and we went on for a while like a pair of ham actors, pausing every so often to gaze and leer.

Then, as I had intended, Marcellus said, 'Hey Drusus; I was thinking. With us going to Lupicinus anyway, why don't we do Firmus here a kindness and take his letter for him?'

'Why not,' I answered with a shrug. 'Friends should help friends, after all.'

'I can't do that,' said Firmus straightaway, in a dogged, wooden voice. 'My instructions are to take the letter in person.'

'Oh well, just trying to help,' said Marcellus. He drank his wine, and returned his attention to the serving-girl, who fortunately for us had not noticed, for she was a drab miserable creature in need of a bath.

In spite of all my efforts, Firmus remained stubbornly sober. Wine, it seemed, was not one of his weaknesses. He began looking about, as if preparing to leave. Quickly I said, 'Anyway, Marcellus, time we moved on. The girls will be waiting.'

'Girls?' asked Firmus, suddenly alert.

'Why, yes. A shame to pass *them* up.' Marcellus, who was never crude, followed this with a vulgar gesture one sees used in camp by the common soldiers. It was so unlike him that for a moment I forgot my act and stared. He caught my eye and blushed, covering it with a sudden fit of coughing. 'But I suppose,' he went on, 'that you'll be wanting an early night, what with your long journey and all.'

'Tell me about the girls,' said Firmus.

Between us we invented some story. As we spoke, his eyes, which up to then had wandered, fixed on us with the keenness of a hunting dog who smells the fox. Then he became talkative, saying he had already tried at various of the taverns that kept whores. None were to his liking. He preferred young types, he said, giving us a significant look and licking his thin lips.

'Ah yes; what else,' I answered. I had heard of his tastes during our long pursuit from London. I sipped at my wine. It was suddenly bitter in my mouth.

Marcellus scratched at his chin, pretending to think. Then he said, 'Well why not come with us then?' and when Firmus was looking away he gave me a quick secret look. We both knew what it meant. We paid and left.

The rain had stopped. The night air was damp and chill, and low cloud obscured the stars.

We walked on, taking a side-street. The close-built houses gave way to larger plots, and smallholdings with yards and walls; the cobbles ended, replaced by dirt track. Beside me Firmus slowed. I could sense his unease, which for a brief time had been suspended by the prospect of what lay ahead. He shifted and muttered. There was nothing courageous about him, even in his whoring.

'Not far now,' I said loudly, in a tone of voice I hoped Marcellus would understand.

At the next corner Marcellus paused. 'I think it's this way,' he said, 'yes, this is where the man told us to go.' He turned off along a grassy path behind the high wooden walls of a barn. We passed a derelict, windowless building and then an open yard. Somewhere in the darkness a dog began barking.

Firmus suddenly halted.

'What is this place?' he muttered crossly. 'Where are you taking me?'

'Not far now,' said Marcellus. 'Wait, I think I see a light – yes; that is the place, just up ahead.'

I had allowed myself to drop back, so that I was a pace or two behind. Now, while Marcellus chattered on, I drew silently near, and reached within my cloak.

Perhaps some god or spirit touched Firmus on the shoulder then. Suddenly, for no reason, he swung round. His startled eyes met mine; and for an instant, standing close, I saw written on his face the knowledge of his own death. My knife flashed out. He gasped once, then choked and fell.

We hid the body in a nearby midden, then made our way back. For a long time neither of us spoke. But when we reached the street with its few glimmering lights Marcellus touched my arm and said, 'There was no other way. You know that.'

'Yes,' I said, 'I know.'

I walked on. Then, after a moment, 'It is pretending to be his friend I hate most of all. I feel it still, like a pollution in my soul.'

'I too; yet it had to be done. We had to stop him. Many thousands will die if Lupicinus marches against Julian. It was in our hands, ours alone.'

At the street-corner I paused under a wall-cresset and by its spluttering light inspected my clothes and hands for blood. In the wet grass beside the midden I had cleaned myself as best I could, but I felt it clung to me still.

'You are right, Marcellus,' I said, when I was done with this, 'and I'd do the same again. But I'd rather the battle-field any day.'

He agreed, and let out his breath in a sigh. I knew that he too had felt the touch of evil.

And there was still the letter.

We had searched the body but found nothing. In the end, supposing he must have left it in his room, we returned to the inn; but we could hardly rouse the innkeeper and ask which room was his. So we crept about outside like thieves, peering in as best we could at half-shuttered windows, trying doors, and, if we disturbed anyone sleeping, feigning stupidity and drunkenness.

At last we found the room we wanted. Inside there was a brown leather satchel, packed with a few possessions. Marcellus emptied them onto the bed and sifted through them – a Mithras-charm; a small rough painting on a folded piece of old wood of a middle-aged woman; a keep-sake lock of golden hair in a little carved box. But there was no letter.

We pulled up the bedding, and felt about beneath the mattress; we tapped the boards, and searched for hidden niches in the wall; but there was nothing. By now the birds were stirring, and the first grey light of a miserable dawn showed through the window.

I blew out the lamp. 'Come on,' I said, 'it's not here.'

Back in our room we stirred up the bed-sheets to make it seem we had slept. Then we sat down and considered what to do.

We had hidden the body quickly, and in darkness. For all we knew, the alley could be a busy thoroughfare by day, and any passing labourer on his way to the fields might discover it. We could not afford to wait for that, with all the attention and questions it would bring. Already, outside, the servants of the inn were moving about under the covered walkway, speaking to one another in hushed voices as they went about their early tasks. And so, in the end, we made our way down to the stables, and took our horses, and rode onwards into the west.

Lupicinus glowered at the document in his hands. It was the letter we had brought him from Julian, recalling him to Paris. I knew from his eyes that he had finished reading; but he did not look up at us, nor did he speak.

In the silence I could hear his breath passing noisily through his nostrils, in and out, like an impatient man on the edge of an angry outburst. Why did he not speak? What was wrong? I waited. I dared not turn my head to Marcellus.

We had finally reached him at the city of Chester, where

he was pausing on his leisurely return south. Now, as I stood before him, I reflected yet again on the many ways Florentius or the emperor could have got word to him: by the sea route to the north of Britain, or across country from the west. I wondered what he already knew that would expose the true nature of our mission.

I realized I was clenching my hands at my sides. I forced myself to relax them. At any moment I expected him to call for our arrest.

In the corner a nervous adjutant was sitting at a desk, shifting his papers pointlessly to and fro while he strained to listen. Through the side of my eye I could see Marcellus standing straight, like a soldier on parade. I decided I must say something; it seemed less painful than the silence. But then, just as I drew my breath, Lupicinus slapped the letter down on the trestle camp-table and looked directly at me, his face as immobile as a statue.

'Why is it,' he asked coldly, 'that the Caesar sent *you*?'

My mind raced. I said, 'I had private business in Britain; it was once my home. And so I accompanied Marcellus, who is my friend.'

He kept his eyes on my face as I answered.

'Is the prefect Florentius in Paris?' he said.

This was a test, I sensed it. I could smell my sweat; I had not had chance to bathe. I said, 'He is at Vienne, sir.'

'Vienne,' he repeated, with a slow incline of his head. I had no idea if Lupicinus had heard that the prefect had already fled from Vienne. If he knew that, then he would know the rest too.

He remained still for a moment. Then he took up the

letter again, and it seemed to me there was an expression of distaste in his pinched features.

'Do you know,' he asked, in a slow, suspicious voice, 'what is written here?'

'Only,' I said, 'that the Caesar asks you to return to Paris.'

'Yes; this letter surprises me.'

'Sir?'

'There is no mention of my victories. Why does it not mention my victories?' He looked again, vain fool that he was. I could almost have laughed.

'Oh,' I cried, 'but we had not heard; no news has reached us for some time. But soon, I hope, you will be able to inform Julian in person; it will be a great triumph for you.' And I thought to myself: so he has beaten back the rabble of Picts and Scots; one might have supposed, from his tone, that he had single-handedly crushed the mighty assembled armies of the King of Kings, and that his name would be written in the stars.

But Lupicinus, as everyone knew, was not a man to understate his achievements.

He eyed me carefully. No doubt he had heard a good deal of insincere flattery in his life. But after a moment he said, 'Yes . . . Well . . . To tell you the truth, I was expecting to hear from Florentius. But you say you bring nothing from him?'

I told him no. He sniffed; then strode to the window with his straight-backed, affected military step, and peered out at the yard.

'Half a month ago, I received a letter from the prefect.

He said little; but he hinted that he feared trouble. Do you know what he might have meant? – No? – Well, nor do I. He gave me no detail; he only said he intended to write more fully soon. Since then I have heard nothing from him.'

He had kept his back to us as he spoke; but now he turned suddenly, as if he hoped to catch in my face some concealed meaning. I looked at him blandly.

'And yet,' he said, frowning, 'you say all is well in Gaul?'

'Well enough, sir. There are rumours the Rhine Germans are stirring again for war.'

'Oh, the Germans are always a problem. It must be some other more weighty matter that demands my presence.'

I agreed, adding, since I knew the sort of man he was, 'I expect the Caesar did not wish to share the details with me.'

'Yes, I daresay.'

Marcellus, in a helpful tone, asked, 'Should we take a message back for the prefect?'

'What? Oh, no; there is no need. Let the prefect contact me himself, if he wishes. No doubt Julian will tell me what all this is about.'

I allowed myself to breathe again.

Marcellus, who had the measure of the man, began asking about the campaign, saying he had heard it much praised, even in the short time we had been in the camp. At this, for the first time, Lupicinus's face brightened. 'Did you expect otherwise? I have never been defeated, and this was little more than child's play after what I have done elsewhere. Why only last year in Syria . . .'

And off he went.

As he talked on I smiled inwardly, and joined Marcellus in laying on the flattery, and for the next half-hour stood dog-tired on my feet, while he crowed to us about his successes against the Scots and Picts. But to be bored by Lupicinus was a relief, for I knew now that we had succeeded.

When later Marcellus and I were crossing the open ground back to our quarters, I whistled through my teeth and said, 'Two days more, and Firmus would have reached him with his letter.'

Marcellus began to speak, then started like a shying horse as from across the square an officer yelled out a reprimand to a trooper.

He glanced at me and shook his head. 'I think I need to sleep,' he said. And then, 'I wonder what Florentius knew. It must all have been in that second letter.'

I nodded, and thought of the messenger dying under my hand. But I did not want to speak of that; so after a pause I said, 'I sense Lupicinus doesn't much care for the prefect. If he did, he might have paid more heed of him.'

'He doesn't care for him at all. And have you heard why?'

'No. Why?'

'He thinks he is arrogant.'

We laughed a good deal at that. It was our first laughter for many days.

'Even so,' I said presently, 'the sooner we are gone from here, the happier I'll be.'

*

But we were not yet free of Lupicinus.

He was a man who, having finally made up his mind to a thing, sets about it at once, in a frenzy of activity. The next morning, in the first grey of dawn, his flustered manservant came tapping at our door. The Master of Cavalry would be travelling south with us; we must make haste, for he wished to make an early start.

Marcellus, half-dressed, smothered a groan. I said, 'Yes; of course.'

We set out soon after, accompanied by Lupicinus and his military escort. His legions – the Herulians and Batavians – would return at their own pace. He had even left his expensive collection of silver plate, which would be sent on after.

At Letocetum he took himself off to the baths – now functioning once more, and surrounded by low-lying wood-smoke that clung in the damp air. Then he retired to his room, saying he wished to dine alone. He left Marcellus to deal with arrangements – and it was just as well: for recognizing us the innkeeper exclaimed how, the day after we had departed, the traveller we had been asking about was found murdered. We expressed proper horror and quickly moved the conversation on. And the innkeeper, seeing our badges of rank, which before we had kept hidden, did not pursue the subject further.

The journey southwards was a constant torment. Every time I spied a horseman approaching on the long straight road my nerves jangled until I could be sure it was not another imperial messenger bringing word from Florentius. Already Marcellus and I had resolved, if the worst happened, that we should strike Lupicinus down with our daggers before he had chance to act. We could do it, for we rode at his side with the escort some paces behind. But it would have cost us our lives. We were two against his entourage of ten; they would have cut us down after.

All through these private fears, with the prospect of death beyond every hill-brow, I had to listen, nodding and smiling, while Lupicinus talked about himself, a subject he never tired of.

I had ordered the cutter that had brought us from Gaul to sail up the Thames to London. It lay waiting at the city quay. We had told Lupicinus that we intended to remain behind in Britain to see to private business. We stood at the waterfront, to see him off; and when, at last, the sleek black vessel cast off into the ebb tide, with Lupicinus standing grandly at the stern, I hardly dared meet Marcellus's eye, in case the relief showed in my face.

Only after the pilot had called out the order for oars, and the cutter surged away towards the bridge, did I let out a long breath and turn to him.

'I wonder,' I said, 'would he have marched against Julian?'

Marcellus returned his gaze to the receding ship. The oar-blades, red and white against the black hull, rose and fell with military precision. Passers-by, who had chanced to be crossing the city bridge, paused at the balustrade to watch, as they will at any fine sight.

'I think so,' he said frowning. 'He has no loyalty to the West. He is Constantius's creature through and through. But I do not believe the men would have followed him.'

Out in the river the cutter was making sail, its great scarlet sheet bulging as it caught the breeze. Lupicinus was standing at the rail, his eyes ahead, his hands clasped behind him in the rigid military posture he affected. I was glad he had not waved or called a farewell. There had been too much deception; and in Boulogne, I knew, the arrest detail would be waiting.

That evening, we dined with Alypius at the governor's palace. We ate our first good meal for many days, drank deep of his fine Bordeaux wine, and told him how we planned to ride out to Marcellus's land.

When the tables had been cleared and the servants had been dismissed, he leaned forward on his couch and said, 'Now that we are alone, tell me, how did Julian bring about his acclamation?'

'He did not,' I answered. 'He was as surprised as the rest of us.' And Marcellus and I recounted the events that had led to the night in Paris when the army stormed the palace.

When we had finished, Alypius said, 'Then it is the same Julian as I remember – I thought perhaps time had changed him. He was never interested in power. All he wanted was to stay in Athens, among his philosopher friends.'

'I believe, sir, he yearns for Athens still. He values it enough to fight for, if he must. But that is not his choice.' And I told him about Eutherius's embassy to Constantius, and how Julian hoped for a settlement.

But Alypius shook his head. 'I doubt Constantius will listen.'

'No,' I said, remembering Eutherius's words to Julian,

'perhaps not, unless he is forced to. It is said he trusts no one.'

'He does not. It is the curse of supreme power, I suppose, and an indifferent mind, and having lived too long with deceivers and flatterers.'

Marcellus asked him if he thought then it would come to war.

Alypius considered for a few moments, the wine-cup poised in his hand.

'I think this,' he said, setting the cup down on the little circular three-legged table beside him. 'Constantius will crush Julian if he believes he can; and his advisers will encourage him, especially that insufferable chamberlain of his. But if Julian can make himself strong, the ground may yet shift.'

Later, over a dessert of fruit tart served with Mauritanian figs softened in sweet wine, Alypius told how he had first met Julian, one summer when he had been visiting philosopher friends in Nikomedia. Alypius had been sitting under the shade of a spreading plane, in the precinct of the shrine of Demeter, talking with his friends, when he had noticed a shy stolid-looking youth, loitering under the colonnade. He had thought no more of it, and turned back to the conversation. But, soon after, the boy had approached and sat on a ledge close by, so he could overhear their talk.

'Seeing him I said, "Come, join us and listen, for there is nothing secret here." And the boy came and sat, until his pedagogue, a Christian priest, came fussing and scolding and led him away.'

He smiled at the memory and continued, 'Years later we met again, and I reminded him of this meeting, and we became friends. In those days he was like a starveling who has chanced upon a rich man's feast, so great was his hunger for knowledge . . . So much,' he added, shaking his head, 'had they kept from him.'

I decided I liked Alypius. I asked him about his home at Antioch; and with longing wistful eyes he described the laurel-shaded avenues, the stepped vineyards rising up the mountain, the libraries and baths and constant pleasure of civilized company.

'I should love to see it one day,' I said.

'Best hurry then, for soon the Christians will have swept away every delight the city offers – the university, the libraries, the theatre, they detest them all. And each year there are more of them, and fewer good men. They will not be content until Antioch is as dull as a desert mule-station.'

And so the conversation turned to the Christians. Marcellus told him we had seen the bishop of London's new cathedral on the hill, in its place on the site of the old temple of Diana, which he had demolished. 'It is all unfaced brick and scaffolding; I had thought it would be finished by now – he has been at it long enough.'

'Ah, the bishop,' said Alypius, and he gave a weary gesture. 'He is fortunate his great ugly edifice is there at all. If I had not interposed my guards, the mob would have torn it down.'

'He used to claim,' I said dryly, 'that the common people were his greatest friends.'

'Such men always do. But the support of the mob is as fickle as a courtesan's love – and as easily bought. He has discovered that for himself, now his funds have run out. They blamed him for their misery. He has done much damage to his cause.'

'The mob should blame themselves,' said Marcellus bitterly.

'Quite. But it is not the way of the vulgar to admit their own folly. So they say instead that the bishop has tricked them. When he could not feed them they went to the same councillors they had once driven from the city, begging them to return. So now the bishop sulks in his great unfinished palace and waits for the end of the world, and meanwhile the people quietly worship the old gods, and the province prospers.'

He ate the last fig from his dish, set it down, and rang the hand-bell for the servant. 'But such are the ways of the ignorant; they will not change . . . Now Marcellus, your cup is empty.'

The next morning, on a day of sharp, brilliant springtime light, we rode out west from London to Marcellus's land, pleased at last to be alone with one another after so much ugly work. All about us the meadows were carpeted with white spring flowers; the wind in our faces was fresh and clean.

By the time we reached the ancient boundary-stone, the sun was sinking on the western horizon into a bank of orange and purple cloud. For some time Marcellus had been silent, and I knew he had been wondering what he would find.

At the stone he pulled up his horse, and frowned out at the overgrown fields.

'No one is working the land,' he said.

I pointed at the ruts in the bramble-fringed track and said, 'Yet men have passed this way.'

He looked, and nodded.

We had asked Alypius, before we left London, if he had heard any word of Marcellus's family and their estates. But Alypius had not been governor in Britain for long, and could tell us nothing. In the chaos that the notary Paulus and the bishop had caused, even the provincial records had been ransacked: ownership and land-title were left unclear, and too many men had been robbed and killed, under the guise of tyrannous law.

Now, as we paused gazing at the untended fields, I thought of the ruins of my father's house and imagined every sort of evil. But there was no need to burden Marcellus with it. We should see with our own eyes, soon enough.

We rode on. At the next ridge we halted and dismounted, and surveyed the green valley below. I came up beside him, shielding my eyes against the flaring sunset, half-expecting to see a blackened shell where the great house had been. But it stood just as I remembered, golden-yellow and ochre behind its screen of elms and poplars. I could see, within the enclosure wall, the blossom showing on the fruit trees in the orchard; and, beside the house, the flowering pale-pink almonds.

'See there!' said Marcellus pointing. Inside the wall two tiny figures were moving between the outhouses, distant silhouettes against the brilliant sunset.

We spurred our horses on, descending into the valley, pausing only at the tomb with its pilastered doorway, where the remains of Marcellus's grandfather lay. The tomb was neglected – all long grass and dense, over-growing ivy. But the ancient structure stood intact. I had feared we should find it desecrated, and Aquinus's bones scattered.

The heavy oak doors in the enclosure wall stood unbarred and open. Within, the figures we had spied earlier were gone. We advanced along the path, leading our horses. The ordered, formal gardens I remembered had gone. The earth had been hoed over. Among the fine orna-mental hedgerows, onions, beans and parsnips had been sown, like the kitchen garden of some smallholding.

Marcellus frowned at these signs of contraction and decline. He turned and called out. There was no answer. We began to walk on; but then he stopped again and said, 'Listen, Drusus – what is that noise?'

I halted and listened. Beyond the wall the breeze stirred the high branches of the poplars. And then I heard it, the sound of muffled scrambling from within the stable-house. I gripped my sword-hilt, and scanned the length of the whitewashed building with its shadowy open arches. Then, at my side, so suddenly that I started, Marcellus let out a shout and sprang forward. 'Ufa!' he cried, as his grey wolfhound came bounding through the vegetable frames to meet him.

I caught him back by the arm. I had seen dark figures move within the shade of the stable.

'Who are these?' I said, as a group of men dressed in brown homespun tunics came filing out into the slanting light.

But then, among them, I recognized old Tyronius the bailiff, and others I had known before.

'Marcellus?' called the old man, squinting against the sun, 'Is that you? We took you for imperial soldiers.' Then everyone crowded round – men who had known him since the day he was born – pressing our shoulders, smiling and laughing with joy.

Presently Marcellus glanced up, and I saw his face grow serious. I turned to look.

Across the ruined gardens, waiting at the top of the wide sweep of stone steps that led to the house, a female figure stood waiting in the deep shade beneath the high pillared portico. It was his mother.

Marcellus turned to one of the young hands. 'Tertius, keep Ufa here.' And then, to me, 'I should have thought. She has been waiting.'

I said, 'Go to her. I will wait here.'

But he answered, 'No, Drusus; come. You belong with me.'

And so, silently drawing in my breath, I went with him, walking at his side.

The fountain in front of the house, with its bronze leaping dolphins, had ceased to flow. The circular pool, on whose wide marbled rim Marcellus and I had once lain side by side considering the night sky, and the deeper mystery of one another, was half-empty, and strewn with old brown leaves. His mother waited motionless until we had mounted the flight of steps. Only then did she turn.

Her long robe was pinned at the shoulder with a single brooch of antique gold; it caught the rays of the sunset. She had not aged, as a myrrhine jar does not age; but her fine-boned face, which had never been weak, seemed to hold a new power, and I sensed a change in her.

'So you have come,' she said coolly, when Marcellus stood before her. She was not a woman given to displays of emotion.

'Yes, Mother. I told you I should return.' Marcellus, I knew, had written to her from Paris. I knew too that he had received no reply. He had not spoken of it after.

She acknowledged my presence with an inclination of her head. Marcellus said, 'What happened here?'

Turning, she took a step forward, and placed one fine hand on the stone balustrade, and looked out beyond the fountain.

'After you were taken,' she said, 'men came and drove away our people. We have managed with what remained – Tyronius; these boys; the womenfolk. The estate is much reduced; but we have survived.'

'What men?' asked Marcellus, his voice hardening.

She gave a slight shrug, as if it did not matter.

'Faceless people, a parcel of hired ruffians, cowards, every one of them; you know how these things are done. The bishop thought he could help himself, with you gone and my father dead. He sent that creature of his, the deacon Faustus. But he forgot whose daughter I am.'

'What did you do?'

'I ordered them away,' she said simply. 'I told them this

239

land has been ours time out of mind, that we have nurtured it across the generations, and I am not going to hand our patrimony to the son of some Belgian bath-attendant who thinks he possesses authority simply because he holds office. The estate will continue, or they must murder me on the threshold of my own house; but either way I stay.'

For a moment Marcellus's eye caught mine. I glanced away and looked solemn. It would not do to smile. 'Yes,' I thought, 'she is indeed her father's daughter.' I could see how the bishop would have misjudged her. A slight, delicate woman; but her character was adamantine.

'We saw the new governor Alypius in London,' said Marcellus. 'He says the bishop is much diminished.'

'He is a broken man. He is nothing without his claque of vulgar followers, and they have abandoned him. It is rumoured he wishes to leave Britain altogether and go to Alexandria in Egypt, where his friends are caught up in one of their perpetual squabbles over their doctrine. They slaughter each other over it, can you believe? Well let him go; we do not need him here.'

She turned back to the great house with its high double-doors like a temple's. Inside a servant-girl was kindling the lamp.

'And the farm-hands?' asked Marcellus.

'Slowly they return – those that can find their way back. This is their home, and their fathers' before them. Soon we shall be able to till the outer fields once more.'

'I never knew,' said Marcellus, 'that you understood so much of farming.' And for the first time he smiled at her.

'There is a great deal, Marcellus, that you do not know.

240

Now come inside, both of you.' And turning to the servant-girl she said, 'When you have finished with that, Livia, you may open up the dining-room. We shall be three, tonight. Tell the cook.'

We ate a simple country meal of bean stew and kid, off plates of old silver. The rooms had never been heavily furnished: Aquinus had always preferred fine, well-made simplicity. The small bronzes were gone, carried off by the Christian mob when they had looted. But the marquetry tables remained, and the old polished couches with their faded covers.

'We are reduced,' said his mother, glancing up and seeing me look.

'I am sorry.'

'Don't be; there is no need. We are not the slaves of our possessions, and we will recover.'

Later, Marcellus asked if she had received his letter from Paris. 'Yes,' she replied, and said no more. But when we had finished she told him to bring the lamp, and led us through the inner garden court, now an overgrown tangle of untended shrubs, to Aquinus's old library.

The door stood ajar, rusted on its hinges so it would not move. The old shelves smelled of mildew and decay. A pool of water had collected under the broken window, in the place where Aquinus's table had once been.

'This,' she said, as Marcellus held up the lamp beside her, 'I have had to leave as it was. I always hated this room, because it took your grandfather from me. But now he is gone, and what he built is all there is. When I return here, I remember.'

Marcellus set down the lamp, and stepped ahead into the long shadows. From the corner beside a shelf he took up a discarded volume. It was torn and broken, just as the mob had left it. At his touch the pages cracked and fell at his feet. He paused for a moment; then turning to his mother said, 'I cannot leave you like this.'

But immediately she replied, 'Yes you can. I have spent too long hiding from the world, and see what it has brought me. No, Marcellus; go back to Gaul and Julian, and do some good. That is what your grandfather would have done, and he was right. The house I can manage on my own.'

She walked on past the high empty shelves, and paused at the frameless window. Then she turned.

In the same firm tone she said, 'This will always be your home . . . It is the home of both of you.'

The lamp flickered and caught her face; and I realized with a start that she was looking directly at me. For a moment she held my gaze. Then, when she saw I had understood, she gave a slight nod and turned away.

I swallowed. I had thought she held no more surprises for me. But now I felt as if my heart would burst within me, and suddenly there was water in my eyes. This was her peace offering, and I knew what it had cost her. At last, after so many years, and by whatever process of painful change, I was accepted.

There remained one other task.

His mother had said, before we left, that the family's London townhouse had been let, she having had no need of it; but the rents had long since ceased to come, and the agents did not respond to her enquiries.

'I will attend to it,' said Marcellus.

We found more than we expected there.

Back in London, we took the familiar street west from the forum, to the suburb by the Walbrook, which I had walked so often as a youth when I went to visit Marcellus or his grandfather. We came at length to the fine old townhouse, with its heavy oak door, set in high, rose-washed walls.

Marcellus knocked and waited. There was a long pause. At last pattering footsteps sounded in the passage; the bolts slid, and the door edged open.

'Yes?' enquired a suspicious black-haired servant.

'I wish to speak to your master,' said Marcellus.

'He has not yet risen. Come later.'

He made to slam the door; but Marcellus had already interposed his foot.

The outraged face of the servant reappeared.

'Then go,' said Marcellus slowly, 'and wake him.' And with the flat of his hand he shoved the door open, adding, 'In the meantime, we will wait inside.'

Even before we reached the inner courtyard with its herb-pots and fluted columns I could hear from the upper storey a man's voice shouting out, 'Lollius! Lollius! – Who was calling? Where are you, curse your eyes?'

The servant, deciding where the greater danger lay, caught his breath and scuttled off; and we stood waiting, hearing from above a hurried exchange of whispered words, followed by impatient grunts and the sound of bare feet on the stair.

Then a bony, harassed-looking man stepped out, clutching a cloak about his body. He was bug-eyed with sleep; his hair was greasy and dishevelled. He began to speak, a loud tirade of self-important protest. But then, looking up, he caught his breath and broke off.

I too was staring; for I knew the man. It was Faustus, the bishop's deacon.

His gaunt face turned pale. He drew himself up. But in his shock he had forgotten to keep a grip at his cloak. It fell open, revealing his white, emaciated body. Quickly he snatched it shut; but his attempt at gravity was ruined.

He knew who we were sure enough. 'This house is mine now,' he cried. 'It is church property.'

Marcellus merely looked at him with firm, aristocratic contempt.

But the deacon had no shame. He talked on, brazen to the last. 'You did not know? Well that can be forgiven; after all, you have been away.' He turned his head and cried up the stairs, 'Lollius! Go and fetch the deed from my study.'

By the time he turned back, Marcellus was upon him, gripping him by his cloak and matted hair, and marching him down the passage to the street.

I heard a yelp, the slap of flesh on stone, and the slam of the door. Then Marcellus returned alone, wiping his hands.

'Lollius,' he said, turning to the gaping house-slave, 'take your master's things and cast them into the gutter. You will find him there.'

Then he took the deed from the cringing servant's hand, and tore it in two.

NINE

WE RETURNED TO PARIS to find Eutherius back from his mission to the emperor. At each city on his journey east he had found himself thwarted by sullen officials. Rooms in quiet inns were found to be full; vigorous horses fell inexplicably lame; carriages which the day before had been serviceable were suddenly discovered to have broken axles, or to have been called away on urgent business.

When at last he had reached Constantinople, he discovered that the prefect Florentius had preceded him, and had journeyed on to Caesarea in Asian Cappadocia, where at that time the court was residing.

I was not present when Eutherius reported back the details of his mission to Julian. But shortly after, when I was at the palace baths, making my way from the hot-room to the pool, I caught sight of Eutherius spread face-down on a slab, while the masseur worked at his broad bear-like back.

I walked on, not wishing to disturb him; for by now the news was all around the palace that his mission had failed. But as I passed I heard his sing-song voice behind me say, 'Though I am lying down, Drusus, I am not sleeping.'

I turned and laughed. 'I thought you were busy with Sophron.'

'Sophron is busy with *me*,' he said tartly, raising his head enough to throw a grim look at the masseur. 'But I am at leisure. Come and sit up here where I can see you.'

So I padded into the side-chamber and pulled myself onto the ledge opposite. After the fierce heat of the hot-room, the damp cool stone was pleasant against my naked skin. From the latticed windows under the domed roof, sunlight shafted down through the humid air. In one corner, water trickled from a lion-head spout into a marble trough. I said, 'I was talking to Oribasius. He told me your journey was difficult.'

He groaned into the slab. 'Difficult? It was vile.'

I smiled and for a few moments watched the slave's busy hands move over his back. I had not seen Eutherius undressed before. He was large and hairless, but not fat. He wore a cloth about his loins even at the baths – a common thing with eunuchs; who tire, I imagine, of men's vulgar curiosity.

'Oribasius,' I went on, 'says Constantius flew into a rage.'

'So he did, and it was a passion unusual even for him. I was lucky to get out alive.'

Then, as I had hoped, he told me what happened.

He and Pentadius had been admitted into the audience chamber. Upon the dais, seated on his gilded and bejewelled throne with his entourage all about him, Constantius sat stony-faced, glaring at them with pinprick eyes.

'As soon as I saw Florentius smiling beside the throne, looking like a cat at the butter, I knew what was coming. But lose heart, lose all. I pressed on and read out Julian's letter.'

Julian had urged Constantius not to heed the gossips and mischief-makers, saying there were men at court whose aim was to stir dissension between them. They must act wisely, and not let enemies drive them towards disaster. He reminded the emperor that he had carried out his obligations faithfully, and explained that when Constantius's notary Decentius had demanded troops he had warned him of the dangers. If Decentius had listened there would be no crisis now. He had not sought to be acclaimed; but, now that it had happened, there would be mutiny if he tried to renounce the title of Augustus, which the troops had pressed on him. And, if he were to try, like as not another less sympathetic to the emperor would be acclaimed in his place, for such was the men's mood.

He asked Constantius therefore to recognize what had been done, and believe him when he said he did not want war between them. His concern remained the security of Gaul, which was still uncertain. To dispatch the best of his army now – even if they agreed to go – would give the signal to the German tribes that Rome was not serious in defending Gaul, and would bring renewed invasion. Nevertheless, to show his goodwill, he would send cavalry from Spain, and reinforcements from the mercenary units, which could be spared without great danger. He invited the emperor to appoint a new prefect to replace Florentius. But as for his other officials, he would appoint men he could best work with.

'During all this,' said Eutherius, 'Constantius sat like a statue, with Florentius inclining his head and whispering into his ear, while the courtiers smirked and raised their eyes to the roof-beams.'

'And Pentadius? What did he say?'

'He spoke after me, confirming it all – and all credit to him, for by then the danger signs were clear for all to see: the purpling cheeks under the face powder; the iron grip of the imperial fingers on the chair-arm; the sequined slipper tapping on the dais.'

'And then?' I asked.

Eutherius sighed. 'Then he seemed to lose all reason. He screamed. He threatened. He jabbed his finger and spat. It was hard to make out the words – traitor, filth, ingrate – but finally that subtle snake the grand chamberlain managed to calm him a little; and when words were once more possible we were dismissed from the Presence.'

He let out a groan as the bath-slave began kneading his shoulders. I sat in silence, considering, dabbing idly at an old white knife-scar on my thigh. Presently I told him what Alypius had said: that Constantius would never trust Julian's promises.

'He will not,' said Eutherius. 'Whatever Constantius decides, it will not be due to trust; the word means nothing to him. No, our only hope is that with the Persians already gathering on the eastern frontier he will see the wisdom of leaving Julian alone, and permit him to keep what he holds . . . That will do for now, Sophron.'

He extended his hand; the slave took it and pulled him up.

'Ah, much better,' he said, stretching. 'Now tell me, Drusus, what do your army friends say?'

I shrugged. 'They expect war. Some of them want it.' I had run into a crowd of Nevitta's friends shortly before. They were talking of nothing else.

'Well, the road to Hades is easy to travel,' said Eutherius with a sigh. 'It is the old men like me who choose peace.'

'Must we not fight then?'

'German barbarians are one thing; Constantius's ironclad cavalrymen and the arrayed armies of the east are quite another.' His eyes passed over my naked body, resting on the scar on my thigh. 'Does it trouble you?' he asked.

I shrugged and took my hand away, suddenly self-conscious. 'Sometimes it itches . . . But the wound was light. There are many men with worse.'

'And tell me, do you hold back in battle because of it?'

I looked quickly up, about to tell him that such a thing would be disgraceful. But then I saw from his face that he had only meant me to think.

I nodded, then said, 'The centurions say: it is the timid that die soonest.'

'And so too,' he said, 'do the reckless.' He smiled. 'And which, do you suppose, are we? Or is there yet a third?

That is what we must decide. After all, it is the wise man that does not deceive himself.'

Seeing my look of confusion he laughed gently, and easing himself off the wet slab said, 'But come, my dear Drusus, and walk with me to the pool. And together we shall consider the timid and the reckless and the brave, and then you can tell me all about your embassy to the noble Lupicinus.'

At the beginning of May, when the first buds were showing on the vines, Constantius sent his formal answer. The messenger was a quaestor from the court. His name was Leonas.

Julian ordered that he was to be treated with respect, whatever message he carried. He wished to show, he said, that he knew the honour due to envoys, even if Constantius had forgotten.

Now, standing in the long audience chamber with its squat stone pillars and old tapestries, we listened as he intoned in a booming wooden voice, like a man reading a proclamation before a crowd, 'The divine emperor accepts nothing of what you propose. I am instructed to inform you that if you care for your safety and the safety of your friends, you must abandon this foolish course.'

He looked up. Julian said, 'Is there more?'

'Yes *Caesar*,' he said, drawing out the final word and pausing deliberately, slewing his eyes around to make sure we had understood the pointless slight. He looked pleased with himself. 'Yes, indeed there is more.'

He had taken Julian's mildness and courtesy for fear,

and was growing haughty. I glanced across at Eutherius. He met my eye, but he had his court face on, a mask betraying nothing.

The messenger returned to the scroll he was brandishing in his hands. 'The emperor,' he declared, 'hereby appoints the following men to your staff. Nebridius is promoted to prefect in place of Florentius; the notary Felix is made Master of the Offices, replacing Pentadius; the general Gomoarius is to replace Lupicinus as Master of Cavalry . . . And Lupicinus,' he said, looking up, 'whom you have under arrest, is to be given safe passage.'

I found, as I stood listening, that my eyes had settled on the threadbare cinnamon-red hangings that hung between the pillars, with their Gallic country scenes of leaping deer, trees in summer leaf, prancing dogs and men in hunting tunics. Behind them, hidden from view in the long aisle, men would be listening, as always. Everything Constantius's envoy said would soon be round the palace and beyond.

Julian knew it too. When at last Leonas had finished he said, 'We shall summon Nebridius and inform him of his good fortune. But for the rest, I will make my own appointments, as I have already said.'

Leonas's eyes widened. He was the kind who reads the surface and thinks he has read the man. I think he had expected Julian meekly to accept what he was told. Now, in a sudden flush of anger, he jutted his head forward and cried, 'Is this how you repay the man who preserved your life and elevated you, a penniless orphan, to the highest rank?'

Everyone stared. By now, even the lowliest clerk knew of Julian's past, and what Constantius had done to his family.

Julian had leaped to his feet with a cry as if he had been struck. 'What?' he demanded. 'Does my father's murderer now reproach me with being an orphan?'

Leonas bit his lip and did not answer. After a pause, Julian, in a quieter voice, went on, 'You wish me to resign – is that it? Very well. I will do so.'

Somewhere behind the hangings a voice gasped. Julian ignored it. 'But,' he said, 'there is one condition: that first you address the troops and persuade them.'

And so, next morning the legions assembled in the open fields beyond the city. It was a day of fraying shifting clouds interspersed with limpid blue; the damp meadows were bright with spring flowers, violets and narcissus and golden crocus, trampled by the men as they gathered. I stood with Marcellus and the other officers, at the base of the wooden tribunal.

Oribasius had argued with Julian, telling him it was madness to place so much in the balance. But Julian answered that he knew his men. 'Besides,' he said, 'without their support I am finished. Better to find out now, don't you think?'

Now, before us, the army waited, cohort by cohort. Sun glinted on the polished standards; the red and gold ensigns swayed in the breeze. Further off, beyond the place where the archers were gathered, I could see Nevitta's troop, with young Rufus in the thick of them, seated on his silver mare and laughing at some joke. Lately, if I happened to pass him in the colonnade, he would deliberately look away, as if he had not seen me. I understood, and took no great offence. He did not want to be reminded of what I knew. It did not square with the new brash self he had become, or tried to become.

Yet even now, below the mask, one could still read the hurt in his eyes. Nevitta's friends were not the type who would notice. Perhaps he knew that too.

Around the tribunal there was a stirring. Briskly, Julian mounted the steps and beckoned Leonas to follow. The envoy, I could see, had lost a good deal of his swagger; but Julian was as he always was: gathered to himself, serious and thoughtful. The vague murmur of the troops fell away; and in the expectant silence Julian spoke, asking the men to listen to what Constantius's messenger wished to tell them.

Then he stepped back. The envoy looked nervously about, surveying the grim immobile faces staring back at him. For a moment, until he grew conscious of it, his left hand clutched at the rail of the wooden platform. He released it as if it were hot and dangerous, and forced his hands to his sides.

Then he began to speak.

The men heard him without a sound. Only when he reached the part in Constantius's harangue where he demanded that Julian should resign did they break silence. Then a great roar of anger rose from them, scattering the birds in the nearby oak grove, drowning out his words, forcing him to stop. On the hillside, beyond the lines, the citizens of Paris had gathered to watch, standing in their coloured cloaks and homespun tunics. Hearing what had been said, they too added their shouts to those of the men, raising their arms and gesturing.

Leonas waited, looking pale and ill at the sight of so much anger directed at him alone. I saw him turn and, over the din, shout something to Julian. For a moment Julian waited; then he stepped forward and raised his hand, and silence returned.

'You have spoken,' he declared. 'You have given your answer and the envoy has heard you. So now permit him to leave in peace, and let him take our answer to Constantius.'

He turned and descended the steps, while all about him the men cheered and surged forward. Leonas, with one last, appalled look at the advancing tide of soldiers, hurried down after him, and stood among us, keeping close in case the men snatched him as he left.

He departed next day with the dawn, taking the troops' message back to the emperor. Julian meanwhile accepted Constantius's nomination of the quaestor Nebridius as the new prefect. For the rest, he made his own appointments. He brought Dagalaif, the German-born commander of the Petulantes, onto his staff; he set Lupicinus free and sent him back to the court, replacing him with Nevitta as Master of Cavalry; he made Marcellus one of Nevitta's lieutenants, and also promoted good-natured, mildmannered Jovinus alongside him, who had served well during the fighting beyond the Rhine.

Then, campaign weather being upon us, we set out for

'Greetings, Nevitta,' I said without expression.

Usually he had little to say to me, and I could think of no good reason why he should single me out now. Besides, I had not liked his tone. I walked on, stepping with my bare feet onto the grass beside the path to avoid his clutch of friends. But as I passed he moved deliberately into my way.

Speaking loud, as much to his entourage as to me, he declared mockingly, 'But I thought you were a fighter. That, anyway, is what Rufus here told me, didn't you Rufus? Yet you volunteer for the armoured foot-race.'

I paused, and wiped the sweat from my brow with the back of my hand, and looked at him. Whatever I did, it was no concern of his, who was not competing at all.

'What you heard was true,' I replied. 'I learned to wrestle when I was young. But I find I do not care for it.'

He pulled an amused, doubting face.

'Men wrestle,' he said with a snide leer, '. . . proper men, anyway. Some might say you were afraid.'

This was going too far, even for Nevitta and what passed for his wit. Ever since I was a boy, certain things have fired my anger, and this was one of them. Before I could stay my tongue, I shot back, 'A fool might say that, Nevitta. My friends, however, know me better.'

His weasel face flinched. One of his hangers-on, a brash youth who had not seen the look in his eyes, snorted with amusement. Nevitta swung round, and the laughter ceased, as swiftly as if the youth's throat had been cut. Even I could have told him that Nevitta, for all his quickness at mocking others, was not a man who could bear to be laughed at himself.

I felt a sudden chill, as if a shadow had touched my soul. Nevitta was not a man to be crossed lightly. The thought quenched my anger. Before he could speak again I said, 'But I am detaining you and your friends, and I could do with a bath; so excuse me.' And with that I stepped firmly on, parting his little band of supporters, who drew back hurriedly to keep my sweat from their expensive clothes.

Marcellus frowned when I told him.

'He had it coming,' I protested. 'If he doesn't like it, he should watch his mouth – and his drinking too. Besides, I don't see what I have done to give him cause. These games are no more than some fun for the men and the populace, and what is it to him which race I run?'

'I don't think this is about you,' he said.

And then he told me what up till then he had held back: that Nevitta was put out because he himself had not been asked to lead the torch-parade.

My first reaction was to laugh in disbelief. 'So that's what all this is about,' I cried.

'That and too much wine, I expect.'

'But the man has just been made Master of Cavalry. He is one of the most powerful generals in the West, and no one else has been promoted so fast. What has he to complain about?'

Marcellus shrugged. 'He likes complaining. He looks for slights.'

We were walking along one of the great curved aisles of the empty theatre behind the forum. I had arranged to meet him there, after my training. He sat down on the stone bench, looking serious. I sat down beside him.

'You should have told me,' I said. 'I was wondering why you had been quiet these last days.'

'Have I? Well, it's nothing; just foolishness. Really it's not worth dwelling on.'

He paused, gazing out across the blood-red pantile roofs of Vienne, to where a boat was gliding down the still water of the Rhone, under oars, making for the docks. The sun of the long summer had turned the fine hairs on his legs and forearms the colour of burnished gold. He sat at ease, trusting and close, unconscious as always of his own beauty.

'Did you say Rufus was there too?' he asked presently.

'Yes; he's always around Nevitta lately. If you ask me, he was drunk. They all were.'

He shrugged.

'Why do you ask?' I said.

'Oh, nothing. He was meant to be practising with the rest of us for the torch-parade, that's all. I suppose he found something better to do.'

I ran my armoured foot-race. I came second, a spear-length behind the leader. As for the boxing, I did not stay to watch. I heard later that the winner was a thickset infantryman from the Batavian legion.

For the rest of those bright autumn days of the games, Marcellus and I relaxed and enjoyed ourselves, which had been Julian's intention. There were acrobats and jugglers to watch, a concert at the theatre, glass-ball games and cock-fights, a troop of dancing dogs with bells around their collars; singers and pipe-players; and among them all, stalls selling food and wine and Gallic beer, and all the gewgaws and trinkets one finds at any festival.

On the final day, at the hippodrome in the valley between the wooded hills and the river, came the chariot race, where Julian was to make his formal appearance before the crowd.

He stood waiting in the anteroom while the slave tip-toed around him, fussing and preening. It was a perfect day, calm and cloudless; beams of sun shone down the stairwell from the terraces, casting brilliant fingers of light over the rose-coloured marble. Beyond, I could hear the buzz of the crowd, tense before the start of the first race, their voices rising and falling as the different factions called out their team's colours.

Nevitta was in the anteroom, talking army business, on and on in his dull toneless voice, all matters that could have waited, none of it urgent. But Nevitta liked to pro-mote himself, and was always telling Julian what he was doing. I could see from Julian's polite, preoccupied, slightly vacant expression that he was not attending; his mind was on the terraces where the crowd was waiting.

The slave sucked the air through his teeth and tutted, and began once more to dab and tug at Julian's collar.

'Haven't you finished yet?'

'But Augustus, it must be perfect. Think of all those eyes on you.'

Julian frowned to himself. The staring eyes of the people was the last thing he wished to be reminded of.

A side-door opened and Oribasius entered. 'Well?' said Julian, turning. He was robed in all the formal symbols of imperium: a white tunic with an embroidered collar; a purple cloak clasped with gold; and on his head a diadem of worked silver inlaid with rubies, newly acquired from the engravers' workshops of Vienne.

'Quite a show,' said Oribasius, raising his black brows, 'you look almost like an emperor.'

Julian grinned. 'Thank Malchos here.' The slave, a dark-eyed Syrian, fluttered his hand as if to say it was all part of a day's work. I smiled to see it. Julian never forgot such people.

'The crowd will like it,' said Oribasius, walking around him and eyeing the gleaming, heavy robes.

'Ah! The crowd. Sooner give me the German frontier, where I know my enemy.' Forgetting to hold still he stepped forward, then quickly reached up and touched at the headgear. 'Is this on right? By heaven, I hardly dare move. I feel like a trussed-up peacock.'

The people in the room laughed; but Julian looked grimly ahead at the sunlit stairwell. He was always uneasy with the urban crowd, saying they were like an untamed beast, fickle and dangerous. He liked to claim he got this from his beloved Plato; but in truth I think it was mostly that he was shy, and preferred the company of a few good friends who shared his mind.

Oribasius said, 'If you keep still it won't fall off. The people have come for a spectacle, and you are part of it. They expect to see a god among men.'

Julian frowned and drew down his brows. 'Then what they want is a lie. An emperor ought to be no more than a citizen, a man among equals.'

'Yes, yes,' said Oribasius, sighing. This was a familiar point between them. 'Once perhaps it was so . . . But now is not the time for such experiments; the people cleave to their myths, and besides—' But the rest of his words were lost in a blare of trumpets echoing from outside.

'It is time,' said the master of ceremonies.

'And soon may it end,' muttered Julian.

He took a step forward, then turned to me, hoping, I suppose, to defer the final moment. 'Tell me, Drusus, what can be more purposeless than spending the day watching chariots circle a track?'

'Go!' I said laughing; and at this he smiled back. Then he drew his breath, like a diving-boy about to leap from a high rock, and slowly mounted the flight of sun-dappled steps.

The rest of us watched his shadow recede. My short-cropped hair prickled on the back of my neck. On this moment, as Julian knew more than anyone, his whole future hung. If he could not carry Vienne he could not carry Gaul, and, without that, the other provinces would surely not follow. This was the citizens' chance to reject him.

The shadow disappeared. There was a terrible silence. Then it began, a great sweeping rising roar, like the onset of battle or a torrent in a flood. It filled the chamber of the anteroom, resounding off the walls, until we could no longer hear our own voices, or our relieved laughter. But we knew what to do, and at the tribune's signal we climbed the steps, emerging into the glare of daylight and the great open bowl of the hippodrome. All around, the people were cheering, arms raised in salute, their bright-coloured ribbons – red and white and green and blue – streaming from their hands. And at the rail stood Julian, with palms upturned, accepting with the traditional gesture their joyful cries of acclamation.

In January the holy day fell which the Christians call Epiphany. The bishop of Vienne, a tall, coarse-featured man who dressed expensively and affected a learned air, made it clear he expected Julian to attend the rite.

'I shall not go,' declared Julian to his friends. 'I cannot continue this pretence. Men will condemn me as a hypocrite.'

'You have only twenty-three thousand men,' said Eutherius. 'There are Christians among them.'

'What of it? Most are not.'

'Those that are not accept you as you already are. It is not the time to stir a dog that slumbers.'

Julian turned to Marcellus. '*You* are not a Christian,' he said. 'Nor are you, Drusus. And the men do not complain.'

'But,' said Eutherius patiently, 'Marcellus is not Augustus.'

Julian frowned. 'Surely they know by now.'

Oribasius, who was also present, said, 'You have declared nothing in public. People believe what they want to believe.'

'Moreover,' said Eutherius, 'at every city along the route east, there will be Christians – and powerful bishops to urge them on. If you anger the bishop here, the others will soon know of it, of that you can be sure. No; too much is in the balance. You cannot afford to find gates closed against you.'

'And thus,' said Julian bitterly, 'bishops rule even emperors.'

But he attended the rite, walking in procession with the smiling, nodding bishop and his acolytes, past the majestic empty temples with their neglected rain-stained facing, like a man on his way to have a tooth drawn.

I do not know if it was this day that made up his mind to go against Eutherius's advice; but shortly after, Julian issued the first of his edicts on religion. Constantius had forbidden, upon pain of death, the worship of the old gods. Henceforth, decreed Julian, men's consciences were free; their minds were their own, and they might worship as they chose. Truth, though one, was many-faceted. It was not for him, nor for any man or any bishop, to dictate its aspect to others.

The bishop of Vienne did not agree. I was with Julian and Eutherius in the great library of the imperial palace, a vaulted light-filled room of book-niches and pink-veined marble columns, which Julian had made his workroom, when he was announced.

The bishop appeared at the far door and for a moment paused and stared. He had lost his bland, complacent look. His face was pinched and harassed.

'I have heard a most troubling rumour,' he cried, hurrying across the vast room. 'No doubt it is nothing more than foolish tittle-tattle, but I have been questioned on it, and thought it best to visit you in person, and lay the matter to rest.'

His eyes passed over the rows of books with a look of

disdain, and then settled on Julian, who was dressed, as usual, in his plain soldier's tunic. Against the bishop's heavy embroidered robe, woven with gold and purple, he might have been one of the servants, or a broad-shouldered minor librarian.

'What is it that you have heard?' enquired Julian pleasantly.

'That you intend to oppress your own church. It is absurd, of course. The noble Julian is a nephew of the holy Constantine, after all.'

'Indeed it is absurd,' said Julian. 'I intend to oppress no one – no one at all.'

There was a pause.

'Yet you are willing to tolerate heretics, and the pagan worshippers of idols.'

'I leave each man free to worship as he will, without fear of persecution.'

The bishop drew in his breath and glared. In a scandalized tone he said, 'Then it is true . . . Must I remind you that idolaters are an offence to God?'

'If that is so, then persuade them by your words and by your example, as Christ himself did. Use the power of your arguments, Bishop, if you have any. But I will not permit men to be dispossessed merely because they do not agree with you, or dragged against their will to your altars.'

The bishop's eyes narrowed. 'These are nothing but a sophist's quibbles,' he cried. 'Men must be compelled.'

'By violence?'

'The sick man does not always welcome the cure.'

Julian paused, and for a long moment the two men looked at one another, uncomprehending, like two figures across an unbridgeable ravine. As for me, a chill had settled on my heart. I had heard such words before, from the bishop of London, on the day I stood as a young tribune in his ornate palace, listening powerless as he announced to me the triumph of unreason.

'The sword or the flame,' said Julian eventually, 'does not change a man's opinion; I should have thought that you of all people, who venerate a long line of saints and martyrs, would have learned that lesson. Or has power made you forget your humanity and your compassion? Power is a strong wine, Bishop; take heed that you do not grow drunk on it.'

But I could tell from the bishop's flushed, hard-set face that he had ceased to listen. He waved Julian's words aside with a snap of his hand, like a man sweeping a troublesome insect from before his eyes. In a stubborn, flat tone he said, 'God gave us power for a purpose.'

'Perhaps you are right. But God gave us reason also, to know how to use that power wisely. There is nothing good for man that is not affirmed by choice. I will govern an empire of citizens, not slaves; men who may speak freely, without fear and without compulsion – as you yourself do now, here, with me.'

The bishop eyed him. 'The Evil One deceives you. I will pray for you.' And then he turned and left, strutting discontentedly out in his shining robes.

Julian watched him depart.

'You should not bait him,' said Eutherius.

'No? – Well; perhaps not. But they will not be content until they have extinguished every glimmer of contrary belief. Intolerance is at the very heart of their piety.'

We spent that winter waiting for fresh word from Constantius.

The new prefect, quiet dark-faced Nebridius, Constantius's nominee, had travelled south with us from Paris. I felt sorry for him: he was a decent, honourable man placed in an impossible position; and though Julian was careful to treat him with courtesy, and permitted him to carry out the duties of his office, he dared not trust him – and Nebridius knew it.

He must also have known, for he was no stranger to the ways of the court, that Constantius would never again trust him either. Thus caught between Scylla and Charybdis, he came to Julian and offered to resign. Julian thanked him, and asked him to remain. Partly this was out of affection: he liked Nebridius and they had always got on well enough; but partly too it was policy, for he knew, if he allowed him to go, that Constantius would assume Julian had driven Nebridius from office.

So Nebridius remained, and acted as any man of honour when forced into such a situation: he stayed loyal to his principles and trusted to his old Etruscan breeding, performing his duties diligently and refusing to be drawn into intrigue, either against Julian or against Constantius. And, as always with such men, there were those who hated him for it.

Marcellus and I passed the fallow time of winter riding

out along the valley, and up into the hills with their oak and ash trails. Returning from our happy expeditions to the pink-stone city beside the Rhone, I wondered if word had finally come from Constantius. But each time there was nothing, and as the weeks passed Julian's well-meant hope of a settlement hardened into contempt.

He talked more often now of feelings he had kept buried: of how Constantius had slaughtered his family and left him to grow up an imprisoned orphan; he recalled the loneliness and fear of his childhood, and how he had been summoned from his happy life among the professors at Athens, where he was no threat to anyone, and sent to Gaul, only to be blamed for his success – which, as he saw it now, had been his undoing.

Then, at last, when the fruit trees in the meadows beside the Rhone were showing their first spring blossom and the green slopes of the hills were speckled with yellow flowers, a messenger arrived from the East.

Marcellus came to find me. I was with a young infantry tribune, reviewing an inventory of new weapons from the workshops of Gaul and Spain. He glanced round the door, threw me a secret smile, and waited till the tribune had left with the scrolls in his arms.

'What news?' I asked, as he strode in across the marble floor. 'Will Constantius settle? He has kept us waiting long enough.'

'I think that was his intention,' he said. His hair, which he had let grow during the winter, had lately been trimmed to a bronze fuzz, soft to the touch, exposing his ears and the white nape of his neck. He ran his hand to it, then looked vaguely surprised that his mane of winter hair had gone.

'Constantius sent one of his tame bishops – a prosing old fool who brought nothing new at all. He says Julian must renounce the title of Augustus; he must dismiss the men he has appointed, surrender himself, and trust in the hope of a pardon.'

'A pardon?' I cried. 'Constantius has shown what his pardons are worth!'

'Yes; that's what everyone is saying. He has delayed us with excuses while he prepares his forces. He intends to destroy us.'

We found Julian standing over the great square map-table in the library. Nevitta was beside him, his face set in an expression of tight-jawed outrage. As we arrived, Jovinus and Dagalaif strode in from a far door. Eutherius was there too. I had not noticed him at first. He was sitting apart, in a patch of shade beside a pool of brilliant southern sunlight, with his large hands folded on the lap of his turquoise robe.

Though no one was speaking, I had the sense that we had walked into the midst of an argument. Turning to me Julian said, 'Has Marcellus told you? – Good. But listen, there is more.'

He took up a heavy formal-looking letter that lay open on the table. I recognized the imperial seal. 'Our agents,' he said, passing the document, 'have intercepted this. Constantius is urging the barbarians to break their treaties and invade Gaul.'

I glanced at the letter. It was directed to a German

chieftain by the name of Vadomar, who held territory in Raetia.

'He has done so before,' I said, and I mentioned the destruction Constantius had brought to Gaul in his war against Magnentius, when he had invited the German tribes in.

Julian nodded vigorously, in the way he did when he was agitated. He hardly needed reminding of it. He had spent the past five years trying to repair the damage.

'It is a deliberate insult!' Nevitta burst out, with such sudden vehemence that for a moment everyone looked at him surprised.

From his chair against the wall Eutherius said calmly, 'An insult perhaps; but there is sense in it also, if we look with a clear head. You cannot leave Gaul with Vadomar at your back, and Constantius knows it. He intends to pin you down until he is ready to march against you.'

Julian turned to the map that lay spread out on the table. For a moment he considered it. 'How soon can we have men at the Raetian frontier?'

'Ten days,' answered Nevitta. He stepped up and jabbed his finger at the map, indicating the road that ran north-east beside the Rhone towards the hills of Raetia. 'The Petulantes know the terrain. Let my man Libino lead them. He is ready . . . and we have waited long enough!' He raised his head and threw a hostile glance at Eutherius. 'Or do you say we should delay, even now?'

All through winter the two men had argued, with Nevitta saying the army should strike east as soon as the passes were clear; and Eutherius gently advocating restraint while there was any chance of a settlement with Constantius. In the midst of this dispute Eutherius had said privately to me, in a rare moment when he allowed his exasperation to show, 'Really, Drusus, our friend Nevitta is not one of nature's listeners. He has never left the West: he has no conception of the forces Constantius commands.'

I agreed. I did not say that Nevitta would have disliked Eutherius whatever the cause, or with no cause. Nevitta had been reared in the rough world of the frontier camps. He had a German father; but his features – dark hair and a pointed vole-like face – he got from his mother, who was said to have been a Syrian camp courtesan. His education consisted only in learning to fight and kill; he regarded Eutherius as a bizarre offence against nature, whose silken words, epicene manner and flamboyant dress outraged his very idea of manhood.

Of course he took care that Julian saw none of this; and, indeed, his dissembling in Julian's presence was the only true self-control I ever observed in Nevitta. But he was less careful among his loud beer-drinking friends in the cavalry mess, as Marcellus knew, having been there and seen it for himself.

Eutherius, I imagine, knew too; for he made it his business to know what lay behind all undercurrents of bad feeling. But he was too polished, too much the politician, and too used to ignorant men, to allow himself to let it show.

Now he returned Nevitta's glare with an urbane smile. 'You are quite right, my dear Nevitta; there is no question that Vadomar must be dealt with. As for Constantius, he doubtless means to unsettle us, and if he is fortunate, to cause us to dispute among ourselves.'

He paused in case Nevitta missed the point; then continued, 'So by all means make war on Vadomar. But let us remember also what Constantius's great weakness is.'

'Well?' said Nevitta crossly. 'What is it?'

'Prevarication.'

Nevitta's face went vacant.

'He delays . . . He cannot make up his mind. Decisiveness is alien to him. Vadomar is a distraction – but we must not let our outrage deflect us from our strategy.'

Nevitta sniffed, disliking Eutherius's tone. He would save his criticisms for later, in the mess room.

Then Julian said, 'Very well, we will send your man Libino to Raetia. Marcellus, go with him. Let Vadomar – and Constantius – see that we do not mean to be taken for fools.'

Two days later, on a clear, chill morning, I climbed the citadel hill that looks out over Vienne, mounting alone the stepped stone path behind the theatre. From the summit, standing on the porch of the temple, I watched the army depart, with Libino at the head of the column and Marcellus riding beside him.

The night before, Nevitta had held one of his banquets. Marcellus, who hated them, had attended, because to be absent would have been noticed. Nevitta expected his officers to join in his drunken feasts. But he had returned as soon as he could, and had come to bed saying, 'Libino will have a thick head tomorrow. He was only just getting started when I left.'

'That sounds like Libino.'

Libino was one of Nevitta's strutting young bloods, newly promoted – by Nevitta – and eager to prove himself. I propped myself up on the pillow, watching Marcellus pull off his clothes. I could smell the wood-smoke and wine on him.

'Still,' he said, padding over to the lampstand in his bare feet and pinching out the flame, 'it is only a fool who celebrates the victory before the battle. I was sitting beside Jovinus. He says the Petulantes are not happy.'

'Well, everyone knows Jovinus wanted to lead them. He thinks he should have been promoted over Libino.'

'Yes, and he is right. Jovinus knows what he's about. He always talks sense. And he knows the men.'

We talked a little of Jovinus. He was a good soldier – not loud or thrusting, not at all the kind of man Nevitta would favour.

My eyes grew accustomed to the dark. Across from me, illuminated by the pale moonlight that filtered in through the shutters, I could see Marcellus staring up at the ceiling, his hands folded behind his head.

'What is it?' I said softly. 'Something is troubling you.'

For a moment he did not answer. Then he let out his breath in a deep sigh. 'Oh, it's nothing . . . Nevitta as usual, I suppose. Those parties of his – I hate all the shouting and drinking-contests, and the courtesans that maul you and bore you half to sleep. And if you don't join in, he thinks you're insulting his taste.'

I laughed. 'His taste? Nevitta would make a barbarian wedding-feast seem like a vigil in the garden of the Vestals.'

In the dim light I saw his mouth move in a smile. 'Anyway,' he said, turning on his side and facing me, 'the Petulantes are good solid fighting men; and a campaign will do me good. I'm sick of winter quarters and all the vaunting talk of what we are going to do to Constantius.'

'Yes,' I said; and after that I fell silent, thinking.

An uneasiness had come over me, like an icy flaw in the air. I had never given much thought to Libino: he was just another of Nevitta's flash hangers-on, and as tedious as all the rest. But now, as I stared into the darkness, I saw him for the dangerous young fool that he was, disliked by the men and promoted beyond his ability. I pushed the thought away, sensing ill luck.

Presently I said, 'You have your own unit to think of. That is enough. Let Libino look after himself . . . Marcellus?'

But he did not answer, and when I listened I heard his gentle, settled breathing.

I smiled. I had been considering whether to creep into his bed to talk awhile, and feel him warm beside me. Better though to let him sleep. Tomorrow he had an early start, and a long march.

But afterwards I lay for a long time awake, staring at the moonlight shapes that cast their twisted shadows across the wall.

It was while Marcellus was away that I next happened to speak to Rufus.

I had gone up to the military stables, and was standing with the quartermaster in the covered entrance to the grain-store where we had been inspecting the supplies, when I noticed him on the far side of the cobbled yard, leading his silver mare.

Marcellus, with his knowledge of horsemanship, could read the mood of a horse from afar. I had learnt enough from him to know at one glance that Rufus's creature was in low spirits. She walked heavily, her ears were laid back, and she pulled and jibbed as she moved. Rufus had always possessed a loving sympathy with horses. I asked myself, as I finished off with the quartermaster, what had become of it.

He had halted, and seemed to be remonstrating with one of the stable-boys. He dismissed the boy with a shove, yanked the mare by her bridle, and when she protested with a high-pitched neigh he glanced round crossly, and with something of a start noticed me watching him.

'Is she sickening for something?' I asked.

'She is heading for a beating, that's what. She's a lazy, awkward bitch, and needs to learn who is master here.'

I cast my eye over the melancholy, resentful horse and then looked at him. His face was blotched; his once-bright eyes were dim and drawn. He had assumed the sardonic, word-wise twist of the mouth that all of Nevitta's entourage wore.

With Nevitta's other friends this seemed to come naturally, as if, in their low pursuits, they had found their true selves. But Rufus wore the mask ill. He put me in mind of a trusting child who apes the manners of a vulgar adult. It grieved me to see his decline, and I thought with anger of Nevitta, who had caught Rufus like a butterfly

275

drawn to a false light, luring him by degrees into gross pleasures when the boy's private pain had made him weak and rudderless.

I returned my gaze to the silver mare. Clearly this once-fine creature had come to hate and fear him. I suppose the stable-boy had known it too. I wondered if that was what he and Rufus had been arguing about.

He had paused, though I had not tried to detain him, and was shuffling about, taking brief, uneasy glances at my face, then looking quickly away – down at the cobbles, or at the horse, or across to the stable buildings with their sand and ochre walls. Perhaps he had understood the thought written in my face, and it had caused him to remember.

I made to leave. I had no wish to force my presence on him. But now, in a sudden rush of words, he said, 'I saw Marcellus you know – he was at Nevitta's banquet – Nevitta invited some girls from the town, enough for everyone.' He made a crude, schoolboy gesture, to make sure I had understood. 'But Marcellus wasn't interested in *his* girl. When she sat on his couch he only talked to her, that's all. Nevitta likes people to join in.'

I think in truth he was doing no more than attempting to be pleasant, to engage me in whatever came into his head. But he had spent too long trying to be clever and sharp, and his words – which I suspect were innocent enough – came out all wrong, like one of Nevitta's ugly jibes. Perhaps he realized, and felt ashamed, for he looked down, and I saw his blotched cheeks redden.

'Yes,' I said, 'I heard about it.' I could not find it in me to be angry with him; but I did not intend to discuss Marcellus, or Nevitta's banquet either. Anything I said would only get back to Nevitta.

So I only said, 'Take care of your horse, Rufus, your life may depend on her one day.'

Then I left him. I felt a deep, world-encompassing sadness. I wished I could change the world for him; but there are limits, I thought, to what one man can impose on another, unless first he wills it. Even so, I resolved to look out for the boy, in case the time should come when he tired of Nevitta's empty charms.

He watched me go, with a face full of unacknowledged grief. And the poor fine creature beside him swung her head and regarded me sadly, with wretched long-lashed horse-eyes.

Meanwhile, at about this time, a merchantman put in at Vienne port with a cargo of Carthaginian oil. The captain came straight to the palace with his news. Gaudentius, the notary who had nearly caused a mutiny when we were fighting the Franks, had been sent by Constantius to Africa with orders to cut the corn supply to Gaul.

'I have family in Marseilles,' the captain explained, 'I told them I was bound for Ostia in Italy, or they would not have let me sail.'

'We are grateful,' said Eutherius, who had received him. He made a note. 'Take this to the treasurer of the household; he will see you are compensated for your trouble.'

As soon as the captain had gone Julian said, 'What do you think? Does he mean to seize Sicily?'

Eutherius shook his head. 'Gaudentius is not the man to do it. He is no more than a bureaucrat and a mischief-maker. Besides, it would take him a year to gather an invasion force, even if he had the ships to carry it. But he can hold Africa against you, and control the grain supply to Rome.'

Then, as the weather warmed and the shepherds began herding their flocks to the upper pastures, traders crossing the newly open Alpine passes told of supply dumps inexpertly concealed in the wooded foothills, and of troop movements in the plains of northern Italy.

'There can be no more doubt,' said Julian. 'The question is whether we continue to wait, and hope for peace, and defend Gaul if we are attacked; or whether we strike first, into Illyricum.'

'As soon as Libino returns we must attack!' declared Nevitta, his close-set eyes gleaming. 'Further delay is madness.'

This time the other officers – Dagalaif, Arintheus, Valentinian – agreed. Already there had been rumours that the Persian king was pulling back from the far eastern frontier. The rumours were still vague. But if they were true, it meant that Constantius had reached an agreement with the Persians. With his eastern flank secure, he could turn the full force of his armies westwards – against us.

'Why else,' asked Nevitta, 'has Constantius returned from the Euphrates to Antioch? He is preparing to strike – it can mean nothing else. Illyricum is rich in men; it is Constantius's recruiting ground. I say take it from him now.'

'And you, Drusus?' said Julian, turning to me. 'What do you think?'

For once I agreed with Nevitta, and said so. 'Constantius means to keep us pinned here, like birds in a snare, until he is ready. That is why he roused Vadomar against us; that is why he sent Gaudentius to Africa.'

Julian rubbed his chin and looked across the room. 'Eutherius? You have not spoken.'

Nevitta's head turned. I saw his jaw tighten. After a pause Eutherius said, 'There are gold and silver mines in Illyricum; and we are short of funds.'

'Then it is decided!' cried Nevitta, bringing the flat of his hand down on the map-table like a gambler who has won at dice.

Eutherius frowned at the sudden noise. He met Nevitta's eye, wholly undaunted by his vaunting loudness.

'Nevitta, the commander of Illyricum is a man by the name of Lucillian. Do you know of him? He is an experienced general – not another of your incompetent barbarian chieftains. Nevertheless,' he went on, raising the flat of his hand when Nevitta tried to speak, 'it is clear now that Constantius is turning his forces westwards, in spite of his attempts to hide it. Such vast changes cannot remain concealed. It will take some time to reorder such a mighty army, and it will be worse for us when it is done. If we are to strike at all, it had best be done before he is fully ready.'

'But we have twenty thousand men!'

'An insignificant number, and the less we shout about it, the better. Constantius can muster ten times as many.'

Nevitta sniffed and fell silent. Julian turned to the map. 'Even so, it will take him time to assemble them. Lucillian is here at Sirmium. He could hold the city for a year or more in a siege: we must not allow that . . . we must surprise him.'

He indicated the Alpine passes into Italy, and, further north, the road that led through Raetia to the western provinces of Illyricum. 'He will be expecting us from here, or here. But,' he said, planting his finger on the wild mountain region that lay between the two routes, and turning to us with bright eyes, 'he will not expect us here!'

We all stared down at the coloured dots and lines and small ink symbols marking rivers and towns, forests, mountains, passes and frontier lines. Even Eutherius left his chair and came to look. But it was Nevitta who spoke first. In a changed voice he said, 'But Julian, no army could pass that way!'

'You are right. No *army* could pass . . . But as for a company of light-armed men, with me leading . . .' He paused with shining eyes, knowing what was coming; and a moment later everyone cried out in protest. The route was untested! It was probably impassable; the forests and hills had not been pacified and were full of barbarians!

'It can be done,' Julian insisted. 'No one will expect us by that route. We can join the Danube here' – prodding the map – 'where the river becomes wide enough for boats; we will be in Sirmium even before Lucillian discovers that we have left Gaul. Jovinus, you will lead half of the army through the passes into northern Italy, making as much noise and show as possible, to ensure Lucillian hears of it. At the same time, you, Nevitta, can go by the northern route through Raetia. Do you see?'

The army, he said, thus divided, would seem more numerous, and Lucillian would be unsure of the main thrust of our attack. Meanwhile, Julian himself would be leading a force of men over the mountains – wholly unsuspected and unlooked-for.

Now it was Nevitta who warned of the risks. What was Julian thinking? If he fell, they would be without a leader, defeated before they had begun. Someone else should lead the men. He himself would go. Or Libino when he returned. Drusus or Jovinus even.

'And you?' he said, turning to Eutherius for support, 'what do you say?'

Eutherius pressed his lips together and looked amused. After a considering pause he answered, 'I have heard you are a gambler, Nevitta. The stakes are high, and now is the time to play or leave the table. We are few, dangerously few; if we are to act at all, then it must be with intelligence, and with speed.'

His eyes moved beyond Nevitta's suspicious, disdainful face. 'But why do I talk on? For Julian has already made up his mind.'

Julian laughed. 'Fortune favours the bold,' he said. And with a happy look he turned back to the map on the table.

TEN

BUT FORTUNE HAD OTHER plans that spring. While the oaks on the high slopes above Vienne were still clothed in their first pale-green buds, Nevitta's favourite Libino returned, not to celebrate victory, as he had expected, but in a clay death-urn, escorted by Marcellus.

I rode out to the walled barracks outside the town to meet him. He looked pale and tired, and spattered with mud from the road. Returning, riding side by side along the avenue of cypress trees beside the grave monuments, he told me what had happened.

Vadomar and his tribesmen had already struck into Roman territory when they arrived. As soon as they heard that our force was approaching they scattered like mice in a barn, out among the many small valleys that make up that region. At that point Libino, if he had been less of a fool, would have halted until the scouts brought in their reports. But he was set on a swift and easy victory.

He attacked even before he knew the dispositions of his enemy. Ranging over the densely wooded hills with an advance party, he was ambushed on a hillside by a band of Vadomar's men. He was one of the first to fall.

Marcellus coughed. He winced up at the afternoon sun as if the light troubled him. 'It's as well the Petulantes were with us,' he went on after a silence, 'they're good, dependable men; they kept their heads and fought on.'

But as word spread that Libino had been killed, the barbarians found new confidence. They began to emerge from their hiding places, and the hilltop lookouts reported columns of Germanic tribesmen approaching through the passes of the valleys. Our troops, seeing they were about to be encircled, reluctantly disengaged, and retreated to hastily fortified positions further back.

'We held the line – just. It was a close-run thing. Libino had not prepared for anything except victory.'

By now we had reached the imperial palace. As he dismounted in the great oval courtyard with its curving sweep of columns, Marcellus suddenly caught his breath. He winced again, and with an involuntary movement caught at his side. I looked at him sharply.

'I took a tumble, that's all. The camp doctor fixed it up. It's nothing.'

Till then I had taken his pale look for tiredness. Now I saw the lines of pain around his eyes.

'Don't tell me it is nothing,' I said crossly. 'Look, there's blood on your hand.'

'I'll attend to it later, after we've seen Julian.'

There was no time to say more, for already Julian was

hurrying out from under the portico. He was never one
to sit in remote majesty, like some eastern despot who
waits for his lieutenants to bring him news. So we went
inside, with Julian eagerly questioning Marcellus as we
walked.

But as we mounted the steps Marcellus stumbled; and
though he tried to cover it, I could tell he was glad of
someone he could rest his weight on.

Immediately Julian summoned a legion out of winter
quarters. He marched to put down Vadomar, before news
spread of Libino's death and the whole frontier from
Raetia to Lower Germany erupted. I should have been
present during this minor war; but Julian, out of kindness, thought up some army matter that would keep me
in the city.

'I can handle Vadomar,' he said. 'You take care of Marcellus. I need him fit and well.'

So I remained at Vienne, worrying the doctor, binding
Marcellus's wound, and bullying him to stay in bed. He
hated being ill; and though he was always gentle towards
frailty in others, he was impatient of his own. Friends
came to visit him – the young men from his troop, full of
concern; Eutherius, trailing eastern scents, and bringing a
box of sweets packed on a bed of ribbons by his servant-
boy Agatho. Nebridius came, ceremoniously sending one
of his clerks ahead to enquire if his visit were convenient.
Even the groom from the stables turned up, dressed in his
leather tunic and waiting shyly at the door, unsure of his
welcome until Marcellus beckoned him in. He adored
Marcellus as much as any lover.

None of these visits surprised me. But I had not expected, one afternoon when I returned from my work, to find Rufus sitting on the stool beside Marcellus's bed, talking quietly, with his chin propped in the flat of his hand.

He had his back to the door and did not see me. With a private smile I left them and continued on my way to the baths.

'I thought Rufus had gone off to Raetia with Julian,' said Marcellus later.

'He wanted to go. Nevitta wouldn't let him. Besides, I think his horse is lame.'

'He didn't mention the horse.'

'What did he talk about?'

'Oh, army gossip mainly. I think he just wanted to speak to someone different. He was asking me about the war, and whether Constantius's ironclad cavalrymen are truly as fearsome as people claim.'

'I expect his friends have been trying to frighten him.'

'That's what I said. I told him fear was a bigger enemy than any mailed horseman. But, you know, Drusus, I think the death of Libino has been a shock to Nevitta's set. They didn't expect it; they thought war was just a game, and an easy one at that. I wonder if Rufus is starting to realize that the crowd he spends his time with are not all they seem.'

I said I hoped it was so, and told him to lie back so I could check his wound.

'But why,' he said presently, as he looked up at me, 'wouldn't Nevitta let him go to Raetia? Rufus is not happy

– it's written all over him. The change would have done him good.'

'Nevitta says his people need to prepare for the march east. That's what he says. But the truth is, he's in a foul mood because of Libino, and he's taking it out on everyone he can, even poor Rufus. He thinks Libino's failure reflects badly on him.'

'It does.'

'I know it does. But as usual Julian accepts Nevitta's excuses.'

I was about to go on, but a sound made me turn.

In the half-open door a slave was standing, holding a tray with a bowl of broth and a loaf. I had sent for it myself; but now I gave a small inward curse that I had not checked the door before speaking. It was not wise to talk of Nevitta where others could overhear, even a servant from the kitchens.

I took the tray of food and sent the man off; and afterwards I talked of other things.

Days passed. The wound in Marcellus's side turned from purple to blue and grey; another grim trophy of war, along with the white seam on his forearm, the old cut on his calf just below the knee, and the mark from a spent arrow beneath his left ear. These were my reminders that he was mortal, if ever I could forget. One evening, in secret, I climbed for a second time the path behind the theatre, to the old citadel on the hill with its ancient neglected temples, and thanked the gods that he lived.

I had seen him grow from boy to man. His muscles had knit strong and hard on his shoulders, firm to the touch;

his arms with their blond feather-soft down had broad-
ened from wielding the sword and javelin. In battle, he
had learned to be tough, as we all had; sometimes, in small
things he did, I saw his grandfather's sternness in him –
in the way he grew chill and distant with those he disliked, or his impatience with baseness and dishonour. This
I understood, for we had seen too much of both.

But towards me he had not changed. There was a gentleness to him, and a need for love. Just as when I first
knew him, he would furrow his brow and rake his hand
through his hair when he was troubled or deep in thought.
And now, with the onset of spring, the sun was working
its yearly magic, turning his curling winter-bronze to gold.
He had lost none of his grace, none of his powerful beauty;
he was still the youth I had always known; bright, generous and perfect.

Nor was I the only one who saw it. He was well liked
among his troop and had many friends. He had admirers
too; and I knew, as one does, that there had been times when
both men and women had tried their luck. What came of
it I never asked. But in what mattered I never doubted him,
or the friendship that was the bedrock of my life. He had
brought to me riches beyond my dreams. In such ways do
the gods touch men's lives, and show their presence.

After ten days of laying up, the doctor pronounced him
safe. Soon after he was back on his horse; and we rode
out together to the upland meadows above the city, where
the air was fresh and clean, and for a while forgot the
clouds of war gathering beyond the barrier of the Alps.

The blow had caught him in the weak place in his side,

where he had been wounded before. If the blade had struck an inch higher, the doctor told me in his matter-of-fact way, he would have died in the hills of Raetia. It was, I knew, no more than the risk we all took, and I kept my deepest thoughts to myself, lest speaking them should give them power.

I needed that time alone with him. I took him for granted. How could I not? Yet it was as if Death with his cold hand had touched me on the shoulder and said, 'Remember me, Drusus, that I am close; each day is in my gift, and I am unforgiving.'

Julian returned from Raetia saying he had dreamed of Hermes telling him that when Jupiter enters Aquarius, and Saturn touches the Virgin, then Constantius would meet his end in Asia. He had written it all down not to forget it, and as soon as he was back in Vienne he referred the details to the city astrologers, who told him it was indeed a portent, signifying that Constantius would die before the year was out. Julian was pleased; but Eutherius reminded me that just then the astrologers were well disposed, having been freed of the restrictions Constantius had placed on their art.

But whatever Eutherius said, the portent had set Julian thinking. Soon after, he paid a visit to the temple of Cybele, for which Vienne had once been famous. Returning he announced, 'I have been talking to the priests. It is time I purified myself and made a fresh beginning. There is an ancient ceremony they told me of. It is necessary; I feel it. I shall arrange it before I go to war.'

I asked Eutherius about Cybele. 'The Gauls call her the Mother,' he said, 'she is daughter of Heaven and Earth, and as old as time itself. You will find her everywhere, though she goes by different names. Even the Christians cannot ignore her, and have given her a name of their own, calling her Mother of God. But her first home is Ephesus – that is where you will find her great temple.'

'I should like to go there one day,' I said.

'And perhaps you will – and,' he added with a smile, 'perhaps I may be your guide, if our young warrior Julian does not first rouse the bishops against him, or tumble into a ravine on his way to Illyricum.'

On the day the stargazers had deemed auspicious we went with Julian to Cybele's temple in Vienne. The garlanded priests intoned their prayers. In the precinct, standing on the steps in the sharp morning sunlight, a choir of boys sang an ancient hymn; and attendants scattered lily flowers across the marble floor. Later Julian emerged from the inner shrine clad in a robe of brilliant white, his hair damp with the water of the holy fountain. Even Eutherius, who did not much like temple ceremonies, commented to me as we walked across the petal-strewn court, 'It seems the goddess favours her new acolyte.' And it was true there was a new lightness in Julian's step.

I said, 'The priests told him he was reborn.'

Eutherius sniffed. 'Is that what they said? Well at any rate he no longer has to dissemble, which is never good for the soul. Maybe one can call that a kind of rebirth.'

'But you do not care for it?'

'I do not care for priests. It is said that the gods choose

their own; I can only suppose they have not chosen me.'

He gave me one of his sidelong looks and then he left me, for he wanted to compliment the little group of bright-faced singers waiting beside the fountain, whom everyone else had forgotten.

Soon after, our scouts reported that the high passes were clear of snow. We made ready to march, and Julian summoned the troops to assembly, to tell them of his plans. He had another purpose too, of which Nevitta privately warned us beforehand, coming to each in turn with the self-important, confidential air of a man dispensing secrets. Julian, he said, intended to ask those present to take the formal oath of allegiance; and we should be prepared.

The oath is sworn only to emperors. It would be a final, public break with Constantius. How Nebridius came to be omitted from Nevitta's warning I do not know. An accident perhaps; though it was no secret that Nevitta disliked the prefect's old-world Italian propriety, and had been trying for some time to persuade Julian to dismiss him.

On the appointed day I walked out beyond the city walls with Marcellus and the cavalryman Jovinus, to the open ground where the army was gathering. Marcellus went off to take his place near Nevitta and the other cavalry officers; I remained with Jovinus, talking of this and that as we watched the last of the troops fall into line.

Soon Nebridius arrived. He paused to greet me in his usual courteous rather formal way; then went to join the deputies from the prefecture, who were standing nearby in a small group under the tribunal. I suppose, after that,

I carried on chatting to Jovinus, not knowing what was coming. It was a fine spring morning. The city showed pink and white in the slanting sun. Light shone on the still waters of the Rhone, and glinted on the military standards with their brazen wreaths and rampant eagles. An expectant hum rose up from the ranks. They had not yet heard the detail of Julian's plans; but they knew that the moment of decision had arrived.

The tribune gave the signal; the trumpets blared. And then Julian mounted the wooden steps, resplendent in his new diadem, his shining dress armour, and his heavy cloak of imperial purple. For a few moments he paused, gathering the men's attention; then he spoke out, reminding them of when he had first come to Gaul, young and inexperienced; of how together they had driven out the barbarians; of how, though they were few against many, and against the predictions of their enemies at court, they had never been defeated. But now, he declared, Constantius was preparing to make war on them, and the time had come to raise their eyes to the east. They must leave their homes, hard though it was: they must strike first, or lose everything.

As his words rang out, the silence in the pauses was so deep that I could hear the birds calling, and the distant noises from the city harbour. He held them in his hand, that close-knit band of fighting men, whose faith in themselves he had restored. All his time in Athens, among the old tomes of Plato and the orators, which his enemies had mocked him for, had not been wasted. He had learned the magic of well-honed words. He had woven his spell around them, not to deceive or beguile, but to hold before each man the promise of his potential. And the mystery was not found in smoke and potions, or incantations and poppy seed, but in the clarity of hard-won knowledge.

'Here then,' he said, speaking to them as a friend and as a comrade-in-arms, 'is what we will do.' And he outlined his plan.

When he had finished he spread his arms and asked, 'And are you with me?' And all together the men broke into a great echoing roar of support, chanting his name and clashing their swords on their shields.

And then, when silence at last returned, he asked them to swear the oath.

Immediately the centurions called out the order. Then, in one disciplined movement, each man raised his sword, holding the long blade to his throat, and in the ancient formula swore to follow to the death. The dark ominous words, chanted like a prayer, or a curse, made the hairs tingle on my neck and arms; and my heart quickened with its power.

Then our turn came. From his place on the wooden platform, Julian glanced at us, giving a slight nod and a trusting smile. Nevitta, taking the lead, drew his sword and brought it up to the exposed flesh above his gilded breastplate; then we followed, pledging ourselves in unison.

Even before I had finished I became aware of hushed muttering and a shuffling of feet. Opposite me, the men behind Nevitta were slewing their eyes, trying to see what the fuss was. But it was no time to turn and stare. Then, through a parting in the crowd, I saw Nebridius. His lips were pressed closed; his proud aristocratic face was rigid with anger and humiliation.

He had refused the pledge.

I lowered my sword, returning it to its sheath. Julian, up on the tribunal, must have heard the disturbance, but had not deigned to look. Indeed I think he would have let it pass if Nevitta had not cried out, 'See! The prefect refuses to swear!'

After that, whatever his private intention had been, Julian could not ignore it. He glared down, more angry, as I believe, with Nevitta than Nebridius. But it was too late now. Nebridius, suddenly the focus of attention, foolishly declared in a clear angry voice that carried far in the silence, 'I cannot bind myself in an oath against Constantius, to whose kindness I am indebted.'

There was an outraged cry from the front ranks. Men rushed forward, pushing past the bewildered centurions and surging round Nebridius. He was not a young man, and he was not a soldier; but he held himself tall, until he vanished within the crowd of shouting men. I did not see him fall; but I saw the swing of boots as they kicked him. Word of what had happened was spreading back along the ranks. More men, encouraged by the first, and taking the passivity of the centurions for consent, broke formation and ran forward. There was a flash of steel in the sunlight. Someone had drawn his sword.

I began to run forward then; but next to me Jovinus's hand locked around my arm. 'No, Drusus. It must not come from us.'

I stared at him in disbelief. Out of all of us he had been the closest friend of Nebridius. I saw his eyes were raised, fixed on the tribunal. And then I understood. At that moment Julian leaped down the wooden steps, taking them two at a time. He rushed to where the circle of men had closed around Nebridius, thrusting his way in, shoving the men aside. They were common soldiers; in the blood-crazed mood they were in, any one of them might have run him through before they realized who he was.

Immediately I raced forward, and Jovinus beside me. Yet even as I ran, I noticed with some other part of my mind that Nevitta, who was closest, had not stirred at all. Within moments it was over. The men stood about blinking; the centurions, remembering themselves, yelled at them to fall into line.

And in the centre, Julian stood with his feet planted each side of Nebridius's body. He had thrown his cloak over him as a sign of his protection. The purple wool was fouled with blood and dust.

I glanced about for Marcellus. Turning, my eyes passed over Nevitta, and something in his face made me pause. I had caught him in a private instant when he had supposed he was unobserved. His expression did not wear the shocked surprise of the rest of us. There was something else – disappointment; anger . . . even pleasure. I could not tell for sure.

Then he turned, and perceiving my eyes upon him he composed his face, as if there had been something written there he did not wish me to see.

But it was no time to reflect, and I thought no more of

it. Julian was helping the shaken prefect to his feet. All around, the men were glaring like dogs held back from the kill. They would have torn him to pieces if they could.

We sent Nebridius back to the city with an escort. Nevitta would have gone with them, except Marcellus interposed himself saying, 'I will see to it, sir.' He must have guessed that the prefect would not have completed the short journey back to the city alive if Nevitta had been accompanying him.

Thereafter, Julian completed the ceremony. Later, when I returned to the palace with him and the other officers, Nebridius was waiting in the courtyard, sitting on the steps with his head in his bloody hands.

'Traitor!' cried Nevitta.

But Julian silenced him, saying, 'You will not be harmed, Nebridius. Get up, and let the physician see to your wounds.'

Nebridius, shaken as he was, and moved by the gentleness of Julian's words, stepped forward, extending his hand. Julian would have taken it, I believe, but for the audience that had gathered.

'No,' he said, a little awkwardly, 'I will not take your hand. What, otherwise, should I have left to offer my friends?'

And then, frowning, he walked on past.

I daresay, if he had been warned beforehand that Nebridius would refuse the oath, he would have excused him from the ceremony and then quietly replaced him. But it was too late now. It would not do, at such a time, to give a public sign of forgiveness. It would have been taken as weakness.

Soon after, we marched to war.

Near Augst, on the Rhine, Julian divided the army as he had planned, sending half across the Alps through northern Italy, under the command of Jovinus, and ten thousand through Raetia, led by Nevitta, with orders to close on the city of Sirmium. Julian himself took a force of three thousand light-armed men into the untamed region that the Germans call the Black Forest. All were volunteers; Marcellus and I were among them.

We ascended foothills dense with fir and pine, up and up, along steep bluffs and past rocky gorges. We forded streams, some only ankle deep; others surging torrents that roared down from the snow-capped mountains, wading through the chill clear water with our teeth chattering and our packs and swords held over our heads.

At one point we passed a flat boundary-stone, white with lichen and etched with old carved lettering.

'What is that?' asked one of the men, pointing.

'Don't you know?' answered a grizzled centurion. 'That stone once marked the end of Roman territory, in the days before we ran scared of the barbarians.'

Men looked about, and frowned. But, stone or no stone, the truth was that these ever-higher slopes and ancient forests belonged to no man, for no man could have held them.

Sometimes, far below, in small green valleys that were little more than crevices between the mountains, we spied signs of life: hamlets and paddocks and smoke from cooking-fires. But Julian kept away from these. We were not here to fight a skirmish war with mountain peasants.

We climbed. The air grew colder. Lacking a mule-train, we slept in the open in what we wore, posting guards at night against wolves and bears, sleeping on a bed of pine-needles, with our kit-bags for pillows.

But our guides knew their work. They led us along the high wooded tracks, and soon the pines and teetering ashes gave way to denser forest again. The mountain streams converged into wider, slower-moving water, meandering through green pastureland. We made our way down, and followed the line of the river; and on the tenth day came at last to a timber-and-brick frontier town, which had grown up at the furthest reach of the river traffic.

Warily we drew near, unsure of our reception, for we were entering Constantius's territory now.

As we approached, the gates swung open. There was a pause; and then the city elders emerged, smiling and making signs of peace and welcome. They gave us the news that, at Rome, the consuls had fled in panic as soon as they heard that Jovinus was crossing the Alps.

Julian nodded gravely, and thanked them, assuring them that their city had nothing to fear from him.

Only when the elders had gone did he say with a smile, 'Remember our old friend Florentius? He holds the consulship this year. It seems that running is in his nature. I wonder if he left his wife and children behind, this time.'

There was laughter.

'Where will he have gone?' I asked.

'To his master Constantius, where else? He has abandoned Italy to its fate.' He shrugged and glanced at the shining water – the upper reaches of the Danube – brilliant in the morning sun. 'Italy has nothing to fear from us; and Florentius knows that. It is his own fate he is worried about.'

Though the mountain crossing had been hard, we did not delay. We proceeded by river in a fleet of small boats, borne swiftly onwards by the east-flowing current. We passed frontier watchtowers, built of stone and black wood, with roofs of thatch. From the high walkways the border troops stared curiously down at us. Some even waved in greeting. We waved back. But, in spite of these friendly signs, we did not forget we were in enemy territory. We put in to shore only at night; and bivouacked beside our boats.

Each day, as we moved east, the river grew wider. The wooded hill-country gave way to the plains of Illyricum, with its fields of beans and yellowing barley. We made swift progress. The winds favoured us; our oarsmen, which included me and Marcellus, were strong and eager. At length, after days on the water, the pilot of our boat pointed to high ground in the distance, rising from the plain. It was Mount Alma, which lies between the Danube river and Sirmium, our goal.

We made landfall at dusk.

We beached our vessels on low, spreading mud-flats. Here we were at our most vulnerable; but apart from a lone goat-boy, who stood with his herd and stared, we were greeted by no one. By now, we knew, the fast imperial couriers would have brought word to Lucillian at Sirmium, warning him of the advance of our main army into northern Italy. He was, as Eutherius had reminded us, an experienced general; he would have sent men to guard the great military highways to the south and west.

'But,' said Julian, 'if the gods are with us, he will not be expecting us from the north.'

Even so, there was no time to lose. We could not remain unnoticed for long. At once Julian assembled a band of light-armed volunteers: fifteen in all, with me and Marcellus leading. Our task was to go swiftly ahead, that same night, under cover of darkness, over Mount Alma to Sirmium.

'Find Lucillian,' said Julian, giving us our orders, 'and bring him here. Let him think our whole army is upon him. He thinks we are still many leagues away.'

We set off under a faint crescent moon, heading south over Alma, keeping the summit on our left and following the farm tracks over the vine slopes.

Venus was rising by the time we descended into the far plain. Our scout paused and pointed. Ahead, across the barley fields, the dark loom of Sirmium's northern wall showed black against the stars.

We pressed on. By the time we reached the suburbs of scattered houses and smallholdings that lay outside the walls, the sky was greying with the first hint of dawn. In the paddocks and market-gardens, people were stirring, going about their early-morning business. They glanced up, but otherwise took no notice of us. They were used to seeing soldiers. We made our way along the quiet paths unhindered.

But at the northern gate, as we had expected, there was a guard.

We approached in an ordered line, like a troop back from patrol. At the gate Marcellus saluted, and said that we were on the business of the Augustus himself, bringing an urgent message for Lucillian. We waited, ready to draw our swords at the first sign of challenge or suspicion. But the guard merely wiped the sleep from his eyes and waved us on. It did not occur to him to ask which Augustus we were talking of.

The streets beyond were quiet still. We passed a public fountain where a few women had gathered to fill their pitchers. In the street a bread-seller with a wooden hand-cart gazed at us. We strode on, with the confident air of troops back from manoeuvres, and made for the centre of the city.

We came to an archway faced with carved marble gar-lands; and passing beneath it we entered a wide oval precinct flanked by colonnaded courts, as large as the hip-podrome at Vienne. The man beside me gazed about and muttered, 'Now what? Where are we?'

'It's part of the imperial palace,' I said. 'Lucillian will be here somewhere. Look like you know where you are going.'

But, of course, we did not know. Already the first shafts of morning sunlight were lancing across the sky in streaks of rose-red against deep blue. We made for the colonnaded walkway on one side of the precinct, where we could pause and consider. From the doorways of the surrounding build-ings people were beginning to appear, men with the look of clerks and bureaucrats. Just then a young mop-haired slave-boy came ambling past. Marcellus caught him by the shoulder and with a friendly look said, 'Tell me, which way are Lucillian's quarters?'

The boy – he could have been no more than ten – regarded us for a moment, his eyes passing over Marcellus's uniform and sword-belt. Then returning his smile with a bright, gap-toothed smile of his own he directed us in his young flute-like voice through a stone arch.

'Good lad,' said Marcellus, ruffling his hair. The boy walked off with a wave, and we went on, emerging into a smaller, marble-paved court. In the middle was a fountain, with a bronze youth pouring water from a pitcher into a circular mosaic basin. Beyond stood a grand house, three storeys high, with a columned porch, and steps, and pilasters topped with golden acanthus leaves.

There was no one about. We strode ahead, quickly mounted the steps, and entered through the small servants' postern.

Inside we paused. We were in a long gallery. Statues stood in marbled recesses upon pedestals of onyx. Between the columns, pale-blue silken hangings swayed gently in the breeze from the upper windows. But there were no guards.

Then, as we were wondering which way to go, approaching footsteps sounded from somewhere beyond the hangings. My hand moved to my sword-hilt. The hangings parted and a middle-aged liveried servant stepped in, humming cheerfully to himself, bearing a great pile of linen on his outstretched arms.

Seeing us he halted and stared. Quickly I said, 'I was told Lucillian was here. I have urgent business.'

He eyed us suspiciously, peering over the heap of folded cloth. Then he said, 'Lucillian is still in his bedchamber. Who are you?'

'It cannot wait,' said Marcellus, brisk but pleasant. 'We have come from the emperor.'

At this the man turned and set down his cargo on a ledge. 'Ah, well; you didn't say. Then I will go and call him.'

He walked off, intending, no doubt, for us to wait. But we followed him, fifteen uniformed men, passing out of the room through high carved double-doors, and up a wide ornate staircase onto a broad landing above.

The servant decided not to comment on this, and presently he halted before a door set within a sculpted marble lintel. All the while his eyes had been nervously, discreetly assessing us. He was washed and groomed, and wore a well-cut tunic of gold and white. He was, I guessed, some high-ranking domestic of the household, who would know procedure and have his wits about him. His frowning glances reminded me how we must have looked – and smelt – after our long journey, with our uniforms faded by the sun and water, and our tanned faces dusty from the road.

Finally, at the door, his uneasiness got the better of him. I saw his mouth firm, and knew what was coming.

'Wait here,' he said. 'This is irregular. I am going to call the head steward.' But before he could move, Marcellus caught him by the wrist.

'There will be no need for that,' he said in a low voice.

The servant's eyes widened, first at Marcellus, then at the dagger I had drawn and was holding up to him. Thereafter there was no more need of pretence.

Marcellus moved the man aside, pressed his ear to the door, listened for a moment, then carefully raised the latch.

Inside was a square, high-ceilinged room whose walls were decorated with painted panels. On one side was a polished writing-table, with papers strewn about, and three or four leather scroll-cases, of the kind used for imperial dispatches. There was a couch with gilded lion's feet, upholstered in green and white, and beside it on a low cypress-wood stand a glass pitcher and golden cups.

But Lucillian was not there.

I raised my blade at the servant. 'Where is he?' I said.

He swallowed, and nodded across the room to where, in the corner beyond the writing-table, plush scarlet hangings, half-drawn, concealed a second, smaller door. I wiped a line of sweat from my brow and stepped quietly across the polished floor. Marcellus was at my side. I gestured to the others, and they crept up behind. I listened. There was no sound within. I cast a warning look at the servant; then, gently, I eased open the door.

The shutters were closed. Morning sunlight shafted through the cracks. From the bed a voice mumbled wearily, 'Not now, Agilo; go away.'

He was lying on his side, the covers pulled up around his neck, his face buried in the white linen bolster.

On tiptoe we advanced and gathered round the bed.

Then, when we were ready, one of the men stooped down and whispered, 'Time to get up, sir.'

For a moment he did not move. Then, in a scramble of twisted sheets, he bolted upright. He froze, staring at the fifteen sword-points bearing down at him.

'Forgive me, sir,' I said, 'for startling you. It is a fine morning, and the emperor Julian would like a word. So be so good as to dress yourself, and we shall go to him directly.'

Thus Sirmium, the mighty imperial city where Constantius had held court only months before, fell to fifteen men. Lucillian put up no resistance. No one else challenged us. All during the short journey back to the Danube, he kept asking how it was that our armies had reached the city without his knowing. We said nothing; and after a while he grew quiet, suspecting, I believe, that he was to be put to death that day and that we had no heart to converse with a condemned man.

But when we arrived at our small rude camp beside the river, Julian greeted him civilly and told him he need not fear for his life, and to pick himself up out of the dust where he had prostrated himself.

At this Lucillian got to his feet, brushed the soil from his clothes, and began glancing around at the tents and pulled-up boats.

'Are you not reckless, Caesar, to strike so far from Gaul with so few men?'

Julian, who had been turning to leave, turned back and looked at him in surprise.

'What now, Lucillian?' he said with a laugh. 'Will you

teach me strategy? Keep your wise words for Constantius. I have not come all this way in order to seek your advice.'

Later that day our force of three thousand marched into Sirmium. Citizens lined the route, holding lights, casting flowers, and calling out blessings.

Julian beamed, waving and extending his palm in thanks. I remembered the time when, as a boy, I had watched Constantius's brother Constans ride into London, gazing straight before him as if his head were held in a vice as he passed disdainfully through the throng of townsfolk.

That was not Julian's way. He meant what he had said in Gaul. An emperor should show himself among his people, a man among other men, leading not by fear, but by the example of his virtue. Here was the nature of kingship – to set oneself above the common people not by force, but by wisdom, and self-mastery, and moderation. In this, and this alone, lay the true title to rule.

He had found these precepts first in books, where wise men had set them down. And for that his enemies had laughed at him.

But, I thought, they would not be laughing now.

ELEVEN

In the great colonnaded precinct Julian received the surrender of Lucillian's forces. He reassured them. They were fine soldiers, he said; he would send them west to Gaul, where he had need of them.

Then, to show himself before the people, as was expected, he devoted the next day to chariot races. He attended at the great hippodrome beside Sirmium's imperial palace, dressed in the heavy purple and gold finery he disliked so much, doing his best to appear engaged as the charioteers swept past the stand in clouds of dust. But the crowd loved it. They roared approval, and waved their green and blue banners, the colours of their favourite teams.

That evening Marcellus and I celebrated with the rest, walking along the cresset-lit streets, pausing at each tavern as men we knew hailed us. Everyone wanted to hear our story; it seemed my cup was never empty.

Later, my head light and carefree from the wine, we left the others and strolled through the fragrant night towards the river.

'Tonight we are heroes,' I said laughing. 'Fifteen men against the might of Illyricum, and we have not even fought a battle.' I threw my arm over his shoulder and pulled him to me.

He said, 'It's what Julian wanted. Only our enemies gain when Roman fights Roman. But Constantius has not given up yet.'

I dismissed his serious thoughts with an unsteady sweep at the dome of glittering stars. 'See, Marcellus, how beautiful they look. Just like you. Do you suppose they hold the answer to all man's mystery, as the astrologers say?'

He smiled. 'Not unless we first know our own souls, and that is harder than any stargazing.'

I laughed and kissed him, and looking up once more I stumbled on the cobbles.

Marcellus caught me before I fell. 'You're drunk!' he cried.

'What of it?' And I kissed him again. 'We have a bed at last, after a month of damp straw and ants crawling in our ears. That's something to celebrate.'

He laughed. 'After so much wine, you could sleep on a midden.'

'And you with me.'

And so our foolish talk went on, leaning one on the other, our voices echoing off the dark, shuttered houses. Presently we rounded a corner and came out in the street of the embankment. Here we paused, leaning on the wall beside the river. The smooth black water shone with the reflected light of a nearby tavern. There was a terrace with tables, and lanterns suspended from a row of plane trees.

'Come, Marcellus,' I said, pointing. 'One more jar of wine, just you and me. Not once this evening have we been alone.'

We sat at a table near the water. A pretty dark-eyed servant-girl brought our wine, and laughed at my drunkenness. We fell to reminiscing, gazing out as we talked at the flickering lights and the darkness beyond. At some point I went off to relieve myself, and returning started saying some thought that had come to me; but Marcellus silenced me with a quick warning gesture of his hand.

I broke off and went up to him in silence.

'Listen,' he whispered, taking my arm, 'but do not stare.' He signalled with his eyes towards the neighbouring table, which was screened from us by a low, spreading laurel growing in a stone pot.

The men must have arrived while I was away. They were soldiers, judging from their talk; but they were not our men. They too had been drinking, but there was no joy in their voices. I edged closer, along the wooden bench.

One, picking up the conversation of his comrade, was saying he could stomach being beaten fair and square, which was the fate of war. There was no dishonour in being trounced in an honest fight. But to be taken by guile, and by an inferior force . . . He paused significantly, and from the others there rose murmurs of agreement.

Another said, 'And now Julian is sending us away to Gaul, like prisoners.'

'He would keep us with him if he trusted us.'

'So I told you.'

'What favours can we hope for now? We are done for.'

Another, with the intonation of a barrack-room sage, pronounced, 'Seldom seen, soon forgotten.'

I met Marcellus's eye. No soldier likes defeat, but I do not know what else they expected. They were two legions and a cohort of archers against our three thousand, and though Julian sorely needed reinforcements, he dared not pit them in battle against Constantius so soon after their surrender.

They went grumbling on. Lucillian, they were saying, should have resisted. He could easily have defeated our rag-tag force. 'And you are not the first to say so,' said another, naming friends of his in other companies who thought the same. Then someone else, speaking in a low, dangerous voice, said, 'We are not too late to do something about it . . . not yet, anyway.'

We needed to hear no more. Ducking down behind the laurels we slipped away.

When we were out of earshot I said, suddenly sober, 'They must be confined to barracks. This will spread like fire in a hay-barn.'

'Yes it will. Come on, we had better find Julian. There will be a mutiny by morning.'

That night, when the troops were back in barracks, guards were quietly posted. Many commanders, at such a time, when all hung in the balance, would have disbanded the men and executed everyone who was suspected. Julian, however, announced he intended to speak to them.

We all argued against it. But Julian countered that the men had given their word. It was better, he said, to credit a man with honour he does not possess, than to take him at less than his worth. So at first light he went to the barracks and talked to them, saying they had no cause to feel shame, that he had true and honourable need of them in Gaul.

When he finished there was a ripple of cheering. Perhaps it was just that the men had sore heads.

But when, soon after, they departed west for Gaul, they went with their heads hanging low, like men being led into captivity.

We were glad to see them go. But we had not heard the last of them.

We did not delay at Sirmium. Soon we were on the march once more, taking the imperial highway eastwards, to the city of Naissus.

Naissus was the final stronghold in the western half of the empire, and it opened its gates to us without a fight. From the nearby heights, Marcellus and I stood with Julian and looked out. Along the river and over the barrier of the mountains lay Thrace, the first province of the East; and then, after that, the great imperial capital of Constantinople – Constantine's city, whom the Christians call 'Great', because he turned away from the old gods.

Julian turned and frowned down at the new-built, bald-domed churches dotted here and there within the city walls. Constantine had built them, with the gold he had plundered from the temples. He had demolished whatever had stood before. The new buildings glared like moth-holes in some fine old garment.

'I should not like to be at court when Constantius hears that Naissus has surrendered so willingly.'

'No, indeed,' I said with a laugh. We all knew that the great Constantine, Constantius's father, had been born in Naissus. It was the ancestral home. Constantius would feel the loss bitterly.

We soon saw that Constantine's loot had been spent not only on the Christians and their grim churches. Three miles outside the city walls, beyond the suburban villas, he had built a summer palace – a complex of high-vaulted halls, mosaic courtyards and marble colonnades as large as a town – and populated it with cooks and chamber-boys, bath-slaves, clerks, gardeners, and men of every trade he could conceive of needing. It was a city of servants, awaiting an always-absent emperor, for Constantine had never found time to return.

Now it was ours, and here we took up residence in glorious luxury among the silken hangings, cascading fountains and echoing marbled halls, and awaited Nevitta and the rest of our army.

In early November, when the first cold winds had begun blowing off the eastern mountains, bending the avenues of cypresses and stirring the fallen leaves in the court-yards, he arrived, riding at the head of the column on his silver-white horse, clad in dyed furs and heavy gold, looking pleased with himself.

'He puts me in mind of a conquering barbarian,' I said dryly to Marcellus.

He gazed solemnly at the advancing column. 'Yes,' he said, after a silence. 'Still, it was we who took Illyricum from under Constantius's nose. That will not please him at all.'

I laughed; but Marcellus continued frowning, drawing down his brows against the bright morning sun. Though he had not spoken of it, I knew what he was thinking: that he would be back under Nevitta's command now.

But whatever we thought of Nevitta, he was bringing Eutherius and Oribasius with him, and we were glad of that.

And with the army came Rufus.

Marcellus saw him first, on the morning after the army's arrival. 'I can't understand it,' he said. He had expected to find him loud and boasting like the rest of Nevitta's entourage; but instead he was sullen and ill-looking and remote.

'Was he drunk?' I asked.

'It was just after dawn.' But then, seeing my look, he added, 'No, I don't think so.'

'He drinks too much.'

'I know. But so do all those friends of Nevitta's.' He shook his head. 'No, it's something else; it goes far deeper than drink. He seems to shun all human friendship. He hasn't been the same since we were taken by the Germans. Before that, the world was full of promise for him.'

He turned, and stood frowning out of the window. Outside, in the vast, bright courtyard of Constantine's lavish palace, a line of gardeners dressed in red and white livery were sweeping up the fallen leaves from between the columns.

I looked at him. He cared about Rufus. I knew he felt in some way responsible; for Rufus had been in his troop when he was captured. He had seen what was fine in the boy, as a man spies gold in ore. It grieved him to see him so diminished.

I drew a breath, ready to tell him what the barbarians had done. But then I stopped myself. I had made a promise, for Rufus's sake. Even now I recalled the boy's broken, imploring face, staring up at me. Something had died in him that day, something in his soul; and in this one thing I was determined to keep faith. I still hoped time would mend him, and for that reason too I kept silent about what I knew, lest I scare off some healing god.

So instead I said, 'I think he has lost trust in himself. That is why he is led by the last person he speaks to.'

'And that person is Nevitta, or one of his worthless cronies. We both have seen the true Rufus, and this is not it. Why don't you speak to him, Drusus? He might listen to you.'

I did not say I doubted it; and agreed to seek him out. But to myself I thought, 'If Marcellus cannot reach him, then surely nor can I.'

And so, next morning, I went to find him. At his quarters they said he had gone off to the stables. But at the stables, the grooms told me they had not seen him.

I was half minded to leave the matter. But then one of the young cavalrymen came up to me and said, meeting my eye, 'Sorry, Drusus, if I am speaking out of turn. But I expect you'll find him in the town. Try the taverns behind the market, the ones that open early.'

I nodded, and thanked him, and went off. After some wandering about, I eventually discovered him in one of the drinking-houses favoured by the meat-sellers, between the market and the abattoir. He was sitting at a rough-wood table, alone, with a pitcher of wine in front of him, staring at it.

Near the serving counter a half-naked flute-girl was playing some drawling, languid piece on a wooden pipe. Most of the market-men had left, so that the tavern was almost empty. Four or five whores remained. They sat at a table near the counter, talking and laughing.

He had not noticed me. I paused inside the door. As I waited, one of the girls got up from her stool, and with the heavy motions of one performing an unwilling errand went over to him. She said something. Without looking up he dismissed her with an angry sweep of his arm. She pursed her lips, gave an indifferent shrug, and returned to her friends.

He was dressed in his smart cavalry clothing – a cream-coloured tunic hemmed with red, and a brown leather belt. The muscles in his legs and arms, once lean and hard, had softened; his young face, which had been so full of light, was sullen and red. Yet, I thought, even now he was handsome, beneath the effects of too much wine.

The girls had noticed me, and so I stepped forward across the sawdust floor and went to him.

He was scowling down into his wine-cup. He did not glance up till I paused at the table. Seeing who it was he gave a start, but tried to hide it. 'Go away, Drusus. Leave

314

me alone.' He was drunk. The sun had not been up more than an hour.

I said, 'Come away, Rufus. You've had enough.'

'What is it to you?' Defiantly he took a long draught of wine, banged his cup down, then cursed and repeated more loudly, 'I told you to go away.'

For a moment I stood looking down at him in the dim grey light. Across the tavern the whores broke into laughter. One of them, mimicking his voice, squealed out, 'Go away, go away.'

He threw them an angry glare and took up his cup. But before it reached his lips I seized it from him and cast it hard into the corner, where it shattered on the stone flags. Then, taking him by the neck of his tunic, I hauled him up and marched him towards the door, past the table of women, who had stopped chattering and were staring with their painted mouths open. In the street outside was a stone horse-trough. I plunged his head into it, twice, then pulled him up coughing and spluttering.

'What did you do that for?' he cried.

'It's enough, Rufus! Do you hear me? Look at you! How can you so abandon yourself, drunk as a camel in some whorehouse when you're meant to be on duty? You ought to be ashamed.'

'Ashamed?' he cried. 'What do you think? You know, don't you, what they did, all of them, out there in the German forest. Would you not be ashamed?' He sniffed, and wiped his face with his hand. 'I hate myself, Drusus, if you want to know; I hate myself and I hate my life. I have made all the wrong choices.'

I released him. He stood looking at me, dripping and forlorn and broken. 'How old are you now?' I demanded.

'Twenty.'

'Then it is time you stopped behaving like a child. Do you think you are the only one who has known pain? What now, are you going to dwell on it forever? Look to what is best in you.'

'There is nothing.'

'Must I duck you again? Of course there is. Everyone has seen it. I have. Marcellus has.'

At this he looked up. His eyes were moist. I thought at first it was the water from the trough.

'Really?'

'How not? You were once the finest in the horse-troop. And you will be again.'

He hung his head. 'You don't know – you don't understand. There is nothing fine about me.'

'Come on,' I said, 'I'm taking you to the baths. You can sweat out some of that wine.'

The city baths of Naissus were close by, a fine building, restored and extended by Constantine, with arcaded galleries, and mosaics of green papyrus and water-flowers.

I took Rufus to the hot-room. He sat silent on the ledge – ashamed, it seemed, even of his naked body. Was that, too, I wondered, something the barbarians had brought him? And suddenly my heart filled with anger – not with Rufus, for all his foolishness – but with all those who had used him for their own base purposes: not only the barbarians, but Nevitta too, and all his hollow noisy friends, who thought themselves so world-wise. Between them they had broken the boy's trust in the world, which had been genuine and true. He has possessed a surefootedness, not yet knowledge, which had been crushed just when it was at its most fragile, trampled like some rare flower, thoughtlessly, unheeded and uncaringly.

I would have put my arm around him then. But even that would be no good. Nowadays he recoiled from any human touch.

I wiped my brow. It was early for the baths, and we were alone.

Presently I said, 'Nature made her creatures stoop down to walk and feed; yet man she made erect, so he might gaze at the heavens, and his soul might know its home.'

At this his young face twisted. 'Fine talk, Drusus; easy for you to say. Look at what you have. Everyone likes you and looks up to you. You're like a rich man who cannot see why a beggar complains of hardship.'

I said, 'My life is not like that. It never was.'

But he merely shrugged. Angrily he said, 'You want to talk of truth? – Then I'll tell you what is true. We are nothing but beasts – low, miserable animals. That is the truth of man, and all the rest is no more than a surfeited dream. Look around you, Drusus! What else do you see, but cruelty and self-seeking?'

I drew the hot air into my lungs. Frowning I said, 'Yes, Rufus, all you say is to be found. One need not look far for it. Do you think I do not know? But there is nobility and love and beauty too, and there is the good, which our souls know for what it is. Beast and god dwell in every man, and every man can choose which he will follow.'

He gave a hard laugh. 'Pious words! But I was there, and you were not.' He paused, and glanced at me, and looked away. In an accusing tone he said, 'You told Marcellus, didn't you?'

'I told no one. What happened that day is between us alone.'

I saw him frown to himself. He seemed about to say something; but instead, after a short pause, he turned his head and spat. Then he pulled himself off the ledge, and for a moment stood motionless, looking ahead.

When he spoke again, all the force was gone from his voice. There was only weary bitterness, and the undertow of pain.

'I'm going now,' he said. 'I don't want to talk any more. Don't come after me, Drusus. You have seen what I am, and that is bad enough. You should have left me to my wine.'

And he stalked off, a naked, forlorn figure, through the curling steam and slanting rays of sunlight.

That night, when I saw Marcellus, he asked me what had happened.

I told him some of it. But not all. Words have power, to summon and dispel. There seemed no purpose in giving strength to such a bleak vision by repeating it.

The morning had left me sombre and reflective, and I had been doing some thinking. Now I said, 'It seems to me, Marcellus, that one man cannot fashion another's life for him, as if he were clay to turn and mould. Such things must come from within, because one wants it; or by the intervention of some god. I do not think he listened to what I said. But, perhaps, one day, he will remember.'

Soon, however, these questions were forced from our minds. Lucillian's legions, which we had sent west to Gaul, had mutinied.

I was with Julian, in one of the vast, grandiose chambers of Constantine's summer palace, when the messenger was announced. The legions had seized the fortress city of Aquileia, and had declared for Constantius.

Aquileia is no insignificant city. It sits on the main east–west highway, and commands the northern reaches of Italy. The danger was great; the Italian cities, which up to now had wavered, would close their gates against us if they saw us falter. And Gaudentius was still in Africa. If Italy turned against us, he could cross to Sicily unopposed and attack our flank.

Julian summoned his officers in council. 'How close is Jovinus?' he asked.

'This side of the Alps,' said Nevitta, 'on the road to Sirmium. He will be with us before month end.' He indicated the place on the map.

Julian stared down for a moment, then began pacing the room. 'Jovinus must turn back and lay siege to Aquileia,' he declared.

At this, everyone began speaking at once. But it was Nevitta's voice that was the loudest of all. 'What are you thinking?' he cried. 'Aquileia has never been taken! It is impregnable – everyone knows it. Jovinus's army could sit there for a year or more.'

There was sudden silence. Nevitta's sharp eyes darted round, looking for support, like a man who has unwittingly exposed himself. His face, always so carefully managed when he was in Julian's company, had doubt and fury written all over it.

And I, who had my own reasons for reading Nevitta's moods, saw something else there too. Not fear, as first I thought. It was calculation. I believe it was at this moment that it first dawned on him that we might lose, and what it might mean for him.

'We have the winter,' said Julian. 'We shall give Jovinus whatever he needs. Men once said that Troy was impregnable, yet it was taken. We must believe in ourselves, and trust in the gods where knowledge fails us.'

Nevitta frowned. He knew what he knew, and had no time for philosophy and gods. But he said no more; he sensed he had said too much already. There followed some talk of details – the requirements for a siege, what could be sent to aid Jovinus, and such things. No one said what was uppermost in their minds – that we were dangerously exposed. There was no point: we had to take the situation as we found it.

Later, when we were outside in the great courtyard, away from the others, I said to Marcellus, 'Did you see Nevitta's face? Last time I heard him, he was laughing at our caution, and crowing that victory had dropped into our hands like an over-ripe fruit.'

Marcellus shrugged. 'He sees he spoke too soon. He

doesn't know what to do; so he strikes out. He's all noise. Perhaps, now, he'll shut up for a while.'

The sun moved behind the clouds. I rubbed my arms, suddenly cold. Already there was a scattering of autumn leaves across the expanse of inlaid coloured marble. It would soon be time for cloaks and long tunics. Across the courtyard, emerging from Julian's quarters, Eutherius appeared, passing along the colonnade, his bright mantle billowing in the breeze. We strode across to him.

'How is Julian?' I asked.

'Troubled,' he said, 'but resolute. He has gone with Oribasius to offer something to Hermes. But I am going to honour the god of breakfast, who has always served me well. Will you join me?'

So we walked with him to his new rooms – a pleasant suite set in its own sheltered garden, with a tall drooping-leaved fig growing up against the wall. We ate seated on latticed chairs on the patio, warmed by the intermittent sun, and talked of the news from Aquileia.

I asked what Constantius would do now.

'Already,' said Eutherius, 'he is hurrying to Constantinople, where the rest of his armies are gathering. He will be delighted, no doubt, at the change in our fortunes. The flatterers and intriguers will be feeding his vanity, like sweets to a glutton, reminding him that he is master of the world, and invincible.'

His manner was light; he did not seem to share the grim mood of Nevitta and the others.

'But Eutherius,' I cried, 'you talk as though it were of

no importance. Yet how can we hope to defeat him now, being so few? Our only hope was speed.'

He set down his cup on the white-painted garden table.

'Drusus, my dear, we must not let the brave Nevitta's sudden anxiety disquiet us. We began this enterprise with open eyes; we chose to follow Julian, and Julian had no choice. He says the gods willed it, and who are we to say they did not? So let us trust in the gods, since our reason offers us no guide.'

He spoke with irony and humour, as always when he referred to the gods. Yet he did not speak with impiety. Rather, it was as if to say that the gods too smile, and we should smile with them. He paused, and watched as a brightly coloured bird, a female goldfinch, came fluttering down and settled on the bough of the fig. It looked about, gaily singing.

'We have had nothing to endure but success,' he went on, 'which any man can bear. Now, when circumstance is against us and we are put to the test, we must bear that too, for it is in adversity that a man truly learns what he is about, don't you think? But look at you, you have lost weight, and since Agatho has been to so much effort to prepare this spread for us, the least you can do is take another honey-cake, or perhaps one of these charming eggs . . . As for Constantius, though he is strong, he is timid. Fear is a greater enemy to him than Julian, and one he has no weapons against. King Sapor is waiting for him on the Persian border, and we are approaching from the west. We hold Illyricum, his main recruiting ground, to say nothing of the gold and silver mines, which he will surely miss. So let us not allow Italy's petulant cities to concern us, nor Aquileia . . . No, Drusus; this contest will be determined elsewhere.'

He took a shelled egg from the little wicker basket, where they sat garnished with green herbs in a neat pile, and pressed it into my hand.

'There!' he said, 'now eat, and trust to what you know.' Then he called for a pitcher of wine and spring water, and another loaf of new-baked bread, and proceeded to ask Marcellus about his horse.

That autumn we seized the Succi pass, which divides Latin-speaking Illyricum from Greek Thrace in the east.

The narrow defile is guarded by a strong fortress, which overlooks the pass and controls the road through. Our forward scouts had returned with the news that the fortress was empty.

Julian summoned the scouts and questioned them himself. He could hardly believe it. A hundred men garrisoned there could hold back a whole legion; it seemed madness that Constantius had abandoned it.

We set out along the river valley to see for ourselves, travelling east towards the soaring snow-topped peaks of Haemus and Rhodope, climbing the road between fruit-tree terraces and goat pastures. Just as the scouts had reported, the fort over the pass had been abandoned.

While our men were busy securing it, restoring the gates and awaiting the mule-train, we rode on with Julian, up the goat-tracks to the summit. We left the horses when the path became too steep, and continued on foot, coming at last to a high outcrop of black rock, dotted with lichen and tiny white mountain flowers. I clambered up the ridge, crouching against the buffeting wind. Marcellus, who was ahead, took my hand and pulled me beside him, onto a flat overhanging ledge at the top.

Turning, I caught my breath. Far below, like a vast blue-green tapestry, the wide plain of Thrace lay spread before me, divided by the distant line of the river Hebrus, glinting like a silver filament in the sunlight.

Julian came up beside us.

'See there!' he said pointing, shouting over the roar of the gale that came rising over the escarpment, 'That is Philippopolis.'

I looked out. The city was as small as a toy, with white walls snaking over tree-covered hills. Among the roofs I could make out the stadium, and theatre, and temples.

Julian's eyes shone. 'It is the key to Thrace,' he said. 'After we take it, nothing will stand between us and Constantinople.'

I gazed down into the valley. Beyond the distant city, the plain stretched out endlessly before me, all the way to Asia. Julian's enthusiasm was catching. It seemed we could do anything, just by trying for it.

But later, back at the fort, Nevitta came up to me, while I was alone, tethering my horse. He crept up soft-footed, so that I did not hear him approach.

'I don't know why Julian is so bright,' he said. His small eyes probed my face, sly and searching.

I looked back at him, wondering what he wanted. Never had he sought me out before. He was overdressed as usual, in a heavy fur-collared cloak, with an elaborate brooch of worked gold.

When I did not answer he went on, 'Constantius has men enough in Thrace, even if the army is in Asia still. It is madness to think he will allow Philippopolis to fall.'

The magic and light-filled power I had felt on the summit bled from my soul. I felt a creeping in my flesh, which I could not account for. I recalled what Marcellus had once said of Nevitta: that he was a killer of dreams. Since the news from Aquileia, a change had come over him. His vaunting had ceased. Suddenly, all about, but with no clear source, there were complaints of the difficulties and risks. I asked myself again what he was seeking from me.

'Perhaps you are right, Nevitta,' I said carefully. 'Perhaps it is madness. Yet we have taken Illyricum, and now we have taken the pass. A man might have said that this was madness too; and yet here we are.'

I turned and busied myself with the catches on the horse's bridle, wishing he would go away. I heard him take a step. At my side, in a quieter voice, he said, 'You have Julian's ear. He calls you his friend.' He made the word sound ugly.

I paused, frowning at the leather strap in my hand. 'We are all his friends, are we not, Nevitta?'

He gave a cool laugh. 'You know my meaning. Some are saying it is time for Julian to make another approach to Constantius. Some are saying we cannot win.'

Out of the corner of my eye I could see him studying me, waiting for a sign of assent, or complicity. I realized my hand was trembling with anger. I left the bridle and turned.

'I will not persuade Julian of what I do not believe myself,' I said in a hard voice I had never used to him before. 'Let those men you speak of go to Julian themselves. Why not? Are they ashamed, as they should be? Or are they merely cowards?'

He sucked in his breath. My words had been clear enough, even for him. I knew there were few things that could have insulted Nevitta more, vain brute that he was.

I turned my back on him, and patted the horse, trying to still my anger.

No one else was about. I guessed he knew that already. He was clever in his schemes, with all the skill of a street-thief. Was he sounding me out, or was he testing me? Either way, he could easily deny it all.

I heard him take a step closer.

'Watch yourself, Drusus,' he muttered in my ear, so close that I felt his hot breath. 'There are no cowards here.'

He did not say more. Whatever he was seeking, he had not found; and after a bristling moment he grunted, and went striding off.

When he was gone I paused for a while and thought. I did not regret what I had said, not quite.

But I had let my anger master me; and I had exposed his pretences for what they were.

It was too late in the year to press on over the mountains into Thrace. Leaving the pass at Succi strongly garrisoned, Julian returned to Naissus for the winter; and there he set about writing to the cities of the empire, justifying to them his move against Constantius. He worked hard at these letters, believing that the cities, when they heard the truth, would support him. But I do not think either Eutherius or Oribasius was surprised when they did not reply, or sent hedging, evasive answers. The Senate in Rome even wrote to say he ought to show more respect to the man who had made him what he was.

'And how much respect,' asked Julian, 'do they think I owe the murderer of my own father, or have they forgotten that?'

But Eutherius raised his eyes to the dome of the lapis-inlaid ceiling and said, 'Ah, the Senate! Behind their guise of principle lies nothing but self-interest. They think they will ingratiate themselves with Constantius with their toothless bite. But if Aquileia falls, the senators will be stumbling over themselves like a herd of startled sheep in their haste to support you.'

'Then I have no use for such friends! Where is their ancient dignity? Where is their sense of who they are, and the great men in whose footsteps they walk?'

'Gone, my dear Julian. Gone. Fear and sycophancy change men. Their dignity was lost long ago. These are no more than grovellers, waiting to kiss the ground the emperor walks on.'

But one city wrote back supporting him – his beloved Athens. It made up for all the rest.

That winter, while we waited, he turned his attention to the business of government, which was always close to his heart.

As with Gaul, Constantius had imposed a heavy tax on Illyricum, which the people could not pay. Julian issued an order cancelling it, and this time there were no fussing bureaucrats to oppose him. Constantius, and Constantine before him, had drawn all power to themselves. Julian's intention was to restore the freedom of the cities, permitting them to see to their own affairs, and raise their own finance as they saw fit. 'How can a man have pride in himself, if he is not his own master?' he would say. 'And as for men, so for cities of men. Each city knows its own needs better than a court of strangers and a distant army of functionaries.'

At the same time, he announced measures to encourage citizens back to the city councils; he ordered public buildings to be reopened – theatres, libraries, basilicas and baths; he authorized funds to restore the crumbling aqueducts – the soaring canals that fed the cities with water, built when men still believed in the idea of Rome.

Winter came on. At Naissus, an icy wind scoured down the river valley from the mountains, and we shivered amid the gilded splendour of Constantine's summer palace. The tall, airy rooms had been built for coolness.

Meanwhile, Marcellus was finding Nevitta harder to bear than usual.

The siege at Aquileia was dragging on. Somehow the rumour took hold that Julian had overreached himself, that he should have slaughtered Lucillian's two legions rather than send them west. It was a foolish idea; but once it took hold it smouldered on with all the stubbornness of a winter fever. Marcellus, who tried to engage the boy whenever he could, first heard it from Rufus.

'He talks without hope, as though we were defeated,' he said, telling me of it.

I shrugged. 'Is that Nevitta speaking, or Rufus?'

'Who can tell? I expect he got it from Nevitta, like most things.'

Nevitta was a man who could not be still. That winter, he was constantly busying himself in pointless activity, and blaming those who served him when they did not do likewise, accusing them of indolence. Whether he singled out Marcellus because of me I do not know; but during that time Marcellus was always being called out on one errand or another – up to the high uplands on manoeuvres in the bitter cold; or needlessly escorting dispatches from Naissus to the Succi pass, or to Serdica, which lay between.

When I saw what Nevitta was doing, I confided to Marcellus his sinister private words to me, and what I had said in return. I had not wanted to burden him with it; but now, seeing Nevitta's petty spite, I felt I was the cause.

'Yes,' he said frowning, 'well, let him play his games; but you are right to keep clear of him. He brings trouble. He may dress like a king, but under all those furs and finery he has the mind of a mercenary.'

I asked him what he meant.

'He cares only for himself – and he doesn't know himself enough to know what he is caring for. I think, in the end, he wants only riches and power. The rest of what Julian is about – the love of wisdom, the good ordering of the soul, or the art of ruling – is all beyond him. Well, you've seen it in his face, the way it goes blank when Julian talks of those things. He is a looter at heart. He does not understand the virtues of a statesman.'

Then, one cold, wind-blown morning, to my surprise Rufus came to me in my workroom – an echoing, absurdly grand chamber of soaring malachite columns and gilded capitals, large enough to hold a hundred men.

I was busy with an adjutant, a young officer called Ambrosius, disposing of the requisitions for a train of winter supplies for the garrison at the Succi pass. I had planned to ride out with Marcellus later that day. He had finally secured a few days' leave, and we had arranged to go up to the pass together.

Rufus waited, shuffling about beside the tall double-doors until I had finished with Ambrosius. I called him in, and asked him how he was.

'I was wondering,' he said, keeping his eyes on a basket of rolled-up scrolls on my work-table, 'who is taking the convoy up to Succi?'

'I am. And Marcellus too . . . But why?'

'I saw Marcellus at the stables. He has had to take a troop of men up into the hills.'

'Are you sure? He didn't say anything to me.'

'No, Drusus; it was sudden. Nevitta sent him. It was something urgent and he'll be gone for some days. He asked me to let you know.'

I shrugged, and silently cursed Nevitta. 'Very well,' I said, 'then I must go alone.' I thanked him for coming to tell me.

Instead of leaving, however, he paused, looking rather

rigid and formal. He had not spoken to me since the day at the baths.

I set aside the papers in my hand. 'Is there something else?' I asked. I expect I had sounded rather cool; so now I smiled, to put him at his ease.

'I was thinking, Drusus,' he said, flushing slightly, 'if Marcellus cannot go, perhaps I could ride out with you instead. Nevitta says I may, and I have nothing else to do.'

I looked at him, surprised. 'Why, yes – yes, of course. But are you ready? We leave at midday.'

'I'm ready.'

'Very well; then good. Go along with Ambrosius and see to the mule-train.' And I added, 'Oh, Rufus, I'm glad to have you with us.'

He nodded, serious-faced; then turned and hurried off.

We rode out soon after, under grey skies, following the river valley, climbing into the foothills of Mount Haemus.

Rufus was civil when spoken to; but otherwise quiet. I left him to his thoughts. His usual silver mare was lame. In her place, he had taken one of the standard-issue army mounts from the common stable, a stolid, dun-coloured creature, as sullen as he.

Still, I thought, it was good that he had come along. His awkwardness would no doubt lift in time.

We reached the pass at Succi without incident. That night, over dinner in the mess, the captain of the garrison – a young officer who had fought with me in Gaul – mentioned that one of his scouts had reported movements. 'Probably no more than local herders,' he said. 'We see them often, ranging along the tracks. Sometimes they call at the fort, with a goat or sheep to sell.'

But Rufus, who seemed eager to see the pass, said, 'We could go up tomorrow and look for ourselves.'

'Why, yes,' I said, 'why not indeed?' So next day, after a fine breakfast with the captain and his men, we set out alone, taking the mountain track up between the trees towards the rocky summit.

Overnight the cloud had moved off. The morning air was sharp and fresh and smelled of pine. High above, golden-brown against the crystal sky, an eagle balanced on the updraught, waiting for a leveret or a rock-rabbit to show.

We trudged along in silence, the only sound our footfalls on the track, and the wind sighing in the branches. I did not burden Rufus with talk; I felt his brooding presence and sensed he had things to say. I would wait till he was ready.

Before long the pines thinned, and we came out at a rocky clearing that overlooked the sheer drop of the pass. I paused, and gazed out at the endless sky. I knew there would be no enemy here; I had wanted to climb for its own sake. On mountain tops I feel the presence of gods; and now the fullness of soul I had felt with Julian returned, and the whole world seemed charged with possibility and promise.

I filled my lungs with the cold air. Somewhere in the distance I could hear water tumbling on rock; and, far below, the sound of the wind as it eddied in the narrows of the pass. 'It is a fine view,' I said to Rufus, who was standing somewhere behind me. 'See there, beside the river? That is Philippopolis; and beyond it all of Thrace, until the sea and Constantinople itself.'

'I heard something!' he said abruptly.

'Oh, I expect it's just a bird, or some mountain cat.'

'No; down there, in the ravine.'

I took a step forward to the edge and looked, wondering at the sudden tension in his voice. Below me I could see nothing but dense trees, and clefts of rock with gathered snow. I was going to tell him not to worry; but already he was moving off, saying, 'It will only take a short while, and we can see better from over here.'

I turned with reluctance from the glittering vista of earth and sky, and began to follow.

'This way,' he called, stepping ahead and vanishing behind a pine-covered outcrop.

I remember thinking to myself that he seemed suddenly sure of his way. Half-serious, I called out, 'Then where is your training, Rufus? You have not even drawn your sword.'

Fool that I was, I had not drawn mine either. Beyond the shoulder of rock, there was a dense thicket of mountain bush. I could not see him. I took a step forward, and spoke his name.

There was a swift movement. Something pressed into my back. It took me a moment to realize it was the point of a blade.

'I am sorry, Drusus,' he said, 'that it had to be like this.'

He called out once. Then, from the cover of the undergrowth and rocks, men with drawn spears appeared and surrounded me.

TWELVE

THEY HELD ME AT bay, like a dangerous animal. Sharp mountain sunlight, slanting through the canopy of pines, flashed on the steel of their blades.

I blinked, unable at first to work out what had happened.

One of them prodded me hard with his spear-end. 'Drop your sword,' he said.

I took my sword from its sheath and let it fall. They were wearing imperial uniform, and some insignia I did not recognize. For a moment, in my confusion, I thought they must be from our garrison. But they were not our men.

'Your knife too,' said Rufus, stepping from behind, 'your hunting knife; the one you keep inside your tunic. The one Marcellus gave you.'

I glared at him, then took the knife from where it was concealed and threw it down. For a moment I had been like a man woken from a deep sleep, who cannot tell where he is. But now, too late, my mind was working.

'You have done this,' I said to Rufus. 'But why? How have I wronged you?'

In a sudden flare of anger he cried, 'Now you will see for yourself how it feels to lose everything that matters.'

I shook my head. Around me the men with spears gazed on.

'This is not your work alone,' I said. 'Who has helped you?'

'No one helped me!'

But he could not hold my gaze, and looking down he went on, 'We are not going to win this fight; anyone can tell you. We cannot win.'

'That sounds like Nevitta speaking.'

'It's not. I can think for myself.'

'Very well.' I nodded at the spears pointing at me, 'Then what is this about?'

'You'll see soon enough. He told me there could be a settlement, if I brought you here.'

'Who told you? Nevitta?'

'No! A powerful man, an emissary of the emperor's.' His voice was shaking. The boy was overwrought. For a moment he stared at me. Then, to my horror, he added with a violent sweep of his arm, 'It is Constantius's personal agent, the notary Paulus. He says he wants only peace.'

My eyes met his. 'By heaven, Rufus, do you realize what you have done? That man is my sworn enemy. He is a torturer and a murderer, and if he wants me, it is so he can kill me. You have been deceived. This has nothing to do with peace, or any kind of settlement. He has used you.'

The leader of the soldiers silenced me with a prod of his spear. From where he stood behind the ring of men, Rufus gave a forced, uneasy laugh. 'What! Is the brave Drusus afraid? Is this now the real man behind all those high words?'

I ignored him; he was no longer important. Already my mind was on my escape. I knew what the notary would do, once he had me in his hands.

The soldiers knew it too. They bound me tightly, with cord of twined leather, and led me off at the point of a sword. We passed a dead man lying among the trees. I knew him. He was one of the garrison scouts; he must have stumbled across them.

We came to a wooded covert where horses were waiting. I was trussed up like a run-down stag, and we set off through the pass, descending eastwards into Thrace.

Presently, after hours of following winding, downward-sloping tracks between the trees, we arrived at a small, walled camp, set among the foothills overlooking the plain. There were a few military tents; and in their midst a tall, square pavilion with the imperial banner fluttering from its pole. I regarded it bleakly, guessing what lay within.

I had tried all the usual ruses as we descended from the mountains – calling that I needed to relieve myself; and, at another time, crying out that the thongs that bound me were too tight and I could not breathe, and did my captors want no more than a corpse to deliver up to the notary?

At this they had briefly checked my bonds. But they were

no common troopers, and were wise to such tricks. Little wonder, I reflected, if they had spent any time working for the notary: they would have heard all manner of pleas for mercy. Seeing this in their hard faces, I did not abase myself further by crying and begging. I knew it would do no good. I tried not to think of what awaited me.

I was unloaded from the pack-horse. My ankles were carefully hobbled, bound one to the other with leather horse-straps. Someone, I thought with grim satisfaction, had decided I was dangerous. I wondered whether they would muzzle me too, like a vicious dog. But this they did not do.

After this, when my captors were satisfied, I was led to the pavilion with its imperial banner.

All the while, Rufus had stood looking on, shuffling and biting his lip. Now the guard-captain said sharply to him, 'You too.'

He almost started back. 'Me? . . . But why?'

'Because he asked for you,' the man said with blunt harshness. They all knew what Rufus had done; and no soldier likes a traitor.

So we advanced – Rufus glancing uneasily about him; and I like a bound animal, with a sword-point at my back, and the dark open doorway of the pavilion ahead of me, like the mouth of hell itself. It was a cold, clear day. Inside, under the heavy leather of the tent, the light was dim. In a corner, charcoals glowed blood-red in an iron basket. There was a trestle table and a chair; and in the chair, sitting as still as a cat, was the notary.

He was half-turned away. Between his long fingers he

was holding a writing-stylus. The guard had spoken; but for a few moments he resumed working at some document spread before him. Then, calmly, with finical care, he set the stylus down on a little stand of carved ivory, eased back his chair, and stood.

His eyes passed over me, taking in the ties and straps. He was wearing a close-fitting felt cap against the cold, and a long robe of featureless black wool. He did not smile or laugh out in his triumph; yet all the same I sensed the satisfaction in his thin, olive-grey face.

His eyes shifted to Rufus, and beside me I perceived the boy's shock. Whoever had dealt with him up to now, it would not have been the notary himself.

'Where is the other one?' he asked suddenly.

I heard Rufus swallow.

'It was too difficult to get them both,' he pleaded, taking a step forward and spreading his hands like a supplicant. 'But this is the one you wanted most . . . the man said this was the important one.'

The notary looked at him coldly, taking his measure, reading his weakness and his fear. The silence unnerved Rufus; he drew his breath and began, 'But I—'

But before he could go on, the notary silenced him with a voice like a lash. 'I asked for both, yet you bring me one. Now one will have to suffice. Go now – get out and leave us. You will be given gold, or whatever it is you want.'

He waited until Rufus had hurried out. Then he turned. Moving with his odd, precise steps, he crossed to the latticed fire-basket with its burning coals. The heat had made the iron basket glow.

For a moment he paused beside it, seemingly warming his hands. Then he reached down, and slowly, from the lower half of the basket, where the fire was hottest, he drew out a metal rod and held it up. It was twisted at one end, like a farrier's hoof-knife, but longer, with a protecting handle, so he did not burn himself.

'Did you think I had forgotten?' he said, turning to me. 'I had not. My enemies never escape me.'

'I had finer things to think of.'

'Ah, yes,' he said amused, 'your philosopher-prince Julian – another young fool, who will soon be crushed.'

He turned the implement in his hand, eyeing it closely, as a gem-cutter might examine some precious stone.

'I can feel your fear,' he said, in his smooth voice. 'I can smell it.'

'You are a monster.'

'I am an artist. And I am powerful. Do you know why? – But no, how could you? You do not understand the depths of power. I am powerful because the powerful need me. I am necessary. The weak, and the fastidious, avert their gaze. That is my strength. I dwell where they dare not look.'

'And,' I replied to him, 'it has turned you into what you are. You take pleasure in it, and seek words afterwards to justify your pleasure. You are corrupt. No man could live with what you do and remain sane. It is only tyrants who need creatures such as you.'

I suppose he had expected me to beg for my life, and I guessed from his face that it was seldom that his victims answered back as I had. Now his mouth hardened. For a moment he was silent; then, with a sudden turn, his arm sprang out and he struck my naked upper-arm with the rod from the fire.

I cried out from the pain. Through clenched teeth I said, 'Is this your proof, or mine?'

'How simple you are!' he murmured. 'I have humbled men far stronger than you. Do you really think you can withstand me with your empty show of bravery? I will flay your dignity away, layer by layer, and you will be screaming out for death long before I have finished my work. You have no conception of how slowly time can pass.'

My mouth was dry. I swallowed. He saw this, and smiled.

'Then have it done,' I said.

'Oh yes, it will be done. But not here.' He set the rod aside. 'Other matters are pressing. We shall wait until Constantinople, where my workroom is. There you shall know the true extent of my art . . . Guard, take him out!'

I was held in a barred, wheeled cage, chained like a captured beast. Seeing I was not to be killed at once, someone threw me an old blanket, and gave me a dish of bean-broth. We set off next day at dawn, down from the foothills into the plain of Thrace, with the men on horseback, and the notary riding in a shuttered carriage. Rufus I did not see.

We came to Philippopolis, and spent the night in a military barracks on the outskirts of the city. The barracks was almost deserted, and I supposed the same must be true throughout Thrace, as far as Constantinople itself. Julian's speed had taken the emperor unawares.

But, for me, this knowledge was of no use. My captors

were taking no risks. No doubt they knew what they could expect, if they failed the notary.

I found I noticed every tiny thing – the wheeling flocks of swallows against the sunset sky; the scream of a kite at dawn. I thought of death, and the gods, and of Marcellus, whom I should not see again. It would be many days before he knew even of my absence, and then he would have no way of telling where I had gone. Rufus – or, more likely, whoever had guided Rufus – had been clever, sending him off to the hills while I went elsewhere to Succi. In my mind, I saw him searching the bluffs and gorges, supposing I had fallen; and for this I grieved.

We travelled onwards, following the imperial highway along the Hebrus river.

At Hadrianople a man in an official's garb with a loud, pompous voice came asking after the notary. I caught no more than a few distant words. When the guard next came with water and food and pushed it under the bars, I asked what the man had wanted.

'Nothing to concern you,' he answered as he walked away. 'Government business. Shut up.'

Whatever it was, shortly after, I saw the notary hurrying off with the official, his gliding form silhouetted against the flaring night-torches. My instinct told me something was wrong. But no one behaved naturally in the presence of the notary; and in the end, when I saw the notary return and everything proceeded as before, I told myself I had allowed hope to cloud my judgement.

In my waking hours I told myself I could withstand the notary's tortures; but with the night came the knowledge of my vanity. Even the guards treated me with a kind of respectful fear, avoiding my eyes, as though I were a bad omen, a portent of dark terrors best kept away.

The following morning we set out once more, along a road lined with tall cypresses and fruit-orchards. It was early still. A daytime moon showed large and low in the cloudless sky. I sat propped against the bars of my wagon, thinking of what Julian had once said: that the heavenly bodies, the sun and moon and stars, were images of the invisible gods, which our minds might touch. A stillness had come over me that morning, and for a short while, even in my wretchedness, my spirit lifted and I knew that the notary's world, for all its pain and power, was a lie – it was a mean, circumscribed, shard of a vision; terrible, but false.

I gazed out, thinking these thoughts. Some way off, descending along a side-track from the low surrounding hills, an old man was leading a train of mules laden with baskets and amphoras. He paused and idly stared, and his eyes settled on mine. Though his face was wizened as the bark of an old cedar, his eyes were full of life and power. I felt it, even from so far; and in spite of myself I smiled and raised my hand. He gave a stern nod in acknowledgement, then looked away and pointed.

It seemed so odd that he should do this that I shifted myself round to see. On the road ahead, from the direction of Constantinople, a company of cavalrymen was approaching, on fine Cappadocian horses with scarlet saddle-cloths and gleaming headstalls. The men were uniformed; but at their head was a man dressed like the notary, all in black.

He gestured for us to halt; then called out, asking for Paulus. I saw Paulus glance out from the little shuttered port of his enclosed carriage; then both men disappeared inside. I could not make out what they discussed; but at one point, from the small square open window, there came the sound of voices raised in disagreement, and I heard the notary cry, 'What, must it be now?'

Presently the two men emerged from the carriage, both with pinched, troubled faces. The second notary's eyes slewed over the line of mounted guards, and rested on the wagon where I was sitting. Turning he said, 'I shall take the prisoner.' But at once Paulus snapped back, 'No, he will stay with me.'

Whether the second man was junior to Paulus I could not tell. But it was clear he was awed by him, or afraid.

'As you wish,' he said, after a pause.

Guards came. One opened the great iron padlock of my cage and ordered me out. He ignored me when I asked what was wrong; but the guard behind him, the one who had brought me food and water at night, muttered, 'The notary must go at once to Asia, to the emperor.'

'And me?'

He shrugged. 'You go with him.'

After this I was bound less firmly, for from here I had to ride, the caged wagon being too slow.

We took the road due south, following the Hebrus river. There was an air of urgency; and, with the urgency, something else I could not quite gauge – fear, perhaps, or foreboding; a sense of something momentous beyond the horizon, which the guards had not been told of. Even the notary was preoccupied and impatient; and I was almost forgotten, though from his place at the front I heard him order that my bonds be checked, and that two men should ride each side of me to guard me.

Eventually we reached the mouth of the Hebrus and the sea. Here a fast imperial cutter was waiting. In the confusion of boarding, I overheard enough talk to know where we were bound: we were going to the emperor. Constantius, it seemed, was returning from Antioch to Constantinople with the court and army. He had paused near the city of Tarsus. But why the notary was so urgently required I could not tell. The pilot was ordered to make all haste; and for three days we proceeded south and east, around the coast of Asia with its inlets and purple, wooded coastline.

But after we had passed the city of Knidos, where we spent the third night, the wind suddenly changed, and from the tiny, barred window of my cell in the hold I saw long fingers of pewter cloud extending up from the south. Soon the vessel began to roll, and I heard the rowing-slaves complaining that the sea was coming in at the oar-ports. But we did not reduce speed.

Presently I heard footfalls on the ladder, and the pilot appeared on the steps. For a few moments he paused in the poor light and regarded me curiously from a distance; then walked across and looked in at the bars of my cell.

I had noticed him on deck when I was led aboard. He was a brisk, grizzled sea-hand, the kind I had met often as a boy when I worked with my uncle in London, the sort of man who knew his trade, and said little that was not to the point. I had seen at once he did not like the notary's over-bearing tone.

Now he said, 'The notary says you are dangerous. Are you?'

'Only to my enemies,' I answered.

He gave me an appraising look, then asked what was it that I had done to displease the emperor. When I told him he said, 'It is rumoured that Julian honours the old gods, even though he was reared a Christian.'

'The rumours are true. The gods are timeless. No emperor's edict can destroy them.'

He looked at me with an expression of frowning approval under his beard. He had respect for the gods, like all sailors. He knew enough sea-wisdom to know that nature will not be tamed by man, like a horse under the whip.

He had not walked off, so I asked, 'Are we in for a storm?'

'We may be – they come up from nowhere in these parts.' He seemed to consider for a moment. Then, stepping up, he unlocked the gate of my barred enclosure. 'Best you come on deck, my friend. You will be safer there.'

The notary was standing at the far rail, glaring out over an angry, lead-coloured sea. When I appeared he snapped round and cried, 'Why is the prisoner on deck?'

'A precaution,' answered the pilot, with a flat edge of defiance in his voice. 'You said he was important.'

Just then the deck lurched. The oars rose out of the water as the ship rolled, and from the oar-decks below I heard the rowers shout and curse. The last of the sun vanished behind grey cloud. Our progress slowed.

'Tell them to row faster,' demanded the notary.

'Fast or slow, oars cannot ply air. I do not know what your skill is, sir, but mine is sailing, and I am telling you that with a roll like this we must alter our course or we shall founder. We will put in at Rhodes until this storm passes.'

The notary gave him a cold, dangerous stare, not liking the pilot's tone. His fingers gripped the rail as the ship tilted again.

'Very well; do what you must.' And he turned away.

For all his effort at control, he could not quite hide his anxiety. I could almost have laughed. Did he fear death after all, I asked myself, this man who had presided over the deaths of countless others?

We struggled into Rhodes harbour with the last of the sunset. I was taken off by the guards and locked in a small stone-walled keep behind the shipyard. I saw nothing of the notary; but during the evening one of the pilot's crewmen came with a dish of fish stew and half a loaf. He was friendly, so after I had thanked him I said, 'You might just forget to lock the door on your way out.'

But he shook his head at this, and told me that guards had been posted all about. 'No one is trusted,' he said. 'Eat your food.'

The storm blew for three days. From my cell I could hear the water roar and break along the harbour wall. By the time we put out to sea again the notary's impatience was starting to show. But eventually, on an overcast afternoon, we pulled in to the port of Tarsus with its great arcaded front, and ashlar wharves, and lines of warehouses and slipways.

As soon as we docked the notary rushed ashore, and for a while I was held on the quay with the guards. The emperor, it seemed, had moved on, northwards to the Cilician Gates – the pass that leads through the Taurus mountains to the high Anatolian plateau.

There followed a long delay while men were sent about the city to search for transport. 'What are these?' cried the notary, when they returned with three gaunt, squalid mules. 'Must I see to everything myself?'

But the vast imperial entourage had requisitioned whatever horses and carriages there were to be had. Even the wretched mules had cost as much as fine riding horses.

We set out north, following the road beside the Kydnus river, with the notary riding on one mule, and his documents and other baggage carried in leather satchels and bound-up wooden boxes on the others. The rest of us trudged after him – I with my wrists bound to one of the guards.

Ahead, beyond the fields and orchards of the sea-plain, the vast barrier of the Taurus mountains surged up, rising in undulating folds of green and grey to high, snow-capped peaks. And, below the peaks, on one of the distant foothills, centred on a hillside village, there lay spread over the slopes like a gigantic patchwork blanket the tents and covered wagons of the imperial encampment.

Night was falling by the time we drew near. Across the encampment torches were being kindled. They flared against the deep blue of the evening sky.

We approached through eddies of wood-smoke from a thousand cook-fires, past cattle- and horse-pens, and store-wagons stacked with all the freight of war. There were tents everywhere, row after row, extending in serried ranks in every direction, until the land sloped away and I could see no more. The air reeked of assembled human-kind, of ordure, and of roasting meat. Men called to one another; dogs barked; and somewhere, among the tents, a shepherd's pipe was playing, picking out a slow lament, amateurish yet haunting, full of simple feeling.

The notary seemed troubled and preoccupied. I hoped that in his haste he would leave me in one of the tents, or chained outside – where, it seemed to me, my chances of escape were better. But he was not so distracted that he had forgotten his hatred. We continued through the sprawling camp to the village that lay at its centre, and here I was taken to a small square building with hewn stone walls like a fountain house.

Inside, set into the floor, was a barred grate, and dark-ness beneath.

'Down there!' ordered the guard, heaving open the grate while another let down a rough wooden ladder.

I climbed down into the blackness, taking unwilling steps. Then they hauled up the ladder behind me, slammed the grate closed and marched off, talking to one another of their dinner.

I blinked and peered about. There had been a torch burning in the building above. Its weak light flickered through the bars of the grate a spear-length above my head. I was in some kind of chamber, a pit with a low vaulted roof like a cistern. Somewhere, in the gloom, I could hear the slow echoing drip of water. The air was damp and fetid. But at least the pit was not flooded, as first I had feared.

I listened to the receding sound of the guards. Then, from somewhere in the surrounding darkness, I heard a stirring and a cough. I swung round. I had supposed I was alone.

'Your fate is fixed,' a man's voice said. 'You must accept it.'

'Show yourself!' I cried, staring and trying to see.

There was a pause, then a stirring, and a gaunt figure came shuffling forward. He moved like an old man, slow and bent; but when he raised his face I saw that he could not have been more than thirty.

'There is no escape,' he said, with a weak gesture at the grate.

'What is this place?'

'A prison.'

'No, I mean before that. It looks like an old water-cistern.'

He shrugged. 'What does it matter? God has brought me here to understand my error. I wait upon His grace.'

His hand shifted, and I saw in his palm that he was clutching a small bronze Christian symbol, which he was kneading and prodding with his fingers.

'Is that so?' I said, eyeing him. His clothes were filthy and torn, but I could see in the dim light the stripes of some echelon of the bureaucracy. 'Well, I for one should prefer to wait elsewhere. If this is an old cistern, there may be a channel or a shaft. Come, my friend, why don't you help me look?'

But he merely gave me an appalled stare, and then shuffled off and crouched down against the wall, like a beggar in the street. He began mumbling some prayer or incantation to himself, and it was clear he would be of no use. He was waiting to die.

I shook my head, and leaving him to his business I began feeling my way along the damp stone walls. The ground was muddy; but beneath the layer of mud was hard rock. All the same I trod carefully. My eyes had adjusted somewhat; I could see there were dark, spreading puddles. Any one of them might conceal a well-shaft or a crevice.

I followed the sound of the dripping water. After a short time, testing each step with my hands and feet, I came to a low brick-built shelf. Beyond it, water had collected into some sort of basin. I sensed a freshness to the air and looked up.

I could see no light; but reaching up I felt a narrow brick-lined shaft, blocked with rusted iron bars. I clambered onto the shelf and tested the bars with my hands. One of them shifted. It made a grating sound that echoed about the chamber.

'What was that?' the man called. When I told him he said, 'But you will only make it worse for yourself.'

'It could not be worse,' I answered. 'I am a prisoner of the notary Paulus.'

At this he let out a gasp, and hurriedly resumed his muttering.

I managed to remove one of the bars. I was struggling with the next, when my companion cried in a low, terrified voice, 'Hush! It is the guards! . . . Oh, what have you done! You have been heard. I told you your meddling would do no good.'

I eased myself silently from the shelf and hurried back as fast as I dared to the place beneath the grate.

'Say nothing!' I hissed. I did not trust him not to betray me.

Footsteps sounded on the stone floor above. Through the bars I saw long distended shadows stretch across the roof, and heard the low murmur of voices. The voices ceased. There was a long silence.

I waited. Suddenly the grate shifted and swung open, and faces peered down, their forms silhouetted against the torchlight.

I gazed up, shading my eyes with my hand. Something was not right. Why were the guards so silent?

Then, from above, a tentative voice called down, 'Drusus? Is that you?'

'Marcellus!' I cried.

Beside him, someone brought up the torch, and I saw his serious face.

'Did you think I was going to forget you?' he said. 'Look at you, you look like a rat in a sewer.'

He glanced over his shoulder, and I heard him ask, 'But how do we get him out? Is there a rope?'

'There's a ladder,' I called. 'It must be somewhere close.'

The heads in the opening withdrew. There were sounds of movement, and the wooden ladder descended.

I stepped up to it; then I paused. 'Are you hurt?' asked Marcellus. 'Wait, I'll come down.'

351

'No; it's all right; I'm coming up.' I turned to the man crouched in the corner. 'Come then,' I said, extending my hand to him, 'you first; your prayers are answered. Here is your freedom.'

But he just gaped up at me with wide pale eyes, and when I advanced a pace to help him, he backed against the wall, whimpering and clutching at his little Christian trinket.

'Who is he?' asked Marcellus, when I had climbed out.

I shrugged. 'I don't know . . . A bureaucrat. A slave. I think fear has broken his mind.'

'Shall I go down and fetch him?'

'He won't come, unless you drag him. But leave the ladder, in case he changes his mind.'

I turned and looked at Marcellus, and at the others who had come. I knew them from his troop. They had disguised themselves in the uniform of one of Constantius's eastern legions. 'But how did you find me?' I asked.

'It was Rufus.'

'Rufus *told* you?'

'No, not quite. He came back from Succi, or wherever he was, and hanged himself. It was one of Nevitta's men who found the body.' He fixed my eye with a confidential look. 'Nevitta, it seems, was more surprised than anyone when Rufus returned. I was away still in the hills when it happened. But Decimus here had stayed behind, and before he died, Rufus gave him a note. He told him to take it straight to me, and mention it to no one.'

I asked what the note had said.

352

'It was filled with self-pity and remorse. He told me how to find you. He said he was sorry.'

I nodded and frowned. 'This was not his work alone, Marcellus. Did he say who helped him?'

'He gave no names. Nevitta asked the same . . . many times.'

As he spoke his grey eyes motioned in the direction of his three comrades standing behind. 'No names,' he said again slowly, 'and Nevitta is very sure he acted alone. Do you understand what I mean?'

I understood. Words have power, and what the others did not know could not harm them. As for our own suspicions, now was not the time. Already, through the doorway, the first red glow of dawn was showing over the Taurus mountains.

Outside, the street was empty. I guessed the guards had decided I was secure enough in the stinking pit where they had left me. We were, I saw, somewhere at the edge of the small village where the imperial army had made camp.

'Where now?' asked Decimus, eager to be gone.

'This way,' said Marcellus.

We set off along an alleyway of tall, stone-built store-houses. At the end of it, rounding a corner, we emerged at the far corner of a small paved square with a fountain. There was an old shrine on one side, and on the steps, under the porch, a troop of men were sitting about, leaning against the columns, dozing and warming themselves at a brazier.

Some of them idly turned their heads as we approached.

353

Recognizing them, I backed into the alleyway, and half-hid myself in the recess of a wall.

Marcellus and the others were dressed in plain military cloaks; but I was still wearing the riding tunic I had been taken in. Its bronze studs and strips of bright scarlet leather stood out among the studied drabness of the others, like a cock-pheasant among hens. I should easily be noticed.

'The notary's guards are with those men,' I muttered. 'They will surely know me.'

Quickly Decimus moved in front to block their view. He heaved up his clothing and began to piss against the wall. The rest of us paused, shuffling about, as though waiting for him.

'Are they still staring?' he asked.

'No,' said Marcellus, 'but better not to test them.' He nodded to a narrow passage between the storehouses. 'We can go that way instead,' he said.

With a deliberate show of casualness, we ambled away down the side-alley. We passed through a crude archway of uncarved stone; and then the village ended, replaced by the much larger area of the military camp that surrounded it.

'Gods below! What is this place?' muttered Marcellus, pausing and glaring at the street of grand, multicoloured pavilions ahead of us, each one decorated with a wide awning of sculpted hide, supported on painted columns of turned wood. As we stood looking, a dapper slave dressed in livery emerged from one of them, carrying in both hands an ornate water-flask of chased silver. He stopped and stared, and seemed about to challenge us. But the burden was clearly heavy, and after a moment he continued on his errand.

'These are no ordinary servants,' I said, eyeing him as he went. It was dawning on me what we had stumbled upon. 'Constantius is here somewhere; this is not a place we want to be.'

We slipped off down a narrow gap between the pavilions. Then, rounding a corner, we stumbled straight into a company of soldiers coming the other way, led by a senior officer dressed in parade-uniform. Decimus, who had been looking the other way, actually managed to tread on the officer's red, carefully polished boot.

'Look where you're going, you oaf!' cried the officer, giving him a clout on the head. 'What are you doing here anyway? You know this area is out of bounds.'

'Sorry, sir,' said Marcellus, stepping up, 'we took a wrong turn.'

The officer glared at him. Then he looked at my clothing. 'Who is this man?'

'He is only a prisoner, sir. We have orders to move him.'

'Is that so?'

'Yes, sir.'

'Then why,' he said, narrowing his eyes, 'is your prisoner not shackled? What is your name, soldier? Which legion are you from?'

Marcellus gave some name or other, then said, 'We're from the Sixth, sir, the Parthians.'

He had dressed like a common foot-soldier, and was trying to sound like one. But lazy, uneducated speech sat on him like ill-fitting clothes. His breeding showed too clearly.

And this fine-dressed officer, suspicious now, was clearly not a fool.

He cocked his head and looked at Marcellus out of the side of his eye. 'The Parthians, is it?'

'Yes, sir; that's the one.'

'You don't look like Parthian men to me. Tell me, where were you last stationed?'

'We were at Antioch,' answered Marcellus, looking at him squarely.

'Well, we were all at Antioch before we came here. I mean, where were you before that?'

Marcellus rubbed his face, like a stupid man thinking. 'Oh yes, sir, sorry sir; before that we were out in Syria of course. Out in the desert, near the frontier. It was hot and sandy; I didn't like the sand.'

Ignoring his prattle, the officer turned suddenly to Decimus. 'And you? Were you there too?'

'Yes, sir. I was.'

'And how,' he said, with a false, conniving smile, 'did you like the Syrian girls?'

Decimus looked blank – for the officer had switched to Greek to ask his question; and Decimus, who had been reared in Gaul, had never been out of it until Julian took him. He did not know Greek from a bird's chirping.

Marcellus, quickly improvising, said, 'Decimus prefers boys, sir,' and at this one of the troopers smothered a laugh.

But the officer was not amused. He looked at Marcellus coldly, sensing the joke was on him, and not liking it. But he seemed pressed, like a man who was about to be late for something, and after a threatening pause he said, 'Get out of here, all of you! If I see you again, you'll be on a charge. Is that clear?'

I had been hanging my head. I allowed myself to breathe again. Then, just as we began to walk away, a voice behind us rang out, 'Hold those men!'

I turned, with a sinking of my heart, knowing already what I should find. Striding towards us with his prancing, cat-like gait, attended by a group of clerks and a score of uniformed guards, was the notary Paulus, his thin mouth pale with pent-up fury.

We were seized, and taken to a patch of open, rocky ground behind the pavilions. The guards held our arms pinned. When he saw we were secure, the notary stepped forward, and walked slowly in front of us, studying our faces, like an officer inspecting a line of men.

In front of Marcellus he halted. 'Ah, so here is the grandson of Aquinus. It seems, then, after all, that I have caught two birds in one net.'

Marcellus said nothing; he merely gave him a look of contempt.

'And now,' continued the notary, 'I destroy you. I regret its swiftness, but there can be no more embarrassment.' He turned to the officer: 'Your knife, if you please.'

The officer reached to his jewelled belt, and passed his dagger. It was a fussy, decorative piece, burnished and engraved, set with a line of gems in the hilt. The notary turned it in his hand. The knife may have been for show, but the gleaming blade was honed and deadly.

Decimus shifted. 'Hold them still!' snapped the notary.

He turned to Marcellus; but then, after an instant of

357

thought, took another step, so that he stood in front of Decimus.

'You first, I think,' he said, in his smooth voice.

Decimus took a breath, and his strong jaw set firm. He was a fine young soldier. He knew what was coming, and was determined to face it bravely.

Even now, out of habit, or out of sheer pleasure, the notary calculated each of his movements to extract the highest terror. It was sickening to watch. Slowly he extended the dagger, raising the point to the soft place beneath Decimus's chin. I heard Decimus swallow, and the sound of a prayer caught in his throat. There was a flash of motion. But it was not the notary that had moved. It was Marcellus. He had struck out with his left arm; he must have freed it from the grip of the guard. He hit the notary with a heavy blow at the wrist, and the dagger fell to the ground.

'I told you to hold them!' cried Paulus. Marcellus winced as his arm was forced back by the guard. The notary stood rubbing his thin, delicate wrist. The blow had hurt him. I was glad of it.

'The futile courage of a comrade-in-arms,' he sneered, regaining his composure. 'To the last you are a man of honour, just like your ridiculous grandfather, full of point-less gestures to long-forgotten virtue. And now you have sealed your death with it.'

'It was sealed anyway.'

'But not the mode; oh no, not the mode. Now your friend here – your *lover* – can watch you die. Will you cry out, I wonder? Will you plead and beg? Now, let us see.'

He stooped to pick up the blade. As he did so, I saw behind him, about twenty paces off, where the line of pavilions stood, that a man was approaching, a heavy middle-aged eunuch, dressed in layered clothes of blue and white and gold, with a felt cap on his large head, and a jewel-encrusted necklet at his throat. He gave a pointed, artificial cough, and at this the notary's head went up. Then, seeing who it was, he stood abruptly to his full height, leaving the shining dagger where it lay.

'What do you want?' he demanded.

'I will take these men,' said the eunuch, in a tone of cold, affected courtesy.

'But these are my prisoners!'

'Do you presume to question me, Notary?'

Paulus looked at him. The sinews in his face had gone rigid, and his pale lips whitened. He drew his breath to speak; but then seemed to think better of it. Everything about this bedizened eunuch spoke of power and supreme authority. He paused, straining to master himself; then said pleasantly, with a face like a man racked with toothache, 'No; take them, Chamberlain, of course. It must be as you command.'

I gazed at the eunuch, remembering Julian's words. Here, then, was the creature who had urged the emperor to execute Julian, instead of sending him to Gaul. And he would have had his wish, except that the empress Eusebia, who had been Julian's friend at court when she was alive, had spoken up on his behalf. I recalled the courtiers' joke which Eutherius had told me once in Paris: how it was said that Constantius was fortunate indeed to possess some influence with his mighty chamberlain. And I saw that even the notary, whose trade was fear and violent death, stood cowed and nervous and subservient.

'Quite so,' the chamberlain now said, with a chill, slight smile.

The notary said nothing. He merely watched in angry silence as, at a motion of the chamberlain's finger, we were hauled away.

We were taken to a large, domed building beyond the pavilions, built within a gravelled court. Here I was separated from the others. Three guards took me off at sword-point, to a bare room with peeling ochre walls and a single wooden bench.

'Strip!' ordered the guard.

I looked him in the face. 'Strip?' I asked, narrowing my eyes at him, remembering, with some part of my mind, what had been done to Rufus.

'Yes, strip. Get on with it.'

I began to pull off my clothes. I said to the guard, 'Have you sunk so low? Remember, you are Roman still, and a man. Even here, some god is watching.'

Taking my meaning he said, 'Don't be a fool. You stink; now get your clothes off. You cannot be brought before the emperor like that.'

I froze. I suppose I must have gaped. 'The emperor?'

'The emperor,' he repeated. 'Now get a move on.'

So I stripped. When I was naked, the three men escorted me to an adjoining fountain-room with a cold stone floor and high, glassless windows, and stood watching while I sluiced myself under a pipe. Then, towelled and dried, and dressed in something clean, I was led out again, to where Marcellus was being held.

'They are taking us to Constantius.'

'I know,' he said. 'They told me.'

I looked at the guard. 'Is this the chamberlain's doing?' But all he would say was, 'No more questions. You will find out soon enough.'

Soon a richly dressed servant arrived, and we were taken to a stone-built dwelling nearby, with a marble pillared porch.

It looked, I thought, like a provincial merchant's house, which was no doubt what it was, until the court had requisitioned it. Long crimson banners bearing the imperial insignia had been hung between the columns; the atrium within had been hastily furnished with rich tapestries, and ornaments too big and grand for the place.

In one corner, beside a heavy, gilded lampstand, a group of portly eunuchs stood gathered, locked in urgent, whispered conversation. Their eyes slewed curiously round as we entered, and for a moment they broke off, staring with grave faces.

'Something is wrong,' I whispered to Marcellus.

He turned his head and eyed the eunuchs in their golden earrings and embroidered robes. They snapped their heads away, put out at his impertinence, and resumed their talk.

'Whatever it is,' he said, 'it is not us they are concerned with.'

I was going to go on and say to him, 'Then why are we here?' But there was no more time to speak.

We were passed into the custody of two discreetly armed military stewards dressed in short formal coats of blue damask. They checked the bonds on our wrists, then led us to a high-roofed antechamber with Persian woven carpets and a goldfinch in a gilded cage. Here we waited, with the two armed stewards standing silently beside us. After a short time, footsteps sounded outside, a door opened, and the chamberlain swept in, attended by a train of robed officials, who fanned out and stood about him, like timid maids around a portly bride.

The chamberlain paused, pretending to look at the song-bird on its little tree-bough of worked silver. His face wore the same pleased, pompous look I had seen earlier. Up close, I saw his cheeks had been touched with carmine, and his black, carefully dressed hair was crimped and shone with oil.

The officials of his retinue waited, their eyes respectfully averted from him. But I had had enough of being toyed with. In a hard voice that set the songbird fluttering I cried, 'Why are we here? What do you want with us?'

He turned then, with an indrawing of his breath. One might have taken him for yet another gossiping eunuch, but for his eyes. They were deep-set, full of shrewd, calculating intelligence. After the painted face and fussy, jewelled clothes, there was something about them that winded one, like an unexpected blow.

I set my mouth firm, and looked back at him. If the rumours were true, this haughty official commanded even the emperor. I could believe it now. Beneath the softness was a core of iron, like a blade concealed in velvet.

And I had another surprise to come, for then he spoke, demanding in his flute-like eunuch's voice, 'I wish to know why the emperor has summoned you.'

At first I stared back at him, not understanding. Then I said, 'You are his chamberlain. If you do not know, then how must I?'

His smooth jaw tightened. He was not a man who was used to being questioned. And it came to me that even though he stood at the very centre of power, he had no idea what Constantius wanted.

'His eternity the emperor shares his every thought with me,' he declared, as much to his retinue as to me. 'You are both accomplices of the traitor Julian. He will wish to question you.'

He gave me a long, penetrating look, as if these words would prompt some answer from me. But I said nothing, and just looked back at him; and after a moment he repeated, 'He will wish to question you . . . You must know, however, that he is temporarily indisposed; he is suffering from a slight fever – nothing serious, for the emperor never ails. But you must say nothing to tire or vex him.'

And then he tried to discover again, using different words as if somehow this would trick me, what it was that the emperor wanted with me. But of course I could not tell him, for I did not know myself.

In the midst of this, a servant stepped in and whispered in his ear. Beside me Marcellus murmured, 'When the beast is sick, it is at its most dangerous. Be careful, Drusus.' And then the chamberlain turned.

'The emperor,' he said, 'is ready now.' And to the military stewards, 'Release their bonds. Bring them.'

The chamber beyond was some kind of makeshift room-of-state. There were more heavy plush carpets; and, against the far wall, a carved, high-backed chair, with a purple canopy over it, supported on gilded posts.

But the room was empty of people, and we passed through to a columned walkway with an open, high-walled garden on one side. Among the forgotten pots and shrubs, great bronze-bound travelling chests and other baggage had been stacked. The building, though large, was clearly too small for the vast imperial entourage. Near the wall, where a lopsided citrus tree grew out of a white marble urn, a small group of officials and slaves stood gathered. They were talking to one another, with grave faces and nervous eyes.

Whatever court business was troubling them, we had troubles enough of our own. I remembered the tales of Constantius's appalling rage, and doubted we should survive the day. We had escaped the notary, it seemed, only to face something worse. I could not imagine what it could be; nor did I want to conjure such an image to life. With an effort of will I pushed the thought from my mind.

We reached a painted door guarded by soldiers with spears. At a gesture from the chamberlain, one of the soldiers stooped and tapped. The door swung open from within, and we were admitted into what seemed at first to be complete darkness.

I paused, blinking. The room was stuffy and hot; the heavy air reeked of scented oil and pungent, healing herbs.

I realized that the windows had all been shuttered; the only light came from fretted lamps which stood on tables by the wall, beside hangings of crimson and reflecting gold.

I cast my eyes about, and perceived with a start that everywhere, among the clutter of furniture, people were standing in silence, their dark shapes emerging from the gloom – servants of the household, lower-ranking chamberlains, a bishop with a massive jewelled cross, military men in their finest uniforms, dark-clad notaries; and, in the midst of them all, a young woman with large eyes and a pale, bland face, dressed in a shimmering green robe woven with bullion, with two female attendants at her side.

For a moment our eyes met and paused. Her small, white hand was resting on her distended belly, and I saw that she was with child. Her eyes turned away, as though offended by my gaze, and settled instead on the low, cushioned couch before her.

And there, at last, I saw him.

He was lying amid piled coverlets of purple and shot silk. His head rested on a high, embroidered bolster; his face was pallid, round and clean-shaven, with curled dark hair matted on his brow.

At first I thought he was sleeping. But then he stirred and coughed, and shifted to look at me. And with a mixture of horror and awe I looked back at him. Here, I thought, was the man who liked to style himself Master of the World. In his sickness he looked no more than a morose child, encased in bonds of amaranth and gold.

He wheezed, and began spluttering again. A surgeon stepped from behind; but with a weak motion of his hand the emperor swatted him away. As I beheld him, all the whispered conversations and nervous, clustering officials now made sense: I saw at once that here was no passing sickness. The vast machine of imperial rule had paused, waiting on this one man.

He pulled himself up.

'It seems,' he said, in a hoarse voice, 'that we are unlucky with our family. Our cousin Julian has brought us much trouble. Are we really so bad a judge of men?'

As he spoke, his eyes, shadowed and exhausted, did not look at me. His gaze was fixed on a place above my head, as if he were addressing some distant crowd. It was disconcerting; but I guessed this was his usual habit.

'No, sir,' I said, 'you are not. With Julian you judged rightly. You should have listened to him instead of his enemies who surround you. It is they, not Julian, who have brought you so much trouble.'

At these words of mine, there arose a general stirring and muttering among the gathered crowd. Constantius made a weak, impatient gesture, and raising his voice cried, 'Julian is presumptuous. He has won a few trivial victories over half-armed barbarians and supposes he is invincible. We have restored him from his exile; we have granted him high office; we have loaded him with favours and honours, yet he turns against us—'

He broke off in a bout of coughing. The surgeon approached once more, but he waved him away.

'It is reported to us,' he continued, 'that he affects the philosopher's beard, like a pagan Greek. Does he imagine, then, that he is learned? And lately it is said that he presumes publicly to worship the old gods, against our express command, and contrary to the Divine Law.'

At this, the bishop with the jewelled cross hissed from the shadows, 'Apostate! His name will be damned forever.'

'Yes, yes,' muttered Constantius, his voice falling away. His heart was not in his anger; it sounded contrived and formal. Now he sighed, laying it aside, and for a few moments remained silent, wheezing as he breathed.

When he spoke again it was in a dull, withdrawn voice, like a man bored by all that surrounded him.

'They say you are his friend.'

'It is true.'

'Do you stand by him, even now?'

'Yes,' I said; and at this, for the first time, his eyes looked directly at me, searching my face in surprise. He looked like an irritated matron, wondering whether to be insulted. But there was something else too: a wistfulness, or envy, as if I had called to his mind the memory of another, better self that had long lain buried.

After a slight pause he said, 'We have attempted to rule with moderation and with justice, yet we are despised. Why do you turn against us?'

He ceased, and waited. And so I said, 'I was not born, sir, when you took up being emperor. But when I was a boy, my father was taken and put to death unjustly; and when I was a youth, you sent your notary to torture and to crush us. There are limits to what one man may command, whatever power he possesses. No one is born with the title to rule: he acquires it, by what he chooses to make of himself. Perhaps, sir, you had that title once. But you have allowed yourself to be misled by sycophants and flatterers, and you have become not a prince but a tyrant. It is time, sir, that you set your rule aside.'

All about me there were shouts of indignation. Over the noise I heard Constantius cry out in a strained, high voice, 'You dare to address us thus!'

'My life,' I answered back at him, 'is already forfeit, so hear it from me, for it is clear these others will not say it. As for you, sir, you are dying; I do not believe either of us will see the next morning, so let us speak truly. Julian had no wish to rule, but you forced it on him. His enemies here intended him to fail; but when he did not fail they whispered in your ear that he was plotting against you. He was not. Julian never cared for power; but he cares for what is just. And so, it seems to me, he is a better prince than you.'

From somewhere I heard the chamberlain cry, 'Take him out and behead him!' And I heard this calmly, for I was ready, and had said what I wished to say. In front of me the young woman in the jewelled robes was weeping, great tears of grief rolling unheeded down her face, glistening in the lamplight. Someone – one of the guards – grabbed my arm; I shook him off and remained still, staring at Constantius on his couch. And he, with an odd, amazed look, was staring back at me.

He made a motion with his hand and the noise fell away. The guard took my arm once more; but Constantius said, 'Leave him.' Then he raised his arm from beneath the silken sheets, and took the grieving woman's hand in his own.

'We have been alone,' he said quietly. 'Even our wives do not survive. We have been having bad dreams.'

Tenderly he touched her swollen belly. Then he said, 'I shall not see my child.'

'No, my lord! You will soon recover!' It was the chamberlain who spoke, and a chorus of voices called out in agreement.

'You see,' he said, fixing my eye, 'even now they lie to me. You are right: Julian never cared for high office. I should have left him with his books, where he was content. Perhaps, after all, as the philosophers say, it is such men who should rule, who care nothing for power.'

The chamberlain said, 'Julian is a traitor, my lord.'

'Is he? So you keep telling me. And what, grand chamberlain, are you?'

The chamberlain stepped back, looking appalled. Constantius's head moved on the pillow, and he gazed up at his wife's stricken face.

'She is innocent of crime,' he said.

It took me a moment to take his meaning. But then I recalled how he had begun his reign with a general slaughter – of Julian's family, and anyone else he thought could oppose him.

I said, 'I believe even now you know your cousin for what he is.'

For a moment he did not answer, and in the silence the only sound was the empress's gentle weeping.

'Yes,' he said eventually, looking at me with red-rimmed, fevered eyes. 'Yes, I believe I do.'

He paused again. Then he said, 'In the end, the great choices are simple. Tell Julian this. Tell him I entrust my wife and unborn child to him. He was wronged, and no act of mine can restore it. Let him rule, unwilling though he is. To him I pass the imperium.'

The chamberlain cried, 'No! That cannot be!'

'Enough! I have spoken, and you will obey this man. Let the scribes set it down, for this is my determined will.' Then, meeting my eye once more he added in a gentler voice, '. . . And it is also my confession. Will you tell Julian that? He will understand.'

'Yes, sir,' I said. 'I will tell him.'

Constantius nodded.

Then he turned to his wife and said, 'Fear not, Faustina. He is a friend of Julian's. He will treat you with honour.'

I found the notary in his pavilion, attended by a grey-clad slave who was packing scrolls and documents into a travelling chest. He was seated at a soldier's trestle table. In front of him lay an open casket, into which he was carefully placing little stoppered flasks like perfume bottles.

When I entered he turned in his chair without surprise. 'You have come alone,' he said. It was not a question. There was a tone of amusement in his voice.

His eyes moved briefly to the dagger at my belt, and he went on, 'You are no longer a prisoner, I see. Constantius is dead, then.'

I said, 'Constantius is dead.'

He gave a slight incline of his head.

The slave had paused. Without looking at him the notary said, 'Leave us, Candidus, we have private business to attend to.' And when the slave had hurried off he said, 'I know you better than you know yourself. That is my strength. You will spare me, in the name of your foolish notion of what is just.'

'Then you misjudge me.'

He smiled. 'I think not. Besides, it seems I serve you now – you and your friend Julian. Once a traitor, now an emperor. There is so little in a name, and so much. You see, my young friend, the lesson that is thus revealed: the only truth is power – how to win it, and how to keep it.'

'I have no need of you. Nor does Julian.'

'You are wrong . . . It is only that you do not know it yet. You are like a poor man who comes into a great inheritance: you see the piles of gold; you sense its promise, like perfume in the air; but you do not know how to spend it. That is why you have come alone. Have you never hungered? – I am the man who can feed that hunger. Has desire never touched you? – I can satisfy desires such as you have never dreamed of. Only consider, for the world lies spread before you. Whatever you want, it is yours for the taking. Let me tempt you. Reach out with that young, hesitant hand of yours and feast yourself on power.'

He paused, sitting back in his chair, looking up at me.

I said, 'What is in those bottles?'

'These?' He turned, looking pleased, like a goldsmith in his workshop, and with his long-fingered hand he gently lifted one of the flasks from the wooden box. 'This one,' he said, holding up the pale-blue phial, 'is aconite – it burns the entrails; it leaves no sign; a useful tool . . . And this' – indicating a brown bottle with fluted sides – 'is henbane; and this is extract of yew. Each has its uses, depending on the need.'

I said, 'Poisons, all of them?'

'Oh, yes. All poison. All deadly. Only the mode of dying is varied. One of them – this one perhaps – will serve for Faustina and the child. You need not trouble yourself with the matter; I shall see to it.'

Outside the day was spent. In the twilight the notary sat still, looking at me unblinking, like a lizard on a rock.

'Thus,' he said, when I did not speak, 'we shall work together, you and I: you as the public face of power; I the hidden one. Both are necessary.'

'No,' I said.

His head moved. 'No?'

'Your poisons lie before you. I leave you to make your choice. Either that, or you will stand trial for your crimes. I think you know what the verdict will be.'

There was a short silence.

'You cannot kill the Hydra,' he said, in a harder tone. 'I am a fact of nature. Others will follow me, to the very end of time.'

'Perhaps you are right. But I too am a fact of nature, and till the end of time there will be men who will resist you.'

The notary sighed. Slowly he took up one of the phials, looked at it, removed the wax stopper, and emptied the liquid into a small glass vessel.

'This would kill ten men,' he said, and he raised the glass, as if to toast me. 'But remember, I am your shadow . . . Your vengeance makes you just like me.'

I paused before I answered. But when I spoke it was in a clear, determined voice.

'No,' I said. 'No, it does not.'

AUTHOR'S NOTE

THE STORY IS SET between the years AD 355 and 361, a century before the fall of the Roman empire in the West. It partly traces the rise of the young imperial prince Julian.

It is often said that it is the victor who gets to write the history. In the case of the classical world, it was the late antique and medieval Church that acted as censor and interpreter of the past. What the Church did not approve of, it suppressed. In an age before the printing press, when the survival of a book depended on slow and painstaking copying by hand, it was the Church that controlled the writing, the copying, and the book burning.

The Church branded Julian an apostate, and that branding stuck, so that even today he is generally known as Julian the Apostate; whereas his uncle, the emperor Constantine, who made Christianity the official religion of the Roman empire, is known as Constantine the Great.

It is thus all the more surprising that so much of Julian's writings have survived. We can reach Julian still, not only

373

from his own words, but from those of his friends and enemies – for he aroused great controversy. From these texts we can piece together a picture of an intelligent and thoughtful young man who dwelt at the centre of power – and challenged that power – in the late Roman empire.

It is perhaps worth mentioning the terms 'Caesar' and 'Augustus'. Originally Caesar referred to Julius Caesar, and Augustus was the name assumed by Caesar's nephew and adopted son Octavian when he became the first emperor. By the late empire, however, these terms had become mere titles of office. An Augustus was an emperor; a Caesar was an emperor's deputy and designated successor – who was often, but not always, a family relation.

Furthermore, at various times, it was thought expedient to divide the vast empire between two or more emperors, each of whom would rule a part (typically the West and the East). So, during the late empire, there was often more than one emperor, each ruling a different region. For the purposes of the story I have simplified the more complicated aspects of late Roman provincial administration.

As far as place names are concerned, I have chosen the modern name where this is likely to be familiar to the reader. So, for example, I have preferred Britain to Britannia; London to Londinium; York to Eboracum; Autun to Augustodunum. For less familiar names, or for names of cities that no longer exist, I have kept the ancient name. Thus Sirmium is modern Sremska Mitrovica; Naissus is Niš; and Letocetum is the village of Wall, just south of Lichfield in England.

The novel follows on from my earlier story, *Cast Not the Day*.